LIMBO

ALSO BY MELANIA G. MAZZUCCO

Vita

LIMBO

MELANIA G. MAZZUCCO

TRANSLATED FROM THE ITALIAN BY

VIRGINIA JEWISS

FARRAR, STRAUS AND GIROUX > NEW YORK

Farrar, Straus and Giroux
18 West 18th Street, New York 10011

Printed in the United States of America
Originally published in Italian in 2012 by Giulio Einaudi Editore, s.p.a., Italy
English translation published in the United States by Farrar, Straus and Giroux
First American edition, 2014

Library of Congress Cataloging-in-Publication Data
Mazzucco, Melania G., 1966–
    [Limbo. English]
    Limbo / Melania G. Mazzucco ; translated from the Italian by Virginia Jewiss. — First
American edition.
        pages   cm
    ISBN 978-0-374-19198-6 (hardcover) — ISBN 978-0-374-70990-7 (ebook)
    1. Women veterans—Italy—Fiction.   2. Afghan War, 2001—Participation, Italian—
Fiction.   3. Psychic trauma—Fiction.   I. Jewiss, Virginia, translator.   II. Title.

PQ4873.A98 L5613 2014
853'.914—dc23

                                                                            2014016985

Designed by Abby Kagan

www.fsgbooks.com
www.twitter.com/fsgbooks • www.facebook.com/fsgbooks

1   3   5   7   9   10   8   6   4   2

The dark night ends in light.

—AFGHAN PROVERB

ACRONYMS

AMX   Aeritalia Macchi Experimental

ANA   Afghan National Army

ANP   Afghan National Police

ATR   Aerei da Trasporto Regionale

BZD   benzodiazepine

CIMIC   civil-military cooperation

CO   commanding officer

COP   combat outpost

EOD   explosive ordnance disposal

FOB   forward operating base

ICOS   International Council on Security and Development

IDF   indirect fire

IED   improvised explosive device

IFV   infantry fighting vehicle

ISAF   International Security Assistance Force

MMPI   Minnesota Multiphasic Personality Inventory

NCO   noncommissioned officer

NGO   nongovernmental organization

OMLT   Operational Mentor and Liaison Team

PETN   pentaerythritol tetranitrate

PIO   public information officer

PRT   Provincial Reconstruction Team

PSYOPS   psychological operations

PTSD   posttraumatic stress disorder

PX   post exchange

QRF   Quick Reaction Force

RC   regional command

RPG   rocket-propelled grenade

SBBIED   suicide body-borne IED

TFC   Task Force Center

TFS   Task Force South

TIC   troops in contact

TOW   tube-launched, optically tracked, wire-guided

VFP   *volontario in ferma prefissata,* or volunteer professional soldier

LIMBO

1

> >

LIVE

Nothing ever happens in this city. There's a frenzy the night that Manuela Paris is to return home—not even a visit from the pope would have caused such commotion. Everyone wants to see her. It's Christmas Eve. The vendors in the piazza have already broken down their stalls, and the rides are closing, too. The cafés lower their shutters, the waiters exchanging holiday greetings with the girls at the cash registers as they turn out the lights, one sign after another going dark. Curious onlookers clump together in front of the Parises' apartment building, huddled against the gate that defends a skinny gravel path. They stare at the intersection—two streets at right angles, like a drawing a kid in geometry class would make on graph paper. Except for the Christmas decorations—arches of colored light suspended between the buildings—there's nothing to look at. Ladispoli's not a very picturesque place. The only monuments, to the fallen in World War I, aren't very compelling: from a distance they look like scrap metal left over from some construction site. The best things about the main piazza are the trees and benches. The houses are nothing special, they don't make much of an impression. Even the Art Nouveau villas along the esplanade, built at the turn of the century when a dreamer prince believed he could transform this barren coast, at that time empty, into Rome's preferred elegant seaside resort, are decaying in the salt and sun. The teachers had encouraged the children living on the same street as Manuela Paris's family to hang Italian flags from their balconies. But school has been out for two days now, and only a few of them remembered, or only a few of them own a flag, so there are only three of them. They're all faded—the last time they were dragged down from the attic was for the World Cup—and so ragged and lonely that they make for a pretty sad sight; it might have been better not to hang them at all. Worse, the biggest one is on the Paris family balcony, so it's really like there are only two. Two flags on a street with at least fifty buildings and four hundred apartments.

So the cameraman prefers not to film them, to avoid giving the impression that Italian people don't give a damn. Manuela's schoolmates—who studied tourism management with her, or say they did, even if they were in a different class and maybe spoke to her only three times in their lives—vie for attention, elbowing to get on camera. But a reporter from the local news is front and center; he is trying hard to explain—in just a few words because the story isn't supposed to run over ninety seconds—that he's outside Manuela Paris's house with the mayor. Only he has to keep repeating himself because of all the honking—cars stuck in the traffic jam. The regular correspondent is on vacation so he's filling in: a young guy nobody knows, with rectangular glasses and a blond goatee. There's a pretty good crowd, though, they'll give her a respectable welcome.

But a sharp, nasty drizzle begins to fall, and Manuela Paris is late, and no one knows if she's coming by train from Rome or by car from Fiumicino, no one knows anything, it's cold, it's getting late, and the spontaneous welcome committee dissolves. A woman in a beaver coat leaves a bouquet of roses on the ground beneath the doorbell, but a neighbor throws the roses away, saying they bring bad luck: they look like those sad flowers people place along the side of the road or on lampposts after an accident, and Manuela Paris is hardly dead. Only the mayor—a woman herself—stays; she really wants to give Manuela a token of the city's appreciation, a little artsy something commissioned from a local sculptor that's supposed to represent the region's traditional product: a golden artichoke. Artichokes have been the pride of Ladispoli since the 1930s, and sometimes it seems as if they're the only thing the forty thousand people who live here care about, even though they're really grown by only a few farms out in the countryside. The rest of Ladispoli's residents work in factories or shops, just like anywhere else. At any rate, the mayor, draped in a tricolor sash, has to present this symbol of indigenous virtue to the illustrious citizen who put Ladispoli on the front page. Because otherwise the city gets talked about only during April, during the artichoke festival. Or if two drunken Bulgarians knife each other in a brawl. Or some retiree drowns on the first Sunday in June. So the mayor stays to deliver the golden artichoke, and to convey the admiration of the entire city council. Majority and opposition may fight each other on everything else, but all agreed when it came to honoring their fellow citizen, a model for young, hardworking Italians—in short, a hope for the future of our country.

The mayor waits under an umbrella with Manuela's sister. Everyone's stunned to see them together, because there's always been a lot of gossip about Vanessa Paris, for all sorts of reasons, and at any rate, the mayor never would have said a word to her if she weren't Manuela's sister. With her platinum blond bob, asymmetrical bangs, green eye shadow, false eyelashes, and bold fuchsia lipstick, Vanessa snags herself an interview with the TV reporter. She's remarkably self-assured, as if she'd been giving interviews all her life. "My sister's totally normal," she says, her cat eyes staring straight into the camera, into the viewers' eyes, "she hates pretentiousness and would never want people to think of her as a hero, or a victim—she was just doing her job, like when a bricklayer falls off scaffolding, or a factory worker gets splashed by acid. She chose that life, she knew the risks, and she didn't let the difficulties get to her, that's why I think it makes sense to talk about Manuela Paris, because young Italian women today aren't all bimbos with no brains or values who only think about money, they're also people like my sister, who have dreams and ideals, and the courage to try and fulfill them." The reporter asks for her number as soon as the sound engineer turns off the mike.

Vanessa Paris will be a big hit when the story airs the next day, because she's still a knockout even though she's over thirty. Prettier than her sister, who dresses like a truck driver and never wears makeup, at least that's what everyone says, but then again, they haven't seen her since she went away, and she was just a little squirt back then, maybe she's changed.

Little by little the houses light up, Christmas trees twinkle behind curtains, and the smell of fish wafts from kitchens. It's strange to see the place so full of life. Usually Ladispoli empties out in the morning, when people leave for work, like a hotel at the end of the summer. For seven months, until the beach clubs open again, all you see are children, old people, and out-of-work foreigners. Manuela Paris's house is the last one on the street, opposite the Bellavista Hotel, on the esplanade. *Esplanade* is a pretty pretentious word for that narrow strip of street that runs between the two drainage canals that define the city center and is besieged from behind by huge buildings that loom over the older villas, as if preparing to crush them. The walls and beach huts obstruct the view, so you only get glimpses of the sea. You can hear it, though. In Ladispoli the sea roars. Open sea, slapped by the wind, always rough. People who have traveled say it's like the ocean. Don't get the wrong impression, though—the place has a certain charm, even if it never did become the hoped-for elegant beach town. To Manuela it had always seemed perfect, and she wouldn't have wanted to be born anywhere else. But when— it's already after eight—she finally gets out of the car, she looks around disoriented; she doesn't seem all that happy to be back.

"We're proud to have you here with us again," the mayor says simply, shaking her hand. Her constituents wouldn't appreciate a lot of pomp, which they're all strongly opposed to. That's why she avoided a ceremony in city hall, agreeing instead to this intimate, informal encounter: hers is a tightrope walker's existence. Manuela doesn't mind, though—in fact, she had begged her mother not to tell anyone she was coming. Instead, to her dismay, she has become a celebrity, and has to endure the ceremony of the golden artichoke and the city pennant. The reporter already used up all his questions on Vanessa, so he merely asks her what she's feeling. "It's good to be home, but I can't wait to go back, there's so much to do over there," Manuela says. Few words, spoken quickly, eyes lowered, not even a hint of a smile. She's always been gruff with people she doesn't know. She hugs her mother. Manuela is a head taller than she is, and Cinzia Colella, minute and shriveled, disappears inside her daughter's big green jacket. "When are you going to let your hair grow back?" she asks, running her hand across her daughter's forehead. She doesn't say "I missed you so much," or anything like that. Just that unfortunate question, which in truth implies another: Do you have to have another operation on your head? Nothing remains of her daughter's long black hair, which used to shine like an Indian's. It's really short now, a crew cut, like a man's. Her chocolate-colored eyes seem too big for her naked face. Her mother hadn't been able to contain herself, because for her, a woman without hair isn't a woman: she's a lunatic from the asylum, a prisoner of war, or terminally ill. Then the chaos starts. Neighbors and relatives, filled with pride, clasp her hand and vie for her attention, a kiss on the cheek, a pat on the back, even her cousins Claudio and Pietro are there, with their kids, and Uncle Vincenzo, the one with the mustache and a hardware store behind Piazza della Vittoria—they all want to kiss her, and her uncle's and cousins' wives don't want to be left out, even though they're not sure Manuela recognizes them, and everyone forgets her mother's instructions—she had begged them to avoid mentioning what had happened—and, adopting sympathetic expressions appropriate to the circumstances, they ask, how are you, how are you, and she answers distractedly, almost irritated, fine, fine, I'm better now.

But she isn't fine at all. She still walks uncertainly, leaning on her metal crutches, hopping on her good foot, as if she's scared to put weight on the other one. Seeing her hobble like that shocks and silences them all, and all their celebrations, all their questions and congratulations stick in their throats. None of them had realized that her injuries were so serious, or that her rehab wasn't over. If the young reporter hadn't mentioned it in the story that will air tomorrow at lunchtime, no one would even know that Manuela has undergone four operations on her foot and knee, three on the vertebrae in her neck, and two on her skull. It's more comforting to think that her convalescence is over and that she is coming to spend the Christmas holidays with her family, like everyone else.

Manuela starts dragging herself up the stairs. There's never been an elevator in their building and there never will be, because the stairwell is too narrow. Her crutches tic-tic mournfully on the stairs, and her mother can't keep from crying. She weeps silently, sniffling and wiping her eyes on her coat sleeve. Cinzia had never resigned herself to the idea that her daughter could get herself killed one day, and for such lousy pay, when she could have become a lawyer or a notary or an astrophysicist. Yet she was the one who, ever since Manuela was little, always told her that independence is everything, that a woman needs to think about herself, choose the profession she wants, and never depend on a man. So if Manuela grew up with those ideas in her head, her mother is partly to blame.

Manuela stops on the second floor because the stabbing pains in her ruined leg are piercing her head and she needs to rest. Vanessa wants to help and offers her arm. Manuela pushes her away, brandishing her crutch like a rifle. "I can do it myself," she grumbles stubbornly, "I can do it." Vanessa thinks that, despite everything, maybe her sister really is better.

At dinner Manuela is seated at the head of the table. They have given her the seat of honor, facing the balcony windows. In the evening darkness, the sea is a sheet of lead that the waves splinter into a thousand slivers of light. The neon sign for the Bellavista Hotel is on, but the shutters are lowered in all the rooms, and the place seems closed. The restaurant is dark. After all, why would anyone come spend Christmas Eve at the Bellavista? Manuela has never seen anyone there in winter. Off season, there are only weekend guests. Clandestine couples usually, married professionals and their young female friends. Manuela tries all the appetizers—the wild salmon, the mushrooms in olive oil, the baby artichokes, the Russian salad, the anchovy and caper rolls, the duck liver pâté, the eel—because the unusual abundance tells her that her mother has spent the entire day in the kitchen, and Manuela is the only person in the world she'd do that for. It's all delicious, but it leaves a bitter taste in her mouth: of salt and waste. She only picks at the linguine with clams, the grouper with capers, the artichokes; she resigns herself to the ritual slice of *panettone*. While Vanessa gets up and, hips swaying thanks to her stiltlike heels, heads toward the kitchen, followed by the bovine stares of the three Colella men, Manuela notices with surprise that a light has come on in the window across the way, on the third floor, behind half-lowered shutters. Someone's there. In the Bellavista Hotel, on Christmas Eve.

Her uncle, cousins, and mother are all shouting, or at least that's what it feels like to her, because she's no longer used to this much noise. In the hospital, footsteps are soft, voices low, sounds muted. You can almost hear silence screak, time breathe. For months all she did was stare at the rectangle of her window, which framed a magnolia tree, and listen to the rustle of leaves and the chirping of birds hidden in its branches. That bright green tree and those chirpy, chattering birds were so unreal, so ridiculous, that at times she would ask herself if she were really alive. The leaves were green in the fall and green in the winter: it was as if time had stopped.

"You should come see me at the store," her cousin Claudio is saying. "I'll let you pick out a dog. It'll keep you company till you're back to regular duty. Toy Russians are really in now—they're tiny, affectionate, totally fearless. I've got one that's perfect, a real purebred, barely six pounds, you can put it in your purse. And I won't let you pay either, it's a gift." Manuela bites into a piece of white nougat, hard as a rock, and stares at him in bewilderment. She wasn't listening. She's wishing she were somewhere else. She had known she wouldn't feel like seeing anyone, and had begged her mother to keep her homecoming a secret, but her mother didn't hold to their agreement, and now she's trapped at this noisy family dinner, as exhausting as a march with a full pack. She doesn't feel like making small talk; listening to other people's conversations interests her even less. People talk merely to air their tongues, and she doesn't want to waste time with that nonsense anymore. It's as if she'd done a kind of detox therapy, ridding herself of everything superfluous. As the months passed, the things that really mattered turned out to be fewer and fewer. In the end all that was left were health, freedom, and life.

"Leave her alone," Vanessa whispers in her cousin's ear, "she's tired." Vanessa has kept an eye on Manuela all evening, and her listless expression puts her on edge—and that's made her eat too much, stuffing herself to ease her anxiety, and now her stomach burns, as if she's swallowed a sea urchin, spines and all. She has missed her sister, tremendously. She doesn't know how to tell her, though, and she also doesn't know if the closeness that once existed between them can ever be rekindled, or if it's gone forever, or if it even still means anything to Manuela. The girl with the shaved hair at the head of the table, huddled in a chair too big for her, looks first at them and then around the room, as if she were lost, as if she were a complete stranger who ended up here by chance on Christmas Eve.

Vanessa uses her nails to rip off the silver wrapping on a bottle of Asti Spumante, shakes it, and pops the cork. The louder the bang, the better the luck it brings. It simply doesn't occur to her. Manuela starts to her feet and goes white as a sheet. Blinded by a flash of light, deafened by a piercing roar, her heart starts pounding like crazy, her forehead is covered in sweat, her legs tremble and give way. She staggers forward, flailing her arms to keep from falling, and a crystal vase goes flying. It crashes to the floor and shatters, flinging water, leaves, and flowers all over her jeans and shirt. A nice vase, one she'd never seen before, the only thing new in a room otherwise exactly the same as when she'd left it, all those years ago. Exactly the same, but aged somehow. She manages to sit down.

"Idiot," her mother hisses in Vanessa's ear. "The doctor told you, no explosions, no sudden noises, Manuela's brain is sensitive." This is what Cinzia says, but in truth she really doesn't know what's wrong with her daughter. She only knows that in practical terms they have to avoid reminding her about what happened. Every time Cinzia went to the hospital to see her, Manuela told her it was too soon, she didn't want to talk about it. But more than six months have gone by since she was repatriated, and not only does Manuela not want to talk about it, but she still loses it when someone pops a bottle of spumante.

"Hey, honey, everything's okay," Vanessa whispers, her hand on her shoulder. "Hey? Are you there? It was just a fucking cork, I'm sorry." She gathers up the shards of crystal from the floor and deposits them carelessly on the soaking wet tablecloth. It's too bad about the vase. It was really pretty and probably cost a lot. Could it be a sign? Youssef had given it to her mother last Christmas. Last Christmas, Manuela was in Afghanistan, and Vanessa's boyfriend had come to wish Cinzia a merry Christmas. Not knowing what to give a woman he had never even seen and whose hostility he sensed, he had bought that Swarovski vase because sparkling crystal makes a good impression. Vanessa is sorry Manuela won't get to meet Youssef. Manuela's a better judge of character than she is, she's good at sizing people up, sees deep inside them, as if X-raying their hearts, and Vanessa wants to know what she'd make of him. If he seems right for her, if their relationship will last, because last Christmas she was convinced it would—if not, she never would have introduced him to her mother—but by New Year's they were already fighting over every little thing, and now she's not so sure that Youssef is the love of her life. If one even exists, and if there's only one. But Youssef won't be back from Morocco until February, and Manuela will already be gone by then.

"Maybe we'd better get going," Uncle Vincenzo murmurs, glancing sympathetically at his sister. Cinzia mumbles something about the fact that Manuela hasn't fully recovered yet, it takes time, the trauma was severe, these things leave deep scars, it's not just the broken bones . . . but she doesn't insist they stay. The Christmas spirit has evaporated. Embarrassed, the cousins and their wives get up, say goodbye to Grandma Leda, but avoid looking at Manuela or drawing attention to themselves, as if they were ashamed of their cumbersome bodies, of their shoes squeaking on the waxed floor. Except for the television, forgotten but still on in the background, a forbidding silence has fallen over the living room, as if someone had died. The flat ring of a phone makes everyone jump. It's music from *Psycho*, the shower scene, and it gets louder with every ring. Very disturbing. Vanessa fishes her cell out from under the cushions on the couch, glances at the display, and decides not to answer. "Is it Youssef?" Alessia teases. "No, sweetie," Vanessa says, surprised. "It's not Youssef."

"Thanks for everything, terrific dinner, I always said you should open a restaurant, Merry Christmas," Aunt Pia whispers to her sister-in-law, while Pietro's wife gets her purse, their daughter, Carlotta, puts on her coat, and little Jonathan stares at the strange girl, white as a ghost, who is panting, mouth and eyes open wide. A rose hangs by a thorn from the sleeve of her blouse, which is soaking wet and completely transparent. Cousin Manuela isn't wearing a bra. She doesn't need one, she's flat as a board, but her nipples are like small buds. His father has to drag him away. One after the other the Colellas leave, apologetically repeating "Merry Christmas, Merry Christmas," without turning around, as if they weren't supposed to see or know, as if they had spied on some forbidden truth.

"Feel better now, hon?" Vanessa whispers, and Manuela nods. The explosion no longer rings in her ears. Even the nauseating smell of burnt flesh is fading. Her heartbeat is slowing, the tingling in her legs is fading. She gives her sister a painful smile, which, instead of reassuring her, pierces her heart. What the fuck did they do to you?! she would like to scream. She plucks the rose from her sister's sleeve, but she can't muster a single word. When her sister enlisted, Vanessa was pregnant. She gave birth the day Manuela was sworn in. Her mother had to choose. She couldn't be in the barracks and the hospital at the same time. Obviously she chose the hospital. Manuela took it hard. Two hundred and fifty female soldiers of the third echelon were sworn in on the parade grounds of the Ascoli Piceno barracks. The army chief of staff was there, along with generals, dignitaries, and family members, eyes wet with tears. Manuela was the only one without any relatives; she had given her classmates the tickets reserved for her family. Not even her grandfather came, because no one could take him. Parkinson's had already destroyed Vittorio Paris, he was all skin and bones, as frail as a dried spider; he weighed all of ninety pounds, and could no longer drive or even take a bus. But it wasn't Vanessa's fault that Alessia was born by cesarian, scheduled well in advance; the doctors don't postpone a C-section just because your sister is swearing allegiance to the flag. To Vanessa, not being there for Manuela that day had seemed like an unforgivable betrayal. She really should have been there. She'd been the first to learn that her sister had enlisted, and, unlike Manuela's mother, or friends, or other relatives, to Vanessa it seemed like the right decision—even if at the time there weren't many female soldiers and everyone said it was unnatural, because a woman's biological destiny is to give life instead of death. But Manuela would reply that human beings have freed themselves from the fierce, obtuse tyranny of nature. People aren't zebras or kangaroos, dominated by instinct, or train cars limited to specific tracks. "We don't have just one path before us—we're free." Vanessa had helped her fill out her application, and had gone with her to the recruiting office. When Manuela disappeared into the barracks, Vanessa bawled like a fool.

Months later, Vanessa had watched the video of the swearing-in ceremony, which Angelica Scianna's parents had taken. All the women looked perfect in their uniforms, with their lip gloss and clear nail polish, the only makeup that regulations allowed. But Manuela, wearing neither lip gloss nor nail polish, her black ponytail tucked under her cap, her expression serious, made the most believable soldier. In the video the women shouted in unison: I SWEAR! and then intoned "Fratelli d'Italia" at the top of their lungs. It gave Vanessa goose bumps to hear the national anthem sung by all those female voices.

At a quarter past midnight, Alessia is asleep on the foldaway bed set up in her mother's room, Cinzia is loading the dishwasher, and Vanessa, cell phone pressed to her ear, is leaning out the bathroom window, because the Bellavista blocks the signal in the Parises' apartment. She's whispering. Manuela is still awake and Vanessa doesn't want to be overheard talking to some guy she met for ten minutes and who's already calling her on Christmas Eve. Manuela is pretty strict. She says a soldier is like a priest: you can't just be religious in church. And so she behaves as if she were in uniform even when she's not. Manuela's romantic life—at least as far as Vanessa knows—is almost humiliatingly monogamous. She only ever brought home one guy, Giovanni Bocca, and even though Vanessa found him uninteresting and untrustworthy, she'd resigned herself to the fact that Manuela was going to marry him. Manuela had already asked her to be her maid of honor. They had talked with the parish priest at Our Lady of the Rosary Church, and had even asked if they could be exempted from premarital counseling. But then, last year, before she left for Afghanistan, she broke up with him. Without telling anyone why.

The young journalist with the blond goatee is named Lapo. He sounds happy, even euphoric. Maybe he's been drinking, or he's popped a pill, or maybe he's playacting, trying to seem cool. He asks if she's busy the day after tomorrow. He's dying to see her again. "I can't," Vanessa hesitates, "I have to spend time with my sister, I don't want to blow her off, she's not doing so well, and besides, she moved up north a long time ago and doesn't know anyone around here anymore." "What if I bring a friend?" Lapo asks.

When all the lights in the house are out and she knows she won't be surprised by anyone anymore, Manuela goes out onto the balcony and lights a cigarette. The balcony runs along the living room, makes a right angle, and comes to a dead end outside the kitchen. It's empty except for Alessia's little bike and a drying rack gnawed by rust. Her mother doesn't care about flowers, and Vanessa is too scattered to remember to water them. The geraniums are dying in their plastic vases, the basil is a shriveled black stump, and the jasmine has lost all its leaves. The nicotine makes her head spin. She smoked the first cigarette of her life just a few months ago, in the courtyard of the military hospital. Twenty-seven years without wanting so much as a puff, not even in school, not even in the barracks, not even at the base, where all the soldiers smoked, and now she can't live without it. What an idiot. She leans on the railing and gazes at the Bellavista Hotel. The light is out in the room on the third floor, the curtains are closed. But someone is on the balcony, in the dark. Smoking. All she can see is the glow of a cigarette—otherwise, she wouldn't even have noticed the shadowy figure in the dark, leaning against the railing, just like she is. It's a man.

The mistral blows the vague scent of aromatic tobacco her way. Manuela taps ashes into the pot and wonders what he's doing there, all alone in an empty hotel, on Christmas Eve. Maybe he, too, suffers from insomnia, and is afraid of going to bed. Afraid that images, smells, sounds, and voices he'd like to forget will reemerge from the darkness. Sounds most of all. *That* sound. At least that's how it is for her. The worst moment of the day is the last, when the light fades and she rests her head on her pillow. She feels fragile in the dark, defenseless against the nightmares—even against the memories. She hasn't been able to get to sleep naturally for the last six months. She puts off going to bed until the artificial drowsiness starts to fog her mind. But now, even with the drops, she remains stubbornly alert. So even after she puts out her cigarette in the damp potting soil and slips the butt into her pocket to avoid leaving any trace, she stays leaning against the railing, watching the man across the way; he's wearing dark clothes, with a lighter color scarf around his neck. He scans the street below—not a single car goes by. From where he stands he can see the Paris family's flag, which flaps against the balcony with every gust of wind. In the silence of Christmas Eve, all you can hear is the rustle of the flag and the sea, which hurls itself against the sand monotonously, maliciously, angrily. But as soon as he realizes that Manuela is looking at him, he starts, tosses his cigarette into the street, moves the curtain aside, and disappears into his room. He doesn't turn on the light.

2

LIVE

On Christmas morning, Manuela goes down to the beach. The doctor recommended walking every day. Cinzia wants to go with her—they haven't said two words to each other since she came home, and she suspects her daughter is avoiding her. But why? Cinzia only wants to protect her, to help her get well. She's convinced that's why the doctor sent her home, to her, that it's her job to cure her. Manuela says bluntly that she would prefer she didn't. That she wants to take advantage . . . "Advantage of what?" her mother asks, astounded. "Of the solitude," Manuela replies, buttoning her jacket. "I can barely remember what it's like now." She closes the door behind her and clambers down the stairs. A soldier's life is lived in the plural. She had zero privacy in the almost six months she was in Afghanistan. Even her underwear was in full view, swaying on the clothesline. They all had less space, and communal life was even more intense than it had been in the barracks. And yet there was something exhilarating about that brutal cohabitation. To get up at the same time, wash your face in the same clogged sink, endure the same hardships, use the same words, the same jargon, fear the same things, share the same experiences, the same daily routine, and store up the same memories is an exercise both in patience and personal growth. You become a cell in a living organism that can't survive without you but that also transcends you. It's reassuring somehow. But now, expelled from the cocoon of a collective existence she doesn't know if she'll ever return to, she feels alone in this city that once was hers but is no longer, alone with her crutches and her shadow.

In winter the beach becomes a carpet of garbage regurgitated by the waves. Old, useless stuff that roams the sea for years, tossed to and fro for thousands of miles, and then, by some whim of the currents, finally washes up on this strip of coast. Plastic bottles, polystyrene boxes, beer caps, Q-tips, diapers even. It would be a waste of energy to pick them up. Sooner or later a stormy sea will take them back again. Objects never die. She walks slowly, avoiding a flip-flop, a dried palm frond, a buoy coated in greenish fuzz. It's a short walk from the Bellavista Hotel to the Tahiti restaurant, a wooden structure with a thatched roof—dark beams, the walls covered with photos of Tahitian gardenias and dugout canoes—which the owners think looks Polynesian, or at least says "Polynesia" to the Romans who come here for fried fish on Sunday and will never make it all the way to Tahiti. When, to catch her breath, she sits on the cement wall that separates one beach club from the next and turns around to assess how far she's come, she sees her footprints, clearly visible in the sand: the tank tracks of her army boot, the smooth sole of her orthopedic shoe, and two lines of what look like crab holes. She feels like hurling her crutches into the sea.

Ladispoli's beach had always seemed beautiful to her. Not that she had anything to compare it to. She'd always spent her vacations here, because here we have the sea for free, her mother would say, it's pointless going and throwing money away somewhere else. She would tell the Alpini who had grown up in the fog and the cold of sad northern Italian cities that Ladispoli's black, ferrous sand, created when pyroclastic material erupted from the Sabatini volcanoes, is renowned for its therapeutic properties. All you have to do is hold a magnet close to it and the magnetite will separate from the green pyroxene. In the summer sun the sand turns red hot and is not only a cure for the bones, but also for the spirit: it teaches you to walk on burning coals. She'd gotten used to it, like the fakirs, which is why the burning desert sand that annoyed the other soldiers didn't bother her at all. They would complain about finding it everywhere—in their teeth as they ate, in their hair, noses, eyes, even in their anuses—but the grit of sand on her teeth and skin reminded her of the happiest days of her childhood, and gave her the feeling that the world was all one, the distance between places and continents almost an optical illusion, and that her current life was a logical continuation of the one she'd lived before. That the military Manuela was the same little girl who would play in the noonday sun, ignoring her grandmother shouting from the window that she should at least put on a hat.

Her first walk was short, but the beach goes on for miles and miles—there's a wooden footbridge now, so you can get across the canal—skirting bays born after enormous cement blocks were dumped in the water to combat beach erosion. Artificial indentations, yet gentle and comforting nevertheless, for as far as the eye can see, until salt vapors obscure the coast, enveloping it in a silvery haze. But the cement blocks didn't do much: the waves continue to eat away at the sand, and winter after winter they consume the beach so that now it's just a thin strip. When she was little, on Sundays when the sea was calm, she would toddle along the shore for hours behind her grandfather, from dawn until the sun was at its peak. Vittorio Paris would go clamming, raking little *telline* out of the sand. People from Minturno who settled here in the 1950s to seek their fortune on the shores of northern Lazio had taught him how. But the *telline* were decimated by pollution and overfishing, and he found fewer and fewer of them, until in the end he gave up.

"Our sand is black," she remembers saying to Zandonà. "Like oil, and even the sea's black." They were stuck in a dune, she couldn't remember the name of the place, or maybe it didn't have one. Zandonà had maneuvered badly. Sometimes he forgot he was driving an armored vehicle instead of a car. She should have reprimanded him, but instead she took the blame. He needed to know she would defend him to his superiors. He needed to trust her. She had to win his trust, his and that of the whole platoon. She wasn't angry or worried. She let the sand run through her fingers. Yellow, almost white. Incredibly fine, like talcum powder. Sand, as far as the eye could see. No buildings. No sign of human life. No shrubs. Or animals or birds or insects buzzing in the thin, dry air. In the absolute silence, only the rumble of the approaching Quick Reaction Force, coming to get them. There was something oppressive about that lunar landscape, that virginal, piercing, absolute beauty. But only now, as she breathes the salty air of the Tyrrhenian, does she realize what it was. The sea, the sea was missing. It was a landscape besieged by the horizon, devoid of exits, of entrances. Of future.

A dark silhouette in a tracksuit, a phantom in a wool cap and sunglasses, whizzes past her while she rests on the wall. For a second his iPod exhales its ethereal music in her direction. It's the voice of Thom Yorke singing "Everything in Its Right Place." She recognizes it because First Lieutenant Russo used to listen to *Kid A* in Afghanistan. He's the one who taught her to appreciate Radiohead. Their music opens a crack in your mind, he'd say, an empty space where your thoughts can hide. A guy who wears dark glasses on a cloudy, gray winter day, not even a sliver of sun, is no less strange than one who spends Christmas Eve at the Bellavista Hotel. It might even be the same guy. Manuela has the feeling he's noticed her. Legs whirling, the phantom races past the Tahiti and grows smaller and smaller, a blue exclamation point on a shore edged with foam.

Teodora Gogean is late. She never bothers to ring the doorbell, she usually just honks three times. Vanessa says she's an uneducated hick, civilization hasn't made it to her country yet, she didn't even know what a doorbell was before immigrating to Italy. Manuela never argues with her sister about these things, partly because Vanessa doesn't have anything against Romanians, just against Teodora. Manuela descends the stairs cautiously, one step at a time: first her crutches, then her broken foot, then the other one. Distances lengthen, space swells around her, even time is distorted. She's like a child again, she's returned to her past. Or she's getting a taste of her future, of old age.

The restaurant at the Bellavista Hotel is open, and she catches a glimpse of the cook's Egyptian face in the square of the kitchen window. But the curtains in the dining room are all drawn. Strange, because the sea view is the restaurant's main attraction; people go there precisely to watch the waves. The corner table is taken. By one person. Even though the curtain obscures his features, it's the same man as the night before, the runner on the beach. A tourist, clearly. But who would come here on vacation at the end of December?

Ladispoli has a bad reputation. Unjust, but reputation is like honor: determined by others and almost impossible to correct. People, places, and races are judged, who knows by whom, and forever. A stupid saying, which pains Manuela but was repeated every time she had to say where she was from, crowns Ladispoli as the ugliest city on the Lazio coast. A clump of apartment houses, each one different, shot up quickly in the sixties and seventies, next to—almost on top of—the tiny Art Nouveau village on the waterfront, built without respect or elegance, renovated, improved with balconies and verandas, but stubbornly ugly just the same. A labyrinth of asphalt, cars, and cement. Manuela would grow indignant, take offense. Arguments would start, from which it could at least be deduced that there was something of a contest for first place. Aside from a fair number of towns south of the Tiber, the strongest contender was Civitavecchia. But the ferries for Sardinia leave from there, whereas Ladispoli doesn't even have a port, it doesn't have anything but artichokes and the sea. Still, the guest at the Bellavista Hotel has decided to spend his vacation right here in Ladispoli. And he's dining alone in the restaurant, a bottle of sparkling water and a middle-aged waiter who stutters for company.

Teodora hugs her tight for a long time. She pats Manuela awkwardly on the shoulders—the only way she knows to express how happy she is to see her. Teodora is a rough, introverted woman, completely incapable of expressing her emotions—if she even has any, which remains to be seen. Manuela fears she is like her. "Isn't Alessia coming at least?" Teodora asks as she grinds the gears, mostly to have something to say, because she already knows that Vanessa would never give Traian the satisfaction of seeing his little niece on Christmas Day. Revenge is best served cold, after it's ceased to matter, when it won't make anyone happy, a belated, futile revenge that gets served up anyway. "Alessia's going with my mother to my cousin Pietro's for lunch," Manuela explains. "She likes to play with Jonathan. They're in the same class at school. But thanks for inviting her." Teodora shrugs her shoulders. She'll never manage to put this family back together.

It's not far to her house. Tiberio Paris and Cinzia Colella never made peace with each other even after the divorce, but they continued to live less than half a mile apart—she in the rectangle of Art Deco villas and he in the new neighborhood behind the roundabout. They walked the same streets, shopped the same stands in the market, drank their coffee at the same café, but when, every now and then, they happened to run into each other, one would always cross the street.

"How's it going?" Teodora asks. "It's hard," Manuela admits. "I'm not used to having nothing to do, I get bored." "Traian wanted to be there last night, to welcome you"—Teodora changes the subject right away. "We had a fight, and he's still in a huff." "Why didn't you let him come?" Manuela scolds her. "I would have liked that." Teodora prefers not to explain: she doesn't want to accuse her husband's ex-wife of preventing her son from welcoming his sister. Manuela wouldn't understand their futile, rotten war. She's happy to see that Traian has hung a flag from his window.

"Why don't you come stay here?" Teodora says as she helps her take off her heavy jacket. "At your mother's you have to camp out, you're like a guest, Alessia had to give up her room for you, you're all cramped, and besides, five women in one house is too many. But there's space here, I can set you up in the laundry room, you'd have your own place. If you wanted to be alone, all you'd have to do is close the door. We wouldn't bother you." "I know, thank you," Manuela says, "but I'm not staying long, after the holidays I'll head back up north, I'm only on medical leave until January twelfth." "You look amazing with short hair," Teodora comments, "you look like Demi Moore." "They shaved my head for the surgery," Manuela responds dispassionately. "Afterward I didn't want to let it grow back. It would have seemed like a betrayal, like I was forgetting. I don't know how to explain it."

"You just did," Teodora says. "And I understand. But you'll forget anyway. Surviving isn't a sin. The dead are dead. You have to bury them. But the living don't have to keep watch over their tombs."

Teodora hastens to light the red candles, to make the table more Christmassy. A large, wooden baptismal cross stands prominently on the sideboard. "Now what will you do, join the police?" she asks, without turning around. "Why would I join the police?" Manuela replies, surprised. "Don't the military get special treatment on the entrance exam?" Teodora wonders. To her, the only reason to join the military is that it's a shortcut to a permanent government job. "What does that have to do with anything?" Manuela asks. "I thought you'd be wanting to leave the army by now," Teodora says. "It's better to be a police officer than a soldier, right? You're still defending your country. Patriotism. It's the same idea." "Being in the army is completely different," Manuela says, blushing because Teodora's words reveal clearly what all her relatives think, though they don't have the courage to say it. Maybe her superiors think the same: she's no longer fit to be a soldier.

"But you're needed more here," Teodora says. "I'm sorry, but who cares about Afghanistan? It's so far away. Italy has more serious problems, the economic crisis that's dragging us down, the Chinese, illegal immigrants, we're being invaded, you'll see, no one goes out after dark anymore, it's like there's a curfew around here. And then there's the Mafia, the Camorra, there's a war going on right here at home, you don't have to go looking for one ten thousand miles away." "Two thousand eight hundred miles," Manuela specifies. "Only a little farther away than

Iceland, but Iceland's in Europe, so it seems closer; geography isn't math."
"Okay, if you say so, you went to school, I don't know this stuff," Teodora
admits, "but ten thousand or two thousand eight hundred, it's the same
thing: you'd do more good as a police officer in Italy, Manuela."

Tiberio Paris would always say that Teodora talked too much, and
worse, she talked without thinking, that she was as rough as pumice and
as sharp as a razor. He would say it was a lack of education, or her Com-
munist education, or something like that. But Manuela, with her military
training, had always appreciated her frankness. She shrugs her shoulders and smiles. But she doesn't respond. In any case, Teodora will never
understand what that feather in her cap means to her.

Last year Manuela celebrated Christmas under a heated tensile structure as sand whirled in the wind and settled on the tent, on their camouflage uniforms, on their skin, in a kind of rough embrace. One long table
for nearly two hundred people, including a Regional Command West
general from Herat, a Task Force South colonel from Farah, the commanders of the Tenth Alpini Regiment and the neighboring ANA brigade, a representative of the American Provincial Reconstruction Team,
and a cable TV reporter. The captain suggested she sit with her men, so
she was at the opposite end of the mess hall, far from the lights that lit up
the scene like a movie set. The head cook, a corporal, had done his best
to make them feel at home. The smell of garlic, tomato, and chilies tick-
led her nostrils. But there wasn't any wine, or coffee even, because supplies arrived in fits and starts. "Not for me, I'm a vegetarian," Jodice said,
removing a dead fly from his mouth. He placed it on Zandonà's spaghetti,
and he, distracted, ate it while the other soldiers brayed with laughter.
They'd arrived a few days before. All Manuela had seen of Afghanistan
was an airport, the road that heads into town, a few mountains sprinkled
with snow, and the perimeter of the base. She hardly knew these two
guys, and still called them by their last names. It had been a happy, even
juvenile Christmas dinner there at the edge of the world, together with
her tribe. With her desire to make a difference. She sat thinking about it
in Teodora's little living room; it was the most wonderful Christmas of
her life. There'd never be another one like it. Maybe that's what it means
to have your future behind you.

Teodora sets a steaming soup tureen on the table and the pungent
odor of liver, kidneys, and pork fat wafts up from it. But there's no sign of
Traian. "It's ready!" she shouts. "It's always the same thing—I have to

call him a hundred times, one of these days I'm going to throw that computer out the window!" Manuela catches her father's meek gaze. His photograph in its silver frame is prominently displayed in the little glass cupboard in the living room. His light eyes, dazzled by the flash in city hall the day of his wedding to Teodora, seem happy. But his hair has already thinned, all that remain are two grayish strands on each side of his head, and he's grown flabby; he certainly doesn't look like someone who's beaten cancer. Looking at his picture now, Manuela realizes he was already seriously ill on his wedding day. Teodora, on the other hand, now seems younger than ever. With her teased hair and shapeless, knee-length blue skirt, she looks like a middle-aged peasant in the photo. But in the years since, she has shed the weight of time. Manuela called her from the base on her thirty-seventh birthday. "Happy birthday, Teodora!" she shouted. "You remembered!" Teodora exclaimed, surprised. Her voice came and went, nibbled by the interference, deformed by the distance. Then the connection went dead.

Teodora was a nurse at the Passo Oscuro hospital. She had gotten to know Manuela's father while adjusting his catheter, bringing him his medications, and serving him his lunch on a tray. Manuela had never understood what she saw in that depressed, emaciated man, ugly with unhappiness, bald from chemo, whose only love was the electrical plant and who had lately developed a passion for windsurfing. It never even crossed her mind that her father, ill and anguished by the approach of death, would lose his head for that rough nurse, or that he could so carelessly and so remorselessly destroy his own life and that of his family for a love that was already all but terminal. As soon as he finished his chemo and regained his strength, he stuffed his shirts in a suitcase and moved in with Teodora. Manuela hadn't seen him leave. When she and Vanessa came home from school, their father was gone. He didn't even have the courage to tell them, their mother had had to do it. Then Traian was born, and in the end Tiberio had married Teodora in city hall. Neither Manuela nor Vanessa was there.

Her mother never forgave Teodora. She's a social climber, she says, ruthless and greedy like everyone else from Eastern Europe who had poured into Ladispoli, in wave after wave, paying exorbitant rents for the second homes that Romans had left empty when they'd started vacationing in Sardinia or Sharm. First the Poles, then the Russians, the Albanians, and, finally, the Ukrainians and Romanians. They'd ruined the housing market. Ruined the atmosphere. Even ruined the families. Cinzia would say that Teodora got herself pregnant with a terminal cancer patient's child in order to get the dying man's money. She went around blabbing to everyone that before his second round of chemo Teodora had him freeze his sperm. They tried four times, but his sperm had grown weak, and in the end they had to do IVF. Manuela was sorry her mother told people these sad, private things, even though she knew they were true. But if Teodora expected a Central Electric employee to have some kind of fortune, she was wrong. After his death, all they found in his bank account were debts. Teodora had fleeced him, her mother noted bitterly, she didn't even leave him enough money for a decent funeral. Her mother was the one who had to foot the bill. And she had paid for his cremation, too.

Manuela's mother was hurt when she told her she wanted to have lunch with Teodora and Traian on Christmas Day. She couldn't explain it, but she had made her peace with her father while in Afghanistan. She had despised him, had kept him from getting close to her, from being part of the important events in her life. She hadn't invited him to the swearing-in ceremony, he never even saw her in uniform. But distance had softened her anger, had made her grudge insignificant: far from her usual routine and all that was familiar to her, she had had to come to terms with who she was, and found that she hardly recognized herself. Finally, lying on her cot in the desert, thousands of miles from home, mulling over her past, she asked herself why she hated him so much. It felt as if she understood everything. And everything was very simple. In the few years he had lived with Teodora, something had happened to the Tiberio Paris she had known—that eternally grumpy, anxious, unhappy man. Her father was now content. As stars burned like flaming confetti in the tar-colored sky, and RPGs exploded against the protective walls of the base, she told herself that her private war against her father and his new family had to end. Wars are never won. Victory consists in achieving your objective. And she had achieved hers.

Traian's room smells like sneakers. His soccer gear is scattered all over the place, a jersey hanging from the window, cleats under the bed, shin guards on the armchair. A poster of Gigi Buffon, the national team goalie, is tacked to the closet door. The walls are covered with Serie A pennants, red, yellow, black, and blue. All that's visible of Traian is a tuft of hair sticking up from behind his computer monitor. Black hair, long and straight. They look alike, Manuela and Traian. She feels somehow responsible for this extra brother, whom she met the day of her father's funeral. A snot-nosed brat with a Giants cap pulled down over his eyes, amused by the confusion and unable to understand why in the world he was in a strange church, listening to a Catholic priest, looking at a dark wood coffin adorned with two flower wreaths whose ribbons bore the exact same message: FROM YOUR WIFE. Traian was four years old, and Manuela had been granted a twenty-four-hour leave. She wore her uniform so that at least on this day of last respects, Tiberio Paris would know who his daughter had become. During the service, Manuela kept turning around to look at Traian. And he looked at her, mesmerized. When she stuck out her tongue at him, he burst out laughing. Teodora reached over and slapped him.

Manuela goes over to the desk, circles behind it, and puts her hands over his eyes. When Traian gets up to hug her, she realizes he's taller than she is now. At least four inches taller than last year. Pimply cheeks, a man's voice, and Paris eyes, the color of blue flax. "I wanted to come see you in the hospital," her brother apologizes, "but Mamma wouldn't let me." "It was far away, and besides, it was complicated having visitors," she says, "so it's probably just as well, Traian." "No," he insists, "I thought about you all the time." Manuela is his idol. She is both pleased and not at the same time. She never did anything to encourage him. She doesn't consider herself a role model, and her brother's devotion confounds her. She ruffles his hair. "Come on, come to dinner, don't make your mother wait, she made blood sausages." As Traian puts his computer to sleep, she glimpses his desktop photo, it's one she'd e-mailed him from Afghanistan. She's happy he liked it. It's of a girl his age, staring sternly, willfully, at the soldier taking her picture. She seems to be asking him what he's doing there, in her village, and yet also to be waiting, almost expecting something. Disappointment and innocence mingle with each other in that gaze, and when Lorenzo—who had taken the photo in Qal'a-i-Shakhrak during an inspection of the school they were building—showed it to her, she had recognized something familiar in it. When the screen goes blank Manuela is suddenly relieved, though she can't explain why.

That afternoon, Teodora wants to go to the movies, to see a comedy, to have a few laughs. At the Parco Leonardo multiplex: twenty-four theaters, plenty of parking, shops, an ultramodern place that doesn't seem to belong in Fiumicino. Manuela doesn't feel up to being with all those people yet, she might have a panic attack. She says so, bluntly, and Teodora apologizes with the same bluntness for not having thought of that, and hastens to say that of course she'll skip it. It's a stupid movie, anyway. But Manuela knows that Teodora wants to go to remember her husband, because that was one of his stubborn habits, the only pleasure he allowed himself. Manuela's father went to the movies only once a year, always on Christmas Day. And Teodora shouldn't have to give that up because, six months after the attack, the daughter of the father of her son still can't handle a crowd. It's not fair. Manuela begs, insists, and in the end Teodora heads off on her own, in her fake fur coat, her hair freshly coiffed, to see a comedy she won't even enjoy, but that her husband would have liked. It's the only way she has of letting him know that she loved him, that she still misses him.

Manuela stays and plays video games with Traian. He lets her choose the game, like a challenger in a duel who lets his opponent choose the weapon. Dubious, she studies the covers, on which square-jawed supermen, armed to the teeth, roar. The titles are all menacing: Assassin's Rage, Battlefield, Call of Duty: Modern Warfare, Medal of Honor. Her brother collects the most brutal shoot-'em-ups, in which he plays the hero who exterminates one human being after another, mowing them down with machine guns, blasting them apart with missiles, crushing them under a tank. Most are set in Iraq or Afghanistan. The protagonist is either a new recruit or a marine. Manuela worries that all the violence is having a negative impact on him. Traian worships weapons. Teodora says he surfs violent extremists' websites, and ordered an AK-47 on the Internet once. Luckily it was a scam, and in the end he just lost some money. "Traian," Manuela says, "I heard you flunked, that you're repeating freshman year." "The teacher and I didn't get along," he mopes. "This year's better, mostly." "Are you doing your homework?" she asks, regretting it right away because she thinks she sounds like his mother. "Can you come see the tournament finals?" Traian asks, slipping a DVD out of its case. "I'm not a sub anymore, I sent the regular fullback to the bench, we're going to win the cup, and if I score I'm going to dedicate my goal to you." In the end he chooses the game: Sniper. Manuela reminds herself that she should tell Teodora to keep an eye on him. Every time she sees him, she finds him more deeply immersed in virtual realities, more indifferent to what's going on around him. But she never does, because she recognizes herself in that willful, wayward boy.

At twelve she was a toothpick with constantly scraped knees, long, wild hair, bangs that hid her eyes, filthy fingernails, a frayed T-shirt, and dirty socks. She, too, lived two lives. In the first, she was the daughter of a working woman separated from—or rather, abandoned by—her husband: a rude girl who reluctantly attended junior high. She used to wonder why in the world she had to waste time writing out equations and learning geometry when—just like the ordinary Japanese girl in the cartoon who discovered she was really the warrior Sailor Moon—she might discover she was a captain, leading her men on heroic missions. During class she would fly away, doodling spaceships and whirling knives in her notebook, hidden behind the scoliotic spine of the kid in front of her. No one knew what was racing through her head. She didn't confide her fantasies and dreams to anyone, not even her grandfather, who would have respected them. Instead, as the years went by, the more important they became to her, the more she disguised or hid them from others. She was afraid they would laugh at or belittle them. That's how it always was, at home and at school. If you wanted something, other people would make fun of you ruthlessly, spoil your dreams any way they could. Her mother did it so she would learn to stand on her own; everyone else just to be mean. People who don't dream are envious of those who do.

Her Italian teacher would call her mother in three times a year. "Manuela's lazy; she could do a lot better—she's quick, intelligent, but she doesn't apply herself. Try and encourage her. It's clear she doesn't get enough stimulation at home." Cinzia wasn't one of those mothers who will defend her children against all comers, no matter what. She would accept the teacher's rebukes and go home feeling mortified, somehow to blame for her younger daughter's disappointing academic performance, even if she couldn't have said why. She was working herself to death in order to give Vanessa and Manuela a decent life, and she was succeeding. She had denied them nothing, except, perhaps, her presence: she was never home. Then it would all turn into a big argument around the kitchen table, as dinner got cold; Cinzia tried exhortations and encouragements, but Manuela would snort and barely listen, because she didn't care at all. This was only her outer life; she was really somewhere else.

In her other life, her imaginary life—the only one that really mattered—she wandered through space and time, through the galaxy and geography, the future and the past: she killed enemy aliens in order to restore Silver Millennium's reign, rode horseback with Napoleon in the Russian steppes, fought with a bayonet in the Libyan desert, or followed Alexander the Great across battlefields, conquering the world. Sometimes, while her teacher was explaining grammar, she was off in Babylon as it burned, and as buildings collapsed in flames, she would flee on the back of an elephant laden with gold and jewels pilfered from the vanquished.

And when she wasn't lost in fantastic battles, she'd be on the beach, even in wintertime, with the kids from the new apartment blocks. They were an unruly, anarchic gang. They'd go explore the abandoned Nazi bunkers along the coast, now littered with porn magazines and used condoms, or peel around on their older siblings' motor scooters, or swim in the surf when the beach clubs were flying the red flag. They had it in for everyone—the people who lived in the villas, the pretty boys at high school, the Russians who sold Soviet junk at the flea market, the blacks who picked artichokes, the Macedonians who grazed sheep for the Sardinians. Out of spite, they'd scratch the sides of cars with rusty nails. They'd choose new cars with powerful motors that belonged to Romans who came to eat at the restaurants along the beach. Manuela was an artist of incision, her marks looked like scars on the metal. They'd steal melons from the co-op fields and smash them on the highway, hurling them from the overpass. Then they'd flee on their bikes, disappearing into the spiderweb of dirt roads that used to cover the countryside. She wasn't the only girl in the gang, but she wasn't one of the ones who just followed the boys. She didn't take orders from anybody. She'd talk back to her mother, or ignore her, as if her mother's very existence constituted some kind of punishment. She dreamed of being free, strong, independent: adolescence was a prison.

Manuela battles Traian in Sniper, Battlefield, Medal of Honor. She beats him every time. He takes it badly, but refuses to give up. Every time GAME OVER blinks on the screen he requests a rematch, loses again, insists, then flies into a rage. She is unmoved. The only thing she can teach him is to learn how to lose. Only at the end—when, exhausted and incredulous, he asks for a truce—does she explain that there was a soldier at the base who did nothing during downtime but play video games. He had beaten all his comrades, and so finally he challenged his platoon leader. She couldn't let herself be defeated by one of her men, could she? So she learned to play. And she beat him. Traian says she can wish him a merry Christmas, even see him while they talk, because he still has Skype even if he doesn't use it anymore.

For the months his sister was in Afghanistan, their Skype calls were the highlights of his days. But when Manuela was in Italy, he didn't hear from her much. She came home on leave only twice a year. Sometimes she'd spend an afternoon with him. Just her, because Vanessa always had something else to do—or at least that's what Manuela would say. As if he cared. He didn't give a damn about Vanessa. Nor she about him, for that matter. Manuela would have him climb on the back of her motorcycle, a crazy Honda Fireblade she'd bought on installment as soon as she got her first paycheck, and they'd go for a ride. Manuela had taken on the role of teacher or mentor or something. Maybe she learned it in the army. Whatever, she took care of him. Manuela had been the one to take him to the Roman Ship Museum in Fiumicino, and to Rome, to see Trajan's Forum. She showed him the hundred-and-twenty-five-foot-high marble column whose spiral friezes recount Trajan's exploits, and explained that the ashes of the emperor who bore his name (or rather the other way around) were once kept there, in a golden urn. One Sunday last year, in Rome, they ran into a soldier from her company. He wasn't in uniform, but he saluted her anyway. It made an impression on Traian that this burly, iron-pumping guy was afraid of his sister, a twig he could have snapped with one hand.

But once she left for Bala Bayak, he heard from her more often. To him she seemed like the protagonist in one of his shoot-'em-ups—a tough marine under evil Afghan fire. He always had trouble getting through to her, but when he finally did, he never knew what to say, because he was afraid that talking about stupid things like school, grades, exams, and homework would bore someone who's in a place where airplanes sow missiles, enemies sow explosive traps, and people are ripped to shreds every day. But Manuela was interested in those stupid things, or pretended to be, and he was happy she found the time to talk with him. He didn't know that time was the only thing she had plenty of. Traian would brag about his military sister. At school he'd show his classmates and teachers photos of her on his cell. Manuela manning the gun on a Lince,

Manuela in uniform surrounded by dozens of ragged children in front of a ruin riddled with bullet holes, Manuela, helmet on, gun raised. And since she'd been blown up, and was all over the news, his classmates had stopped calling him "Romanian."

"Thanks," Manuela says, "it's a nice idea, but they're in a different time zone, they're three and a half hours ahead, Christmas is already over. And besides, the Spaniard's not there anymore." "Well, call the other guys then," Traian insists. "It's night now, they'll be in the mess hall," she says: "And besides, I don't know anyone anymore, my regiment came home in mid-June." She was supposed to come home with them. Instead she returned early, on a stretcher, drugged with sedatives.

She remembers every interminable moment of the journey out. The roar of the C-130 engines, deafening despite her earplugs. The Siberian cold—there was no heat—the uncomfortable seat, which meant she had to huddle against the wall, the jolting of the plane, which upset her stomach, though she, unlike the guy next to her, had managed not to vomit. The embarrassment over the bathroom—there was only one, makeshift, surrounded by a curtain; the men peed in bottles but the few women, after trying to hold it, finally resigned themselves to clinging to the cloth and squatting. The emotion of that slow, blind, nocturnal flight, unable to see anything because the only window was nowhere near her, but aware she was flying over a mysterious and unknown continent. The exit from the rear hatch, feeling her way in a darkness so impenetrable it was like she'd gone blind, going from blackness and noise into the rarefied silence of the desert at the Herat Airport runway. Afghanistan revealed itself to her only three days later, when all the procedures were complete, the last exams passed, when she got her new International Security and Assistance Force ID, and her company finally received authorization to be transported out to their destination. The helicopter flew over a mustard-yellow plateau, tinted pink by the first light and hemmed in by impassable, solitary, smoke-colored mountains that seemed to float on the horizon. A sight that took her breath away. The trip back is a black hole. Maybe that's why she sometimes feels like she's still there.

"When are you going back to Afghanistan?" Traian asks her. "I don't know," Manuela shrugs, feigning indifference. "It depends on how my doctor's appointments go. You can't have a gimp private, let alone a gimp sergeant." "Why isn't the war over?" Traian asks. "Why haven't we won yet?" Manuela hesitates. She's about to say that according to the latest

ICOS data—the International Council on Security and Development—the Taliban controls eighty percent of the territory. But data has to be interpreted. You have to consider that the international coalition's fewer than seventy thousand soldiers are scattered over a territory the size of Germany with a population of thirty million, and if you bear in mind this overwhelming and unfavorable statistical reality, the situation suddenly looks very different. In short, the situation on the ground is far too complex to be captured by numbers. But Traian's only twelve, he wouldn't understand these subtleties. So she only says that it takes time, the transition isn't complete, and besides, it's not a war, so there can't be a victory. Traian studies her, disappointed. Apart from her pale skin and the white line that runs across her skull from temple to nape, his sister doesn't seem so sick. But she doesn't seem to be the proud, self-assured woman who said goodbye to him last year either. Maybe they turned her brain inside out over there. "Why did he do it?" he asks.

Traian had downloaded every article about the attack—in truth not that many, and concentrated in the three days after it happened, before the story disappeared and wasn't talked about anymore. People talked about the war in Afghanistan only when someone died—if it bleeds, it leads, is the golden rule of journalism—and since another soldier died a month later, the story of her attack was no longer interesting. Traian had queried the major search engines: the name "Manuela Paris" got 160,000 hits. He saved all the pages that provided some new information—most merely repeated what was written by the agency that first broke the news. He read them all, without finding the answer to the only question he would have asked if he'd had the chance. What do they have against you? What makes them lay those traps in order to kill you? What's so wrong with digging a well, repairing a street, or building a school? Or even arresting a murderer? What's wrong with that? Then he downloaded everything onto a pen drive and put it in a light blue envelope.

Manuela had no desire to read the newspapers, and, apart from her report to her superiors and her testimony for the state attorney's investigation, she didn't want to know anything more about the attack. It was as if it had happened to another person. Someone she had known, whose misfortune she pitied, someone she stood in solidarity with, but still couldn't quite bring into focus. She didn't remember anything about that morning, and she had said as much to the man who questioned her. She didn't remember her last journey to Qal'a-i-Shakhrak. Not the village or the school, not the dilapidated houses, not even the ruined minaret that he mentioned more than once. All she remembered was the noise. A rumble that seemed to erupt from the center of the earth, from deep down inside her.

The psychiatrist at the hospital where she was being treated said that her strategy of *avoidance*—as it was called in psychiatric jargon—was keeping her from working through the trauma; a symptom of PTSD, essentially, which she had to strive to overcome if she didn't want it to become chronic and cripple her forever. He was even making her write about her military experience and the trauma: her *homework*, as he called it. Manuela was supposed to work on it over the holidays and turn it in to him in January. When he had spoken to her about it, she couldn't help but smile. But he had cautioned her not to underestimate the assignment. Despite the childish, scholastic term, her homework was serious, perhaps the only therapy that could really help her. The only way she would be able to distance herself from the pain was to talk about it. Otherwise it would grow, spreading like a weed, extending its roots in the dark, until it destroyed her. Manuela had promised to take it seriously. She had bought a notebook, but she still hadn't written a single line in it. She kept telling herself it was only because she wasn't used to writing anymore. The only things she still wrote by hand were coordinates, code names, temperatures. To write about yourself you have to think, and she didn't want to think.

"There're some photos of you, too," Traian says, inserting the pen drive in his computer. "I don't know who gave them to the newspapers, we didn't give them anything because we couldn't ask your permission, and maybe you wouldn't have agreed—do you want to see them?" "What photos?" Manuela starts. Her hands tingle, her heart races, and there's that sensation again, of a sharp nail boring into the nape of her neck. "There's one of you with an old Afghani woman, you're standing close together, talking." "It must have been retouched," Manuela says. "Women don't go out there, they're invisible, in six months I must have seen two at most. And they certainly don't let themselves be photographed. Neither do old people, they think you're trying to steal their souls." "You came out good," Traian insists, clicking on the thumbnail of the photo. The envelope the pen drive was in is on his desk. In his neat, childish handwriting he had written SERGEANT PARIS in felt-tip pen.

The photo is of Manuela and an Afghani woman with a shriveled face and skin wrinkled like a rotting leaf standing in front of what seems to be a grayish metal cage—prefabricated modules filled with sand and inert material that form Sollum's impenetrable protective barrier. The woman is wearing a dark men's overcoat, and the scarf wrapped around her head and neck leaves only her eyes, nose, and mouth uncovered. She and Manuela, slightly out of focus, are looking at the photographer, both of them surprised, almost annoyed, at having their picture taken.

The image resurfaces from somewhere infinitely far away. Manuela had forgotten that face, the reason the woman came to the base, the incredibly brief instant of contact that the photographer froze in time. But the photo sparks the memory of the memory. And the vivid, indelible impression that woman—the first and only Afghani woman she had the chance to meet—had made on her. She can't remember her name, though she's certain she knew it once. The soldiers cruelly called her Skunk. All Afghanis stink, they'd say, from the lowliest shepherd to the highest-ranking general. Irritated, she had pointed out that after only a few weeks in the desert, they stunk, too. That woman's proud bearing, the dignity of her callused feet and angular face, the vertical furrows at the corners of her mouth, her wild, mute desperation, reminded Manuela of her mother at a precise moment in her life: the day she was laid off from the fish factory. It was the summer of 1996. The economy was stagnant, unemployment was rising, financial pressures were suffocating them, and then the company outsourced its mackerel operations to Tunisia. Manuela was thirteen, Vanessa sixteen. Their future had been decided by the company manager, who had never set foot inside the factory, had never met the women who worked there, had probably never even eaten a mackerel in his life. You never see it in restaurants. Mackerel is the fish of the poor.

Shadows had dimmed her mother's eyes; vertical furrows were carved around her mouth—indelible. Cinzia had always dreamed her daughter would graduate from college. Manuela's junior high Italian teacher told her that her daughter was a natural student; she had a rare mastery of language and an authentic intelligence, which consists not in the ability to memorize but in the ability to make connections. She was rebellious and her grades were poor, but Mrs. Colella shouldn't give up or let herself be fooled: she just had to give her time to get to know herself, to accept who she was. She urged her not to waste her daughter's talent, to consider it her inheritance—a fortune, in other words. And not to listen to people who say there's no point in studying Greek or philosophy, that Italy isn't America and social mobility doesn't exist here. Manuela's future was in her head. Cinzia, who had only finished junior high and had started working in the factory when she was fifteen, felt proud.

After she was laid off, and the factory closed, she couldn't make ends meet. She had to swallow the humiliation of accepting a monthly check from her ex-husband. Manuela enrolled in a vocational school that specialized in commercial and tourism management, the branch at Palo Nuova, so she could get there on the Cotral bus. It was a practical degree, good for getting a job. Her mother understood, and she didn't stand in her way. Sometimes, in the morning, she would take her to class herself. But she never asked her daughter anything. In five years she didn't go talk to her teachers even once. Stooped, tense, always tired, she never smiled. In that Afghani woman who dragged her plastic flip-flops in the dust at the base, Manuela had recognized the same discontent, the same rage, the same shame at not being able to offer her children something better that had disfigured her mother's face.

"She wasn't old, Traian," Manuela says. "I thought so, too, but it turns out she was my age: twenty-seven." Traian doesn't seem particularly struck by this revelation. The photo of an unsightly beggar holds no interest for him. He prefers those of military vehicles, Freccia wheeled tanks, or Dardo armored battle tanks. But now he's looking for another one. "Look at this, from inside a Lince," he insists, clicking on the last jpeg of the series, "you're talking on the radio." Manuela looks away too late. The news had made the front page in every newspaper—local, national, and online. Headlines in big letters. Next to the photo her brother wants to show her is another one, in color: a heap of burned metal, tires, rags, boots. In the foreground a blood-soaked helmet. Manuela rips the mouse out of her brother's hand and closes the program. The taste of rust in her mouth. Traian insists she take the pen drive, a present, he really wants her to have it. He collected those articles for her, it's her story. It must be cool being famous. He wants to end up in the newspapers and on TV one day, too, wants people to recognize him on the street and say, Hey, look, there's Traian Paris. Manuela should explain to him that celebrity has no value, it doesn't mean anything, but she doesn't have the strength.

For the rest of the afternoon, until Vanessa comes to get her, as she battles Traian in Sniper, she keeps asking herself who could have taken that photo of her in the Lince. Every soldier had a camera or cell phone, they were always photographing everything. But at times like that they had other things to think about. They concentrated because a mistake or a distraction could cost them their lives. Alert, mouths dry, their stomachs in knots. It wasn't nostalgia they were feeling, wanting to be somewhere else, or to go home. Eyes fixed on the square of the windshield, all they looked at was the road, which cut across the plateau: the fresh furrow of the tires, a straight, naked sign in the yellow, naked sand, no reference points, no trees, no poles, nothing at all. They looked at that simulacrum of road that unfurled before them, exactly the same for miles and miles. Searching for obstacles, metallic glints, unnatural bumps, turned earth, abandoned vehicles, unusual swellings, spots, shadows, carrion. And now, from all those months spent in Afghanistan, only one image remains lodged in her memory. That dazzling streak of light—ignited by the sun, swept along by the wind. The cloud of dust coming toward them, which they enter as if entering fog.

The guest at the Bellavista dines alone in the hotel restaurant and retires to his room at nine thirty. Manuela peeps at him through the living room curtains, and keeps eyeing the hotel all evening while, sitting on the couch next to Alessia, she pretends to watch a cartoon on TV—a story of enchanted castles, witches, and talking scarecrows. It's a good movie, with great animation and surprisingly sophisticated dialogue, but she can't manage to follow the plot. Images flash like lightning in her mind and superimpose themselves on the scenes she's watching, the voices in her head blending with the characters' voices. She's sitting in her mother's tiny living room, and yet she's not. Swallowed by vertigo, she clings to the arms of the couch so as not to faint, a whirlpool grabs her by the legs and drags her under, down to the bottom of who knows what. She feels like she's falling, and her foot's numb again. Her amygdalae—the endocrine glands at the base of her brain—are to blame; her doctor explained it all to her. They create abnormal hormone levels, and the neurotransmitters that act on the hippocampus are affected as well, eroding her memory. A neurological phenomenon, perfectly understandable. Nevertheless, as she watches the movie, her foot is no longer there. And her skull is being crushed with iron tongs.

The guest at the Bellavista Hotel is watching TV, too: an intermittent azure light filters through the shutters, lowered almost to the floor. To judge from the reflections and the colors projected on the walls, it's the same movie. He doesn't go outside to smoke. He turns the light out at eleven. He doesn't suffer from insomnia.

3

> >

HOMEWORK

The forward operating base at Bala Bayak was called Sollum. The name was in honor of a famous WWII battle, and was meant to infect us with the courage of those who had defended the front in the Libyan desert seventy years before. But the base itself reminded me, more than anything else, of a Zen garden: an open box of sand raked by truck wheels and helicopter blades, which stirred up a sandstorm during takeoffs and landings. The following conclusion appears on the first page of the diary I kept while in country. I wrote it on December 23, two hours after our arrival, sitting on my pack, still not sure where I was supposed to bunk: "Arrived at FOB. We're in the middle of nowhere, surrounded by nothing."

Ninth Company, Tenth Alpini Regiment was deployed on a rectangular island just under 1,000 feet long and just over 150 feet wide. The perimeter, punctuated by guard towers, was surrounded not by sea but by clouds of barbed wire and other protective barriers that obstructed the view and created the unpleasant sensation of being under siege. To the west stood a mountain, its sharp ridge a woman's profile, like Monte Circeo, but completely devoid of vegetation. Sollum's commander, Captain Paggiarin, observed with pleasure that our desert FOB reminded him of the Roman encampments beneath the walls of Masada; seen from the rock cliffs above, the camps in the sand below must have looked like squares drawn in the middle of nowhere, frighteningly vulnerable. Yet it was precisely from those encampments that the Roman legions had gone out to conquer the rebel city. I didn't know the story of Masada, and didn't say anything. But to the insurgents lying in wait atop the imposing mountain that dominated the plain, the impression our FOB gave was probably exactly what he'd described: a little fort in the middle of nowhere and—despite the vast number of high-tech weapons—frighteningly vulnerable.

The officers were quartered in small barracks that were either prefabricated or improvised as best as possible out of the ruins of a former Soviet airport, while the enlisted men were in inflatable tents, constantly besieged by the sun. They were not thrilled with their new homes. I'd hear them grumbling among themselves, but they'd go quiet whenever I came near. "I can't decide if it's more like a Boy Scout camp or a gypsy settlement," Rizzo commented sourly. "What were you expecting, a hotel?" Pieri laughed. "So how is it that the guys from the Fifth are in Shindand while the Tenth ended up in this shithole?" Schirru muttered. A friend of his assigned to Shaft had extolled the beauty of the immense, fertile valley as well as the carpets of a certain Abdul, who was allowed a stall inside the Task Force Center base. A market was held there every Sunday. Here, nothing but dust and desert. "Clearly the Tenth has no guardian angel," sighed a lance corporal whose name I hadn't learned yet. Even in Bala Bayak, conspiracy theories served to explain every injustice. "It was worse in Somalia," Masera, the QRF sergeant, assured them. "But it's better in Lebanon," Santapaola muttered. "They've even got the sea."

I gathered up my gear and, with feigned self-confidence—it weighed fifty pounds—dragged it over to the infirmary. Housing for women is always a problem at FOBs. The officer in charge of logistics, after counting out the tents and the names on the rosters, put the three of us in the same corner of the base, in a container fifteen feet long and six feet wide. On my right, the more sheltered side, was First Lieutenant Ghigo, medical doctor. On my left, the side most exposed to dust and drafts, behind a curtain hanging from a clothesline, Corporal Giani, Quartermaster. I took the middle. I was an NCO, the link between enlisted personnel and the commissioned officers: the middle was my place, my job, and in a certain sense my mission. There were almost two hundred people at Sollum, but only three of us were women. A gunner had been replaced at the last minute because of a cavity in her molar. No one in our medical corps specialized in dentistry so they didn't let you deploy if you were in danger of getting an abscessed tooth.

I slapped the dust from my cot, unrolled my sleeping bag, folded up my duffel and my pack, took out my bathrobe, and headed for the showers. Guys were in line for the john. There were only twelve of them: chemical toilets, squatters. A few were in line for the showers, too, but I had the key to the one reserved for women. As I walked past I could feel their hostile gazes on the back of my neck. I didn't give them the satisfaction of turning around. I knew what they thought about privileges for women.

As soon as it got dark, I slipped into my sleeping bag. Though I was exhausted from the trip, I couldn't fall asleep. The incessant hiss of the generators and the sound of vehicles maneuvering in the square kept me awake. And adrenaline made my blood tingle. For the first time in my life, I was exactly where I wanted to be. This was what I'd been hoping for ever since that evening in November 1992, when the Manuela Paris I recognize as myself was born: the story that led me to Bala Bayak begins way back then. When I was nine years old.

Even though I preferred sports and playing outside to fairies and toy kitchens, I could never even have imagined becoming a soldier. Strange as it may seem, dreams need an echo in reality; you can't dream of something you can't conceive of, something you don't know. And when I was little, Italy was the only country in Europe whose armed forces still didn't take women. Even Portuguese women could enlist. When it comes to civil rights, Italians are always last. That evening my life lit up. Sprawled on the couch, a greasy cardboard box on my knees, I was dining on pizza, Coca-Cola, and potato chips. Alone, because my mother was racking up overtime at the fish factory, my father was in the hospital recovering from an operation to remove a tumor in his shoulder, and my sister, Vanessa, was rolling around on her bed with a boy in the next room. She had just discovered that her unripe figure made her irresistible to men, whose attention she craved. I kept the television on with the volume cranked up to avoid hearing their grunting. In short, I was at home, alone, wedged between the cushions on the couch, confused, and bored as only a nine-year-old girl who has finished her homework and played with all her toys can be, another day gone without anything happening, the same as yesterday and the day before and tomorrow—when all of a sudden, smiling Amazons appeared on the television screen.

Not the ancient Amazons my grandfather used to tell me about every now and then, woman warriors who would cut off one breast, who had fought at the walls of Troy, and whose captain, Penthesilea, was killed by swift-footed Achilles. No, these were modern Amazons, practically my contemporaries. The news was reporting on an experiment entitled "Italian Women: Soldiers for a Day" or something like that, which thirty young women had participated in. It showed them in uniform, marching in a barracks in Rome. Ordinary women, and yet, to a young girl watching wide-eyed from her tiny living room in Ladispoli, they were already bathed in a mythical glow. In truth it was only a publicity stunt; it would still take several years for the armed forces to accept women for real. But I didn't know that then, and staring at those women marching happily around the parade grounds, I was overwhelmed, first with amazement and then with joy. I knew instantly that that was where I belonged. And for the first time I let myself think I wasn't simply some hopeless mess of a girl.

From that moment, since the only books in my house were *Reader's Digest*s my mother had bought who knows when, and which sat gathering dust on the top shelf in the living room, I started going to the public library in the piazza. I became a compulsive reader. I would devour encyclopedias in search of stories about female warriors and was delighted to discover that there were lots of them, in every era and in every part of the world. I diligently copied out their stories in a small notebook, on the cover of which triumphed the powerful and invincible Sailor Moon, the warrior of love and justice whom I'd by then discovered in TV cartoons, and with whom I identified completely. But Sailor Moon was the invention of an ingenious Japanese writer, also a woman, whereas the female warriors whose deeds I recorded had really existed—or at least that's what those books made me believe. There was May Senta Wolf Hauler, nicknamed Little Wolf, who in 1917 fought as an Austro-Hungarian infantry soldier in a mountain battle and took defeated Italians prisoner. And the Amazons of Matitina, an island in the Caribbean, near Guadeloupe, where, as Christopher Columbus learned from the natives in his retinue, only women—deadly with bow and arrow—lived; they coupled with males only once a year, no doubt making them take care of the fruits of their union, unless of course they were girls. The Matitina Amazons had fought hard against the Spaniards. But my favorite was an Italian like me, Onorata Rodiani, who at twenty became a soldier of fortune after killing the man who tried to rape her. In the fifteenth century, this woman, disguised as a man, fought for thirty years under several captains, until she was mortally wounded in battle. I never showed that secret notebook to anyone, and when I was twenty, in the throes of depression, I threw it away. I still regret it. But I never forgot the bellicose companions of my youth. For it was with them that I spent those years while I waited to grow up so I could enter the barracks in Rome. The world would still have to change, the laws would have to be reformed, and the Italian army reorganized, but I wasn't in a hurry. And knowing I'd been born neither too early nor too late, but just at the right moment, gave me a strange strength—the certainty of having a destiny.

And now there I was, in the desert, with my people. At the NCO Academy in Viterbo, when it was time to indicate our preference, I didn't ask to join the paratroopers or Lagunari—the amphibious assault regiment—the posts my classmates coveted most. I asked to join the Alpini, who were trained for mountain combat, because I was convinced that, throughout our history, they had formed the democratic base of the army, the true infantry of the people. In every Italian war, the Alpini were the only ones who showed they knew not so much what duty was, but what the fatherland was: they communed with the land their fathers and grandfathers had tilled, hoed, and farmed for centuries, with the animals they knew how to raise and slaughter, with the trees they knew how to prune, fell, and turn into firewood and charcoal, with the stones that became roof tiles and walls, with the rocks and mountains that marked Italy's borders. In short, they really knew how to be Italian. Since I graduated near the top of my class, I got my wish even though I wasn't born in Alpino territory.

I put my earphones on, the volume low. Death metal is so repetitive it sends me into a trance. I listened to Gory Blister's *Graveyard of Angels* CD, just right for the naked yellow cemetery that stretched for miles and miles around me. I dozed off, only to be roused by Giani's screams. A scorpion under her pillow! First Lieutenant Ghigo grumbled that the sting of an Afghani scorpion is rarely fatal. "But girls, I told you to keep your mosquito nets closed and to inspect your bunks. This place is full of scorpions and camel spiders, it's no fun finding one in your sleeping bag. Just kill it, okay?" she snorted. But Giani was in a panic. "But how?" she kept repeating. "How? It's huge, it grosses me out." Ghigo didn't move. She was thirty-four, a first lieutenant, an elder, to her we were newbies.

In the army, seniority is everything. I unzipped my bag, put on my slippers, and switched on my flashlight—shielding it with my hands, because the base was in blackout. I whistled in astonishment. The scorpion was gold, like a coin, and as big as my hand. It waved its poisonous stinger like a flag. A war machine created by nature. Perfect in its own way, and perhaps necessary in this environment. A sting probably wouldn't be fatal, but I didn't feel like finding out. We two were incompatible. Giani's wide eyes told me it was up to me. I certainly couldn't ask the guys for help. I was their commander, they would have teased me forever. And besides, they were too far away. I sent the scorpion flying to the floor with a towel and then crushed it with my rifle, thrusting the butt into its abdomen with all my might. I heard a crunching sound, like glass shattering. I was sorry that that scorpion was the one to welcome me to Afghanistan—and that that was how I reciprocated.

My first days were a battle of logistics and bureaucracy. The rotation of brigades and regiments was rusty. Phone booths, mess refrigerators, shower pipes, protective barriers, concertina wire—everything needed fixing, cells had to be organized, jobs assigned. TFS and PRT commanders briefed the FOB commanding officer, Paggiarin briefed the officers, and the officers briefed the platoon NCOs. Even though special forces had been at Bala Bayak until just recently, Tenth Alpini Regiment wasn't on a combat mission. Our mission was routine: convoy escorts, guards, roadblocks, arms requisitioning, outreach, identification and neutralization of threats and hostile elements. It could all be summed up in three words: *security, reconstruction, governability.* The Ninth Company's operation name was a good omen: Reawakening.

Captain Paggiarin briefly recapped the situation. "We have to support the reconstruction of a province that is forty-eight thousand square kilometers—the size of the Veneto, Friuli, and Lombardy combined—population almost half a million, with less than two thousand men. We started pretty much at zero, after thirty years of anarchy: no public services—no water, no light, no sewers—no schools, no courts, no army, no police, no institutions. We've made remarkable progress. But it takes time. There's an Afghan proverb that says, 'a frog that leaps on a clod of earth thinks he can see Kashmir.' We have to humbly imagine that we're that frog, all the while knowing we'll never see Kashmir. But we still have to leap on that clod." The concept was crystal clear.

Headquarters wanted us to demonstrate flexibility and movement in order to testify to our presence even in the remotest villages. Interaction with the locals was essential, but we always had to be conscious of the risks. We were advised to be patient, take it one step at a time, keep in mind that it takes only one stone to destroy a glass house. Respect for the local population and private property meant we had to be extremely diplomatic. Ninth Company had approximately ten weeks to get oriented. Winter operations were usually not particularly complex. But spring was coming, and when the snow in the mountains melted and the roads, now impassable, reopened, and especially after the opium poppy was harvested, an increase in hostile activities was expected. Men, drugs, and arms would start moving in April, attacks would intensify, casualties would increase. Insurgents would undoubtedly engage us in armed conflict, which meant we had to train rigorously every day. But I knew all this already, and while the captain spoke, my gaze wandered outside the shed. Sand as fine as powder, kicked up by the wind, whirled among the tents. All that mattered to me was that I had been assigned to S3—operations—and was responsible for thirty men.

Pegasus platoon expressed surprise at having a female commander. Everyone feels insecure when faced with something they're not used to. The men greeted me with curiosity, but I had learned to look inside people, and knew how to decipher the language of their evasive eyes, even the skepticism in their voices when they said, "Yes, ma'am." Without even knowing me, they'd already judged me. I could guess what they were saying. Little Miss Graduate, fresh out of school, unsuited to such a delicate operative role, unfairly promoted by the army general staff, protected by some bigwig at the ministry, or the lover of some high-ranking officer. I was determined to ignore their resentment, which in any case I understood. But I would win them over. I would treat my subordinates as I wanted my superiors to treat me. I would lead without coercion and instruct with behavior rather than with words. I would be firm and consistent; I would delegate so that my subordinates felt involved: I merely had to identify my most capable men. I would face problems calmly, and with the utmost self-control. More than anything, I wanted to appear sure of myself. But I knew I had to earn their respect. That's how it always is when you're a woman. You have to work three times as hard to prove you're worth half as much as a man.

And besides, I'd already been through it. I'd spent twelve months in the rank and file. At eighteen, I survived it. At twenty-seven, I considered myself strong enough to deal with Afghanistan and my platoon's prejudices at the same time. In a Sollum perennially enveloped in a cloud of sand and smoke, I sought the joy and enthusiasm I'd felt during my first months in the armed forces, and which I thought I'd lost. I was nostalgic for those ten weeks of basic training in Ascoli Piceno, in a barracks reserved for women. We slept in a dorm, six beds to a room, like at summer camp. My bed creaked and my locker was small, but it didn't bother me, because I really didn't have much. Apart from my underwear, gym socks, rubber insoles for my boots, seal fat to keep them soft, apart from my sweatsuit, flashlight, padlocks, toothbrush, shower shoes, toilet paper, multi-outlet for charging my cell phone, gel Band-Aids for the blisters on my feet, and a hairnet to hold my hair in a bun, all I had was one change of clothes for when I was off duty: a pair of jeans. The prohibition on colored nail polish—which upset my fellow soldiers, who considered it an offense to their femininity—left me indifferent: I'd never used it.

Life followed an elementary, repetitive rhythm. Reveille at 0630 hours, fall in, flag-raising, marching, military theory, push-ups, training, guard duty, firing range, fall out, lights out at eleven thirty, like when we were kids. The other women were done in by the marches in the rain, the training runs where we had to follow the instructor all around the barracks and then along dirt roads, but I enjoyed them. (I was a cross-country champion when I was young, and I might have kept at it if I hadn't found out that my father had been a good runner. I didn't want to have anything to do with that worm.) The overnight field training exercises—three days in the woods with a tent, a sleeping bag, and a pack—thrilled me (I'd always dreamed of going camping). Being away from home, which for many was the cause of tears and sobbing, turned out to be good for me, because my family was made up of rancorous, unhappy, and confused individuals who unloaded their frustrations on one another, punishing each other for imagined wrongs. The only one I missed was Vanessa. We'd grown up together: her voice and her laugh had been the soundtrack of the first eighteen years of my life. But Vanessa—even though she was pregnant and for some reason I can't remember anymore wasn't supposed to drive—would take the car and come see me on Saturdays. And a few hours of her talking nonstop—she's a real motormouth—was more than enough. Communal living, which the other women considered agreeable at first but increasingly trying as the weeks wore on, was for me a pleasant surprise: I'd felt very alone growing up. The discipline didn't seem oppressive to me, as it did to more than half my companions, who dropped out; on the contrary, it relaxed me, because for the first time in my life someone was telling me what to do, and I had no choice but to obey. I had to accept the rules or be punished or excluded; I had to zip it, even if I was convinced I was right. In short, it was as if I was always wrong, no matter what: a total demolition, from the bottom up, of everything I'd ever been. Up till then, I'd always made my own decisions, and the more someone tried to force me to do something, the more I'd resist. I'd never made my bed before; at most I'd pull the covers up over the pillow, and by morning the crumpled sheets would have left zebra stripes on my skin. I had never cleaned up my room, never cared what condition my clothes were in. But in the barracks—after three savage scoldings—I complied. My bunk was perfect, my uniform pressed, my boots polished. When I went home months later, my mother said I was so changed she hardly recognized me.

Loyalty and sacrifice, the watchwords that became the cornerstones of my new existence, reminded me of my grandfather's lectures, and they rang true. Lies and subterfuge, which I had resorted to many times, were now repugnant to me. As for sacrifice, I already knew that nobody gives you anything for free, neither respect nor affection. To sacrifice myself for something more noble—my country, as my instructors kept telling me, even though I didn't think I had one—made me feel important: me, a complete zero, a grub, a gnat, a provincial girl born into a dysfunctional family that couldn't offer any kind of future.

And then there were the weapons. The first time they put an AR70/90 in my hands and I held it in firing position, I knew we would get along. My drill instructor told me I had to care for it as if it were my child. That seemed somewhat excessive. Besides, I didn't know how to take care of a child. But he was right. I liked everything about my Beretta assault rifle—its awkward stiffness, its deadly weight, its pointy edges, its oily smell, even the abrasion it left on my neck, the bruise the belt made by pressing for hours against the same spot on my skin, so that my arm swelled like a drug addict's for three weeks. But the sound it made when I loaded a magazine or chambered a round, the crackle of the volley, thrilled me. In that suspended second when—before pulling the trigger—my eye focused on the target in the crosshairs, I felt I owned the world, could blast anything. Even though the weapons were complicated, and difficult to handle, assemble, and maintain, even though the pineapple-like grenades loaded with deadly compound B were heavy in my hands, and the noise of the mortars absolutely terrifying, I quickly developed a real passion for our squad's weapons. I learned everything about them, about automatic pistols, calibers, bullets, sights, rounds per second, cartridge capacity, maximum effective range, triggers, and even bullet speed. I spent hours cradling my rifle, disassembling the bolt, polishing, oiling, and lubricating it, and cleaning the bore with a brush. Then I would chamber a round and load the drum. I even talked to it. When I finished basic training and had to return it to the armory, the parting was painful, as if they were cutting off one of my limbs. You never forget your first rifle.

I didn't know what to do when I was off duty. Civilian life now seemed disappointing. On Saturdays the other women would stroll down Ascoli Piceno's main street, meet their boyfriends, go window-shopping, do laundry at the coin-op. I usually stayed in the barracks, reading tank magazines. People started saying that Manuela Paris was a fanatic.

I got the second-highest score on the physical and practical tests and on the military science exams. "You would have been first, if Angelica Scianna weren't so blond," my roommate Guglielma Ruffilli teased. But I wanted to be friends with Angelica so I didn't take offense. Besides, they had assigned us to the same unit, same detachment, same regiment, and so we headed off together. She from Sicily, me from Ladispoli, both of us headed north, hundreds of miles from home. It was the first time so far away for both of us. That first night, sleeping in the same dorm room, we wondered what would happen now that we were finally in a real barracks.

A few hours were all it took to disillusion me. The soldiers looked down on newcomers. Merit counts less than seniority, and I was the newest arrival. I'd have the right to take it out on a new bunch of recruits a few months later. Such were the unwritten, unchangeable laws of the group, in place from time immemorial, and I had to accept them. Uphold them, even—along with the pranks, the abuses of power, and the bullying. My superiors were either paternalistic or brutal, nothing in between. But my future depended on their assessments. I was evaluated constantly. I had to have them on my side if I wanted to stay in the army, to reenlist when my twelve months were up. My five female companions were competitive—and one of them, the beautiful and clever Angelica

Scianna, in fact, was obsessed with excelling. Each hoped the others would fail so she could be the only one to succeed. I had been raised as a boy in a family of women, and considered myself amphibious: I was comfortable with women, and they often confided in me, especially when they had relationship troubles, but I was comfortable with men, too. Separating people based solely on gender seemed an old-fashioned approach, as arcane as the debates on the sex of angels. I never would have imagined I'd be rejected by the men and considered a rival by the women.

In a co-ed environment, the lack of privacy turned out to be humiliating. Latrines stinking of stale urine and whipped by icy drafts; rusty sinks, dreary showers. Narrow, uncomfortable beds. Senseless discipline. Exhausting physical combat training. It was no longer a question, as it had been in Ascoli, of jogging after an instructor at a modest pace, so as not to humiliate the overweight women who, poor things, were showing such goodwill. And there were quite a few of them. The weight cutoff at enlistment was one hundred and seventy-five pounds—generous enough to include even the obese. But here you had to complete grueling marches on impassible trails, crushed under the weight of your pack and weapons. A rifle alone weighs eight pounds, but with ammunition it comes to seventeen, and that's not counting grenades and other equipment. Perhaps only Vanessa, swollen out of proportion during her pregnancy, could understand the effort required for someone as slight as me to drag around such ballast. The first time I had to slither through the mud on my elbows and climb a rope to get over a ditch, I was left behind. Incredulous, I hobbled through the rest of the course, coming in last, out of breath and spent. This one's not going to make it, I read in our trainer's eyes; give her a month and she'll quit. She doesn't have the physique. Or the head. When he bawled me out in public because I was the worst of the platoon on the rifle range—it was like I was cross-eyed, I couldn't hit the target even once—I cracked. I felt so humiliated, so disappointed with myself that I started to cry. And I didn't even have a Kleenex.

"Emotions, Paris," the drill instructor reprimanded me, planting himself in front of me, his legs wide. "A soldier keeps them to himself." I sniffled and stared at my boots. "Do I have to put in your character report that Corporal Paris is unable to control her emotions? That what Paris knows how to do best is cry?" "It won't happen again, sir," I swore. After that, I saved my tears of dejection for the bathroom. I'd lock the door and flush to make noise, crouch down, and have myself a good cry. A soft sob that choked in my throat. Then, as the months went by, I found I couldn't cry on command anymore. So I stopped.

Only during theory classes did I shine. They thrilled me. Strategy. History. Religions. I had hated school, but in the barracks I discovered I liked to study. I listened openmouthed to the officer lecturing. I took notes. "Write it all down, write it all down," Corporal Zappalà would tease me, "maybe the sergeant will hire you as his secretary."

I didn't socialize with the short-term service guys: twenty-year-olds who ended up in the barracks because they had few other options, Neanderthal braggarts, dumb as rocks, whose only way of speaking to women was to make vulgar jokes. Except for those two or three sentimental soldiers who took themselves too seriously and hid ungrammatical love letters in our bunks, the men viewed us as sexual distractions, there to keep up the morale. If I happened to run into one in some secluded corner of the barracks, he'd try to grab me. Angelica and I would always go to the bathroom together at night; we'd watch each other's backs. All the women responded in their own ways to the unwanted attention— either by passively putting up with it, crying, or feeling flattered. I returned the insult. Foul language has never intimidated me. "Kiss my ass," I said to a soldier who pushed me into the mess hall storage room and tried to feel me up. I realized right away that the only thing you shouldn't do was complain to your superiors: you'd be considered a pain in the ass, a whiner, weak, unable to take care of yourself, and therefore unfit to wear a uniform. They'd tear you apart in your character report, so you couldn't reenlist. In short, they'd screw you.

The guys divided female soldiers into three categories: lesbians, whores, and trolls. I wondered which was best. The lesbians were picked on and provoked a desire for revenge. The trolls, too ugly to spark pornographic fantasies, were left in peace, but ignored by their comrades and superiors. The whores, who only fucked the instructors and officers because they wanted to get ahead, were badmouthed but feared, because at the end of the day they really did move up the ladder. To Angelica and me, it seemed the lesser of all evils, so that's the category we chose. We learned to seem flattered and smile at the officers, most of them potbellied older men who courted all of us, even me, though I'd never considered myself attractive, with an old-fashioned and—all things considered— harmless gallantry. In the latrine, unrepeatable epithets accompanied my name. But in truth I never did more than offer strategic little smiles and cause a few hearts to flutter. A sergeant with amorous eyes, whom I refused a kiss, told me I wouldn't get far because I didn't understand that I needed the protection of a man. "We'll see" was my insolent reply.

But the most dangerous ones were the male chauvinists, who insisted that the officers favored the women, made things easier for them, and surrounded themselves with cute co-eds like African tribal kings. Women catalyze the attention of the media, make the Italian army appear modern, and help attract funding. But other than that, they're not worth a damn, all they do is cause problems, because having women live with twenty-year-old guys whose testosterone levels are through the roof is something not even the Americans have been able to figure out, and they've had women in their ranks for decades.

They'd make fun of us, calling us officers' pets. And they'd try to crush us during the physical tests, to show that, even though we held the same rank, we would never really be equal to them. It was all smoke and mirrors, women were nothing more than mannequins for parades who would all end up in the orderly room, the medical corps, or behind a desk. And I began to suspect they were right; when, at the end of training, I was sent to my detachment and assigned to an office, I felt insulted.

But I couldn't protest, I couldn't point out I had indicated a preference for placement as an armorer or machine gunner—because a soldier must obey above all else. I wanted to prove that the men were wrong, but I didn't know how. Lying in my bunk at night, in an enormous dormitory in the wing of my new barracks reserved for us women—privileged, protected, or simply pets, perhaps not even that; second-class soldiers in any case—I sensed I was in the wrong place. If this was all the army could offer me, if being a soldier meant saluting the flag and then counting down the hours behind a desk, answering the phone and scheduling appointments for the commander, I preferred to pack it in, request an honorable discharge, and go home. But I didn't have the courage. The army was my dream. And I didn't want to betray it.

The Americans came to Sollum. They had held the province until the year before and still ran the PRT at Farah. It seems they were satisfied with our work, and that made our commanders cocky. Paggiarin dreamed of a visit from General Petraeus, but he chose another base, and never made it to ours. The regular Afghan army generals came. The police chiefs came. Hours and hours spent exchanging information about regional commands, councils, cooperation with the civil components of government organizations and NGOs involved in the reconstruction of infrastructures—only a faint echo of which reached me. After flag salute, roll call, and the morning briefing, other than filling out paperwork, oiling my rifle and cleaning out the sand that threatened to jam the mechanism, other than making sure that my platoon was active—unrolling concertina wire or on guard duty in the towers—or supervising them on the firing range, I didn't have much to do. I'd never expected to be bored in Afghanistan.

At dawn, as I inspected sleepy Pegasus faces, I'd repeat to myself the names of my classes at the NCO Academy. Leadership. Daring. Honor. Loyalty. Duty. Firmness. Will. Drive. Pride. Dignity. Tenacity. If I managed to represent—and communicate to my men—all those things, then I really deserved to be here. To be a leader means to be responsible—like a father. If even one of them made a mistake, the company captain would punish me. He didn't seem to trust me yet. He kept me inside Sollum longer than all the other platoon leaders. On the list for patrol duty, he put Pegasus last. I was disappointed. But I was ready.

4

> >

LIVE

The guest at the Bellavista Hotel does nothing but run, apparently. On Christmas Day he ran in the direction of the Tahiti, and on the morning of the twenty-sixth Manuela sees him running in the direction of the Piazza of the War Dead; he's back on the beach again in the afternoon, but this time running toward the tower. He exits the hotel quickly, from the back door, in a blue tracksuit, wool cap, headphones, and sunglasses. Manuela notes that he never leaves at the same time and always goes in a different direction. As if he were deliberately randomizing his movements. It's a professional deformation of hers: she has learned not to overlook the smallest detail.

She runs into him that same evening as, tired and slow, she finally reaches the Tahiti's Polynesian hut. He's coming toward her, still running at a good clip. He has taken off his wool cap and sweatshirt, and his T-shirt is wet with perspiration despite the cold. He has the lean physique of someone who exercises constantly. Manuela is pleasantly surprised. From a distance she had thought he was middle-aged. He sees her, too—there's no one else on the beach—just the thin girl with the shorn head sitting on the cement wall, watch in hand. Manuela checks to see if it took her less time today than yesterday, if she shaved off a few minutes. Negative. He glides past her, slowing slightly. Manuela can hear his labored breath. About thirty years old. Nearly six feet two. Muscular. Wide shoulders. Rolex on his right wrist. Left-handed, like her. She follows him with her eyes as he heads back up the beach toward the hotel. An easy stride, a fast, steady pace, and he stops only when he gets to the glass door of the hotel. There, the guest at the Bellavista turns, hesitating for a second. Manuela can tell he's looking at her.

Dinner at eight thirty at the restaurant, alone, always the same table. The waiter stops and talks to him whenever he brings him a dish. The guest listens distractedly, and responds only now and then. But the waiter's chatter doesn't bother him, in fact he smiles frequently. At nine twenty he goes up to his room, turns on the light, but doesn't raise the shutters, which remain lowered, level with the balcony railing. "Are you playing, Aunt Manù?" Alessia tugs at her sleeve, rousing her from her reverie. "Of course I'm playing, what kind of holiday would it be without tombola?"

Christmas at the Parises' is always the same. A fake tree with red, green, and white lights, a forest of spiral candles from the supermarket, the nativity scene on top of the TV cabinet, with brown hills made out of packing paper and the star of wonder Scotch-taped to the grotto. That nativity scene is at least of legal age, because ever since Manuela can remember, it would reappear every December 8, looking exactly the same, in the usual corner between the two windows. Even the little statues are still the same ones. Every year, before her father left, the whole family would go to Rome for the holiday of the Befana, and she and Vanessa would get to buy one new figurine at the stalls in Piazza Navona. It was absolute bedlam, a practically impenetrable swarm of people, and they had to worm their way around big people's legs and backs, around spinning merry-go-rounds with music blasting, balls of pink cotton candy, colorful balloons in the most astonishing shapes, and Befana witches trying to convince the little ones to get their picture taken with them. They constantly risked losing sight of their parents—and when they did, they would burst into tears until someone handed them back to their mother, who was so happy to have found them that she forgot to spank them. They would squabble about which figurine to choose, Vanessa wanting the little shepherdess or washerwoman, and Manuela the shepherd, but in the end Manuela would win out, because when she wanted something it was impossible to make her change her mind, and Vanessa had learned to let her sister have her way when it came to little things so she could control the more important decisions.

Twenty years later, the shepherds in the Paris living room seem disheartened. The wise men are already lying in wait on the top shelf, even though it's still ten days till Epiphany. There are only two of them, though, because black Baldassare, with his turban and red cape, is missing. "Did you do the nativity scene?" Manuela asks her niece, intercepting her as she drags the big tombola box to the table, huffing and puffing. "Who else was going to do it, Grandma Leda, who's blind as a bat?" says Alessia the know-it-all. She has lost her two front teeth and is embarrassed about it, so puts her hand over her mouth when she talks, which makes her practically incomprehensible. Manuela hadn't seen her in a year, and finds she has grown ungainly and as chubby as a sausage. It's too bad she lacks Vanessa's feline beauty. Maybe she takes after her father. The perfidy of nature is depressing. Alessia's pointy profile and frizzy hair are the mark of an imbecile unworthy of leaving even the slightest trace in her sister's life. Vanessa is a good soul, she didn't deserve this kind of punishment. "On Epiphany I'll take you to get a new figurine at Piazza Navona," she promises her. "What's that?" Alessia mumbles; she's never been to Piazza Navona. Manuela can't believe it. She respects traditions, in a family they're everything—or almost everything. They're like the mortar that binds the bricks and strengthens the walls. Otherwise, it's like building on sand. At the first gust of wind, it all collapses.

Manuela would like to ask her what grade she's in, if she likes geography, if she has an atlas or a globe, so she can show her where she's been all this time and why she hasn't been able to come see her, but she doesn't remember how to talk to children so she doesn't say anything. "Is it true you're leaving after the holidays?" Alessia startles her by asking as she drops the box on the table and flings the cover onto the couch. "Are you sorry?" Manuela flatters herself, smiling. "No, then I can have my room back," her niece responds sincerely. "All my toys are in there."

Alessia dumps the cards on the tablecloth. The old tombola game! The cards sticky with sugar, and orange peels for chips. Manuela's eyes well up with tears at the sight of those cards, the grid of numbers and pictures. She's annoyed that she's become so emotional. She gets up, turns her back to the table, and pretends to adjust the curtains, fiddling with the cord, because she doesn't want her mother to see her like this. Her mother tells everyone that she'll be Italy's first female general one day. And that Vanessa has to be there that day, even if she has a cesarean scheduled. Manuela has given up trying to dissuade her, even though she knows that the first female officers will have to serve twenty years before they can even be considered for promotion to brigade general. And she isn't even an officer.

"I don't feel like playing tombola," Grandma Leda snaps. "It's for Alessia," Vanessa whispers, lifting her eyes to the skies, "to celebrate Christmas, she has fun, do it for her, Grandma, there's no harm in it." "Christmas is invented, and besides, it's important to protect yourself from the wicked world," Grandma insists, drumming on the table. Behind her thick lenses, her eyelids lower over her eyes, like a salamander. A sign of hostility. The guest at the Bellavista comes out onto the balcony to smoke, elbows resting on the railing, eyes peering into their living room, their tombola game, their life. Manuela goes back to the table but leaves the curtain open, aware that he's watching her.

Her mother takes the chart and the bag full of numbers. Grandma flings the card that Alessia has placed in front of her onto the floor. "I'm not playing, I'm not playing!" she repeats obstinately, crossing her arms. "I could kill her when she acts like this," Cinzia sighs. "What an awful thing old age is. Please God, let me die with all my teeth in my mouth and my brain still working . . ." "My brain works better than yours," Grandma cuts in. "I'm not playing, because games are a tool of the devil." Manuela tries to remember how old Grandma Leda is. Eighty-five, maybe. And she looks it. She never saw a woman that old in Afghanistan, where female life expectancy is no higher than forty-four. Life doesn't become a habit there. Cinzia took her mother in when Manuela enlisted, saying she wouldn't be coming back, because a soldier's home is her barracks. Her mother was convinced the apartment was big enough, four spacious bedrooms, all with windows, two with balconies even, and that sooner or later Vanessa and her daughter would find a way to get their own place. But you forgive things in a daughter that you don't in an elderly mother, and their cohabitation quickly degenerated: Manuela's mother and grandmother fought constantly, viciously, and it didn't any get better when Manuela returned. Grandma Leda repeats stubbornly that she doesn't want to celebrate Christmas, a blasphemous, pagan holiday. "Fine, Mamma, do as you like," Cinzia gives up. "We're going to play tombola."

She shakes the bag noisily, the numbers rattling around inside. Then, after a strategic pause, she extracts the first one. "Fear!" she announces with a kind of solemnity. "I got it!" Alessia rejoices, placing an orange peel on number 90. "Seventy-six, ladies' legs," Cinzia says, ignoring Grandma's furtive movements; she gets up, scraping her chair legs on the waxed floor, gives her daughter, her granddaughters, and her great-granddaughter a disgusted look, and then, wobbly yet proud, head held high, exits the room without turning around, without saying goodbye. "Death that speaks, forty-seven." "Two in a row!" Alessia shouts, incredulous, snatching the coins from the pot. Then, with increasing avidity, she pockets the prizes for four and five in a row as well. "Don't forget about us when you're rich!" Manuela says sweetly and then winks at her mother. Cinzia always lets the kids win. She can tell the numbers with her fingers, so she feels around in the bag for ones on their cards. She must have done the same for Manuela once, too, though she never realized it.

Alessia's pile of coins grows, and every once in a while she hides one under her card, so she won't have to give it back if her luck turns. Alessia doesn't know it, but Manuela has left her half her treasure: the earnings she had set aside for a future that might never have arrived had she not returned from Afghanistan. It's not a lot, but it's all she has. Before she deployed, Manuela had both her funeral arrangements and her will notarized. She had written it all out by hand, block letters on a sheet of legal paper, because Sergeant Piscopo of S4—logistics—had told her, who knows if he was right, that handwritten wills are considered more valid. "I leave my savings (9,750 euros in my account at the Banca Popolare of Verona, Branch 52) and the indemnity owed me if I die during my tour of duty to my brother, Paris Traian, and my niece, Paris Alessia. I leave my jewelry to my mother, Colella Cinzia. It's in a safe deposit box in my bank. I leave my Honda CBR 1000 motorcycle to my sister, Paris Vanessa; it's in the parking lot at the Salsa barracks in Belluno. I leave the white gold and sapphire ring that Giovanni gave me to Gogean Teodora; she knows which one it is. To Paris Traian I leave his grandfather Paris Vittorio's medal and photographs, they're in box n. 1 in the attic at Via Garibaldi. I'd also like him to have my army things, if he wants them. Bocca Giovanni can have my computer. I would like Vanessa to give something of mine to my friend Scianna Angelica, but she's not required to do so. If it's legal, sprinkle my ashes in the sea in front of the tower."

The guest at the Bellavista stays on his balcony all evening, watching the four Paris women play tombola. Evidently he has nothing better to do.

The local TV reporter shows up behind the wheel of a Mercedes 1800 and takes them to the countryside, to a farmhouse near Cerveteri, perched on a hill above the Etruscan necropolises, with stables and a pool. Vanessa agreed to go out with him as long as he chose somewhere relaxing, no crowds or commotion. Manuela's nerves are frayed. "I don't know if you've ever heard about posttraumatic stress disorder, but she has a meltdown at every loud or sudden noise." "It's peaceful there," Lapo swore.

On the way there, Lapo tries to impress the provincial Paris sisters by lecturing them on his fascinating profession, the world of TV news, communication in the Internet age, global information, et cetera. Manuela doesn't even try to look interested. She hates reporters. There's no military culture in Italy, reporters don't understand soldiers, they're interested in them only when they're unloaded from a plane in caskets, and while they're interviewing you they're thinking to themselves that you're an ass or a fanatic—in any case a fool who's been dazzled by propaganda, while they, who know the whole truth about international politics, are superior, enlightened. Vanessa's afraid her sister's hostility will hurt her own chances. Which seems unfair. Lapo is cute, nice, and not a caveman at all, she doesn't get to meet people like him very often. The guys she picks up online inevitably turn out to be inarticulate sex maniacs with brains the size of fly shit, she's already gone out with the men in the weight room at her gym, and the ones who take her group dance class are either losers or have male menopause. And besides, it would go against her professional ethics, and she prefers to avoid complications. She interrupts Lapo's monologue to ask him his sign. "Scorpio." "Well, what do you know," Vanessa rejoices, "I'm a Scorpio, too. Manuela's a Gemini, though. You two wouldn't get along even if you were the only two survivors of a nuclear holocaust."

Lapo invited a friend along, just like she'd asked him to. He's waiting for them at the farmhouse, flipping through a newsmagazine in front of the fireplace, and when they walk in he looks at his watch, as if in a hurry to get this over with. His name is Stefano, he works for an NGO in Mozambique. He's a nurse, with a specialty in obstetrics. Single. As tall as a lamppost, bundled in an ugly braided wool sweater, corduroy pants, with a metal stud in his eyebrow, and features so anonymous, it's as if they'd been partially erased. Vanessa sizes him up: morally rigid and boring. But he's lived in war-torn places and so is perfect for Manuela. It seems like something arranged by a dating service, and Vanessa whispers in Lapo's ear that she'll give him a commission if it works out. Lapo replies that he's trying to fix himself up, not Stefano. Vanessa laughs.

The farm organizes horseback riding in the hills. With docile horses and expert guides, so even beginners and children can go. They won't need a guide, though, because Lapo swears he can lead them, he's been riding since he was a kid, he's practically a horse whisperer, like Robert Redford in that movie. The Paris sisters confer. Vanessa wants to go, even though she's never been on a horse in her life, but Manuela is reluctant. "I can't ride, and besides, I should ask Doctor Brazzi permission." "What are you, a minor, you have to ask permission?" Vanessa snaps. "The army doesn't own you. So call him, if you really need his okay." Vanessa insists because she wants to have fun and do something different. Between her job, her daughter, and Youssef, she feels trapped, wilting like a rose without water. Lapo, on the other hand, is young, he doesn't even look twenty-five. And Manuela's funk is starting to get on her nerves. Afghanistan sent her back a sister she doesn't recognize—standoffish, weak-kneed, a stranger. They've barely said a word to each other in nearly three days, and they used to share everything, absolutely everything, even the most intimate, secret things. Manuela locks herself in her room for hours, listening to twisted music—screaming heavy metal, bestial braying, an out-of-tune guitar and a paranoid drummer right out of the asylum. Or stands out on the balcony smoking cigarette after cigarette. She's smoking, the girl who used to sniff your clothes, interrogate you if you smelled of smoke, who could spot a speck of ash on the bathroom floor . . . A guy called her, nice-sounding, with a northern accent, from the Dolomites, said he was from her platoon, in Rome on vacation with two friends from Pegasus, they wanted to come see their platoon leader. But Manuela didn't even want to talk to him, screamed at her to tell him she wasn't home. She'd even been cold to Alessia, whom she used to adore: when she came home on leave she'd smother her with presents. But now, nothing, not even a kiss. Indifferent, almost hostile. The change is so noticeable that last night, as soon as she went down for a walk on the beach, Alessia asked her if a bomb fragment had pierced Aunt Manuela's heart, like the glass shard in Kai's heart in Andersen's fairy tale *The Snow Queen*. Vanessa didn't remember the story, but she said yes. There were so many shards in Manuela's body, they couldn't remove or even count them all. The doctor said they would bother her at first, hurt her even, but eventually they would be absorbed, they would become part of her flesh and bones.

"I don't want the colonel thinking I came home just to have fun,"

Manuela whispers. "What's wrong with that?" Vanessa snorts. "It's un-
wise, and it's inappropriate," Manuela elaborates. "Enough already,
honey, fuck!" Vanessa explodes. "You've got to snap out of it!" Manuela
glares at her ferociously. "Of course we'll go, but you have to help us,"
Vanessa chirps to Lapo, "because it's not like we're Amazons exactly."
The owner of the farm leads them to the stables. There are a dozen or so
inoffensive-looking horses in the stalls, their muzzles buried in oats.
Lapo sticks a carrot between the yellowed teeth of the friendliest-
looking one, a white beast with big, round, sad eyes. "Paris sisters, let me
introduce you to good old Adam, my horse. He lives here." "You have a
horse! So you're rich!" Vanessa exclaims. Manuela's not surprised by her
enthusiasm, because her sister has a way of feeling at ease with everyone.
Whereas she feels at ease only with her comrades now. And not only
with other NCOs. With her platoon mates as well. Vanessa has dated an
Albanian fisherman and the son of a notary—class has never been an issue for her. "People are just people," she always says. "There are rich
bastards and stingy bastards, angels who have college degrees and angels who are illiterate. I look at a person's soul." Manuela doesn't believe
in anything she can't see, whose existence cannot be proven scientifically.
She only believes in facts. And she has already condemned this Lapo
without appeal: a daddy's boy, conceited and full of himself, completely
soulless.

"I'm afraid I have to disappoint you," Lapo parries. "I'm only a fledg-
ling journalist with a lousy temporary contract. The regular's on mater-
nity leave, God bless her." "There's a good chance she won't come back,"
Manuela comments bitterly. "Seventy-five percent of Italian women
leave their jobs when they have children." "Well, clearly I'm not Italian,"
Vanessa laughs. She started working only after Alessia was born. She'd
never even considered it before. And if it were up to her, she still wouldn't.
Work really gets to her. She's never lasted more than a year in any job. "I
don't feel very Italian either," Lapo says, misunderstanding. "Actually,
I'm ashamed to be Italian now. If I could, I'd emigrate or defect. Italy has
become a country of zombies, thieves, and pimps. Being twenty-five
here is like having some incurable degenerative disease." Manuela realizes he hasn't understood Vanessa's allusion.

The owner helps the Paris sisters mount lazy horses, and then escorts the improbable group of riders to the head of a trail that cuts
through woods and along steep tufa cliffs. "It'll take you half an hour to

get to the Lions' Tombs," he explains. "They're well worth seeing if you haven't already."

Stefano the obstetrician spurs his horse and takes the lead. He doesn't look back at the others, who straggle behind. He acts as if he only came to do his friend a favor. The other three move slowly, cautiously, the Paris sisters clutching the reins, Lapo constantly reining Adam in. He doesn't want to give Manuela the impression he considers her superfluous. He wants to make conversation, but he doesn't know what to talk about with someone who has survived a war. He worries that if he doesn't ask her about it, she'll think he's superficial, but if he does, she'll think he's invasive. Based on what he's gleaned from the movies, veterans complain that no one is interested in their exploits, but at the same time, they don't want to talk about them with civilians. "When I studied sociology in college," he tosses out, "I read that there are three kinds of female soldiers: the paleomodern, the modern, and the postmodern. The paleomodern's reasons for enlisting are classic, to serve her country, family tradition, things like that; the modern enlists in order to find a job; the postmodern to test herself. What kind of soldier are you?"

In a bad mood because she let herself be dragged along on a risky adventure that could compromise her rehab, Manuela responds dismissively that she doesn't believe in such distinctions. There are good soldiers and bad soldiers, just like in any profession. "And I'm a good soldier."

"I'll quote you on that," Lapo says, refusing to be discouraged. He's not the kind of guy who gets offended when he's told he's made a mistake, or feels pleased when he's told he's right. Besides, he doesn't accept easy labels himself. He always gives the wrong answers in a survey or opinion poll, trying to sabotage the system from within. He's starting to relax, savoring the pleasurable realization that Vanessa didn't agree to go out with him because he works in TV. She didn't seem disappointed to discover he isn't famous, that he'd only been on air for thirty seconds thanks to his interview with her and the mayor, that he's still very junior. The truth is, he doesn't know why she agreed to go out with him, and he starts to worry it was in hopes of finding a boyfriend for her traumatized sister. But if he's understood anything about Vanessa, it's that he can't get to know her better without making Manuela like him. He flanks Manuela's phlegmatic horse, and, to encourage her to open up, tells her he always dreamed of being a reporter: when he was little he'd imitate the TV newscaster, talking into a funnel in front of the window. His parents and grandparents were theater actors, and they didn't understand where he got the idea. They made fun of him all the time. And they still do. "And you?"

"Look, I don't give interviews," Manuela smiles. "Not even if I asked you to, to help me out?" Lapo lets slip. "If I pitch a story on female soldiers they'll go for it, it's always a big draw. I only have a temporary contract, I have to come up with something to get myself noticed. They've stationed me in the northern outskirts of Rome, it's deathly boring there. No organized crime to speak of, only a bit of Camorra infiltration lately. Very few homicides, all robberies or immigrants, at most a strike at the power plant or the port at Civitavecchia, commuter protests, poachers' vendettas—they chop up wild boar and hang the pieces on people's gates—nothing interesting. There's no news, I'll never get any national coverage."

"I'm sorry," Manuela says sympathetically, "but I can't help you. I would need authorization from the PIO, which I don't have." Lapo doesn't know what the PIO is, but imagines it's the office that handles public communication, so he gives up. He could never do a job where you're not allowed to say what you think to whomever you like. He wouldn't feel free. Manuela gives in to the repetitive rocking of her horse, careful merely to duck as they snake their way beneath low-hanging branches, noticing only the buzzing of insects, the call of magpies, the shuffle of hooves over rocks and puddles. Italy is surprisingly green, moist, inhabited. Birds—raptors, maybe—perch on the high-tension pylons and wires. The sight of oak, holly, and ash, of dark fields and clouds is so sweet it hurts her eyes.

Vanessa's bright voice blends with the crackle of crows, her words forming an intimate, familiar music, laced with memories. What a shame to have grown so far apart. And how peaceful the clatter of the horses' hooves, how soft the earth, how warm the color of the rocks, how gentle the shape of the hills. "I wanted to be a ballerina, I drove everybody nuts, I wanted to be the next Alessandra Ferri. Mamma had to take me to the opera house in Rome, to see *Swan Lake*, *Giselle*, you know, those ballets where it's all a flutter of tutus, and Manuela was bored to death. But I'm not pulling my hair out because I didn't live my dream. You should never live your dreams, it's actually a huge mistake." Lapo suspects he's too young to understand what she really means.

They've come to a clearing. The high cliff is full of holes, like Swiss cheese. The tufa looks solid, but it's actually soft and crumbly, you can carve it with a spoon. Stefano halts his horse, hops down, and helps Manuela dismount. He gets her crutches from the backpack behind her saddle and hands them to her awkwardly. "It's worth having a look at the necropolises," Lapo says, "even though the grave robbers have taken everything. There's no money to fence in the tombs or protect them somehow. And then there're so many of them around here, they don't know what to do with them. But you can still see the frescoes above the doors." Vanessa hops down boldly, deliberately falling into Lapo's arms. "That's not why I didn't become a ballerina," she clarifies. "I'm not like my sister, I've never liked things that require too much work." "Well, so what do you do?" Lapo asks as he takes a flashlight out of his backpack. "I'll wait for you here," Manuela says, sitting on a rock. "I've already seen the tombs. And besides, I can't walk on such uneven terrain. But don't worry, I'm happy I came. I'd forgotten how beautiful it is here."

Vanessa and Lapo venture down the slope. "A bit of everything. I worked in an appliance store selling refrigerators and stoves, I was a sales rep—pots and pans—I danced with an avant-garde troupe, the Flying Ghosts, maybe you've heard of them, they're pretty well known on the festival circuit. But then I fought with the choreographer, so I quit. I regret it now, it was a mistake, but I'm too proud to go back. After that I spent six months in Ancona, as a secretary in a chimney flue factory. But I missed my daughter too much, so I quit. I have a seven-year-old daughter, I don't know if I told you." She hadn't, and the news isn't particularly welcome. "Now I teach group dance in a gym in Civitavecchia, there's still room if you want to sign up. Oh, I also do the bookkeeping for my friend Youssef, he's a professional electrician, he has his own company and a ton of sites to manage. I schedule the jobs and keep track of the bills. I have a boyfriend, we've been together for fourteen months, which for me is a world record, I don't know if I told you." She hadn't, and the news isn't particularly welcome. "All in all, I net six hundred a month," she concludes. "I think I'm one of what's called the new poor." Lapo laughs, even though there's not much to laugh about, and pushes her into the dark tunnel. Vanessa Paris smells of strawberries and the sea, a scent that causes a painful sensation in his groin.

Heads bent, they move forward under the vaulted roof of the tomb. The flashlight illuminates walls dripping with humidity, putrid puddles, Kleenex. Vanessa is simply too likable to let him get discouraged by all the negatives she tried to communicate so cheerfully. And besides, if she described the length of her relationship as a world record, maybe she was sending him a message. Message received. He shines the flashlight in her face and as soon as she closes her eyes he kisses her on the mouth. She doesn't push him away, and Lapo switches off the flashlight.

Manuela gets up. She hazards a few steps on the path, but doesn't feel safe. She's afraid that her knee will give way, that her ankle will crumble. That her twenty-one bone fragments will separate. She feels like one of the old plates from her mother's set of good china. Held together with glue, it still looks nice, but no one would dare eat off it. Noting her hesitation, Stefano feels obliged to ask her how her physical therapy is going. He has stayed behind with her instead of exploring the tombs only out of politeness. Though nature really doesn't do much for him, and he can't understand why she gazes at the ferns and nettles in the gorge more enraptured than if she were looking at rarities in a botanical garden, and why she follows so eagerly four finely spun clouds as they streak across the December sky. Manuela replies that the military doctors are excellent, specialists, and that, given how serious her injuries are, things are going as well as could possibly be expected.

Lapo and Vanessa have been in the tomb for a while, and Manuela and Stefano stand there next to the horses, watching puffy clouds race over the hills of Cerveteri, talking about decomposed fractures, cranial sutures, ankle and knee bones, cartilage, surgeries, the difficulty of treating tibial plateau fractures, articular plane reconstruction, titanium plates. Stefano notes that the prognosis is bad, but a body as fit as hers will certainly recover. A normal person would be permanently disabled. Manuela says she is a normal person. Not a champion skier or marathon runner. Stefano calmly asks if she is always so argumentative. "No," Manuela responds, stabbing an acorn with her crutch. "I never express my opinions and I don't talk a lot. I've learned to keep quiet. But I'm not on duty now. And maybe I *am* permanently disabled and don't like you reminding me. It's taken me a lifetime to become who I am."

When Vanessa and Lapo emerge from the tomb and get back on their horses, wanting to continue their trek at least to the top of the hill, Manuela says she would rather head back. Stefano offers to ride with her to the farmhouse, and then take her home in his car. After a quick, silent exchange with her sister, Vanessa accepts. She has put a piece of mistletoe in her hair. She's excited, her nose red from the cold. She'll see the reporter again, and she won't ask Manuela to go along next time. That's how Vanessa is. She dives headfirst into life. She's never satisfied, she's always searching for something. She's capable of throwing away a stable relationship that has lasted fourteen months for some twenty-five-year-old she barely knows. Manuela has never been able to decide if it's a sign of freedom or of a perverse form of slavery. But she has never been able to dissuade her. "Don't do anything stupid," she whispers in her ear. "I'm on the pill," Vanessa responds with a wink. "But don't worry. Nothing's going to happen today anyway, I'm on my period."

In the car, Stefano turns on the stereo, and Manuela is grateful because she doesn't have the energy to bear the weight of a conversation. She has forgotten how to be with other people. For months she talked only with doctors, nurses, and other patients at the military hospital, and all they talked about were drugs, therapies, operations. The wounded lose the rhythm of life, they fall out of step, nothing really interests them anymore. She didn't even watch TV. Everything that lay beyond her injuries, her problems, beyond her limited horizon of drug dispensation and doctors' consultations, was out of reach. But now just talking about her fractures nauseates her. The stereo is playing Arabic or Indian music, something Oriental. A repetitive, hypnotic lullaby. It grates on her nerves because it reminds her of something, even though she couldn't say what, but she doesn't ask him to turn it off. "Lapo told me you were at Bala Bayak," Stefano says out of the blue. "Did you know about it when you left? Were you told? Did you ever think about it?"

"About what?" Manuela asks suspiciously. "About the massacres in May at Ganjabad and Gerani," Stefano says. "Those villages are only a few miles from your base, you must have seen the ruins." "I didn't get there until over six months later," she responds, tensing up. "And besides, we Italians had nothing to do with it. The Alpini were inside the base, they were still setting it up, the Americans had only transferred control of the province to us a few weeks before." "But it was a huge deal!" Stefano exclaims. "In the U.S. they compared it to My Lai in Vietnam. According to the Red Cross, at least eighty-nine civilians died."

"That figure is exaggerated, there's been a lot of misinformation about the whole episode," Manuela replies. She would rather spare herself the effort this is costing her. "According to the American report, there was a

Taliban gathering, and after the first bombing they scattered throughout the village, hiding in houses." "What does that mean?" he interrupts her. "You don't kill the dog to crush the flea." "The world has changed," Manuela says. "Fire burns friend and foe, it doesn't ask for your ID first. In World War I five percent of all victims were civilians, in World War II fifty percent, in the wars in the second half of the twentieth century, eighty percent. But in today's wars, it's sometimes impossible to distinguish between combatants and noncombatants. The same person, depending on the circumstances or the season, may be one or the other. Insurgents don't wear uniforms. They dress like everyone else. Even as women. Sometimes they send the children ahead. There are children everywhere, they come up to you, surround you, tug at you, ask for candy, they have nothing, they're the poorest people on earth, truly the lowest of the low, and you'd like to pat them on the head, give them a high five, even just look at them. But instead you have to fear them. Like in that sci-fi film, *Screamers*. I saw it at the FOB, on a friend's computer. We watched it to remind ourselves not to get too sentimental, to remain vigilant, circumspect. It's really scary." "I've never seen it," Stefano says. Manuela doesn't say anything else. She doesn't want to think about Afghanistan. The word itself is a thorn in her flesh. But it's been tattooed on her forehead; it's as if she's been branded, people can't help but talk to her about it.

"Sixty-four were women and children," Stefano insists, "twenty-two of them little girls. The youngest, Sayad Musa, was only eight days old. I saw the photos on the Internet. I've been wondering what you thought when you met people from those villages. Every one of them must have lost a relative in the bombing. It must have been hard—for them, but for all of you, too." Manuela's leg starts to tingle. She has never been a person who believes that whatever she thinks is right and whatever others think is wrong, she has always enjoyed sharing and debating opinions. But right now she's fighting an irresistible urge to punch Stefano. She bites her knuckles, leaving teeth marks on her skin.

"I'm not judging you," Stefano clarifies. "I can imagine your take on it, otherwise you wouldn't have enlisted. But only the person who believes in something has the right to question it. Disillusionment is the privilege of purists. Did you ever feel you were in the wrong place, Manuela? Like a card in the hands of a card shark? Didn't you ever wonder if you were being used? If the politicians are trying to recoup some international credibility by sacrificing your skin? I know you weren't the ones who bombed those villages, but I'm wondering what the point of rebuilding them is if there's still a war going on. Okay, not officially, but in practice, which is the same thing. It's like poisoning the wells and then handing out bottles of mineral water." "Twenty-two were Taliban," Manuela replies.

But one morning their convoy had passed a yellowish expanse of earth at the foot of a hill on which there had once been some buildings. Nothing remained but ruins blackened by fire. The hill was strewn with rocks, and here and there stood reeds, with green rags on top, fluttering in the wind. The ground swelled gently, with what seemed to be natural undulations, like ripples of erosion—or explosion craters. Lance Sergeant Spina explained that they were graves. "The cemeteries here make me sad," he had said to her. "They only dig as deep as they need to, because the ground's as hard as crystal, then they quickly cover the bodies with a layer of sand and at most a pile of rocks. They don't put any names, no marker other than maybe an oblong stone, they don't bring flowers. The desolation is unbelievable."

"Maybe it's not because they don't care," Manuela had observed, staring dumbfounded at the empty expanse. "Maybe they're all dead. Maybe there's no one left to come visit." Parallel hollows in a land as arid as ashes. Graves too big to contain just one body. Common graves. And more than twenty-two of them.

"After all that's happened, now that you're back," Stefano continues, even more animated now, "don't you think that twenty-first-century Italians should break the spell of history that compels them to act like servants in other people's wars? It's been this way since even before Italy existed as a nation. The Crimean War, World War I, World War II, Yugoslavia, Somalia, Iraq. We go to war so as not to be left out, but without any real reason, which means we end up being there without real conviction, without the consensus of the people. It must be frustrating to be a soldier in a country that makes war that way." "But I don't make war," Manuela says. "I'm a soldier of peace."

Stefano looks at her perplexed, and is about to say something, but she seems so forlorn that the words die in his throat.

In front of her house, he opens the car door, retrieves her crutches, and helps her get out. "I'm sorry if you didn't think I was very nice," he says.

"The fact is, maybe I'm not very nice. And besides, you intimidate me a little, because of what's happened to you, because you're a soldier, or in the military, sorry, I don't know these things, it's all new to me." "You're not the first person to say that to me," Manuela says, extracting herself with difficulty from the low seat and grabbing her crutches. "You're the most interesting woman I've met since I've been back," he goes on, embarrassed. "You must not have met very many women," Manuela cuts him off without even a glance, digging in her purse for her keys. "I'd like to see you again," he hazards. "I'm sorry," Manuela says, "but I'm not looking for anyone. I want to be alone. Vanessa really wanted to go out with your friend, and she never would have gone without me. I'm sure it seems strange, but we're really close. I'm sorry."

The concierge at the Bellavista Hotel is watching TV in the lobby. All the keys are dangling on the board. All except one. The guest is out on the balcony, on the third floor. It's cold, but there he is, wrapped in his scarf, his cap pulled low on his forehead, and a cigarette between his fingers, as if he were waiting for her. Manuela gives him a smile.

At seven in the evening Manuela goes down to the beach. Vanessa's still not back. "I'm going to do my exercises," she says to her mother. She feels suffocated inside the house. The sea is stormy. A cold wind blows from the west, fraying the crests of the waves and slapping the sand. It's dark. The lights of the Tahiti, obscured by the mist, quiver faintly, like stars in some far-off galaxy. The streetlamps along the esplanade give off a soft glow and cast long yellow shadows on the black sand. But the darkness thickens as she heads toward the shore. Manuela pulls her jacket tightly around her and tries to light a cigarette. But the tiny flame from her lighter dies in a gust. "Face into the wind," a male voice suggests, making her jump. Her heart pounds against her chest. Pounds with fear, with the habit of fear, but maybe with something else, too. "I see you haven't been smoking long," the voice says. "Don't turn or try to shield the flame. You have to stay face to the wind. Like this." A spark of flame lights a cigarette, which seems cradled by the night. When the embers catch, she sees what she already knows. It's the guest at the Bellavista.

He lights Manuela's cigarette as well. The smoke spirals up and dissolves. In the dark, the guest at the Bellavista stands close to her, one hand in his coat pocket and his mouth buried in his scarf. He smells good.

"Are you on vacation?" he asks after a bit. "More or less," she says. "And you?" "Me, too, more or less." Manuela turns to look at him. She can just make out the contours of his face, the cloud of rumpled hair, square jaw, a big, strong, slightly crooked nose. He's nearsighted, his glasses gleam in the dark. Flashy red frames, the Tom Ford logo visible on the temple. A black, expensive-looking coat. "I don't need to look at you now," he says, continuing to stare at the water's edge. "Because I already know you. I can see your house from my window. You're thin and don't eat much. You're the last to go to bed and the first to get up. You sleep with the light on. Sometimes you wake up and pace around your room. You wear a white T-shirt instead of pajamas. And don't ask me that question. The answer is no. I'm not a psycho."

"I know you, too," Manuela says, strangely neither offended nor embarrassed at the idea that the guest at the Bellavista has spent three days spying on her from behind his shutters. After all, she was doing the same thing. "You drink seltzer water. You read a book before turning out the light. You spend hours surfing the Internet on your laptop. You run well. You smoke too much. You don't get phone calls. You're afraid of habits. You're waiting for something."

The guest at the Bellavista smiles. Then, she leaning on her crutches, he jamming his fists in his coat pockets, they head slowly toward the glimmering lights of the Tahiti. Physical proximity makes Manuela dizzy, but she doesn't shrink from him. Raked by the icy wind, silenced by the bellowing sea, they don't say much more, nothing important, anyway. Unessential information, uttered lightly, as if it were all superfluous already. At eight she leaves him in front of the glass door of the Bellavista. She doesn't want her mother, sister, and niece to see her emerge from the dark with a stranger. She wouldn't be able to explain. She says goodbye without ceremony. He's expecting her at the hotel restaurant tomorrow at one. His name is Mattia.

5

> >

HOMEWORK

Lance Sergeant Spina was my deputy. Short and squat as a cork, balding, Ray-Bans even after sunset, a voice like a crow. Several years older than me, he made a show of being both protective and deferential. I was grateful but also wary, because I suspected that he really wanted to undermine my authority. The soldiers really respected him, they'd done other tours of duty together. I was just beginning to sort out the Panthers of the Ninth. Only a quarter considered themselves true Alpini—those actually born in the region of the regiment. They called the others—*terroni* from the south who'd enlisted to make a living—mercenaries, and not always jokingly. And they made fun of me because I was born on the coast and was like a fish out of water among mountain infantrymen. I wore the brown feather in my cap just like they did, but I would have to eat a lot of sand and snow in order to consider myself one of them. During training, in Italy, everything went fine. But I knew I'd have to start all over again once we were in country. My first words, my first orders, would prove decisive. If I made a mistake, I'd never be able to make up for my initial error, even if I did my best later on. Most of the guys in my platoon were veterans, professionals. Some already had wrinkles and a touch of gray hair. These men grew old before becoming career soldiers or being promoted to sergeant, and very few got even that far, so I could understand their frustration at seeing the gold stripes on my shoulders.

I don't remember all of them. I've already forgotten the names and faces of some, and others I get mixed up. The only thing that sticks in my mind about Abbate was his dysentery, which debilitated him to the point that he couldn't leave the base. He was so ashamed. All I remember about Curcio, Montano, and Zanchi is how competent they were, they knew what to do even before receiving orders. About Fontana and Pedone, their incredible aim: they were my best shooters. Giovinazzo, his burbly laughter and kindness. They called him the Good Egg. Morucci, the awful, incredibly vulgar jokes that never got so much as a smile out of me. But the other Pegasus guys, good or bad, friends or enemies, became a part of my life. Puddu was my team's radio operator, but I never knew his real name. Everyone called him Owl because he played chess against the computer at night. The riflemen Rizzo and Venier—known as the Cat and the Fox—I pegged right away as two slackers. Whenever they had a free moment, they'd lie down and start tanning: "We're at over three thousand feet," Rizzo would say jubilantly, "the sun really cooks here, it's like being in the mountains." Had it been up to me, I never would have let them deploy. But supposedly we were short of men, so they took whoever signed up. Pieri, a machine gunner with a sculpted physique, reminded me of the Belvedere Torso at the Vatican, but the others called him Michelin Man because he was so pumped. He'd knock himself out in the gym tent, really went crazy with the chin-ups—he could do twenty in a row without breaking a sweat. He was first-rate and I made him my squad leader.

Zandonà was the youngest of our platoon, of the entire company. Small, super thin, rust-colored hair that formed a crest like a hoopoe bird's, freckles, and a smooth face. The northerners called him "Boy," the southerners "O Bebè," everybody else "Baby." I rebaptized him "Nail" and in the end it stuck. He photographed everything, like a Japanese tourist in Rome: he wanted to get into PI—public information—so he documented our every move. He never spoke, not even a mute says less. He was twenty, but looked even younger. The platoon chose him as their mascot, but the company targeted him right away as the preferred butt of their jokes. They picked on him, teased him. In the space of three days they pinched his toilet paper, requisitioned his sunscreen, and shat in his helmet. At the end of our Christmas lunch, they made him stand up and sing "Jingle Bells." Zandonà could carry a tune, so he pulled it off. The fact that he was a driver made me think he was an ignoramus who'd only finished junior high. They had no imagination at Army General Staff. Those with hotel management degrees were assigned to the mess, those with high school diplomas to headquarters, junior high graduates were all shooters or drivers.

Jodice was big, strong, and swarthy. He had bushy sideburns and a mane of curly hair. A gladiator tattooed on his right biceps, and a woman's name, Imma, on the left. He complained that the phone card he bought didn't work, that cell phones were blocked at the FOB, and that they were allowed only one hour of free Internet a day—but there weren't enough computer stations, headsets, or webcams, so the guys fought over them, which bred discontent. "A soldier comes all this way to hell and gone, he deserves a little respect," he would protest. An arrogant and self-centered braggart, he always did the talking, and he knew everything, not even an old general was as wise. His name was Diego, but everyone called him the Spaniard, like the gladiator tattooed on his arm. Spina had warned me that he was the alpha male of our platoon. Even though he wasn't older or higher ranking, he had a powerful charisma. The others followed his lead. What was right for him was right for everyone. I told Spina I wasn't interested in ethology, I preferred psychology. Spina said that soldiers are just like a pack of jackals, lions, or wolves, and I'd do well to remember that. I reminded him the soldiers of the Ninth Company were called Panthers, and panthers don't hunt in packs.

But I should have listened to him. Spina soon let me know that Jodice was determined to make the guys aware that this was his fifth tour of duty, and his second in the Stan, whereas Sergeant Paris had only been in Kosovo, and the riskiest mission she'd had to perform there was to escort an Orthodox patriarch through the beautiful green countryside and a sleepy city full of shops to church. That he'd grown up on the street, in a place where they'd had to establish a curfew and where people gunned one another down in video arcades, and he'd seen plenty of people shot and killed, while she was born in a beach town where not a damn thing ever happens, and had never even seen blood. That at age fifteen he was already making criminals respect the law, while she, with that schoolgirl face, wouldn't even know how to get kindergartners to obey her. That he was a corporal and she a sergeant, but that he had bigger balls than all the students at Viterbo put together. That my rank was higher, but that experience is the only rank that really matters, and so by that logic Sergeant Paris was worth zero point one, and he'd shit on my gold stripes. Right from the start, during those months of consolidated training at Belluno, I'd marked him as someone who would make life difficult for me. I tried to keep him at a safe distance.

The third day, Jodice showed up for evening roll call blatantly listening to his iPod and crooning none too softly. I knew perfectly well that he was trying to provoke me, but I didn't feel like yelling at him, calling him out for insubordination, or confining him right away to the barracks for five days. I simply held out my hand and made him give me his earbuds. "Do you like Gigi D'Alessio, Sergeantess?" he asked me as he handed them over. "Sergeant," I corrected him. If he thought he'd get a hysterical reaction, he was mistaken: I smiled. I wanted to assert myself mildly. "And anyway, no. I prefer Gory Blister. I'm okay with Krysantemia, Delirium Tremens, or Katatonia, but the rest is sweet candy pop for little girls." Pegasus exchanged astonished looks. They'd never imagined a woman could withstand the reverberant rape of death metal.

I don't look for conflicts; I usually avoid them. Maybe because I'm a woman, and because I can't stand a frontal attack. I've always preferred strategy. My technique is siege. Attrition. Infiltration behind enemy lines. But this time I couldn't wait. Alpha male or not, he had publicly shown me a lack of respect. I knew how to retreat to defend myself, but I also had to show him I knew how to advance to check him. I'm not rigid, but I am firm. Flexible but not weak. But this thing was just between me and Jodice. I never would have humiliated him in front of the others. So when he came down from his watch in the tower, at five in the morning, exhausted and numb with cold, I summoned him. "Your sideburns are too long, Jodice," I noted. "Regulations don't allow it. Shorten them, shave them, whatever, but I don't want to see them again." Jodice protested. He said that no one gave a fuck about regulations around here. That we were in the fucking Afghan desert, not the June 2 parade on the Fori Imperiali. "You look like a hobo, or a terrorist," I insisted. "The regulations impose decorum. Get rid of them." "You don't give a shit about my sideburns, Sergeant, you want to emasculate me," Jodice said, staring me insolently in the face. "Get rid of them." I kept smiling, unflappable. When a superior tells you something, you have to do it. Period. Jodice shaved his sideburns.

———

Our turn finally came, and Pegasus was allowed to leave the base. In a darkness already giving way to milky dawn, the soldiers loaded crates of ammunition, readied the flares, and took their places in the Linces, crossing themselves beforehand. I was team leader for Lambda team, with Zandonà. It was my duty to be in the vehicle with the youngest driver. And to convey calm and confidence to my team. The soldiers get nervous if they sense their leader is nervous. "So, Sergeant, why do you think we Italians head out so early?" Jodice asked. "Because we have a long way to go," I answered, without even turning around. The thing with the sideburns had remained between us, but Jodice had pumped himself up with negative energy. In other circumstances, had we faced a real war, I think I would have been in danger. But I wanted to show him I wasn't afraid of his arrogance, so I put him on my team. Art of command, or something like that. "Because we're the biggest losers," he sneered. "Those crafty Afghanis wait till the sun's already high before they head out. The first to take a road left unguarded during the night is the first to be blown up." "You didn't listen to the briefing, Jodice," I silenced him. "Bombs here are all remote controlled. If they want to get you, they'll get you."

Zandonà activated the mine lock on the doors. I buckled my seat belts. "Initiating movement, over," Zandonà said. Then he put the armored vehicle in gear and drove through the gates of the base. I hoped he really was as skilled and experienced as the captain had assured me, but his freckles and beardless chin didn't exactly inspire confidence. It wasn't easy to drive that six-ton beast down streets pocked with bombs and tank tracks, control it crossing fords, and keep it from getting stuck in the sand. The thing that would have upset me most was to be injured in a road accident, in Afghanistan. That would have been ridiculous. But it could always happen.

So here we are, a column of armored vehicles one behind the other, going ten kilometers an hour on a track riddled with craters, passing burned-out vehicles and mud villages dotted with pestilent human excrement and animal carcasses in various stages of decay, and crisscrossed by people pushing carts piled high with jerry cans of water, children prodding goats, old people riding even older donkeys, or in decrepit, unrecognizable cars, the doors a different color than the body, jam-packed, people crammed even in the trunk, and vehicles with the steering wheel on the right instead of the left, driven by hostile-looking men in turbans with no respect for the rules of the road. The villages we drove through without stopping had no electricity or running water. Nothing but rubble everywhere, ruins, and absolute, radical poverty. The farther we got from the base, the rarer the signs of reconstruction became, until finally they ceased entirely. "The magnitude of this disaster is unimaginable," I confessed at mess that night to First Lieutenant Russo. "It'll take a hundred years at least to get this country back on its feet." "Things are improving," he assured me. Russo was in charge of the CIMIC cell. An optimist, a humanist, and an anthropologist, he had faith in progress. No obstacle seemed insurmountable to him. "The first time I came here, in 2003," he said, "there wasn't even an airport in Kabul anymore. The terminal had been destroyed—by the Russians, I think. Burned to the ground. The only thing that had survived the bombs was a billboard that said 'GOOD FLIGHT.' That paradoxical slogan expressed the desire to soar again. To fly. We have to make this country fly." "That's why we're here," I replied.

But the idea of spending one hundred and eighty days in that desolate, alien landscape, as if on another planet, filled me with anxiety. I couldn't wait to make contact with the locals. The ANA soldiers, the ANP officers, the interpreters and truck drivers aside, I hadn't seen a single Afghani in two weeks. The forays outside Sollum—whether to patrol the territory or simply to escort convoys of trucks filled with fertilizer or saffron bulbs—turned out to be much more stressful than I could have imagined. The invisibility of the threat made it absolute, almost metaphysical. We had orders not to stop. We'd get off the paved road as soon as we could. It was a new road, surrounded by an almost surreal emptiness, but it was too exposed: we called it the Road to Hell. We'd head down poorly marked paths that petered out in yellow stubble, climb steep hills and cross riverbeds that were now merely muddy brooks slithering among the rocks, only to pick the road back up a few miles later, and then leave it again, entangling ourselves in laborious, exhausting itineraries. It's called randomized activity: we followed different, unpredictable routes so as not to give the enemy any point of reference. In the evenings, we would spend hours in the shed that served as the operations room, planning itineraries. I had studied topography and cartography at Viterbo. It was one of the most dreaded exams. A third of the students failed, and since we had only two chances to pass it or be expelled, we studied like mad, even at night. I adored maps and charts, and by then I could read them like musical scores. I'd been practicing patrol activities, orienteering, and ground movements since my first year. I'd demonstrated a real spatial sense—I'd call it an instinct even—though Afghanistan was nothing like any of the places in Italy where I'd been dropped in order to test my capabilities. Afghanistan was an inhospitable labyrinth of sand and stones.

Captain Paggiarin listened patiently to my ideas, but he never accepted my suggestions. Still, I felt up to taking on that responsibility. I wouldn't have had my men take the wrong road, we wouldn't have ended up off the map. "Tell me the truth," I said to my counterpart Vinci, the Cerberus platoon leader, after swallowing the umpteenth "we'll see." "Are we supposed to plan itineraries so as to avoid running into any and all problems, or to reach our objective?" Sometimes, in the evening, I would fantasize about drawing insurgent fire, only to repel it, earning the attention of the captain and RC West. The incident might even make the papers, and we'd be awarded the merit cross. I longed for that stupid cross as much as I'd longed for command of a platoon. I beat back those fantasies as if they were some grave offense. I had to detach myself from my own self, from my interests and passions: I hadn't come here for personal satisfaction. I had to forget Manuela and become my rank. "To minimize the risks," Vinci said, a cunning smile fluttering across his lips. "We have six months to reach our objective."

D+15, one hundred and sixty-five days to go. We crossed the province of Farah, sealed in our Lince as if in a submarine, until we came upon a broken-down medical truck and had to stop. Aragorn, the code name for our onboard radio, ordered us not to get out of our armored vehicles, because an IED had been found in that village three days earlier, and it could be a trap. We sat there for roughly half an hour, doors locked, while the onboard computer connected to the cameras on the unmanned Predator aircraft that escorted us from the sky beamed back images of the village and surrounding hills to the small screen inside our vehicle: a cemetery of sand, not even the air was stirring. "When I was in Bosnia I got stuck in the mountains once," Jodice started in. His voice came from the turret. "There wasn't a damn thing there, only some cows. So I head out on foot to a mosque, it's open. I stick my head inside, and there's this old guy." "That's enough, Jodice," I commanded, "concentrate." The video cameras hadn't picked up any hostile movement, and the truck radiator needed water. CIMIC was bringing medicine to a village not far from there: their first village medical outreach mission had been set for that day, they wanted to go, the village elders were waiting for them, it was important not to let them down like this, right from the start—we were new, we had to earn their trust, otherwise the regiment would lose face.

I received orders via radio to get out so as to coordinate operations and repair the breakdown. I explained that Sergeant Serra and Zara, the bomb dog, weren't with us; they'd stayed back at the FOB. The dog had worms and was really sick. They were waiting for a helicopter transfer to the veterinary hospital in Farah. We still hadn't received a substitute dog. They authorized me to repair the breakdown. The gunners at the head of the column had verified that everything was under control. "Roger, received, here I go." "Don't be nervous," Jodice joked. "It's no great loss if you get blown up, noncommissioned officers are useless ballast, a corporal can handle just about everything." "Don't kid yourself, you're going to have to put up with me till the end," I answered. "Be careful, eyes on your feather," Zandonà whispered. I was happy that he'd used that Alpino expression with me. "You, too," I said as I got out. "Eyes open and asses tight."

Hindered by ten kilos of weapons, bulletproof vest, and helmet, I made my way toward the truck. I sensed a slight movement. Reaction time, a fraction of a second: I brought my rifle to firing position. But what appeared from behind the wall was only a group of children. Covered in dust, barefoot, filthy. Some blond, others with dark Tibetan hair. I looked at them, surprised but happy. And they looked at me. The littlest, probably five or so, stared at me as if I were from Mars. The older ones made a gesture that seemed decidedly obscene, but which I preferred not to decipher just then. They shouted something at me. I felt a pain in my calf. Then I realized they were throwing stones at me. That evening, when I took off my socks, I had a bruise the size of an apple.

6

LIVE

On the morning of December 28, Manuela brings her grandfather a sunflower. The florist suggested she choose something more appropriate—chrysanthemums, Gerbera daisies, carnations—but she couldn't be convinced. Sunflowers are tall and straight and always follow the light, they only bow their heads when they're ready to offer up their seeds and die. "That's how he was, and that's how I am. I couldn't bring him any other flower." Vittorio Paris rests in peace in the city cemetery, in the corner closest to the Aurelian Way, in a structure six stories tall that looks like a cross between an apartment building and a dovecote. He wouldn't have liked it, but he never worried much about eternity, not being convinced of its existence, and didn't leave enough money to be buried in the ground. His niche is way at the top, and in order to place the sunflower in the vase, Manuela has to drag a heavy cast-iron ladder down the hallway and carefully climb its rusty rungs all the way to the top. It's quite an effort with her bum foot and fragile knee, held together with steel pins and titanium plates. And Alessia's no help. She's still sulking because her mother, on the one day she doesn't have dance class, has dragged her to the cemetery instead of taking her to the amusement park. She stamps her feet against the cold and asks every five minutes when they can leave. Vanessa observes Manuela's maneuvers, perplexed, and when Alessia brings the sunflower to the foot of the ladder, she slips out into the sun. She calls Lapo, to cancel their date for today, she doesn't have anyone to leave Alessia with, her mother works until three, and she just found out that her sister is busy, unfortunately.

Balanced precariously at the top of the ladder in front of the niche, Manuela fusses with a rag. Vanessa can't stand this cold, damp edifice that smells of rot—dead flowers give off the same foul smell as dead animals, and dead humans. And anyway, she didn't get along with her grandfather, a stern, overbearing, old-fashioned old man who ruined their father's life and would have ruined hers as well, if he could have. When he died, her first thought was that his cottage at Passo Oscuro would be empty now, and she and Alessia could move in: she could finally stop being a daughter and a girl-mother and become an adult. And it would already have happened if only her father hadn't had another child. They each inherited a third of the house, but couldn't agree on what to do with it. Teodora wanted to sell Traian's third, but Vanessa didn't have the money to buy it, and Manuela preferred to sell, too, because by now her life was in Belluno and she wanted to buy a house near the barracks. So they ended up going to court, but they have no idea when the trial might be, since the case is still languishing in some courthouse filing cabinet. That empty cottage, exposed to the elements and left to crumble, is an insult—and a declaration of indifference.

Vittorio Paris was tall and blond like a German, and maybe he really did have some German blood in him, because Vanessa seems to remember that the Parises were originally from a village in the Alps and came down to Ladispoli to grow artichokes after the marshes were reclaimed in the 1930s. He was as rigid and inflexible as a German at any rate. When he wasn't barricaded in a nearly impenetrable silence, he would criticize her miniskirts, her nose ring, her boyfriends, her makeup, or hold forth on homeland, duty, justice, and dignity. Those sermons annoyed her so much that she finally told him—he was the one who had taught her not to lie—and, to her surprise, he didn't take it well at all; he found it inconceivable that a young girl would allow herself to contradict her father's father, sixty years her senior, a wireless operator who had fought in the war and had even received a medal of valor.

But to Manuela, Vittorio had been like a father. She practically grew up with the old widower, such a solitary eccentric that everyone called him Badger, after the animal who lives crouched in its burrow. When she was little, on the weekends, while Vanessa was parked at her maternal grandmother's, Manuela would go to Passo Oscuro. He didn't have any grandsons, so he had to settle for this wild, sullen girl, skinny as a toothpick. He helped her with her homework, read the *Iliad* to her, taught her to swim and play briscola, even how to handle a knife. When his chicken got sick, he ordered her to wring its neck. Manuela did it, but with tears in her eyes, because that bird—everyone called her Pina— was like a person to her, maybe even something more. Vittorio lauded her Spartan determination. He told her that Pina had been put out of her misery and that she was a brave girl. Which made her worthy of his respect, since courage is the only thing that can't be taught. Either you have it or you don't. They buried the carcass at the foot of the pine tree and placed a stone over it to keep the stray cats from digging it up.

But best of all, when he put her to bed at night, he would tell her stories about the war. He was sent to North Africa in 1940. He told her how his platoon, shoulder to shoulder with Libyan troops, defended an outpost four miles from the nearest oasis, how they held out against an entire enemy division, the front crumbling all around them, how they were surrounded but stood their ground, defending the desert, the Libyans wanting to go home and protect their families, and the lieutenant repeating "nobody gets through here, hold out till the bitter end, fight to the death." Vittorio defended that frontier garrison, convinced that he, too, was defending his family in his homeland far away. Artillery fire by day, bayonet attacks by night, disembowelings and desperate raids in the dark, it just kept getting bloodier and more horrible. A hundred and twenty degrees in the shade, no provisions coming, nothing to eat but a donkey's hoof crawling with worms and a heart of palm knocked out of a tree with a hand grenade. Hunger, brackish water, dysentery, bodies mummified in the desert sand, water bottles filled with piss like hot tea, the shinbones of less fortunate comrades used as hoes to fortify the lines of defense. Minefields all around them, grenades, bombs falling from the sky, ripping off hands and heads, a soldier's brains splatter his face, and after an explosion an officer turns to him and says, "Did something happen to me, Sergeant? I can't see anymore," and he answers, "You've been wounded slightly, sir," and the officer feels his face while his eye dangles from its socket, bobbing as if on a rubber band. And then the Australians raid the garrison, tanks appearing like monsters in the night, crushing, shattering, smashing everything, vehicles, sandbags, weapons, bones, bodies. And afterward a dreadful silence, the attack has been repelled but the order is confirmed, fight to the death. And then the radio tank he's in is hit by a 47 mm antitank gun and bursts into flames, his friends are burned alive, and he—how, God only knows—manages to drag himself free, and, his clothes on fire, roll around in the sand like a human torch, a hole in his heart.

Manuela made him tell her those blood-curdling stories a thousand times, and she listened to them as attentively as other children listen to fairy tales of princesses and dwarfs, always demanding the same stories, the same actions, the same deeds—and her grandfather would repeat them, exactly the same, but each time more exaggerated. One dead soldier became a heap of cadavers, and the defense of his garrison became a matter of national importance. In the end, it seemed as if Vittorio Paris had singlehandedly fought off the enemies at Garet el Barud, like Hector at the walls of Troy. Burned and broken as he was, he was evacuated on the last plane out, just before the siege cut them off, and repatriated. Months later, back in Italy, he learned that his comrades really had held out till the end, but in vain: Libya was lost, and they were all dead or taken prisoner. He was still in the hospital, but he and his comrades were talked about on the radio, and even in the movie theaters. But the celebrations disgusted him, something had snapped inside him, and after the September 8 Armistice he joined the partisans fighting alongside the Allies, those same Australians and New Zealanders who had massacred the Italians at Garet el Barud and who respected him precisely because he'd been there. He fought his way up the peninsula as far as Bologna, and only returned home in 1946. "I gave six years of my life to my country," he would say. "When I left I was a student, and when I came back I was already too old for everything. I couldn't finish college, I didn't have the head for it anymore, my nerves were shot, I started picking fights with everyone who hadn't been in the war and thought they could order me around, and by then we were too poor, we had nothing, so I drove trains, even though I would have been a Greek professor if it hadn't been for the war. No one can give me back those years, they were stolen from me and from my family, too, but I'm glad I experienced them. I did something for my country. Life's not worth a thing if you're not prepared to lose it."

Manuela would gaze endlessly at the rare photographs of him in uniform, in the desert. A twenty-year-old kid, with a blond forelock falling rebelliously over his forehead, and crafty eyes. She knew his eyes were a cold, clear blue, but in the black-and-white prints they looked dark and mischievous, like those of a Neapolitan urchin, like hers.

Manuela balances on the ladder and reaches out to dust off his photograph, stamped on porcelain, removing the dark crust of spiderwebs, dead bugs, flower petals, and dirty water. The photo had been taken a few months before he died, at eighty-six. Shrunken, bald, his scalp speckled with warts, enormous, fleshy ears, and a big beak of a nose, yet that shadow of a man was identical to the twenty-year-old soldier with urchin eyes. Manuela had never loved anyone with the same tenderness, admiration, and innocence with which she had loved her grandfather. For many years, he was the only adult—and the only man—she had any respect for. He never expected anything of her, never scolded her, let her do whatever she wanted. He didn't explain right and wrong to her, insisting instead that it was better to make a lot of mistakes than none at all. "But you have to take responsibility for your actions," he would say. "It's a fact of life, you can't grow up without making mistakes. But when you do, you have to pay. That's what it means to be human. You can fix your mistakes, though, and turn them into opportunities." It had taken her far too long, but in the end she finally understood what he was trying to teach her. Grandfather knew it, and was glad, even though he never told her so. For her, his death was a threshold; her true entry into adulthood. And even though almost three years have passed since the day he died, she thinks about him often and talks to him as if he were still alive. The first time she set foot on the rocky crust of the desert, she felt his presence, like a protective shadow, shielding her from sun and danger.

Grandfather would have understood. She wouldn't have had to tell him anything. They would have sat in silence and she would have shown him her scar. Once, when she was ten, he took off his undershirt and showed her his. Manuela stretched out her hand. A raised seam, like a thick thread, ran across his burned and shriveled skin, from his kidney to his armpit. "Cannon shrapnel." It had gone in one side and out the other, right through his lung. It missed his heart by two inches. "If I'd been a little shorter, you never would have existed, Manù. Life's a miracle. One inch can be the difference between life and death, between everything and nothing." But even half an inch is enough. The shrapnel Manuela took stopped half an inch from her brain.

The waiter from the Bellavista restaurant, who seems on familiar terms with the hotel guest, informs them that two tables have been reserved, one for a large family, the other for a group of friends celebrating a birthday. Mattia suggests they go somewhere else. His car is in the garage: she can choose another restaurant, a pizza place, whatever she likes. "Mountains or the sea, city or country, I'm open to anything." Manuela says she doesn't know any restaurants around here or anywhere else, she hasn't lived here for years, so it doesn't matter to her where they go, and besides, food isn't that important to her, she's always eaten little and poorly. She prefers to go with him down to the garage instead of coming through the front door, because she didn't tell Vanessa whom she was going to see. She didn't want to explain that she had agreed to go out with some guy whose name she barely knows. She's criticized her sister too many times for going to bed with someone on their first date. She's always blamed Vanessa's bad luck with men on this lightness of hers: she never gives them time to want her, to fall in love with her. A fruit that ripens too quickly soon begins to rot. A house that goes up in a few days lacks a solid foundation. It takes time to build something, an entire lifetime, even. She regrets having lied to Vanessa, but it's too late now.

Mattia's black Audi is brand-new, it still smells like the dealership. And looks as if it just came from the car wash. Not a speck of dust on the mats or upholstery. Nothing left under the seats, no umbrella or crumpled newspaper, no plastic water bottle. Not even a map in the door pocket. An anonymous car, that seems to belong to no one. Mattia's clothes seem new, too. He's not new, though. From close up, he looks a lot older than thirty, the age Manuela had wishfully given him. Thirty-five at least, if not forty. Manuela considers men who are forty old. His hair, which might have been blond once, is now tired ash, definitely edging toward gray at his temples. His big nose is charmingly crooked. A tall, reassuring man. Old, but still quite attractive.

Mattia turns the radio on low and pulls gracefully onto the back road that cuts through the countryside toward the hills. He drives smoothly. It's only when she notices they haven't encountered any cars for quite a while on this weekday in December that she realizes she hasn't asked where he's taking her. She'd trusted him. But she doesn't know anything about him. He really could be a psycho. Or dangerous. He behaves strangely. Maybe he's a criminal, a wanted man, hiding out in an empty hotel off season. They should have stayed at the Bellavista. She made a mistake getting in a car with a stranger. Even agreeing to go out with him was a mistake. She has to choose her friends wisely. She has to remember every day that she's not merely Manuela Paris, that she represents something larger. For a soldier, irreproachable conduct and impeccable morals are as important as military qualifications. A soldier can't hang around with just anybody. A soldier has to choose, select, and if necessary, know how to retrench. Her political science professor at Viterbo, a major, once told her, without mincing his words, that Giovanni Bocca was not a suitable companion for a young woman like herself, in whom the army was investing so much. He hadn't wanted to explain why. Manuela got it in her head that they had followed Giovanni and discovered something terrible about him. The thought ate away at her. She never really trusted him again. Maybe that was when she had started to leave him. But now she's in a car with a total stranger, and the car's not even his, there's an Avis sticker in the corner of the rear window.

Mattia notices she's staring at the sticker and smiles. An easy smile, surprisingly innocent for a man his age. "Yeah, it's a rental," he admits, "but it's insured. If we flip and end up in a ditch they'll pay up as if we were new, even though we're both pretty well used." Manuela laughs and shrugs. No, she's not afraid of this man. She saves her fear for more serious things. Betrayal. Illness. Death. It had been months since a man made her laugh.

Mattia wants to talk. He talks nonstop, like someone who's been alone too long, like someone who needs to hear the sound of his own voice. He talks about cockroaches (the Bellavista hosts a whole colony, and at night they emerge from the shower drain), boots (she wears only one, on her good foot, black leather with a low heel, and he finds the asymmetry alluring), hotels. He's a world expert on hotel rooms, he could practically write a guidebook. There's one thing that's never missing: the Bible in the nightstand drawer. And one that's always missing: silence. It's incredible how irritating noises can be, even in an empty hotel. Moaning elevator cables, slamming doors, burping bathroom drains. And then the temperature. It's always either too hot or too cold. The pillow is too flat or too fluffy. And the TV remote? It's almost always some old model they stopped making ages ago. And the welcome chocolates? Mushy and melted, or as hard as rock. And the bathrobes? And the terry-cloth slippers? Is there anything sadder than a hotel shower curtain, a scrap of dull, limp plastic, which the backs and behinds of hundreds of unknown guests have rubbed up against? And the hairs in the sink? That slimy, grayish muck that clogs the drain? Bits of beards and bikini lines from who knows who. And the mirrors? Sometimes, when they fog up, words fingered who knows when reappear. Hotel rooms are a land of ghosts. You have to live with them, and sometimes it can even be pleasant. He has grown fond of the ghosts in room 302 of the Bellavista. What signs do they leave? A cigarette burn on the carpet that suddenly surfaced near the foot of the bed. The circular stain of a glass that emerged on the minibar. In the morning, when he shaves, he feels like the face of the guest who stayed in that room before him might appear in the mirror.

The car, humming softly, glides quietly up and down brown hills, between rows of bare plane trees and fields dotted with sheep, horses, and cows, and Mattia talks moodily about all sorts of strange, stupid things, and Manuela isn't sure if he's being playful or sad. But she likes his calm, deep voice. The guest at the Bellavista seems vain and pleasantly superficial. Someone who has traveled the world and knows how to enjoy life. Manuela has never met anyone like him before. Her boyfriend was studious, serious, and pedantic: at sixteen he already lived like an adult. And perhaps she, too, had stopped being young too soon. By the time they reach Lake Bracciano, she's convinced she has met a real pro, who has just been thrown out of the house by his wife who found out he had been cheating on her with his secretary. Well-off, a businessman, a lawyer, or maybe in a more creative field—an architect, a conductor, an artist, much more highbrow than the people she's used to spending time with, from the north somewhere—but his accent is too slight for her to place it. He hasn't asked her what she does, and for that alone she's already grateful to him. She doesn't want to lie to him, but she doesn't know if she would have told him the truth either. You freak a guy out when you tell him you're in the army.

The perfectly round lake sparkles silently under the faint December sun. On the distant hills, wrapped in a bluish haze, is the broken tooth of Trevignano Castle, and farther to the right, in a bay sprinkled with houses, the Anguillara fortress. Dozens of tiny white sailboats plow the waves. Manuela says she never comes here, even though it's not far from Ladispoli. Lake water is treacherous, and she hates the clumps of algae that surface here and there, stirred up by the current, those thorny tentacles that cling to your feet when you swim. She prefers the Tyrrhenian, open to the horizon. The sea is honest, it has no secrets; lakes are deceitful somehow. And this is a volcanic lake, fed by underground springs and invisible basins. It's disturbing to know that lurking beneath that idyllic blue seethes turbid molten rock that could gush up at any moment. Mattia says that's exactly why he likes lakes, and Bracciano in particular: they don't breed familiarity; they aren't what they seem. No one knows the depths of a lake.

The restaurants strung along the shore are all closed, chairs stacked in corners, piles of uncollected mail, menus written in chalk months ago. Glassed-in terraces, gazebos, verandas suspended over the deserted beach strewn with rotting ditch reeds. Paddleboats are piled up and chained together, row boats turned upside down. The only life seems to be three swans waddling across the earthy sand. "We'll have to go up into the town," Manuela says. "Things will be open there for sure." Mattia says he doesn't feel like shutting himself up inside a restaurant. He spends so much time between the four walls of his hotel room, he needs some open space. He suggests they take a paddleboat out and have a rustic picnic in the middle of the lake. "The boat rental places are all closed this time of year," Manuela objects. "But there're some guys doing construction over at Pino's," Mattia responds. "They'll rent us one for sure. I'll do the pedaling, obviously. You just have to let yourself be taken around. Let yourself go. Do you even know how?"

It's not a good idea. It's cold, and the pale sun seems about to vanish altogether. And besides, there are only a few hours of daylight left. But Manuela agrees, and half an hour later they're already a hundred yards from shore, jostled by the tiny waves the breeze stirs up. They eat their salami sandwiches moored precariously to a buoy and surrounded by the silent dance of sailboats from the Bracciano sailing school. The kids at the rudder look at them with surprise as they sail past. Mattia and Manuela drink a bottle of Cerveteri red they bought at the supermarket, which tastes slightly corked. She hardly ever drinks, but today she doesn't feel like saying no to anything. They take turns sipping right from the bottle, without wiping off each other's saliva. Planes heading to the nearby Fiumicino Airport materialize from behind the Sabatini Mountains, inscribing white lines across the sky. Just above the paddleboat, they bank and drop slowly, beginning their descent right as they fly over the lake. There's a plane a minute. At any other time, that thundering roar would have panicked her, set off the piercing pain in the back of her neck and the cramping in her stomach, but now their powerful, regular rhythm cradles her like a metronome, like the beating of a mechanical heart.

The paddleboat lurches scarily whenever either of them moves, so they climb onto the deck and sit next to each other on the damp plastic surface. Manuela hadn't thought to wear a hat, and her forehead, ears, and shaved head are cold. Mattia forgot his gloves in the car and rubs his hands together, blowing into them. He has smooth hands, with long, thin fingers. He has no idea the blisters and calluses a gun makes. When he realizes she's shaking, he takes off his scarf, wraps it around her head, and knots it under her chin. He says that from room 302 he can see everything going on inside the apartment directly opposite him. A family of women live there, women who speak loudly, shouting from one room to the next. The old woman, a plucked chicken with glasses bigger than her head, the skinny woman with the gray hair, the young woman with the platinum blond bob, and the pudgy girl always dressed in candy pink. They have normal lives, they go to work, or school, sometimes they fight; like everybody else, they don't seem particularly happy or unhappy. But then all of a sudden, on Christmas Eve, the girl with the shaved head appears. A thin girl, as slender as a shadow, as promising as a dream, such an improbable presence within those walls. A sad girl who smokes in the dark, like a criminal. He spied on her for three days, telling himself it was a shame he would never meet her, get to know her, talk to her, and at a certain point he realized he was glued to the balcony, spying on the cars that tear up and down the shore, petrified that one would stop at her gate, that this strange girl was waiting for someone to carry her off. "I'm not a girl who lets herself be carried off," Manuela says.

But then she regrets it, because Mattia doesn't say anything else. She can't seem to find the right tone for talking to people anymore. She's always too stiff, too brusque, or too aggressive. The truth is, his words embarrassed her, because she had the feeling he wasn't just saying them, wasn't just being playful or sarcastic, but that he really was interested in her. And she doesn't know how to behave anymore. But Mattia doesn't seem that upset; in fact, he smiles. He puts his arms around her waist and brushes his fingers gently across her lips. Eyes closed, he touches her temples, her cheekbones, her forehead, as if he wants to fix the contours of her face in his mind. Or see her with his hands. At a certain point they kiss. Manuela likes to think he's the one who started it. But in truth she can't really say how it happened.

Between a Boeing from Malaysia and a creaking twin-propeller from Corsica, Mattia uses the excuse of warming his fingers to slide his hands

under her sweater. Manuela, obsessed with maintaining her irreproachable conduct, pushes him away. She jumps to her feet, upsetting the boat
so they nearly flip, and to keep from falling overboard they grab on to
the plastic seats and each other. They burst out laughing and Mattia
regains his courage. He kisses her again, and when his tongue is tired
he slips his mouth and nose under her sweater as well. Just then the enormous shadow of an Airbus covers them, five hundred people who could
look down into the dark mirror of Lake Bracciano and wouldn't see
them. No one can see Sergeant Paris, who lets herself be touched, licked,
sucked, caressed by a stranger on a paddleboat. She is invisible. There's
no smoke when wind fans the flames. Reprehensible behavior. A black
mark on her record. What the hell, she's on leave. And she doesn't even
know if she's still in the army.

After about a dozen Alitalia ATRs and many more kisses, her nipples
are numb with cold and her lips are chapped from the wind that blows
toward Trevignano, which has been carrying them away from the buoy
and out into the middle of the lake. The boat slaps against the waves that
ripple the surface of the lake. The light is fading, the sun disappeared
behind the battlements of the Orsini castle a while ago. They have to
head back to shore, but they don't want to. The gentle rocking, the wind
in their faces, the feeling that nothing bad can happen, have made her
forget for a few minutes—or has it been hours?—the stabbing pain in
her neck, the tingling in her legs, the fear. She feels good. Not a care in
the world. She's no longer Manuela Paris, she's simply a mouth, a tongue,
a warm body. Mattia presses his cheek in the hollow of her collarbone.
As if he wanted to hide himself in her. But she doesn't want to hide. Manuela Paris is incapable of lying. You can't build anything authentic on a
lie, an omission, or a compromise. Honesty above all. That's what they
taught her. So it's better to put it all out in the open right from the start.
Better to lose him today than tomorrow. Tomorrow might be too late.
Even a spark, if it's not put out, can burn a forest down. By tomorrow I
could have fallen in love with him.

"My sister says you've been at the Bellavista since the eighteenth,"
she begins, looking him squarely in the eye. Blue eyes, like the petals of
a flower in Afghanistan whose name she never did learn. "Didn't they
tell you anything?" "About what?" Mattia asks with surprise. "About me."
Mattia admits that the waiter, Gianni Tribolato, who's really a good
guy, is also quite a gossip. He was shocked that Mattia didn't know, so he

revealed that the brunette with the shaved head in the house across the way was Manuela Paris, the platoon leader wounded in Afghanistan, the Italian hero of the hour. Manuela looks up suddenly. "So you know?" she asks with alarm. "Of course I know," Mattia says, nibbling on her ear. "It's all anybody talks about. Pretty soon they'll erect a monument to you in the piazza. Ladispoli has a real obsession with war dead, I've noticed. Victory Piazza, Piazza of the Fallen ... But the most heartbreaking one is in the little piazza in front of the Church of the Rosary, a plaque for the captain who was awarded the Gold Medal of Military Valor, the pilot, what's his name, Valerio Scarabellotto, who 'fell from the sky over Malta on July 9, 1940, year eighteen of the Fascist Era.' You've probably walked past it a million times, the landscape we absorb as children is tattooed on our hearts. But the truth is, I really don't have any idea what a sergeant does." Mattia smiles. "Is that all you're going to say?" Manuela asks. "What do you want me to say?" He laughs. "I never would have imagined that I'd kiss a sergeant one day."

It's not so easy getting back to shore. Mattia pedals like a madman, going against the wind and the waves. His forehead is dripping with sweat. She lets herself be carried. She's not in a hurry. The shore comes closer. She can see it clearly now, the modern apartment buildings on the crest of the hill, the skeleton of an abandoned hotel, the bare branches of the chestnut trees, the olive trees whipped by the wind. The line of buoys. A family of loons. The coots bobbing among the reeds. The black strip of sand. The paddleboats piled under the eaves. The narrow street on which the occasional car passes, headlights already on. It's almost dark by the time they dock. They pay the construction worker triple the price, apologizing for staying out so long.

Numb with cold, they take refuge in the only open bar along the lakefront, a square hut with a slanted roof. Through the windows, darkness swallows up the shore, but the water shoots up orange reflections of sunset. Mattia puts on his sunglasses before going in, and then heads straight for the corner table, far from the bar and the other customers. "Are you famous or something?" Manuela asks, astonished. "Is there something I should know?" Mattia says there are lots of things she should know, when the right moment comes for him to tell her. "Well, the right moment is now," Manuela observes. "We've been an item for an hour already." "We're an item?" Mattia asks. "It seemed that way to me," Manuela says, "but maybe I was hallucinating. That's been happening to me a lot lately."

Mattia looks at her, unsure if she's joking or not. No, she's definitely not joking. Soldiers have no sense of humor. Sergeants even less than the rest. Sergeants are always authoritarian and mean, real hard-asses. He remembers the bloodthirsty Tom Berenger in *Platoon*, and Hartman, the ruthless, inhuman drill sergeant in *Full Metal Jacket*. Even the only Italian sergeant who comes to mind, Mario Rigoni Stern, the Alpino who fought in the Russian snow, was as authoritative and thorny as a pine tree. Maybe Manuela Paris is that way, too. "If you have something to tell me," she orders, all serious, "tell me now." Mattia tries witty evasiveness. "I won't submit to an interrogation without my lawyer." "There are two things I could never forgive," Manuela warns him. "If you're married or have another woman, or if you're in trouble with the law. Everything else is negotiable."

Mattia asks the waiter to bring two hot chocolates with whipped cream, rubs the tuft of hair on Manuela's forehead, and says she has quite the imagination for a soldier. In his mind, soldiers are practical types, not susceptible to introspection and melancholy, who live day by day, acting without asking themselves too many questions. He had hoped Sergeant Paris was one of those soldiers—which would be a real rarity for a woman, practically a miracle. But no, he's not married and never has been. There's no abandoned wife waiting for him somewhere. And he's not a criminal. But he doesn't want to talk about the past, the past doesn't exist, he wants to live in the present, enjoy every instant as if it were his last, just do things. He downs his hot chocolate quickly, pays, and asks her if she wants to go home. Yes, she does.

As they cross the bridge in Ladispoli that leads to the shore and join the long line of cars searching slowly, attentively, yet in vain for a parking space, Manuela is wondering how to tell him that she can't go up to his room. That she likes him, a lot, but she just can't. Can't let herself go like that, so soon. She's not that kind of girl. Not anymore, anyway. When she was twenty, maybe, but army life has changed her, she's a different person now. But Mattia stops in front of the gate to her building without asking her anything. His high spirits seem to have evaporated. He looks at her as if he'll never see her again, as if it's all already over even before it's begun.

Manuela stalls for time, rummages in her purse, pretending to look for her keys. The Bellavista sign casts bluish reflections on the hood of his Audi. The digital clock on the dashboard says 6:14. Manuela has nothing to do. She sees before her a long evening, empty as the blank pages of the notebook that sits waiting for her: pointless conversation, questions she can't answer, silence, and then, night. Insomnia, anxiety, benzodiazepine, torpor, nightmares. She doesn't want to leave him right now. She really likes this large, older, secretive man. "It's better if you just go," Mattia says.

Manuela retrieves her crutches from the backseat and opens the door. Mattia doesn't even turn his head. He stares dully at the dashboard display, the red seat belt light, green for headlights, yellow for heat, the oil gauge, gas gauge, odometer. Anything so as not to meet Manuela's velvety, disappointed eyes. Tottering on the narrow sidewalk, one elbow resting on the roof, leaning into the car as if unable to tear herself away without a real goodbye, without a plan to meet again, as if they hadn't just spent three hours in the cold in the middle of a lake, glued to each other, thinking of nothing else. "Is something wrong?" Manuela asks him. "I'm a totally normal girl, even if I know how to command a platoon. And I'm also the kind of soldier you were talking about, I don't dwell on the past and I don't ask a lot of questions. I prefer action." Her voice is uncertain, choked by too many unspoken questions. Mattia hesitates for a second too long, and she has already straightened up. Erect and proud on her crutches, she waits, expecting an explanation, and she deserves one. "I'm sorry, Manuela, but it's better if I just keep watching you from the balcony," Mattia says. "Better for whom?" she demands, stiffening. "You don't know anything about me!" She slams the door and walks away without turning her head.

"Giovanni called," Cinzia announces as soon as she realizes her daughter is home. "He'll call back." Manuela heads straight for the bathroom so she won't have to meet her mother's gaze. The mother who, since she's come back in pieces, treats her like she's sixteen, and thinks she can still control her daughter's life. But I don't need her help or her pity. She turns on the hot water in the tub. She's chilled to the bone. Bathe, wash away Mattia's smell, the traces of his saliva. Never see him again. There's nothing more humiliating than being rejected.

"He still loves you," her mother comments, shuffling down the hall in her slippers. "You can't just throw away such a long engagement like it was nothing. I don't understand why you don't get back together with him. You're almost twenty-eight. It's time you started a family. A house. A husband. Children. A normal life." "Mind your own business," Manuela cuts her off, slamming the door. Her mother steps closer, is about to knock, but then hesitates, her hand resting on the handle. She doesn't understand Manuela anymore. She had hoped this tragedy would open her eyes. But that's not the way things went. Manuela doesn't want to think about the future. And yet she has to muster her strength and accept that it's over. She has to go it alone, ask to be discharged, collect the money she's due, and use it to make a new life. It's not going to be an X-ray that convinces her she can't be a soldier anymore. "I told Giovanni you were out with Vanessa," she shouts so as to be heard over the water rumbling in the tub. "I know it's not true. I'm not asking you who you were with, you're an adult, it's your own business. But I decided to lie for you because you'd be happy with Giovanni. He's a good guy, and he even has a steady job now. A permanent contract."

Manuela pretends not to hear. She undresses quickly, and throws her clothes in the hamper. She catches her reflection in the mirror over the sink, already steaming up from her bath. Shimmering in the oval fog is an angular, bony body, unnaturally white, still bearing the traces of a tan. Forearms and neck slightly darker than the rest: the only parts of herself the spring Afghan sun had unintentionally settled on during her downtime. But the bright red scars on her right leg stand out against that sickly, white flesh, as if drawn in blood.

As she eats dinner, sitting in her usual place, looking out on a sliver of stormy sea, Manuela recognizes Mattia's outline in the shadows. He's on the balcony of the Bellavista, smoking, and staring at the lights in their apartment, at the Christmas tree which is still up, the shabby couch, the ugly paintings, the calendar from the bank. And at her. Manuela draws the curtains and shuts him out.

At ten Giovanni calls back. He had tried her several times when she was in the hospital, but she never answered. They quickly run out of things to say. Her head, her leg, the operations to reduce and then stabilize her fractures, the metal wires to hold the fragments together, the cement injected in her weakened bones, the shrapnel fragments still inside her. "They might be able to remove some of them, maybe, with more operations. But most will never come out. So now I'm made of steel." "You've always been a bionic woman," Giovanni says. And then the conversation dies. In the silence, Manuela recognizes the whimper of Giovanni's griffon Champagne. He's probably holding the dog in his lap. She gave the dog to him when he was just a puppy, right before she left for Kosovo. He was all ears then, a ball of bristly, honey-colored fur. She'd bought him in her cousin Claudio's pet shop, to keep Giovanni company during her tour of duty. He sent her pictures almost every day. "Let's raise our dog until it's time to have a baby," he would say, "we can practice on him." Manuela loved Champagne. Dogs ask for so little—food, some petting, a bit of attention—and give back boundless loyalty. Giovanni asks her why she hasn't updated her Facebook profile in months. He kept checking her page, but there were no new posts, the last one was from June 7, just a few words, he still remembers them, he'd read them a hundred thousand times. "48° C in the shade. Just before sunset, and the sky is a deep blue, like the bottom of the sea. We rotate out in 13 days. Too bad, I could stay here a whole year, I'm happy here."

Manuela says that her life stopped on June 8, and now the thought of telling her 258 so-called friends on Facebook what she's up to seems completely absurd. "But I'm not one of your so-called friends on Facebook," Giovanni interrupts, surprised. "You were supposed to marry me in the Our Lady of the Rosary Church. You already had a ring." "But we didn't get married," Manuela says. "You can have the ring back if you want, it's too tight, I never wear it."

Giovanni prefers not to push it. He asks her when she's going to come see him. He lives in Civitavecchia now, he bought a house, his parents helped him out. "Did you get your degree?" Manuela asks him. No, in the end he dropped out. He only had five more exams, but the fees were too high and he just couldn't juggle work and school. When he won a place as a regional employee, category C, he started working eight hours a day, and he just couldn't do both. The last exam he took was two years ago. Manuela says it's a shame not to finish university after all the effort he put in, especially when he was so close. She thinks he should reconsider. Giovanni says it's not worth it now. "This is what studying like crazy all those years got me, Manuela—all through our twenties, our best years. Do you realize that the reason I could never visit you in Viterbo was I had to get my engineering degree? It kills me to think I lost you for a civil service job in the Civitavecchia jail."

"That's ridiculous," Manuela interrupts him. "It just didn't work, I wasn't the right wife for you. In fact, you know what I think? You don't need a wife. It's the last thing you need." Giovanni swallows the insult, but insists she at least come see his place. It's brand-new, 700 square feet in a new development, terraced homes, with a yard, a view of the sea, she'd like it. Manuela won't settle on a date, but promises she'll call him in the next few days. Cinzia, who has been eavesdropping on bits of their conversation, sighs with satisfaction. Her daughter will change her mind by January 12.

Manuela dilutes her benzodiazepine drops in a glass of water and gulps them down. Vanessa's not back yet so it's up to her to put Alessia to bed. She helps her get into her pajamas. They're acrylic, so as she puts them on they give off a crackling wave of sparks. Manuela can't fall asleep. Tension makes her spine crack, her muscles ache, and her neck burn. She has a headache and nausea. Today of all days, the first time since June 8 that she hasn't once thought about Afghanistan. Not in the Audi, not on the paddleboat, not in the café. No sickly sweet taste of blood in her mouth, no sound of the explosion, no stink of burnt flesh. Today she had been her old self again, as if it really were possible to forget what had happened. Push a button and erase it all—painlessly. And reconnect with her interrupted existence.

Mattia is still on the balcony. He's waiting for her. But what more is there to say? Whatever it was he was searching for in her, he didn't find. It all went wrong, though she doesn't know why. She reads the first chapter of a story about a mouse to Alessia, but the girl wants her mother. Vanessa's still not back, what a wild one, she certainly knows how to dive headfirst into life. Alessia lies stiff under the covers, her fists clenched, listening for a noise on the stairs, waiting for her mother. She struggles to stay awake, though sleep closes her eyes. "Go, Aunt Manù," she says every once in a while, "go away." She doesn't fall asleep until page seven. Manuela doesn't go out onto the balcony to smoke. Instead she goes back into the pink bedroom, the walls covered with Hello Kitty posters. She's dazed but awake. The drops don't do anything for her anymore. She should increase the dose. But she needs to take it slow. The bottle's almost half-empty and she can't refill it without a new prescription. She won't be able to sleep tonight and she's afraid she won't be able to control her anxiety. That she'll feel sick, vomit until she rips her insides out. She places a plastic tub next to her bed, just in case. She undresses in front of the window. She takes off her jeans, then her sweater. She stands there naked. The shutters are open. She hasn't drawn the curtains, and her bedside lamp is on. She knows he's there, on his balcony at the Bellavista, and that he's looking at her.

> >

7

HOMEWORK

The first time I heard Corporal Zandonà's voice was on a Sunday. The army chaplain was celebrating mass in the big tent, and all the company soldiers and officers at the FOB who were free went. Some out of conviction, some out of boredom—nothing else to do—others out of fear that their absence would be noted. I was going, too, for that very reason. But I was running late. I'd washed my hair and that day the water had barely dripped from the showerhead. I shivered for a long time under a trickle too meager to rinse out the shampoo, my teeth chattering because even though the sun was hot during the day, spring-like almost, at night the temperature dropped below freezing. The cold froze the pipes, drained camera batteries, jammed the heating units in the tents and containers, turned puddles into ice. The chaplain's booming voice, distorted slightly by the speakers, echoed in the unnatural silence of the base. All of a sudden I heard music. Notes dribbling out, staccato, a vague melody I thought I recognized. It was coming from the soldiers' tents. I stuck my head in the last one as I rushed past on my way to mass. The soldier with the red hair, the mute, Boy, O Bebè, Baby, Nail—Zandonà, in other words—was sitting cross-legged on his cot, strumming a guitar. He kept playing the same chord, but the melody eluded him.

His sleeping bag was all scrunched up and his bunk was a mess. A clear sign of a lack of both initiative and responsibility. I should have pointed it out, told him he risked getting written up. That's what another commander would have done. Some officers issued warnings, reprimands, even restricted soldiers' movements for much less. Once, when I was a private, my squad sergeant had said, "I'm not seeing my reflection in your boots, Paris." And then he canceled my leave.

I hesitated at the tent flaps. Tightly rolled sleeping bags, neat cots, orderly lockers. The fetid smell of grease, sweat, men's dirty feet. The smell of every barracks in the world, perhaps the most disgusting aspect of military life. It had followed them all the way to the desert. "You play, Zandonà?" I asked him. "I used to play. Now I just practice, so I won't lose the dexterity in my fingers. Music keeps me company. Music is free." His unexpected burst made me move closer. Amid the cookie crumbs on his cot was a tattered paperback with a seagull on the cover. "Are you sure everything's okay?" I asked him. "If there's a problem, if some of the older guys are picking on you, you can always come talk to me. I'm here to help you, I want you all to be okay." "If I tell you everything sucks, Sergeant, what will you do, ship me home?" Zandonà asked, lifting his fingers off the strings for a minute. "We just got here, Nail, you want to go home already?"

"I called at seven this morning," Zandonà said glumly. "It must have been three in the morning in Italy. The phone just rang and rang. My girlfriend didn't sleep at home last night. And her cell was turned off." "It was Saturday, she probably went out dancing," I said. "You can't expect her to live by your watch, it doesn't do you any good to assume the worst right away. You have to try and keep your jealousy in check. Otherwise, what are you going to do three months from now?" "She's mad at me, she didn't want me to leave. But I wasn't about to ask her permission. She told me I was an ass." "I don't agree," I said. "I was wrong to come, it's nothing like what I thought it would be," Zandonà said. "I don't like anything here, this is an evil country, one huge reeducation camp, we came here to liberate them and instead we're being held prisoner by the very people we liberated." "No one's holding you prisoner," I corrected him. "If you want to be repatriated, talk to the psychiatrist. You wouldn't be the first and you certainly won't be the last. This place is for people who are motivated." Zandonà didn't reply. He tuned his guitar and played the whole refrain this time. "It really got to me the way that Afghani looked at us yesterday," he said in a low voice. "I can't get it out of my head."

It was our first Afghani. The first one we were afraid of. The kids had stopped throwing rocks. The commander had spoken to the village leaders, who must have been quite convincing. Now they waved to us, and if any of them approached, it was to ask for a snack or a bottle of water. It happened during a zigzag convoy around the Ring Road. We were escorting a diesel generator, a current transformer, and a 100-kilowatt immersion pump for the well in a village five kilometers from the base. In our first in-country briefing, Captain Paggiarin informed us that Operation Reawakening's primary objective was to expand the security bubble around the FOB. It was supposed to be twenty kilometers by the end of June. But he wanted to achieve our objective well before then, to score a quick win, maybe even exceed it, to demonstrate initiative, skill, and prudence to the brigade's general commander. And he wanted to do it all without losing a single soldier, and if possible not a single vehicle either—the cost of a Lince made it just as precious as human life. Our superiors were highly competitive; they gambled with their careers in Afghanistan. Anyone who stayed in Italy was convinced he'd been wronged; he worried there wouldn't be enough time for his own company to deploy, that he would miss out on the war. Paggiarin didn't want to give his disgruntled colleagues the slightest cause for complaint. He was hoping for a quick promotion to major. I could understand his ambition. Paggiarin was known for having no particular talent, but for surrounding himself with competent subordinates. Since he'd chosen me, I hoped it was true.

At the moment, he told us, the bubble around Sollum didn't exceed five kilometers. There were no insurgents, weapons, or suspects within this perimeter, which had already been searched and cleared. But as soon as we went beyond that invisible boundary, we entered hostile territory. So it was necessary to enlarge the security zone as soon as possible. He was planning on extending it one kilometer a day. The Ninth and the Afghani Kandak soldiers were patrolling the sixth kilometer, and had already started to make the first arrests. Unfortunately, there were IEDs everywhere, and they had to keep stopping to defuse them, so the operation was advancing slowly. Just five kilometers! I thought to myself. That's a lot less than the range of a mortar. How much time would it take to build outposts and secure the FOB? But the transformer and pumps had to be delivered right away. If we were too generous, the village chief would consider us weak, wouldn't respect us, would deceive us. But if we weren't generous enough, he'd nurse secret hostilities. "He who begins well is already halfway there," Paggiarin would say. So we pushed on toward the village, at the edge of the security zone.

Even though our vehicles were painted with camouflage so as to blend in with the sand, even though we carried only the gear that was absolutely necessary so as not to appear openly aggressive, our column moved too slowly to remain invisible. I've always liked looking through the sight of a rifle, but knowing I could be in someone else's sight was nerve-racking. We had to assume we were surrounded by a malevolent presence, an attitude that could, over time, cause paranoia. Jodice was in the gun turret of the Lince. His record indicated that he had performed well on his previous five foreign tours of duty. His obvious state of nervous excitement worried me, but I did my best to control myself. "Zero-three, Aragorn reports a Toyota Corolla approaching," the radio crackled all of a sudden. "Aragorn reports a Toyota Corolla approaching."

It was always the same damn make, in every attack. It was the most common one, after all. The most anonymous. It had made *Corolla* one of the most unwelcome words in the Stan vocabulary. "From where, Aragorn?" I asked. "Victor Papa right, two hundred meters, it's advancing toward you, zero-three, advancing." "I can't see a damn thing," Zandonà cursed. Even though he was keeping regulation distance—twenty-five meters—from the vehicle in front of us, the dust those armored vehicles kicked up was as dense as fog. He was driving blindly. Then I heard Jodice shout something in English. We were approaching the intersection, and he was ordering the driver of the Toyota Corolla to stop. The rule was that no civilian vehicle could ever join a column—not for any reason. But the car kept approaching at a steady speed toward the critical point, and it wasn't stopping. Jodice, this time his voice frantic with fear, again ordered it to stop or else he would shoot. The echo of machine-gun crackle inside the Lince. Jodice's Browning fires off an entire belt. "God, no," Zandonà prayed, "please don't let us be the guys who get one on our third time out."

The car has stopped, the door is open. Thick smoke that smells of gas and burnt oil is billowing out of the muffler. The driver is right there, standing next to the car, completely still, his hands up. Jodice didn't lose his head, he followed procedure, he fired into the air. The Afghani who had caused the panic was a twenty-year-old kid. He wasn't wearing a turban or a *pirhan tonban*, the traditional white outfit, but a normal checked jacket and a pair of jeans ripped at the knee. He didn't have hostile intentions, merely the stunned expression of someone chewing *naswar*, his lip puffed with a small ball of the opium-and-tobacco mix. He hadn't heard the order to stop because he had the radio on full blast: music pumped through the open door into the dumbfounded silence of the desert. The whistling refrain, intoned by a mournful male tenor, was right out of a Sergio Leone spaghetti western. A romantic melody that probably spoke of love.

"Do you know who that song is by?" Zandonà said. "Is that what you were trying to play?" I asked, curious. "Ahmad Zahir, a real star in Afghanistan in the seventies, kind of like Little Tony, an overweight Al Bano with a big nose and sideburns. His father was a prime minister and he became a musician, he sang, played the accordion, gave concerts all over the country; as if Berlusconi's son were to become a pop star. He died when he was thirty-three, just like Christ, assassinated maybe, that was thirty years ago, but people still listen to his music. You can hear it on YouTube, his fans post super-low-fi videos—tulips and beaches with palm trees, I don't know why, since they don't have any beaches here. The arrangements are really basic—trumpets, drums, piano, sometimes strings. But Zahir had a beautiful voice. The lyrics run along the bottom of the videos, karaoke style, I think they're taken from classical poets, like if Iva Zanicchi had sung one of Petrarch's sonnets at Sanremo. They've never been translated, but I like them even though I can't understand the words. Music doesn't need a dictionary."

Even after we drove past, that Afghani kid just stood there on the edge of the road, his hands in the pockets of his jeans and the ball of *naswar* in his mouth. The song followed us for a few minutes, as we paraded, as if in slow motion, down the empty road. That spaghetti western whistle suited the scene—the dust, the soldiers, the rifles, the endless horizon—but at the same time it seemed to mock us. "He looked at us as if we were an inconvenience," Zandonà said, "the way we'd look at the lowered bar at a railroad crossing."

Those first weeks at Sollum really tested me, as a soldier but also as a person. The responsibility wore on me, the physical exertion exhausted me. I was afraid of disappointing myself and my superiors, of not being suited for command, just like that officer had predicted many years ago. A soldier's first duty is discipline. If someone of higher rank tells you to do something, you have to do it. Period. And when I was a corporal I obeyed. I was in the army, but I worked in an office; I Xeroxed, answered the phone, and brought my boss coffee, just like a secretary. But I was never fully resigned to it. Angelica Scianna showed me the way out. I didn't even know the Modena Academy existed. Angelica was as blond as a Norman, as slender as a gazelle. We were born on almost the same day, the same year, so we thought of ourselves as twins. I shared a room—and a whole lot more—with her for nearly a year. We recognized each other, loved each other right away, like Sailor Uranus and Sailor Neptune, the warriors of the wind and the deep sea we had both adored as girls. We loved each other the way you can only when you're eighteen, a despotic, exclusive love. We lived together in infantry barracks in Friuli. We trained together on steep Alpine trails, and together we tamed the mountains—we who had both been born on the coast. Together we made photocopies and answered the phone in the public relations office, and we smiled at the barracks commander who thought we were cute (Angelica much more than me, to tell the truth) and called us his Praetorians. One night, while we were doing guard duty at a dump in desolate terrain in southern Italy where our regiment had hastily been detached, she said that we were only in an unpleasant holding pattern; the two of us couldn't keep wasting away in the heap of dead bodies that constituted the rank and file. No, we would become—at the very least—parachute officers or fighter pilots.

I started to think of my twelve months' enlistment as a sort of purgatory, a boring but necessary apprenticeship. Modena was my goal. I sent in my application. I wanted to get a degree in strategic studies. There were almost nine thousand candidates for one hundred and two places. I had no confidence but plenty of hope, and hope is stronger: as irrational and irresistible as faith. In February I was summoned to the Selection and Recruitment Center in Foligno, to take a preselection quiz. I'd never even heard of Foligno before, I had no idea how to get there. But Foligno rhymes with tomorrow: it sounded like a promise. The train station was deserted, just clusters of kids in winter coats roaming the platform and spilling into the large piazza out front, marching toward the hotels where they would spend the night.

Angelica and I slept at the youth hostel. There was a group of boys from Naples in the room across the hall. Still in their last year of high school, they didn't even have their diplomas yet. They wanted to hang out, but Angelica and I ignored them. Even though we'd applied as civilians because we hadn't accumulated enough service time to apply as internal candidates, we already felt like soldiers, whereas they were still children. And besides, we didn't feel like making friends. *Mors tua, vita mea.* We hoped they'd all fail the next morning. At nine thirty I was already at my desk. I didn't take my eyes off my paper for two hours. But I knew that Angelica was seated somewhere behind me, and her presence comforted me. The room was freezing cold, and there was a ghostly silence, all you could hear was the rain tapping on the roof, and a subtle sigh—like a collective breath. The results would be posted at four, so Angelica and I decided to wait and catch the last train home. But four became five, and then six, and in the end we raced to the station without knowing if we'd ever be in Foligno again. We boarded the Intercity, and I stood in the back of the car, my nose pressed against the window, staring at the lights of Foligno as they twinkled in the darkness like in a nativity scene. A Recruiting Center employee called the following day to tell me that Paris Manuela had scored 26,176 points. "You came in fifth, you're in," he explained, "you'll get an official letter, you'll need to come back for more tests." I let out a whoop as soon as I hung up. Angelica beamed. All she said was I told you so.

At the end of April I returned to Foligno for physical and aptitude tests. This time I stayed at the barracks: candidates were given room and board. I might be there for a week or for two days, it depended on how the tests went. It was a sort of elimination competition. Eight hundred of us were left. Just over a hundred would make it to the training. There were still too many of us. Too many women, too. I counted sixty-five. We joked cordially in the dining hall, traded advice. This was the third time for some, who were respected as veterans. But I tried to see them through the selection committee's eyes. Some displayed a less than soldierly rotundity, others an anorexic frailty. "After all," a rubicund girl from Sassari said, "an officer has to have more brains than muscle, which is why you get fewer points for the physical. In theory you can get thirty on the written quizzes, but you can't get more than six total on your physical." I said I agreed. Still, as soon as I'd submitted all my documents and certificates, I put on my sweats and went for a run on the track, to keep in shape—I had to capitalize as best I could my excellent physical condition because, if I made it to the next level, I'd have to take the math test, and I was sure I'd only score a few points there. On the evening of the second day, all happy, I called Vanessa to tell her I'd passed the physical: I'd run a thousand meters in three minutes and thirty-seven seconds and completed the set of push-ups in two minutes—even though the other women let me know that our superiors were willing to turn a blind eye if we crumbled. I chose to do the optional tests as well, so I jumped a meter twenty and climbed a four-meter rope. I earned five and a half points.

That evening my companions shared their anxieties; they envied my height, my agility, my fitness. They had asthma, or were allergic to mites, or had celiac disease; they had flat feet or scoliosis with a Cobb's angle over fifteen; they were nearsighted, or had had laser surgery to improve their eyesight. They had very little chance of passing the medical exam. Yet not one of those women gave up. They kept trying; they had my same determination. They were even prepared to lie. I'll never lie, I told myself, scandalized, how can you build a career based on a lie? If I were lacking some essential requirement, I would simply accept that I had to give up my dream. Forgive my intransigence. I wasn't even twenty years old.

The doctors examined X-rays of my bones and my lungs. In those translucent films clipped to the light wall, I saw myself dead. It was a strange sensation. I didn't want to die, I'd never felt an attraction to death, life was bursting inside of me. Then they moved on to the joints in my hands, back, and feet. They asked if I'd ever broken any bones or had surgery. "I've never set foot in a hospital my whole life" was my arrogant response. "Next they'll check my teeth, like a horse," I joked later with Vanessa. "But they didn't find a damn thing. I got four point five, the top score, physically I'm a hundred percent." "What is this, eugenics?" Vanessa laughed, "not even the Nazis went that far." "No, it's more like a video game," I said, "they eliminate us one by one. Only the best survive." "Strength and Honor, sister," Vanessa joked. "You bet, I'll call you tomorrow," I replied.

By the evening of the third day, the center had emptied out. Twenty-six women were left. We were awaiting the psychological aptitude test, the most feared, because the psychologist's evaluation was absolute, final. No appeal, no second chance. If he tore you apart, if he wrote "introvert" or "rigid personality traits," it'd be all over. The other women kept saying that the psychologist would give us the third degree, try to make us crack. He'd insult us, keep us waiting, standing in the hallway for three hours, just to throw us off. He'd treat us like idiots, or spoiled children. You had to stay calm, not take the bait, ignore his provocations.

Above all, don't bite your nails or drum your fingers, and do not sweat. They never take the ones who sweat. Other women said those were all just myths. The key was to show you were motivated, but not a fanatic. And above all, don't lie. Don't pretend to be someone else. "Be yourself," Angelica urged me, which is what her brother, an airman, had told her, "and it'll go just fine." That might have been easy for the blond Angelica. But I didn't know who I was yet.

That night I was seized with fear. Being so close to my goal made me suddenly realize that I might fall short. I couldn't sleep. I washed my face with cold water and at nine stepped into the meeting room, pale and tense. But I had dry palms and enough grit to tear the world to pieces. I closed the door and sat facing the military examiner behind the desk. He was close to retirement, with a short, pointy beard. "Did you close the door?" he asked me. I nodded with a smile. I already knew that trap. A big blond kid from Matera, who'd fallen for it the year before, had told me about it in February. If you turn around to check, it shows that you're anxious and insecure, and that you don't remember what you did five seconds ago. You're not trustworthy, you'd never be able to command or become an officer. They kick you out right away. "I shut it," I answered, looking straight at him. The psychologist's eyes were gray and inexpressive, like reinforced concrete.

I told Vanessa very little—and even that unwillingly—about the psych visit and the aptitude test. "I didn't understand anything about it, all I did was answer, they asked me a ton of questions, to trip me up, I think. I was supposed to answer true or false. I was supposed to tell the truth, but maybe I contradicted myself, it was embarrassing." "What kind of questions?" Vanessa was surprised. "I don't know, if I ever lie, if I'm bothered by being teased, if I have nightmares, if I feel inadequate personally, if I worry about what others think of me, if I believe in myself." "And what did you say?" "I tried to make a good impression," I answered. My sister waited in vain for me to phone with the results. I never called.

I crowded around the bulletin board with the other women who'd made it this far. Standing on tiptoe, craning over the shoulders of an aspiring officer shorter than me, I scanned the list of names, my heart in my throat. Pacini, Parenti, Paris. Paris Manuela. *Unfit.* I read and reread the list, hoping there'd been some sort of mistake. That I'd read it wrong. That the *unfit* was Parenti Tiziana, or Pastore Margherita. But no. It was me. I felt I was dying. As I stared at my name, so tiny behind the glass clouded with fingerprints, my future passed before my eyes with piercing clarity. The companions who could finally have become my friends, but whom I'd already lost, having only just met them, a group of young women like me who would finally have made me feel like I was part of something, who would have torn me from my solitude, from that feeling of floating in a void that had made my adolescence so liquid and listless. It was the work I felt I'd been born to do. But no.

I slipped away silently, making my way past the lost friends of my future, my true friends, the ones you choose, with whom you share the most exhilarating years of your youth. The name Scianna Angelica—fit to command—burned before my eyes. Me no, her yes. It was all over. I walked to the station, and this time I knew I would never return to Foligno. That name would be forever hateful to me. Foligno rhymes with sorrow. I boarded the train almost without realizing it, like a sleepwalker, and without realizing it I got off in Rome. I let myself be swallowed by the escalators that sank into the abyss of the subway tunnel, by the crowded subway car where a dark-skinned man was playing the accordion, begging in vain for change. I emerged into the open air, and walked toward the bus station. The bus for Ladispoli already had its motor running. But I let the automatic door close, and watched as it disappeared down the end of the street. I wanted to be alone. Because the pain was all mine, and I didn't want to show or share it.

But the bus station was on a street swarming with people, gushing out of the subway like water. I couldn't go home. Or to the barracks. Not like this, not having been defeated. I started to run along a broad street lined with ancient plane trees, furrowed by clanging trams and orange buses. I passed a high school with students milling around out front. I kept running, through intersections and stoplights to where the trees seemed to draw back like a theater curtain, framing a slice of rosy sky. That open space signaled the end of the street. Rome began again on the other side. In between was the river.

The Tiber slid by below, imprisoned between massive walls. A turbid brown line flowing swiftly south. A plastic bottle bobbed along, carried by the current. To be that bottle, carried off by some powerful, dark force, unable to put up any resistance. Till then, I'd spent my life swimming upstream. It's easier to accept your destiny. Just let yourself go. It was already evening, and the riverbanks were deserted. I hurled myself down the steep stairs, sliding on wet leaves that had turned to slimy muck in the rain. I fell and banged my knee, and didn't even notice the pain. After all, I'd always known how to endure physical pain. It was the other kind of pain I didn't know how to deal with. I kept running along the riverbank, bridge after bridge, until I was out of breath. Then I stopped and let myself fall. Flat on my back, arms open wide, hair fanning out among the trash and the leaves the wind had ripped from the plane trees, some green, others rust-colored or as brown as the earth. Above me, interlacing branches filled with screeching birds, the city lights flickered, the first car headlights crossed the bridge. An incessant flow, a current from which I was excluded. Blocked, extraneous, rejected. *Unfit.*

What's wrong with you, Manuela Paris? Which response was the one that screwed you? Or was there more than one? The MMPI test—Angelica had explained—measures the subject's tendencies to falsify the results of the test, or to provide a self-image that is socially acceptable. Everyone denies feeling aggressive and having malicious thoughts: but if you deny them too much, then the responses are assumed to be false. Did the examiner notice how much the question about somatic problems, about fears and anxieties, bothered you? And yet I didn't lie: never lie. I calmly told him about the fainting spells that would come over me in class now and then, during a disastrous oral exam, or in the middle of a party that I couldn't make myself enjoy. Or the question about family problems? Why did I tell him that I felt hatred for my father, whom I knew I should love and who was dying? Or was it the question about sex? The examiner wanted to hear that I had a stable relationship, that I fucked normally, why hadn't I realized that? No, I don't have anyone, I'm too young, I don't want to tie myself down with a boyfriend. And when he asked me if I felt an aversion to sex I'd answered boldly, no, the opposite actually. What an idiot. Or was it the one about my faults: How would an enemy describe you? I thought about it, and I wasn't sure if I was supposed to tell the truth, and reveal my weaknesses, or tell an innocuous lie, to protect the real Manuela inside of me.

Your enemy, someone who hates you, would say that Manuela Paris is insecure, a girl who hides her fragility by feigning aggression, who feels alone even when she's with people, who sometimes has crying fits she can't control, who gives up when things go poorly, saying that she really didn't give a shit anyway, who avoids disappointment by saying no to things ahead of time. Who seeks out unpleasant experiences just to make sure she can feel something. Who let herself be deflowered by an industrial technology student at a school friend's birthday party, in the room where all the coats had been put, on top of the other guests' scarves and purses, because at sixteen she was sick and tired of feeling weird for never having slept with a boy. Who, after that fleeting, disappointing experience, had experimented with just about everything, only to conclude in the end that she could get the same result without having to put up with a stranger's body, breathing, idiotic conversations, and sticky sperm. Or maybe I was wrong to tell the examiner I don't go to church, I don't believe in eternal life, not even in God?

Unfit. How was I different? Did I tell too many truths or too many lies? Did I talk too much or too little? Did I have strange thoughts? Maybe I was crazy. Maybe insanity isn't feeble-mindedness, maybe it's not the broken, raving monologues those desperate people you see wandering around outside the train station have, maybe it's this irresolvable difference that separates people like us from other men and women: the hope, the dream, almost the expectation of having a destiny. Of not being a shadow without a history, a ghost who slides through the world without leaving a mark; of wanting to do something important with one's life.

The wind whirled the leaves. It tore at the plastic bags that had been tangled in the shrubs growing along the banks of the Tiber since the last flood. But I didn't move. I'll never get up again, I thought. A cyclist riding along the banks swerved so as not to hit me. He thought I was drunk, didn't stop to ask if I needed help. No one came near me. The rare passerby veered around me, like an obstacle. Who knows how long I lay there among the leaves, my eyes wide open, staring at the evening and then the night sky. A handful of dim stars came out. I was still lying there, immobile, drained of all energy. I had no future anymore, since I couldn't live the only life that was possible for me. I could die that very evening. Throw myself into the river. Let myself be carried away by the muddy water of the Tiber. It didn't matter to me at all. It was all over. The only thing keeping me alive was the hatred that rose up in me every so often. I would have liked to get up and go back to Foligno, plant myself in front of the Recruiting Center, rip the flesh off the psychiatrist who had destroyed my dream. Tear him to pieces, force him to admit that he'd made a mistake, to ask my forgiveness, to pray for mercy. That was my destiny, that guy with the beard, a failed, bored officer—he hadn't understood the first thing about Manuela Paris; or had he in fact understood everything? Damn. Damn you. I hope your heart rots. That your testicles get gangrene. *Unfit*. Not you.

When I heard foreign voices emerging from the darkness and footsteps coming closer, I finally got up. I didn't want to be raped, and, all things considered, I didn't want to kill myself either. I wanted to get revenge on that medical officer with the pointy beard, on every officer in the world. That thought gave me the strength to get shakily to my feet. When I returned to street level, I was surprised to discover that while I lay as if dead down along the riverbank, nothing had happened: cars continued to line up at the stoplight in order to cross the bridge; in reality only two hours had passed. Manuela Paris had been assassinated, but Rome continued to live, indifferent to my tragedy. The last bus for Ladispoli had already left.

I took the subway back to the station and waited for the train. I got a seat near the window, the car was practically empty, the commuters were already home by now. The coastal train heading north stopped at every station. Tuscolana, Ostiense, Trastevere, San Pietro, Aurelia, Maccarese, Torrimpietra, Palidoro. And between one stop and the next, I saw the houses outside my window lit up, fleetingly framed little living rooms, all exactly the same, families at the dinner table, people sitting on the couch watching TV—the spectacle of other people's lives enraged and infuriated me, but also left me indifferent, because I no longer had a life. They'd stolen it from me.

Vanessa came to get me at the station. I must have looked really awful, because she didn't have the courage to ask me anything. Reading the disappointment in my sister's eyes was almost worse than reading *unfit* next to my name. "I didn't make it," I whispered. "Assholes!" Vanessa swore, devastated. "I was deemed unfit. I can't be an officer," I explained, kicking a soda can. "It's their loss," Vanessa said. But she was frustrated, too. She'd been hopeful, convinced I was meant to fulfill all our dreams: she had delegated hers to me as well, since she was too lazy to follow them herself.

That night Vanessa slipped into my bed. "You have to try again, Manù," she said. "You didn't prepare enough, and besides, at nineteen it's normal to drown like an ant in a glass of water. You have to learn to handle yourself better. Get someone to explain how those damn tests work, the things you shouldn't do. You'll ace them next year. You'll pass with flying colors." "Try again? Not over my dead body," I swore, and I kept my promise. I wouldn't have been able to bear another failure.

At the end of my year of service I was honorably discharged with the rank of corporal and good character notes on my record, but I didn't ask to reenlist. I left the army angrier than when I'd joined. More aggressive, more hostile, more everything. I threw away my military magazines, my Sailor Moon notebook filled with stories of Amazons, the photographs of me with my classmates, of me in the barracks. I spent weeks holed up at home, like a leper, even refusing to answer the at first sympathetic and later concerned phone calls from my friend Angelica. Corporal Paris had been killed at Foligno—killed by friendly fire.

There's no trace of my anxiety either in my e-mails or my diary. I couldn't let it seep out. From Sollum I sent vacuous, reassuring messages about the food and the cold, as if I were on vacation. The truth is that I understood Corporal Zandonà more than he could possibly know, even if I never could have told him. The initial euphoria had worn off. I, too, felt as if I were in prison. But I couldn't fathom what crime I'd committed, and I couldn't imagine how my presence there could be considered offensive. I'd gone there in order to do my part to rebuild a country, but I spent my time guarding the base, wearing out my eyes staring at the desert, at herds of goats roaming among the rocks, grazing on thorny tufts of grass; I fixed my binoculars on old men in turbans shuffling around in their slippers in the sand and lighting fires, perhaps sending smoke signals about our movements, and droves of barefoot children collecting scraps of metal and dragging water tanks and perhaps spying on us for their fathers. I spent my time practicing at the firing range, shooting at nothing, saluting the flag that fluttered in the wind, calling roll morning and evening, and filling out forms and patrol reports. I'd never written so much in my life. I wrote with principle and precision. At Sollum I learned the value of words. I told myself that even writing was important, because what I wrote would be sent higher and higher, up a long chain of command, all the way to the NATO heads—and a piece of information that seemed insignificant to me might prove essential someday. But I would never know. I studied maps and occasionally— too infrequently for my tastes—traveled in an armored vehicle, in relative tranquillity at night, and with a great deal of anxiety during the day, and patroled a road that our very presence assured would immediately be deserted. At times, filing past long lines of stopped cars, all I could read on those faces resigned to our passing by was patience. The patience with which a peasant endures rain and droughts and locusts, knowing that this, too, shall pass. You'll pass, too: that's what I read on their dusty faces, which were framed for a second in the windows of our Lince, as we filed past them at ten kilometers an hour.

But I hadn't gone all the way to Afghanistan just to file past. I wanted to do something for those people. It is the duty of civilized countries to help less-fortunate populations. Is it possible they didn't understand that? And yet, in March alone, 721 makeshift devices exploded. Between American and various coalition soldiers, there were twenty-eight casualties. Nearly one a day. And I waited, without really knowing anymore what for. I cleaned the delicate workings of my rifle, recalibrated it, polished the scope, brushed my uniform, which was so encrusted with sand and sweat it could practically stand upright on its own, worked out elaborate itineraries on the map, chatted with First Lieutenant Russo while Radiohead sang malaise, listened to Jodice's unending anecdotes and First Lieutenant Ghigo's stories. She'd been in country the year before, in Herat, where she saw dozens of civilians every day, there was always a line in front of the base's first aid station. It was the most gratifying experience of her life. She'd even managed to send two children with cancer to Italy, where they were cured. Here, no one. No one from the nearby villages came.

The truth is, nothing ever happened. I'd come to make peace with war, or to make war to establish peace—I'd been training for it for years. It's why I'd studied political science and economic geography, applied machine mechanics, and chemical weapons, why I'd parachute-jumped and perfected my shooting and become a first-rate patroller. And it's what I'd always wanted. I wasn't born to wear out a chair in the comfortable office of some provincial barracks. I wanted to change things, get results. And I was prepared to pay a very high price. But we Italians moved with a caution and diplomacy that I understood but that still annoyed me sometimes. We didn't want to alienate anyone. We would negotiate and bargain even with bandits, people who couldn't even really be considered insurgents, just ordinary delinquents. We honed our patience with an almost Oriental focus. It was our way of gaining respect: everyone has their own strategy: some prefer a show of force, others dialogue—but it seemed like a waste of time to me. Proof of how middle class the military had become. Its ranks were full of respectable people—competent, educated, qualified—who were not looking for redemption or liberation; back in Italy they had comfortable homes, they were well-off and content. Giuseppe Lando, a chubby, taciturn rifleman, burst into tears when he heard his mother's voice on the phone for the first time in ten days.

My neighbor, Giani, the quartermaster, chose me as her confidante. She had no one else to talk to: First Lieutenant Ghigo was standoffish because she outranked Giani, and some things only another woman could understand. She was afraid she wouldn't make it till June. She missed normal life, missed going to the beauty parlor to get her legs waxed, missed having a bidet or even a toilet where she could sit down instead of a Turkish toilet where she always had to squat like a medieval peasant, missed letting her long hair hang loose, wearing a dress and high heels, in short she regretted having to put parentheses around her life as a civilized person and as a woman. Sokha Giani was a graceful twenty-four-year-old of Cambodian origin—the soldiers called her Angkor—with lithesome movements and luscious, long black hair that was offended by the Afghan sand and by the military regulations that forced her to keep it tied back at all times. But I wasn't much help. I had never cared in the least about high heels, hairstyles, or waxed legs, and a month after my arrival at Bala Bayak, I sat down in front of Sergeant Corvia, the barber on the base, and ordered him to cut off my braid.

"No," Corvia refused. "I'm not going to do that to you, Paris, your hair's the prettiest thing about you." "It'll grow back," I said, "long hair's just a pain in the ass here, and washing it wastes water, and we don't have much. Cut it just below my ears, hurry up." Corvia cut my hair. He was no hairdresser. He was used to shaving the men's limp hair, and didn't know what to do with a woman's. He improvised an androgynous cut that made me look like a pageboy in some Renaissance court—or, more prosaically, like an elf, as the guys joked. Zandonà called me Mulan, after the Chinese woman warrior in the cartoon who cuts her hair to pass as a man and fight in the army. I never managed to shake that nickname. I gathered up my braid, put it in a jar, and placed it on top of my locker. First Lieutenant Ghigo pointed out that it attracted flies, and that flies could transmit horrible diseases, so I threw it in the trash, no regrets.

If I sit still for too long, though, first I get depressed, and then I explode. I need action, and I'd trained for a high-risk mission. I'd expected to have to shoot in order to defend a position or a protected site, or to avert an attack, and I was prepared to do it. Peace can be boring sometimes, but so can war. I never imagined it could become a routine, a sequence of empty actions, an interminable pause. I was waiting—but for what? Waiting to get started. But I never did. January came and went, then February, then March began, I lost all sense of the flow of time, and after a while I wouldn't have been able to say what exactly I was waiting for.

The Afghanistan I had dreamed so much about was hostile—the stones, the climate, the roads, the people: all hostile. Even the animals were hostile: there weren't very many of them, and the caracal, that rare wildcat also known as a desert lynx, which I hoped to see and whose tracks I searched for in vain, remained elusive. Apart from the occasional turtledove or sparrow, all I saw during those months were gerbils, desert mice, scorpions, vipers, snakes, ticks, flies, millipedes as long as my finger and whose bite—I learned the hard way—would make your foot swell up like a balloon. But the most unwelcome of all these visitors turned out to be the honey-colored, humpbacked camel spider, with too many legs and long, antenna-like claws. When I had to get dressed in the middle of the night, I would inspect my boots carefully before putting them on. The camel spider loves the dark. Light kills him. And if you happen to flush him out, he hides in your shadow, follows you, clings to you, like a bad dream. I killed dozens of them, and dozens of them ran after me. What do you want? Why are you following me? Go away! I'd say to each spider in turn, prodding it with the tip of my boot. Every country has its totem, be it the kangaroo, the raccoon, the kiwi, the reindeer, the tiger, the bear, or the wolf. For me, that furtive, bellicose spider became Afghanistan's totem. So I decided not to kill them anymore, but to coexist with them. When I found one hiding in the expanded polyurethane foam of my helmet, I would simply shake it out into the sand. It would run away so quickly, following the line of the shade, that it wouldn't even leave tracks in the sand.

The sounds in Afghanistan were hostile. The crackle of the machine gun, the buzz of the attack helicopters that flew right over us toward the mountains, the roar of the cargo planes that delivered provisions, the thunder of the fighter-bombers, the hiss of the unmanned aircraft that accompanied us like an ethereal cloud. The smells were hostile. The stench of shit, of animals, and of men who aren't used to washing regularly or don't have enough water, of motor oil, leaded gas, kerosene, grease, rusty metal. The colors were hostile. Afghanistan—or at least that small corner of it that had been given to me—knew only primary colors. A sad, monotonous yellow prevailed. I've always believed that colors affect our soul and produce a spiritual vibration. Yellow, I thought, had a disturbing influence, like a warning signal. I associated it with traffic lights. Those yellow traffic lights that blink all night long at deserted intersections had always made me nervous. Even though the yellow here wasn't uniform, but changed with the seasons and the intensity of the sunlight, and the tone varied from mustard to peach, from lemon to sawdust, it was still alienating, it upset the mind and could drive you crazy. The sand, the hills, the mountains, and often even the sky were yellow. Yellow was my uniform, desert yellow were the armored and tracked vehicles, light yellow my helmet; my boots were yellow, and so was my sand-covered skin. The country flaunted its foreignness; it was as unfamiliar as the moon—everything seemed corroded by time, as if nothing could possibly last, and that erosion, that disintegration of all things, became the only possible reality.

Everything spoke of death. Skeletons everywhere, of trucks, cars, and tanks—only the burned-out shells remaining—skeletons of homes, schools, mosques, and shops, skeletons of sheep, donkeys, and camels, rubble, ruins, rust. Broken, shattered, useless things. A country without time, where, I learned quickly, a village might be in ruins because of Enduring Freedom bombs a month ago or because of Tamerlane's army six centuries ago. Where people looked like ghosts. The women were invisible or erased by black veils or burqas, but so were the men—anonymous, all dressed in the same traditional white outfit, buried under beards and turbans. We were ghosts, too, driving by in our armored vehicles, erased by our uniforms, made anonymous by our helmets, our bulletproof vests, our sunglasses, by the kaffiyehs we wrapped around our faces to protect them from the sand. I began to feel as if we were already dead.

But it wasn't the fear of death, that would come later. It was like a time lag, a displacement: a sense of total remove from what I was doing, and even from my own self. The feeling that I'd already passed by, that I was moving about not in reality but in a dream. In a dream no one hears your voice, your actions make no impact, and their consequences are unpredictable. Words don't mean what they should. Distributing medicine, toys, and notebooks to people whose houses had been bombed by planes or who had shot at us a month before seemed hypocritical to me. Our checkpoints—controlling a deserted intersection in the middle of nowhere, rummaging through some poor shepherd's pickup, commandeering empty gas cans, accusing him of transporting them in order to resupply drug traffickers, while entire caravans of jeeps loaded with arms and drugs slipped past behind our backs, on mysterious mountain tracks—seemed like a pointless act of theater, like trying to empty the ocean with a leaky pail. I didn't have the courage to talk about it with anyone.

"Our real enemy is time," I dared to say one evening to First Lieutenant Russo: a skinny, lightweight man with a mustache who didn't roll his r's—I'd singled him out as the most intelligent of the officers—in love with Afghanistan and with his work. "We have to bring home results immediately, back home every member of the coalition faces elections, internal arguments, operational and human costs, and every piece of bad news cancels out a hundred positive developments and shortens the time we have. It never makes the news when we thwart an attack, but every single loss makes the public think we're losing. But the Afghanis have all of eternity ahead of them. It's paradoxical, but time is their most powerful weapon. And the only one we can't fight against."

First Lieutenant Russo gave me a surprised look, asked me if I remembered the philosopher Zeno, and switched off his laptop. I always wondered what he was writing, but we never became close enough for me to ask. I shook my head. "They don't teach you philosophy at tourism management school." "Our first year of high school, we covered the Greek philosophers," Russo said. "One of them was Zeno of Elea, which is near Salerno supposedly, and my mother's from Salerno, so I took a liking to him. He lived during the fifth century BC, and was a disciple of Parmenides. He invented dialectics. He taught how to take apart your adversaries' theses, reduce them to absurdity. Zeno wanted to show that the universe is made up of one unique and immutable being and that movement does not exist. He used paradoxes to do so. The most famous is the one with Achilles and the tortoise. Achilles is incredibly fast, the tortoise incredibly slow. But Achilles will never catch up with a tortoise who starts even a little ahead of him. By the time Achilles reaches the point where the tortoise started, the tortoise will have already moved farther ahead, and even if the distance is practically imperceptible, Achilles must reach the tortoise's new point of departure, and in the meantime the tortoise will have gone even farther, and so on, until infinity. In short, Zeno said that space and time are infinite, so it's impossible to make up the distance. Becoming and movement are absurd if examined with the tools of logic and reason."

I wasn't sure I understood what First Lieutenant Russo, or Zeno of Elea, meant, or if by telling me this story he wanted to say he agreed with me—or, on the contrary, show me that I was wrong and warn me to not ask too many questions. But I didn't want to be Achilles and chase after an objective I would never reach. I was beginning to ask myself what would happen when we were gone. "Will we leave behind solid institutions?" I asked him. "Or a sand castle? Will the country hold? Will what we're doing be swept away? Will it be like we never even existed?" Russo smiled and spread his map out on the table. "Our duty is to extend the security bubble to twenty kilometers all around Sollum. To secure this village, and this one, and this one"—he pointed with his pencil to nearly invisible dots on the map. "That's all." The dots circled in red indicated where IEDs had been identified, or where—in the previous months—Italians had been attacked. The map had measles.

I was crumbling under contradictions and solitude. For years my relationship with my family had been halfhearted, but now I found myself anxiously awaiting the moment when I could call Ladispoli. I'd get in line for a computer, send e-mails, post silly little things on Facebook, look at my friends' pages, study their idiotic photos snapped furtively at a party or a pub, or in the snow. I'd Skype my sister, my mother, even Traian. I'd make them tell me about themselves, in order to cling to something real, because my life wasn't.

Little by little, though, it was as if the thread were being cut. The important people in my life began to fade, became even more unreal than the ghosts around me. I'd call Italy once a week, then even less frequently. I discovered nostalgia. Once I was surrounding a village with my platoon while CIMIC coordinated a swap. The villagers would give us their weapons—ammunition belts, rifles, mines—and in exchange we would distribute useful items. Actually, we made the ANA soldiers distribute them: it was up to them to make contact with the population, and people were happier to receive things from their fellow country-men. Hoes, farming equipment, sacks of seeds and rice, used clothing, shoes. You never gave anything away for free here, it was a country without compassion. A soldier picked up a pair of women's boots. Brown leather, fake snakeskin. Identical to the ones my mother wore the day of my first communion. Those boots had walked for twenty years to reach me over there. But they didn't reach me. The soldier gave them to an old man in exchange for a hand grenade, I never figured out what good they did him. Three months after my arrival in Afghanistan, the Italian life of Manuela Paris was already the dream of a dream.

In March it snowed. A tentative but persistent snow, which turned to mush in the tepid midday sun, and then froze over again in the night-time cold, creaking ominously under our boots. The whiteness erased the towers, the protection barriers, the barbed wire, the road, the ruins of the village opposite the base. The bad weather shut us up in the FOB: convoys, outreach missions, and joint operations with ANA soldiers were all suspended. "When I was in Bosnia," Jodice told the soldiers shoveling snow to clear a path to the bunker, "a storm hit us. So much snow fell that it trapped us inside the huts. We were buried alive. We had to climb out through the chimney. My commander was so fat he got stuck. I had to go at the chimney with a pickaxe to get him out. Later they handed me the bill. For damaging military property, they said."

Then the rains came. The desert bloomed: a downy green coat, in-tangible and ephemeral, covered the sand—for a few hours. But even the rain was hostile. It gushed violently, cruelly from the sky, and when it hailed, the balls of ice that hit my head were as hard as rocks. Torrential rains lashed the tents and flooded the base. The sand turned to mud, and the mud became a dense slime, thick as cement, which clung to our boots and stuck to the ground, so it was an effort to take even a single step. The rains flooded the fields, erased all tracks, swept away the frag-ile village houses, swallowed up sheep, goats, trucks. We were cut off for days, not even our provisions—which arrived only from the sky—could reach us. The mess kitchen closed. We ate precooked rations, crackers, canned ravioli and sauce, and flavorless medallions of beef. "When I was in Lebanon," Jodice told us, "I'd had it with those shitty K rations, so I ate a jellyfish. The cook and I put it in a pot and boiled it for an hour, like an octopus. Then we ate it, little bites, with sugar. It tastes good, kind of like aspic." There was no time to comment on Jodice's recipe; the mournful howl of the siren sounded. The FOB was under attack. We ran to get our weapons, then to the bunker or our battle positions, hurriedly but also somehow calmly. Everyone knew where to go. They'd warned us it would happen. And it did. We knew what to do. "Lebanese jellyfish aren't edible," I said to him after the alarm was over. "You don't believe me, Sarge?" Jodice asked, astonished.

The warnings became an everyday occurrence, and anxiety spread, as contagious as a cold. I slept little, alarmed at the slightest sound. An officer sneezing in the next container was enough to make me leap to my feet. Then I didn't sleep at all. Awake on my cot, I listened to the symphony of whistles, snorts, coughs, hisses, and snores that rose, with varying intensity, from the officers' huts and the soldiers' tents: everyone snored, their noses and lungs were clogged with sand. Eyes wide open in the pitch black, I tried to imagine the men hiding on the mountain facing us, in position in the cold, busying themselves with the weapons they'd learned to handle as children. I asked myself what they truly hoped for, if they hoped for anything. People here didn't give the impression they were waiting for anything. I wondered who they were; how many they were. If they attacked us with any kind of coordination at all, we would be in trouble. One hundred twenty soldiers and one dog—with no drone support, held hostage by the weather, confined to the hangars by the rain, the helicopters hundreds of kilometers away, grounded by the storms, stuck on an isolated base in the middle of nowhere—as solitary as shipwrecked souls. The night was impenetrable, and the silence, broken only by rifle shots in the distance, was frightening.

They attacked us for seven days in a row, raining 107 mm rockets on us: the mortar platoon leader was given authorization to respond to their fire. I saw the shells launch. They rose into the air, making an arc like a comet. The first one moved me, the second upset me, and then after a while the spectacle left me indifferent—like a habit. We were hoping to neutralize the threat. But *threat* was merely an abstract word used to domesticate a concept. The threat was people. Yet it all seemed tremendously normal. Every soldier tranquilly performed the necessary gestures, as if it were a drill. Myself included. But I always felt like I was dreaming. None of this was real. When, after the attack on the fourth day, it was my turn to send two teams to comb the area, I almost couldn't believe they might actually encounter insurgents. And in fact they didn't—even though they searched for them for hours, staying out all night.

Captain Paggiarin congratulated Pegasus for the coolheadedness and discipline we showed in our baptism by fire. Other platoons hadn't been so efficient. "Buy us a drink, Sarge," said Zandonà, "we deserve it." The beer had run out, so with the last bottle of Coke we toasted Saint Hesco Bastion, Saint Beretta, and Saint Lince. "Our sergeant doesn't smoke, doesn't drink, and doesn't fuck, so let's drink to Saint Manuela," Jodice proposed. We were toasting my supposed virtue when a rocket landed near our vehicles. "Looks like God disagrees," Jodice laughed, kissing the Padre Pio medallion he wore around his neck. "Sarge is no saint, even she has her sins." I told him to knock it off. There was nothing to laugh at. The splinter effect of a 105 mm shell is fifty meters. In other words, the rocket just missed us. Everything faded into a dreamlike unreality. But the shells were real, as were the shards of broken glass, the flat tires, the craters in the sand.

I started to feel afraid. An irrational fear of dying in the desert, two thousand eight hundred miles from home, without having accomplished even one of the things I'd come here to do. I wanted more time. In that suspended moment between the whistle of the rocket and the rumble of the explosion, I thought this could be the final second of my life. I looked at the yellow tents, the milky sky, the soldier closest to me—Zandonà, with his freckles and boyish face—and the moment took on a bitter sweetness, a bottomless melancholy. And the more I felt afraid, the more the wild beauty of the country pierced me, like shrapnel, deeper and deeper, entering my veins, hurting me. The more Afghanistan repulsed me, the more it tried to crush and annihilate me like an insect, the more I began to love it, this naked, essential country, in which even a nail is important.

LIVE

I t rains on December 29. Drops tap against the windows. On the deserted beach a fisherman, sitting in a folding chair under a big black umbrella, surveys his lines: the rods planted in the sand, the bait in the still water, the taut nylon slicing through the air. His soggy dog keeps him company, tail wagging happily. The stubborn loyalty of dogs. Giovanni is loyal, too, in his own way. But Manuela doesn't know what to do with his loyalty. For her there's no going back.

Mattia must have gone out early: the shutters to his room stay closed all day. Manuela tossed and turned all night, restless, haunted by Ahmad Zahir's music, Lorenzo Zandonà's melancholy smile, the blood-soaked tampon on Diego Jodice's pillow, Mullah Wallid's angular, arrogant face, the call of the muezzin in the village of Bala Bayak, the taste of Mattia's saliva, the crunch of the yellow scorpion under her rifle butt, the dripping water in a camp shower, the furious buzz of a Mongoose helicopter, the crackle of a machine gun, the crash of an antitank missile against a rock. She didn't fall asleep until six in the morning, so not even three hours of anguished, unsound sleep. She wakes up five or six times, sweaty, trembling, even screaming once.

She goes to the bathroom and rinses her face. Vanessa's already there, brushing her teeth. "Did I scare you?" she asks. "Not at all," Vanessa replies, spitting a blob of toothpaste into the sink. "You scream every night, we're used to it by now. You sound horrifying when you scream, it's not your regular voice. Remember *The Exorcist?*" "I'm sorry," Manuela says, "I can't help it, I can't control it." "It won't last forever," Vanessa reassures her.

"I spotted him first, you know, the guy at the Bellavista," she adds, elbowing her sister conspiratorially. Then she starts to gargle, her voice becoming an incomprehensible mutter. "Amazing blue eyes, great body, nice ass, too, broad shoulders, pretty hot." She drools, spitting a rivulet of whitish water into the sink. "But I'm happy he likes you better, hon." "He's a wuss," Manuela says as she sticks her face under the freezing cold water. Vanessa turns to her, surprised. Her sister's angry response strikes her as a good sign. So it's true what Grandma said! Vanessa had thought she was raving, but Manuela really did go out with the guy from the Bellavista, who knows how she managed to snag him, he doesn't trust anyone. Vanessa had lain in wait for him for three days, and only managed to catch him on Christmas Eve, in the street in front of the hotel garage. She asked him to help her unload her car and carry the presents upstairs. They were heavy, she had only two hands. He kindly carried her packages, but didn't ask her anything or offer any conversational opening. She invited him in for a coffee, but he declined. "Not today," he said, "at any rate, now that I know where you live, we'll see each other again." Vanessa had the impression he liked her. Her skin tingled, his eyes twinkled—little things, but she was rarely wrong. He hadn't sought her out, though. He went for Manuela instead. Who would ever have thought. Just for a second—the time it takes to dry her mouth and look at herself in the mirror—she envies her sister, that lunar face standing behind her. And she's surprised, too. She's usually the one who snags the guy.

Manuela drags herself back to bed. She sleeps another hour. At ten she vomits in the conveniently placed tub. Mattia still isn't back.

Only Vanessa's home for lunch. Her mother's at work, Alessia's at a school friend's, Grandma's with the Jehovah's Witnesses. Manuela didn't know her grandmother had converted. "Two years ago," Vanessa says. "A sort of preacher came to lead the community, beard, sandals, talking like a prophet. Grandma's crazy about him. Their church is in a garage in the industrial park, behind the Vaccina River, just past the car dealership. There must be two hundred people there. Mamma says they seem possessed, but they're really just normal people. The fact is, Grandma's much calmer since she started going. She goes around proselytizing and sell-ing magazines door to door. She's tried to convert us all." "Has she had any luck?" Manuela asks, increasingly astounded. It's only then that she realizes she was away a really long time, and that she's not the only one who's changed. Vanessa doesn't answer.

They unearth a block of hamburgers, fish filets, and a package of baby peas from the freezer. "Damn!" Vanessa remembers all of a sudden, "I promised Mamma we'd go grocery shopping!" They defrost the ham-burgers in the microwave. The block disintegrates into a pile of bovine mush, devoid of any consistency or flavor. Manuela says she ate better at the mess in Bala Bayak. Still, she doesn't have the right to complain, be-cause she doesn't know how to cook. In the barracks there's always some-body to cook for you. It's one of the advantages of military life. While Vanessa keeps an eye on the espresso maker, Manuela spies on the Bel-lavista restaurant through the curtain. Mattia is having lunch at his usual table. He's reading the paper, which he has spread out across the whole table, as if trying to fill up the space someone left. The waiter Gianni comes over, removes the cover from a dish, and waits for Mattia to comment on how wonderful the chef is. Mattia gives him a sad smile and goes back to his paper.

The discount supermarket, in the basement of a shopping center wedged between the Via Aurelia and the tollbooth, is the size of a city. As she loads the shopping cart with colorful, plastic-looking vegetables, frozen cod, pork from who knows where, Tunisian tuna, Greek olive oil, Bel-gian mustard, Czech beer, German mozzarella, and precooked gnocchi, Vanessa asks Manuela if she wants to go to a New Year's party with her, in a former industrial area, the old gas company. It's expensive, tickets cost fifty euros, but the music is real mellow, the best techno-dance DJs around taking turns. "No way," Manuela says. She hasn't gone dancing in years and it doesn't seem like a great idea now that she's on crutches. And besides, blasting music would rattle her nerves. Vanessa doesn't re-alize what Manuela is capable of when she really loses it. She's afraid of becoming seriously unhinged. It happened to another Alpino, a soldier named Cadin Edoardo, from her same regiment. She never met him; the story was already years old when she joined Ninth Company. Captain Paggiarin let slip that after returning from Kabul, Cadin Edoardo had done some nightmarish things and been discharged. By "nightmarish" Paggiarin meant that he tried to kill himself: he shot himself in the head with a pistol.

Vanessa says that she won't go either, then. She has a better idea, in fact. "Let's eat dinner at home, that way we'll make Mamma and Alessia happy, and then ring in the New Year at Passo Oscuro. Mamma doesn't know, but I stole a set of keys—I go there with Youssef. He lives with his cousin, but we can't see each other at their house because Youssef has a wife in Morocco, I don't know if I told you." "Vanessa, no!" Manuela exclaims, but her sister just shrugs. "We never knew where to do it, the car is gross, I'm not some slut he picked up on the Aurelia. Grandpa's cottage is all run-down, it's falling to pieces, the roof leaks, but with a little imagination it can be quite charming, and it's only a hundred feet from the sea. We bring a boom box and dance to our favorite music, just the two of us."

"I thought you wanted to go out with Lapo on New Year's," Manuela says. "I couldn't care less about New Year's!" Vanessa blurts out. "I don't believe in holidays, for me it's like any other night. I want to be with you. You're important to me." Surprised, Manuela stops the cart in the middle of the aisle. Under the harsh neon lights, her hair an unnatural color, her skirt too short, her shoes too tall, Vanessa looks fragile and lost. She's never said anything like that to Manuela before.

"When I first heard about the attack," she says, tossing a huge bag of paprika potato chips into the cart, "because I was the one who opened the door when the guys from the army showed up, I thought: Now what do I do? I don't want to live without Manuela. We grew up together, she's the only person who really knows me. And she's the only one who knows the good things about me. I never even told her I love her, because it's embarrassing to say stuff like that, and you think there'll always be time, but saying later is like saying never, and all of a sudden, boom, it's all over. We die so quickly, we're like leaves dangling from a branch. When you were over there my heart would stop every time the doorbell rang because I was afraid it was about you. When it happened, the army guy said to me, he was so polite, you could tell he'd been trained, he said, 'I need to speak with Miss Vanessa Paris, I have an urgent, confidential communication.' 'That's me,' I said. He told me it would be best if I sat down. So I knew. I was holding my cell phone and I threw it against the wall, it shattered in so many pieces I had to buy a new one, and I started crying like a crazy person. I was sobbing so hard, I couldn't breathe, I was suffocating. 'Sergeant Paris requested that you be the person to contact in case of an accident.' He explained it was up to me to tell the other members of the family. But I couldn't bring myself to call Mamma. 'My mother's at work,' I told him, and so he says, 'Can't you call her office and tell her to come home right away?' 'Office?' I said. 'What office, she doesn't work in an office, we can't call the roadside diner, my poor mother's making coffee for the truck drivers, she'll have a heart attack, this is going to kill her.' So I called that fucking gypsy woman. 'You tell her, Teodora,' I said, 'you're probably glad, one less Paris to deal with.' I was screaming, I bet I sounded like I'd lost my mind, 'You tell my mother that her daughter, her youngest daughter, is dying.'" "I'm sorry," Manuela mumbles. "I'm sorry I put your name on the form, but I didn't want some stranger to tell her, I'm sorry."

Every time Manuela left the FOB she thought: If something happens to me, how will they tell my mother? She knew the procedure, the protocol. She knew the words, the formulas, but it was the miserable, banal everydayness into which those words would erupt that she found so devastating. Ironclad inside the Lince, ironclad in her uniform, helmet, and body armor, automatic rifle in her hands, she'd be thinking about the rest stop on the Rome–Civitavecchia highway two thousand eight hundred miles away. Morning in Afghanistan was dawn for Cinzia Colella. The lights of the rest stop dispelled the darkness of the asphalt. The pull-off would still be filled with tractor trailers, dripping with the night's humidity, and the first truck drivers, sleepy, with prickly beards and bloodshot eyes, would be at the counter, and her mother would already be at work, in her white uniform and her cap with the company's red logo. Manuela dead, disemboweled, decapitated, butchered in the desert, and her mother at work, an ordinary day, flattened by the news while the coffee machine oozed black drops into little espresso cups, and speechless customers watched that shriveled-up shadow of a woman who had once been attractive weep desperately, that middle-aged woman who just a minute before had been joking with them and accepting their crude compliments delivered in a rough Italian with Lithuanian or Slavic or Turkish mixed in, and who was now devastated, destroyed, crushed. Manuela knew she was her mother's shot at redemption, the good daughter, the accomplished daughter, the daughter who had lifted herself out of poverty and ignorance, whose success made her own wasted youth packaging frozen filets in a fish factory, made the millions of cups of coffee prepared on the side of the highway, the truck drivers' compliments, the loneliness all worthwhile. Manuela couldn't die without killing her mother as well.

She could almost see her after receiving news of Sergeant Paris's death, fallen in the line of duty. It was such a horrible thought, and so obviously possible, that she crossed her fingers and hoped that, if something did happen to her, it would at least be on a Sunday, when her mother was home. Then she remembered that for her mother, just like for herself, there were no Sundays, only shifts. So she wished that nothing would happen to her. And the more time passed, the closer she got to leaving Afghanistan, the more she gave in to the presumptuous certainty that she would survive.

"You think you're the only two people in this world? So rude! Let me by, you jerks." Their shopping cart is blocking the way. A woman complains; she's in a hurry, or thinks she is. She tries to wedge past them, and the wheels of her cart catch Manuela's crutch and yank it out of her hand. It crashes into the shelf, knocking over cans of hazelnuts and packets of toasted almonds and pistachios. "Bitch!" Vanessa yells. "It was to save your lazy ass and protect your shit life that my sister got her leg blown up!" Her eyes glisten and a tear trickles down her cheek, tracing a pale path in the thick layer of rouge. She kneels, picks up Manuela's crutch, and hands it to her. "You know I prayed?" she says with a smile. "God, did I pray, honey!"

Manuela doesn't know what to say. She doesn't believe her, but she can't let her sister know. "I swear," Vanessa insists, "when you were in a coma in the hospital in Farah. In Our Lady of the Rosary Church, under those weird paintings you like so much. They look to me like the artist was on ecstasy, but you always said they spoke to the heart more than Raphael's paintings did, being so simple and colorful, so I went there thinking of you. I did the via crucis—Mary and Elizabeth, the shepherds, the temple—I prayed for you under every station of the cross, then I knelt at the high altar, I gazed at Christ in the Last Supper, and I'd say, 'Jesus, you came back from the dead, you made your friend Lazarus come back from the dead, make her come back, too.' And then I'd start all over again. I'd do the whole church until the parish volunteers locked up the place and threw me out." To prove it was all true, Vanessa crosses her fingers, kisses them, and presses them to her lips. The same gesture from when she was a little girl.

Manuela pushes the cart down the detergent aisle. Vanessa quickly grabs bottles of soap, laundry detergent, and softener, without letting herself be distracted by the "3 for the price of 2" offers or the throng of carts at the cash register. She doesn't care at all that she's talking so loudly everyone can hear her. Only Manuela exists right now, Manuela and the interminable anguish of those damned days; her sister doesn't even know about them but they made Vanessa realize that she didn't want to live without her. That—damn it—she loves her. "But you didn't get better, nothing happened. You didn't wake up. Finally I went to the Jehovah's Witnesses," she confesses, her voice cracking. "It's not like I converted, but I can't deny what happened. The day after I went to the Kingdom Hall, which is like their church, God heard me. Because Jehovah is supposed to be God, I don't know if I told you. Jehovah is the name of God. If you say God, just God, it's like you're saying engineer or lawyer or doctor, a generic title, but God told us his name, which is Jehovah. It's written in the Bible, I can't remember where. If you need to call someone, you have to call them by name, or else they won't answer you—maybe that's why when I prayed before he didn't hear me. Then I called him by name and he answered me, see? So I made my peace with God. I respect him, I believe in him. I'm convinced he exists now. I'm convinced it was God who stopped that shrapnel."

"I don't think God has anything to do with it," Manuela says, admiring the cashier's ability to type in bar codes at such a phenomenal rate. A girl Manuela's age, with nails like claws, purple lips, and a curious star-shaped cut on her cheek. Why does a girl like that settle for such a monotonous, unrewarding job? Ever since she was little she knew she'd leave home one day, and come back only when she could offer herself, her mother, and Vanessa a different life. A real life, one worth living. The cash register vomits out a mile-long receipt. Forty-three items purchased. A total of 4,570 points on their card. They need another five thousand and something in order to get the reward, a set of pans. Vanessa doesn't have enough cash. Manuela takes out her ATM card. When the cashier lifts her head to hand her the card reader, Manuela recognizes her. It's Samantha, an old classmate. Manuela gave her that scar on her cheek years ago, back when she was a thug. An act of revenge. Samantha had offended her so she sliced her face with barbed wire. Back then Manuela believed it was up to her to mete out justice on her own. She didn't have any allies, and it seemed as if the whole world were against her. After that incident, she was reported to city services for being "psychologically disturbed" and "difficult." They sent a social worker, but her mother refused to open the door. So after a while they left her alone. Samantha deserved it, but she's sorry you can still see the star-shaped scar on her cheek. Samantha doesn't recognize Manuela, though, she's changed too much. And besides, she never looks at the customers. She moves them through one after another, all she cares about is finishing her shift and going home.

"It was pure chance," Manuela explains as she fills humongous plastic bags with meat, fish, cheese, vegetables. "The technical term, in ballistics, is divergence. I was supposed to be in a certain point, at the intersection of a series of lines, a point determined by a logical, mathematical chain of actions, decisions, movements, gestures. But by pure chance, I wasn't there. I was ten paces back, even though I shouldn't have been, and the explosion blew me apart, but not completely. I'm alive because of that divergence."

"I can take you there, to the Kingdom Hall, if you want, the meetings are open to the public, first they sing, then they explain the Bible, then they pray," Vanessa says, ignoring her sister's meditation on ballistics. "It makes you feel at peace. Their God, Jehovah I mean, is omnipotent but he's human, too, I don't know if I'm explaining this well." The glass doors open and they are expelled from the supermarket. The smell of tar and carbon monoxide rises from the asphalt. Vanessa wedges her pear-shaped cart into the last cart in the line, and the little device on the handle returns her coin. Vanessa automatically drops the coin in the empty can that the pregnant gypsy girl with a newborn in her arms holds; she's begging next to the row of shopping carts. The girl has stationed herself at the point of convergence. Excellent choice. "You have to hear them pray," Vanessa insists. "You have to read their magazine, it's really simple and easy to understand, it explains all sorts of things. The most important is that God knows you, God knows your needs, God cares about you."

Manuela isn't much of a help; her hands are busy holding her crutches. Vanessa staggers under the weight of the shopping bags, but she's used to it. No one has ever helped her. It doesn't even occur to her that someone might. "God isn't some abstract force," she says, "but a person, with a personality and feelings, there are things he loves and things he doesn't. The other important thing is that Jehovah is happy. That's what Timothy writes, I don't remember where, because it's not like I've read the entire Bible. But I'm touched by the idea of a happy God, what can I say. I got chills when I read it, because I understood that the difference between God and us is just that, happiness. Only God can be happy. I don't know if I'm explaining this well. I have the magazines at home, all this year's issues, I hide them in my underwear drawer because Mamma doesn't know about this thing with the Jehovah's Witnesses, I don't know if I told you. Chance has nothing to do with it, you'll see. It means something that you were saved. It's a message."

I'm alive because the 120-day winds quieted down and there wasn't a sandstorm and the helicopter was able to land, Manuela wants to say. And because the surgeon at Role 2, the American camp hospital at Farah, didn't have too many wounded in action that day, and so he wasn't tired and his hands were steady and he removed the shrapnel before it sliced my brain. But she can't find the courage to tell Vanessa. Vanessa doesn't know a thing about probability computations and divergence theories. That's all soldier talk. Ravings caused by nostalgia, solitude, and fear. Nonsense invented during night guard duty, at the outpost on the hill, buried in a trench, watching burning fireballs sweep across the sky; they looked like tracers, rockets, or searchlights, but they were actually stars. Gigantic stars. Meteors, planets, celestial bodies dressed in fire, crisscrossing the horizon and sinking into a sea of darkness.

During those 167 Afghani days, Manuela received word of the accidental death of an army engineers sergeant attached to the Alpini at a nearby base, crushed by a Buffalo during a maneuver, and of the death of a major, whose heart burst during a visit to an outpost near Badghis, in the north, perhaps because of the harsh February cold. There was a blizzard that day, and the helicopters couldn't take off; he might have survived if they'd been able to get him to the FOB. And of the wounding of an Alpino from a different regiment, shot in the head at close range by an Afghani police officer shouting "Allahu Akbar": the bullet had merely grazed his scalp. Then there were 321 attacks without casualties and fifteen thwarted attempts. Explosive devices, sown along the very road she had to travel. Traps waiting for her. That hadn't exploded. Or that were detected in time. Reported by a peasant eager to collaborate in hopes of peace, or identified and neutralized by their jammer. Death didn't obey any rules. She knew it was absurd, her survival completely random. So she became convinced that every event was the result of a convergence of facts, an intersection of all the other infinite events scattered through time and space, distant and independent, yet somehow strung together like pearls on a necklace.

Every day each one of them performed a series of insignificant acts and irrelevant movements, what might be called the simple business of living. All without knowing that each one of those acts and movements was converging toward a center, a sort of black hole that swallows and annuls matter. That center is the focal point into which everything inescapably falls. It has nothing to do with probability computations. It's a point, a lightning flash, the climax of a lifetime, its end and perhaps its significance. Irrelevant, insignificant acts and movements performed a split second earlier or later can cause the divergence, prevent from happening what has been determined by logic and mathematics. A divergence of this kind must have occurred at Qal'a-i-Shakhrak, because, of the five of them who got out of the Lince, only she was spared. The others found themselves at the point of intersection—but not her. She must have carried out some insignificant act, some irrelevant movement that allowed her to deviate from the trajectory pointing to her death, and saved her. But that morning had been erased from her memory, leaving behind a crater no less deep than the one the plastic explosive made in the sand at Qal'a-i-Shakhrak.

Manuela finds a letter for her in the mailbox. No stamp, so it wasn't mailed. Written on hotel stationery—there's a stylized drawing of the Bellavista on the top left, with the address, phone number, and three stars. Only three. Manuela thought it had more. In the envelope there's a photograph Mattia took on his cell. The light is milky and the image blurry, but it's clearly of her—a close-up. Mattia hadn't yet cocooned her in his scarf. The water sparkles all around her, encircling her in a kind of halo. It's not easy to photograph a person. Everybody takes pictures, but in order for them to really say something about the subject, the person taking them has to know how to see beyond the subject's features and momentary smiles. He has to convey something of his own gaze. To capture the unique light that that person, and only that person, emits. To love, perhaps. Mattia's Manuela is wild, but not hidden. She offers him her bare face, her protruding ears, her nose red with cold, her lips folded into the beginning of a smile, her eyes glistening and wide with curiosity and trust. An ingenuous but determined Manuela, never before seen, even by herself. It's a pity to lose a man who looked at her like that.

On the back of the photo is written in black ink: "If every day were December 28, I would ask you to come up to my room. The things that have never been last forever. Don't look back." He didn't even sign it.

She slips the photograph into the book that Colonel Minotto recommended she read, a manual on the psychophysical rebirth of the veteran, published by some American university. She gave up on it after the first chapter. Either because medical-psychological English is difficult, or because she doesn't like thinking of herself as a veteran when she's not even twenty-eight. She's too tired to think, or to do much of anything. She doesn't even know if Mattia's sibylline and hypocritical note has wounded or consoled her. Or what it really means. All she wants is to relive those few hours on the paddleboat, which are already fading, clouded by infinite distance. To feel that hypnotic rocking of the waves again and the heat of his body against her own, that dawning intimacy, timid yet brazen, the foolish way her heart leaped after such a long time. She dilutes her drops in a glass and falls asleep right away. The next morning her mother doesn't have the heart to tell Manuela she didn't sleep a wink because her daughter's anguished cries kept her up all night. No one in the house was able to sleep, in fact. Alessia climbed into Vanessa's bed, weeping. Even Grandma woke up. And when her daughter asks her, Cinzia lies and gives her a tired smile. "No, Manu, I didn't hear you screaming last night."

9

HOMEWORK

On April 3, we were expecting a freelance reporter and photographer at Sollum. The brigade PIO had given his approval, and Pegasus was chosen to flank them for a story on Alpino activity in the province of Farah. The other noncommissioned officers resented this privilege. Rightly so, because I hadn't done anything to deserve it. But the explanation was simple: Captain Paggiarin knew the presence of a female platoon leader so deep in hostile territory, at such an exposed FOB, guaranteed visibility. Freelancers usually managed to sell their stories only to small magazines, or local papers where the regiment was stationed. I had no desire to waste time letting reporters who wouldn't even be on the base for twenty-four hours play war, but obviously I said, "Yes, sir." When the reporter, wrapped in a blue shawl, climbed out of the helicopter and ran across the landing pad, we saw it was a woman.

She was blond, plump, and pretty. Not so young that she was just chasing after adventure but not so old that she'd lost her taste for it. The soldiers stared at her as if she were an apparition. They hadn't seen a woman who wasn't armed and bundled in camouflage for three months. The combination of no sex and a whole lot of masturbation was making them hallucinate. The captain cursed under his breath. He didn't want civilian women at the FOB, they only caused trouble. When, the year before, the ministry, hoping to raise morale on a less-exposed base, packaged up a show—complete with the requisite scantily clad dancers, TV entertainers of some kind, who were supposedly very popular but whom he'd never even heard of—he had refused, horrified. An Alpino regiment is not a circus. But this time they'd screwed him. "It's Daria Cormon!" First Lieutenant Russo exclaimed with a smile. "I know her, she's a good-luck charm, she's been traveling the front for years. When she's around no one dies."

Pegasus didn't leave the FOB. Intelligence had issued a car bomb warning—a Toyota Corolla station wagon—on the S17 heading toward the village, so the captain canceled the outreach mission. The situation was too dangerous. Cormon, who hadn't been told why there was a change in the program, begged, insisted, implored. She was prepared to sign a release form. "I'm visiting the village at my own risk, if they kill me, it's my own fault. Just let me go." "Absolutely not," Paggiarin repeated. "I'm not risking my men for some newspaper article." "Of course," Cormon sighed, "I understand." It was only noon.

The distressed reporter ate combat rations with First Lieutenant Russo, Lance Sergeant Spina, and me. Russo asked her if it was true that in Kabul they called her the Blue Fairy. "I don't know," Cormon said, "but I wouldn't mind if they did. I'm not a vampire looking for blood, I'm not here to make a name for myself on your backs." The disheartened photographer took some pictures of the bomb dog, and then of Angkor: she was without a doubt the most photogenic member of the company. "A quartermaster who doesn't even know what a machine gun is," Jodice lamented. "They've never done a story on me. What kind of fucking image are they spreading of Italian soldiers, we're not nurses here to hand out candy."

But the guests didn't have time to get bored, because they got to experience an antitank missile attack. Cormon had been in Sierra Leone, Pakistan, and Rwanda; she didn't scare easily. She followed us into the bunker, not frightened in the least. Civilians usually panic at the first explosion. I don't know why, maybe some kind of gender solidarity, but I was glad that everyone at Sollum agreed: that blonde had balls. She had to interview me for her story. She told me so flat out. "I cover all my expenses up front," she said. "If I sell a piece, I get paid, if not, I'm out that money. I'm thirty-nine, it's not an easy or comfortable life. But I'm free, you know what I mean? No one tells me what to write." "No one tells you what to write, but you can't choose what you get to know," I observed.

Cormon smiled. "Okay," I conceded, "but let's not waste too much time. The situation's critical, as I'm sure you noticed. I'm very busy."

We got off to a bad start. "Why did you join the military?" I was dismissive: "Everyone always asks the same thing, as if it were a weird choice. To me, that's a sign of a country's cultural backwardness. No one asks a female judge why she decided to become a judge, yet until forty years ago even the judiciary was off limits to women. I don't have to explain or justify anything. It's my profession." "I know," Cormon said, "and I agree. I asked because that's what people want to know." "I don't discuss my personal life," I specified. "But I think it was an encounter with a colonel that really changed my life. He treated me so badly that I wanted the ground to swallow me up. But what he said stuck with me. In a certain sense I'm here today because of him."

"Your mentor?" Cormon was curious. "No," I answered, "it was at a party thrown by the army, I was still in school, he wouldn't even remember me. The girls from tourism management and the kids in their last year of high school at Ladispoli had been invited to some patriotic event—a November 4 victory celebration. To be honest, I couldn't remember which victory we were supposed to be celebrating, but I was curious to see some soldiers up close, so I went. There was a band playing the national anthem and a flag unfurled on the wall. I didn't know then that the flag is a symbol, like the body of a nation, and that soldiers salute it every day. I felt like I was at a soccer stadium. They'd set up a buffet on the other side of the hall, but the snacks, pizza, and drinks were covered with a tablecloth, and you couldn't go near it until the speech was over. The officers explained to the group of kids how the Italian Armed Forces are organized, that the army is made up of six branches—infantry, cavalry, artillery, combat engineers, communication, transport and materials—and three corps—administration and commissariat, health, and engineers. When the kids heard the word *cavalry*, they sneered and stopped paying attention because they couldn't believe soldiers still rode horses in our Internet age. I listened attentively, even though I pretended to be as indifferent as the others. Because of the ruckus I couldn't understand the difference between the light and armored cavalry, or what the connection was between the railroaders, pontoniers, sappers, pioneers, and the dog unit. I was hypnotized by all those specialized terms. The speaker concluded by reminding us that mandatory service would soon be abolished and that Italy, too, would then have an army of professionals. Volunteers would be dynamic, responsible young people ready to face new challenges and experiences, build character, and discover whether they were fit for military life. He wanted us to know that being a soldier in the twenty-first century would mean taking part in a good, modern profession that would offer an interesting and economically rewarding life of service to the community, or rather to the homeland—in other words, Italy. 'Be proud to be Italian.' When he finished they distributed fliers and brochures.

"The kids had fun because they got to skip classes that day, but they didn't really listen, and their brochures ended up in the trash. But I put mine in my pocket, folded in quarters like a Kleenex so no one would notice it. I feigned the same couldn't-care-less attitude the others had. When a group is too tight-knit, it's never a good idea to be the only one to take the other side. It's better to pretend, and to act without the others knowing, so that no one will try to get in your way. Leaning against the wall, I drank Coca-Cola and spied on the officers. Their uniforms, boots, berets, and stars. They all seemed so sure of themselves. I furtively approached an old officer with a walrus mustache and a nose like a lumpy carrot. He was a colonel, but I didn't know that. His shoulder loops, ribbons, and insignia didn't mean anything, to me they were just scraps of fabric. I didn't know that soldiers wear their history on their uniforms, like a book. 'What do I have to do to enlist?' I found the courage to ask. 'Do I need to train? I'm a good swimmer and I run like a shot, but I don't know how to ride a horse.'

"The colonel turned around, surprised. These propaganda pilgrimages to schools, which the Ministry of Defense required, were like forced labor to him. I can understand his annoyance and frustration now, even imagine what he was thinking. Young people today are apathetic cowards—dead dogs, as we call them in the military. They don't want to work hard. Concepts like honor, dignity, and steadfastness haven't touched them. The girls from tourism management preferred to flirt with the guys from the NCO Academy in Viterbo. And those big, horny boys took the bait. They'd been holed up in the barracks for months. But they'd been brought along on these school visits to serve as testimonials, because the young never listen to the old. The colonel looked me up and down. Back then I was skinny as a rail, black bangs hiding my eyes. Dressed like a million other kids in nowhere towns all over the world:

jeans four sizes too big, a faded hoodie, a tattoo on my neck. 'How old are you?' he asked me. 'I'll be seventeen in May,' I answered, trying to seem important. 'So study, get good grades, graduate from high school.' I shrugged my shoulders and blew the bangs out of my eyes. That's what my mother always said to me. But I expected different advice from a military man. 'We need to construct an elite army to represent Italy throughout the world,' the colonel said. 'We need mature, aware, motivated youth, not soccer hooligans.' I turned red. I felt as ashamed as if he'd spat in my face. I disappeared into the crowd that was attacking the buffet table.

"Basically, he made me realize that to become a soldier, you have to go through a selection process, compete, just like when you enter the workforce. And to earn a place you have to know things. Read, become informed, learn your history and geography. So I got it into my head that I'd never become a soldier if I didn't fill the gaps in my education. I've never lacked willpower. My grades improved dramatically. In the end I surprised everyone—especially my mother. I got one hundred percent on my high school exit exam. I applied, ready to crush the competition. I became a volunteer for one year, what's known as a VFP1. To me it was really something, but it was only the lowest form of military service. The first thing they told my echelon was that this year was a kind of test. To see if military life was right for us. That explanation annoyed me. I didn't need any tests, I knew already. I didn't consider myself just some volunteer passing through. I already felt I was a professional soldier. Private Paris."

Daria Cormon smiled. Maybe she wanted me to keep going, but to me it seemed like I'd talked too much already, and besides, I had things to do. I rushed through the rest of the interview in ten minutes. The usual questions, the usual answers. Is this a passion for you or a vocation? What does the fatherland mean to you? What's it like commanding a platoon, have you encountered any difficulties as a woman, do you have a boyfriend, do the men respect you, are you afraid? It felt rehearsed. Cormon would have liked to ask completely different questions, and I would have liked to give completely different answers. But we couldn't. Both of us knew it, so we kept to the script. I never asked if she was able to sell the interview, or if she'd send me a copy. The first time I was interviewed, back at the NCO Academy in Viterbo, the only woman in my course, I bought forty copies of the paper and gave them to friends and relatives. But I never recognize myself in the words they attribute to me, so I gradually stopped caring about my public image. I do my job and try to do it well. The rest is not my concern.

Then Daria Cormon asked if I could show her the squad weapons. I stared at the tape recorder on the table. It was still running. In a conflict a reporter, even the most famous correspondent, never mind the lowest freelancer, is like the lowest-ranking soldier. You have a very limited view of the playing field, like when you're seated behind the goal at a soccer game, or when you're the ball boy. You get very little information, and you can't verify it, can't put the pieces together, you're a puppet maneuvered by strings you can't even see. You travel forty-eight hours to spend one day holed up in an advance base, buried in the sand, and maybe you won't even sell your story. I had them call machine gunner Pieri. He was the best of my men, he deserved to have his picture in the paper, or an interview, some kind of recognition.

Michelin was over six feet tall and ripped like a decathlete. An incredibly gentle soul despite his disturbing Terminator look. When, during training in Italy before deployment, he discovered that his commander was going to be a woman, he told the others—Nail, who had become my confidant, perhaps without even realizing it, told me—that he found the idea intriguing, he wasn't upset at all by the strangeness of it. It was a new challenge, and he liked to set goals for himself. He came running, drying the sweat that ran down his cheeks from under his helmet. I authorized Private Pieri to accompany our guest to the shooting range. "Yes, ma'am," Michelin said, without even lifting his eyes to look at her.

Michelin didn't sleep in his tent that night. I should have punished him, because it was strictly forbidden, and if he'd been found out or if something had happened, I would have paid for it. Steadfastness, honor, duty, integrity. But also good sense. Flexibility is the key to every human relationship. I pretended I didn't notice. The visitors left at dawn, the grumpy photographer with a long beard, and smiling Daria Cormon, her hair wrapped in her blue shawl. At roll call Michelin had a hickey on his neck and was falling asleep. At the morning briefing Paggiarin asked me if Cormon's visit had caused any problems; he was staunchly against outsiders at the FOB, but they didn't understand that at the ministry: sometimes the media's perception of the operation seemed more important to them than the operation itself. But it matters what you do, not what you say you do. "No problems, sir," I said, "the platoon is very grateful to have been chosen."

That evening, in the mess, the men called me over to their table and offered me a glass of prosecco. Cormon had smuggled in the bottle, she knew that the scarcity of alcohol at Sollum was demoralizing. I accepted, just a token sip, to show team spirit. But Zandonà filled my glass and I downed it. Later I learned from Nail that the platoon's respect for their leader had increased after the Blue Fairy's visit. Paris didn't humiliate them just for the sake of it. She wasn't like the college graduates, or the other parasites who kiss the officers' asses to get even with the soldiers. She was on their side.

"Tell her, Spaniard," Michelin goaded him. "Tell her, tell her," the others prodded. Jodice, sitting at the far end of the table, refused, protested, made them beg. "No, I'm not going to, women go all soft, she might think I'm doing it so I can ask her a favor, no." "Tell her, man," Zandonà insisted. "Paris is all right." I didn't understand what they were talking about. They were all excited. Giani's eyes were wet with tears. "Spaniard scored," Owl said with a wink. "Sarge," Jodice finally said, "my heart's melting." Zandonà turned the laptop toward me so he could show me the DVD. From the soldiers' expressions, I could tell they'd already seen it, and they were stunned.

A sort of black funnel appeared on the screen, slashed horizontally by clearer streaks, lines almost. In one corner of the funnel was a spot. It was pulsating. I didn't understand. "It's my baby," Jodice said. "This is the ultrasound, the Blue Fairy brought it to me from Herat, if I'd waited any longer for the mail to arrive, Imma would have already given birth. If you look, you can already see his little weenie, it's a boy."

I couldn't imagine what he must have been feeling, two thousand eight hundred miles from home, his son on a DVD, and rockets overhead. I'm not easily moved, and anyway, I had learned to keep my emotions under control. Besides, that microscopic dot that I could barely make out didn't seem human to me or even alive; it was more like a star. I didn't know what to say, or what all the soldiers pressing against me expected. I did know that their sharing their secret with me was a kind of initiation.

"Congratulations, Diego," I said. "You must be glad it's a boy, you don't really like women." "It's weird, right?" he said. "Here I am showing you the ultrasound, all emotional, like it's me who's pregnant, and you, Sergeant, you're looking at me like I'm some sentimental little lady because you don't give a shit. Either the world is turning upside down, or one of us was born the wrong gender." "I don't think so," I said, "and it's not true that I don't care. If you toe the line, I'll send you to Dubai to see your girlfriend." Jodice understood that it was a pact, not a promise. I held out my hand. He shook it, hard and for a long time. It was the coarse, callused hand of a soldier.

No sooner had the supply planes started making deliveries again, and spaghetti with tomato sauce and frozen fish started showing up in the mess hall again, no sooner had the snow melted on the mountain passes and the tracks were passable again, and the waning moon became a crescent, a sickle, a line of light, and finally nothing, then the order I'd been waiting for all winter arrived. This time it was for real. It was our turn. Ninth Company Panthers—Mars, Cerberus, and Pegasus platoons—departure at 2100. Cordon and search. Operation Goat 4.

> >

10

LIVE

On December 30, the roadside diner is unusually quiet. Every now and then someone comes in for a newspaper or cigarettes, but for most of the morning, Cinzia doesn't have a lot to do. She heats up a few sandwiches on the grill, and between customers she enjoys the company of her daughter who—for mysterious reasons she prefers not to ask about—insisted on coming to work with her. The persistent smell of mortadella, coffee, and disinfectant wafts through the vast space. The radio plays the latest hits. Tomorrow's the last day of the year, the DJ keeps insisting, how are you going to celebrate? And don't forget to wear something red, something old, and something new. Manuela wandered among the shelves, perused the stuffed animals, maps, and outdated CDs on sale for a few euros, then flipped through the books heaped in a metal basket. Then she moved a bar stool behind the counter and for hours has simply been staring hungrily at the cars zooming by. Her mother is afraid she's bored, but Manuela reassures her: the only thing she wants to do is sit right here.

The customers are in a hurry, they keep turning around to check on their cars through the window; they talk about insignificant things or important things, all without noticing Manuela or her mother. "I warned him, but he wouldn't listen," a woman says to her son. "There's not much snow, but the lifts are open," a kid says to his friend. "I barely even saw my Christmas bonus." "He went to Germany, makes three times as much, but the Germans are awful and the weather's miserable, so now he wants to come home." Lives light up for an instant—voices, people— and then the place is deserted again. The customers look at Cinzia Colella without actually seeing her. For them, she simply doesn't exist. Maybe because she's over fifty, or maybe because she's a waitress. She's simply an efficient machine, one of the restaurant's appendages. This discovery both offends and moves Manuela. Her mother exists only for her.

Her co-workers turn out to be nice. The other woman who works the counter—a redhead, thirty years old, with ample breasts that must make the truckers happy—keeps discreetly to herself. But Manuela isn't here to discuss the meaning of the universe. She wants to make up for her absence in the past in some way—and for her absences in the future. Because she wants to go back to Afghanistan. She wants to see that damn school. To start patrolling that endless road again. So, in a way, she has come to take her leave. "Teach me to make coffee," she says all of a sudden. Cinzia is surprised but agrees. She explains how to bang the cylinder on the edge of the base once, to loosen the wet grounds so they drop into the trash. To use your wrist to turn it. It's simple, a child could probably do it. Nothing like the things Manuela does. Here the biggest danger is being held up by a drug addict or yelled at by a drunkard. But that's never happened to her. Besides, there are video cameras. Apart from that, her life has been reduced to just a few actions and even fewer words, always the same. Make coffee, heat up sandwiches on the grill, tear the receipt in such a way that the customer can't get served twice, say good morning, say goodbye. The biggest challenges are slicing lemons for tonic water and pouring a beer—it can't have too much head, which her customers don't like, or too little, which her boss doesn't like. The proportions have to be just right. She doesn't have anything else to teach her daughter.

But Manuela seems to be enjoying herself, and wants to make coffee for the gas station attendant who comes inside to soak up a bit of warmth. "It's good," he assures her. It took her less than ten minutes to learn. Her mother says she shouldn't spend too much time behind the counter, people might recognize her, it's better if she doesn't let herself be seen with her. "Why?" Manuela asks with surprise. "It's not very heroic," Cinzia responds confusedly. What she means is that she doesn't look like the mother of a hero, that she's worried she might diminish her daughter's glory. But she doesn't know how to explain. The words get all tangled up inside her. When the redhead disappears into the bathroom, Manuela bends over her mother, who is intent on working the coffee machine, puts her arms around her waist, and kisses her neck. Cinzia starts, frightened. When Manuela was little and her mother would bend down to kiss her, she'd make herself into a ball, offering the smallest possible surface area. Manuela was so tall, dry, and closed that Cinzia would jokingly compare her to the artichokes that thrive in Ladispoli's volcanic soil: hard, compact, and closed up. She would remind her daughter, who was allergic to her outbursts of affection, that Ladispoli artichokes are famous because they're sweet and don't have any thorns. But Manuela still wouldn't let herself be kissed. "I must be a different species," she would say. So Cinzia realizes that something's about to happen, and an oppressive sadness washes over her. Her daughter is the only precious thing in her miserly life. Incongruous in this world of cheap goods. So determined and so intransigent. So rare. But how can you keep a daughter from following her own path?

Manuela calls the Bellavista and asks to be connected to room 302. Mattia never gave her his cell phone number. "I'm sorry," the concierge says listlessly, and slightly annoyed, "but there's no one in room 302." Yes, there is, Manuela, who is on her balcony, is about to say, I can see the light on in his room. But she's not quick enough, he has already hung up. She dials the number again, and lets it ring twenty times. By the third ring, she gets the impression the concierge has unplugged the phone.

The lobby of the Bellavista is as big as the waiting room at a train station, an empty space where two red armchairs, one on each side of the entrance, float as if lost, as if begging to be remembered. A runner, also red, covers the slightly yellowed marble floor and then ventures up the stairs, stopping on the landing in front of four identical doors. The ballroom, perhaps, or dining hall, or conference center. Manuela had never set foot in the Bellavista before, and it strikes her as a cold, pretentious place. Mattia has been living there for more than ten days. He must be lonely, as lost as one of those armchairs. There's no one at the reception desk. The keys to every room dangle on the wooden rack. Every room but 302. In the little box for 302 is a piece of paper, folded in half. Legal-size paper, a fax, maybe. So Mattia isn't in hiding, someone knows he's here. Office managers, bosses, suppliers—that's who faxes you. Perhaps he's merely in Ladispoli for work. Manuela leans over, reaches for the fax, but isn't able to grab it. She wants to read it, right away, as if it might hold the key to Mattia's bizarre behavior. But she stops herself from taking it, because that would be like stealing. Honesty. Honesty above all.

She rings the bell and the concierge emerges from the office in the back. His face conveys the same listless boredom as his voice. "Please tell Mattia in room 302 that Manuela Paris is here." She uses the same decisive voice she would when giving orders to her soldiers, and the concierge, even though he wants to object, decides to pick up the phone. She hears Mattia's voice. "Yes?" "Miss Paris is here," the concierge says, eyeing her with ill-concealed disapproval. Manuela doesn't lower her gaze. "He says he'll come down," the concierge announces as he hangs up the phone.

Manuela paces the length of the lobby two or three times. Brochures for local tourist attractions, car rentals, and train schedules for Rome are scattered on the glass table. There's also an Italian guidebook in English. Mattia doesn't come down and Manuela flips through it distractedly. She turns to the chapter on Rome, the one that gets consulted the most. She reads that the Vatican Museums are closed on Sundays, except for the last Sunday of the month, when they are free. Official taxis are white and have an illuminated sign on the roof. A subway ticket is only good for one ride. Before being deployed, she had bought a guidebook on Afghanistan from the same publisher, to see what it said about the region where the Tenth Alpini Regiment would be operational. It was a few years old, but there weren't any more recent ones. She'd read it on the bus to the airport, forcing herself to concentrate while Ninth Company sang and made a racket as if they were going on a school field trip. She read the introduction on the flight to Dubai, until she fell asleep. She started up again in the crowded hangar where they waited thirteen hours for the cargo plane that was to take them to Herat, amid a confusion of voices and baggage, and then kept reading as the C-130 maneuvered on the runway while the roar of its four engines made the walls shake. She read in darkness during the flight, using her headlamp, but eventually she had to stop because the old cargo plane tossed terribly and the words danced before her eyes.

The first pages were color photographs of the country's most spectacular sites: the great Buddha of Bamiyan, the bird market at Kabul, the sharp peak of Mir Samir, the rocky spires that tower over the lapis lazuli lake of Band-e Amir. Herat—the seat of the Italian command—was described as Afghanistan's artistic capital. The guidebook dwelled extensively on the country's complicated history, but it also provided practical advice about tourist attractions, hotels, and restaurants. There was a section on shopping. And phrases in Dari and Pashto in the back. Do you accept travelers' checks? Where may I find a room, please? Thank you, you're welcome, good night. Manuela was stunned to learn that in the 1970s Afghanistan was a tourist destination. Hippies came by motorcycle or bus, or hitchhiked, and lingered before heading to the Himalayas or India, charmed by the friendliness of the people, for whom guests are sacred, the beauty of the gardens, and the sweet slowness of life in the tea salons. But that was all before she was born.

Yet some people thought it was possible to travel again there. The guidebook said that after the Taliban were expelled, the war ended and the situation, though still evolving, had stabilized. It suggested trekking itineraries through the enchanting Hindu Kush mountains, visits to archaeological sites, museums, mosques, citadels, villages. Reliable local travel agencies organized unforgettable excursions through this largely uncontaminated country: tourism was sure to become an asset to the country and a great spur for further development. The guidebook didn't say that the infrastructure was almost nonexistent, that there were no roads other than the Ring Road, that you couldn't take a single step off the existing tracks without the risk of losing one or both legs on a mine. That there are more mines than people in Afghanistan, as many mines as stones: and worse, the mines are gray and made to look like stones, so as to blend in with the landscape. That a mine costs fifty cents and can weigh as little as four ounces—three slices of mortadella—and can cause shock waves that travel at twenty thousand feet a second. Or that a mine remains active years after the person who made it is dead. That a minefield is cleared two inches at a time, by mine clearers wearing suits that weigh sixty-five pounds, and that no matter how good the mine clearer is, he can't clear more than thirty square feet a day, so that, optimistically speaking, to clear all the mines in Afghanistan—even if they could all be found, which is impossible because most of the minefield maps have been destroyed—would take three thousand years. It didn't say there were parts of the Ring Road where even troops in armored tanks wouldn't travel, or that there were roadblocks every ten miles—manned if not by policemen, by Afghan National Army soldiers, by one of the forty nations that made up the international coalition, then by soldiers without a uniform, from some shadow army, who would cut your throat and feed you to the dogs. That the taxis, jingle trucks, and buses traveled only in convoys in an attempt to discourage bandits. Or that in the out-lying cities no one dared poke his head outside after sunset, and no one knew if they'd wake up the next morning. That the villages, many of which were still abandoned, were made of mud, rubble, and dried animal dung that crumbled in the wind. That the museums had been sacked, the statues disfigured by bazookas, vandalized, or stolen and sold secretly to collectors from the very same countries that had sent their soldiers to rebuild the place. That, in truth, the only museum a foreigner really had to see was the mine museum at the Kabul airport.

She hadn't been there, but First Lieutenant Russo had, and he told her about it once, while they were trading food and medicine for weap-ons with the inhabitants of a village. He said that there were dozens of models on display, of every shape and size—butterfly mines for chil-dren, cylindrical mines for tanks, rock-shaped mines for men—between nine and twenty centimeters in diameter, each with an explanation of how it worked and where it was from. And he kept reading Made in Italy Made in Italy Made in Italy. And even if we, as opposed to, say, the United States and a few other countries, have signed the Ottawa Con-vention banning antipersonnel mines, and have stopped producing them, seeing Made in Italy on those mines in the museum made his stom-ach turn: he didn't sleep for days. Manuela turned over the unexploded mine that a little boy had traded in for a packet of aspirin: a TS-50, Made in Italy.

The province of Farah, where the Tenth Alpini Regiment was to be deployed, wasn't even mentioned in the guidebook. At first she inter-preted this absence as a sign that there weren't any monuments or tourist attractions there. But when she landed at the FOB, the thought struck her that there might be another reason. The province couldn't be in a guidebook because it was considered out of control. "A key area" in mil-itary lingo. A war zone. "We'll sit at the bar," Mattia says to the con-cierge, making Manuela jump. "It's closed," the concierge informs him. "I know," Mattia says, "that's okay."

Mattia steers her through the glass door. The room is dark but he doesn't turn on the light. There are a dozen or so couches and chairs around low tables. Mattia sits in the corner chair, where he can keep an eye on the door. He slips a piece of paper into his pocket. Manuela recognizes it—the fax. She catches a glimpse of the number it was sent from in a corner, but can only make out 06, so Rome. There's a chessboard and a deck of cards on the table. The dust is so thick she could write in it with her finger. He doesn't want me to go up to his room. No intimacy. He's keeping me at a distance. The heat is off and it's cold. Manuela doesn't even take off her gloves. In the thick shadows, she observes that he's nervous, he crosses his legs, wiggles his foot, keeps touching his hair. He wasn't expecting her and seems thrown off. He didn't have time to prepare his next move or organize his defense. Military tactics. Strategy. Daring. Impetus. An attack works well only if it's a surprise. Only if your enemy isn't expecting you. You can't defend yourself from something you're not expecting. He's not my enemy. Still, I want to conquer him.

"I'm sorry about what happened at the lake, Manuela," he says without looking at her. "I made a mistake and I apologize." He stares at the photographs on the wall above them: the Etruscan necropolis at Vacuna, the gold-plated silver fibula in the shape of a cicada, exhumed from a tomb at Piane di Vaccina, a young Ostrogoth woman who died in the fifth century. As if that barbarian object were somehow more reassuring than she. He almost seems afraid. Only now does Manuela realize that the local archaeological treasures are mortuary trousseaus, and there's something unsettling in the discovery that the art of her homeland is linked to the journey to the other world. For the Etruscans, as well as for the barbarians, life is something we merely pass through; death is everything. One thousand five hundred years of so-called civilization at Ladispoli have left behind a ruined watchtower, a prince's impregnable fort, and fields of artichokes—nothing more. But she is still alive.

"I'm waiting," Manuela says, using that same decisive tone that had worked with the concierge. "For what?" Mattia asks, surprised. "For you to tell me something; you choose. Why we kissed. Why you wrote me that idiotic note. Why you won't take phone calls." "Too many things," Mattia says, forcing a smile. "Choose one." "Why you don't want to see me anymore," Manuela says.

"Because I can't get into a relationship with you," Mattia says, "and I realized that you're not the kind of girl I can be with for a day or a week. But that's all I have." Manuela counts thirteen days until the twelfth.

Not many, but not so few. If her doctors' visits on January 12 don't go well, she will hurl herself into the sea and drown—the Tyrrhenian is unsparing in the winter. She doesn't want a life outside of the army. It'd be the same as dying; it's better to actually kill herself. To believe—like the Etruscans, like the barbarians, like the Taliban—that life is something we merely pass through, that death is everything. She would ask to be buried in her uniform, they can't take that away from her. In the hospital, she'd often thought angrily that it would have been better to die with the others. At least she would have had the funeral chapel at Camp Arena in Herat, the honor guard, her comrades' heartfelt tears, the flag-draped coffin with her feathered cap resting on top, the state funeral, the red carpet, the military band, the president of the republic comforting her mother, the posthumous promotion, and everyone's respect, forever. Maybe they really would have erected a monument in her honor on the promenade at Ladispoli, and a hundred years from now the inhabitants of her city would remember her, thinking her no less worthy because she gave her life for a cause they didn't understand. She doesn't want to go back to being just Manuela Paris on January 12. There's nothing behind that name—an ordinary woman, without a future, or with one she already rejected, years ago: as a tour guide, the wife of an office worker, the discontented mother of children fed on her regrets. She doesn't want that kind of life. Thirteen days before she finds out if she is alive or dead, Sergeant Paris or no one. It's not worth giving up something for nothing.

"It's not like I want to marry you, Mattia," she says. "I'm just passing through, my work comes before everything else. The army, Italy, my Alpini, my family. Those are the things that matter to me, in that order. I don't know what you do and I don't really care. I don't know if you chose it or simply stumbled upon it. For me, work isn't something I do to fill my day or to earn a salary. It's a part of me. In fact, it's the truest part of me."

"But you don't even know me, and if you did, you wouldn't like me," Mattia observes calmly. "And I don't know you, and if I did, maybe I wouldn't like you. I don't remember who said it, but whoever the genius was, I agree with him: of all the things mortal man has made, the one we must fight, flee, avoid, and avert, in every way possible, is war. There is nothing more profane, futile, wasteful, squalid, and long-lasting than war. For me *Italy* is a suspicious word that I associate with the rhetoric of those who want to impose their laws on me in order to pursue their own interests. I would have much rather been born French, or Swedish. At least I could have had the illusion of living in a country of rights and duties, instead of this corrupt place with its attitude of 'I don't give a damn.' Furthermore, I detest soldiers, I didn't even do my military service. When I was eighteen, it was still required, you still had to give a year of your life to Italy. But I don't want to pass myself off as someone I'm not: I wasn't a conscientious objector either, working for, I don't know, Caritas; I didn't do anything noble, like help the homeless, cook them hot meals or cure their scabies, or teach disadvantaged children. I just got a friend of my father's to have me declared unfit for service. I imagine that in your eyes, I'm a slacker, a coward, a deserter. I've always tried to mind my own business and be happy, and I've succeeded, too. I've never paid much attention to the injustices of the world, to other people's problems; my own were plenty. And the mere thought of putting on a uniform and saying 'yes, sir,' of obeying an order I don't understand or don't agree with, of shooting, killing, even if only in self-defense, goes against my conscience."

"I see I've gotten myself into a real mess," Manuela laughs. But strangely she isn't offended. In fact, the more he finds her life absurd or incomprehensible, the more she wants to defend it. It's precisely when she's faced with someone who deems her life pointless or misguided that it makes the most sense to her. "It's cold in here," she says. "Don't you have heat in your room?"

The key to room 302 is a silver-plated metal plaque, the same size as the one that holds together the bones in her knee. The elevator's busy, the cleaning staff are moving trolleys around. So they take the stairs, their footsteps muffled by the threadbare red carpet as they climb from floor to floor without stopping, Manuela maneuvering her crutches and gazing at Mattia's wide back, his bare neck, his ruffled hair thinning on top. His shoes are new, the leather soles still smooth, not even a scratch. There's something helpless about that purity. He closes the door without making a sound.

A ray of light suddenly pierces the lowered shutters and casts a bright line on the comforter. A streetlamp has come on outside, along the promenade. Manuela, lying on the bed, her head on Mattia's chest, has lost all sense of time, and is amazed that it's evening already. She should go, she left the house saying she was going down to the beach for her usual walk to the Tahiti, and her mother has undoubtedly started to worry. But she doesn't move. The walls of the room begin to emerge again confusedly from the shadows, the rectangle of the window, the bathroom door, which was left ajar, Mattia's shoes, upside down on the mat, her crutches across the chair. Room 302 of the Bellavista Hotel is furnished with that functional impersonality common to every three-star Italian hotel. The double bed is jammed between two nightstands made of mahogany-colored plywood, Mattia's balled-up underpants tossed on the one on the left. The mattress, a little soft, dips in the center, tumbling them into a cozy pocket and forcing them to sleep on top of each other. The walls are painted a soft blue. On the other side of the room hangs a black-and-white print of the Lazio coast in 1910, with the Palo Castle and three fishing boats on the shore. The only things on the desk are a computer, an ashtray, and yesterday's paper. On the 1980s armchair near the bed-side lamp are their clothes, removed in a hurry and tangled in a color-ful heap. Manuela doesn't see a suitcase. In the half-open closet hang a gray wool suit and a pair of jeans, as if Mattia were only staying for a few days.

Mattia fusses with the phone, but he can't make out the numbers. He turns on the light. Manuela was the one who had turned it off. She had begged him not to look at her. Because of the red scars that disfigure her leg. But also because of her soldierly modesty. Her habit of treating her body like an instrument, one that must be kept running efficiently, but that must also be handled with care. To be trained, protected, and, above all, used only for indispensable tasks. Mattia presses 9, reception, and orders room service, dinner at nine. Spaghetti with clams and a bot-tle of Fiano. "But I have to go," Manuela protests, "I'm leaving right now." "If you want," Mattia says, and turns out the light.

She doesn't leave, and they start again. The first time it happened too fast, impassioned clutching interrupted by unpoetic words of prevention and precaution, a belated shyness because they don't have any condoms and the pharmacy in the piazza is closed for vacation—but by then it was too late to stop, best just to trust her good luck, his prudence, or simply destiny, a collision of tongues, elbows, knees, and bones, the other's body like a strange mechanism. "I want to be on top," she whispers, embar-rassed, because she's too shy to tell him she can't strain the vertebrae in her neck. But even that position is complicated because she can't bend her knee or ankle, and in the end she clings to the headboard, one leg dangling off the bed. Too uncomfortable a position to free her mind of thoughts. The second time they go as slowly as they want. "I'm sorry, it's hard for me to move," she whispers, "I'm all broken and they put me back together with superglue. If I twist the wrong way I'm afraid I'll fall to pieces. I even cracked my epistropheus." Mattia says that *epistropheus* is too sweet-sounding a word to describe something awful. "I hate it, though," she says.

She discovered the existence of the word *epistropheus* at the base, one evening in spring. "Sergeant," Puddu had asked politely, "what's the epistropheus in the human body?" "I don't have the faintest clue," she had answered, barely lifting her head from the book that First Lieutenant Russo had lent her. Written by an Englishman who had traveled across Afghanistan in the 1930s. All the author was interested in was architecture, and even though he claimed to appreciate the dignity of the Afghani people, their self-confidence, their proud detachment from western culture, and their dramatic fierceness, he described them as comical, as basically ridiculous. She was having trouble getting through it. Once, back in Italy, before she deployed, she had been told she shouldn't take part in a colonial war. Italians should be the first among the last rather than becoming the last among the first, and sharing in their colonialist disdain. A people of emigrants, peasants, and workers couldn't ape Bush's imperialism. Among the many objections that people raised, this was the most hurtful. Her book propped on her dinner tray at the mess hall, she was trying to carve out some space for herself, get some distance. "But you passed the NCO exam, the questions haven't changed," Puddu insisted. "It's number twenty-five in the study booklet. The choices are: a vertebra, a gland, a pathology, an excess of sugar in the blood." "I really don't know, Owl," she said. The correct answer, given in the back, was A: the epistropheus is a vertebra. It was a tough question, worth four points. The author of the manual explained that the human neck contains seven vertebrae: the first, the atlas or C1, supports the head; the second, the epistropheus or axis, allows the head to rotate and incline. "So it's this one," Zandonà said, resting his dusty fingers on the nape of her neck. He lightly touched her seven cervical vertebrae, barely perceptible beneath her T-shirt. "What the hell are you doing, are you high?" she said, brushing his hand away. "Seven, like musical notes," Nail said lyrically. "I could play you like a piano. The epistropheus is the second note, D. You're a symphony in D minor, Sergeant."

The second time she heard the word was in a hospital bed in Farah. The radiologist was showing the orthopedist an X-ray of her spinal column: there was some problem with her epistropheus. The doctors debated the issue out loud, sure she either wasn't listening or wouldn't know what they were talking about. No, not my vertebra! My leg, okay, but not my C2, please don't let it be my C2. The thoracic, lumbar, and sacral vertebrae are important, too, but the cervical vertebrae are essential. You can't move your legs or arms if they're damaged. You can't even breathe naturally. Terrified, she tried to stand up. But she couldn't even lift a finger. Epistropheus. Correct answer, four points. "Am I paralyzed?" she screamed. The violence of her voice surprised her as much as it did the doctors. She had come out of a coma less than two days before. Epistropheus. The doctors looked at her in awe but didn't answer. Her epistropheus had only a very minor crack, but it took three months to heal. Three months immobilized in a military hospital bed, with that word stuck in her head. She hates the word *epistropheus*. Some words you just can't forgive.

"I'll go slowly," Mattia whispers. He rests his fingers right on her epistropheus, as if he already knew what it was. But the feel of his fingertips on her sensitive skin is so stimulating that Manuela doesn't mind. He caresses her, explores her gently, almost in awe, with his fingers and lips, he sucks her and tastes her inch by inch—all down her spine, her seven cervical vertebrae, her ribs, the secret architecture of her bones, the constellations of her moles, her dark downy hair. And then every fold, every cavity. The religious devotion with which he explores her reveals a true veneration of the female body. He knows what to look for, and how. He must have had a lot of women, and loved several of them passionately, but just then the idea doesn't upset her. In fact, it means he has put his forty years to good use. Something melts inside her. It takes a few minutes for her to realize that the guttural, bestial whine echoing throughout the room is coming from her throat. Ashamed of making noise, she buries her face in the pillow.

Afterward, as they wash off sweat and semen in the shower, Mattia says she didn't have to stifle herself, the neighboring rooms are empty. He's the only guest in the entire hotel today. The whole Bellavista is his.

There was an agricultural machine rep here yesterday, but he's already gone. He saw the guest book. Vacant, completely vacant. But tomorrow, unfortunately, the restaurant is throwing a New Year's Eve party. If they want peace and quiet they'll have to find somewhere else to go. It occurs to Manuela that they could go to Passo Oscuro, to her grandfather's cottage. Then she bites her lip because she promised Vanessa to go there with her. And even though she hasn't said anything yet, she has already betrayed her. While Mattia dries himself off in the bathroom, Manuela tiptoes over to his pants, which he left on the chair. She looks for his wallet, because she feels she now has the right to know who is this man whom she has allowed to know her so intimately.

She hasn't had a lot of experience—at least not much pleasurable experience. Before Mattia, she'd only slept with her boyfriend, Giovanni, and a dozen or so guys whose faces she can't even remember, guys she met before she was subject to military ethics. Quick couplings—in changing cabins at the beach, in the bathroom at a club, in single beds in tiny rooms still decorated for a child, on the front seat of a car, with the gear stick jabbing into her thigh and her back pressed up against the dashboard. She recorded each one in a notebook, grading their performance. More than anything, it was a way of taking possession of the world, of exploring and subduing it, a human geography, a comparative anatomy. She remembers only one name, a last name—that of a lanky retiree from Arkansas with a baseball cap, in shorts that showed his toothpick legs, and white sneakers: one of the guys from the cruise ships. Brandishing her red umbrella, she had accompanied her group to the catacombs, but then Mr. Garret—that's what was written on the plasticized name tag he wore on his T-shirt—started feeling sick, or at least that's what he said, and she had accompanied him back to the ship, which was anchored at Civitavecchia. She found herself in his cabin, then in his bed. The ship was empty, even the sailors had gone ashore. Mr. Garret was at least fifty years older than her. It was to him that she owed her first multiple orgasm and the discovery of the existence of her clitoris.

Only once did she make the mistake of going with a fellow soldier, whom she'd met during summer training in the Dolomites. A laconic Alpino with a lumberjack beard. Between orienteering training and a march with a full pack, an attraction was born. They'd done it—rather brutally—in a pine forest, in the dark, on a tent tarp. The grass, the thistles, his beard—all pricked her like nettles. The rocks grated her skin.

She had scratches and bruises for days. Afterward, she was so ashamed that she never spoke to him again. She was afraid of ending up like so many other women who had lost their careers and the group's respect, those sly, devious types she had always despised and who reflect poorly on all the other women. Some guys would record those fucks on their cell phones to show their buddies, would boast about them for months. Fortunately her lumberjack was a rugged Alpino, an honorable mountain man, old-fashioned, mute. He kept the memory of Manuela Paris's body stretched out on the tarp, her camouflage pants rolled down to her ankles, and her timid breasts naked in the moonlight, to himself. He got assigned to another regiment and she never saw him again.

Still, it was never like this before, not with Giovanni or Mr. Garret or the lumberjack. Some corner of her brain had always remained conscious, aware of her surroundings, her body, her secrets, her possibilities. She had never let herself go before, never given herself up to someone else—to herself—as she had with the guest at the Bellavista. But there was no wallet or ID or anything in Mattia's pants pockets, only a two-euro coin.

"The fax says I have to go to Rome tomorrow morning, I've been called in for a work meeting," Mattia says calmly, as if searching his pockets was a completely logical thing to do. "I'll be back around two. So don't make any plans, I won't either." "I'm sorry," Manuela mumbles. "It's fine," Mattia smiles. He comes closer. He's still naked and his chest hairs glisten with water. There are teeth marks, ruddy and fresh, right on his breast. She doesn't remember biting him. "I told you what really matters to me," Manuela says. "Now you have to tell me." "Right this minute, nothing matters to me except you," Mattia responds. "Don't lie to me," Manuela pleads. "I can't stand it. If you don't want to answer, then don't, but don't make fun of me. It's so disrespectful I just can't stand it." "I know you don't believe me," Mattia says, "but it's true. You're all I need. Wherever you are is everything for me."

The waiter knocks twice but then comes in right away, without waiting for an answer. He avoids looking at them—she draped awkwardly in the curtain, he naked, indifferent, and standing casually in the center of the room—and sets the dinner tray on the nightstand. Manuela informs her mother that she'll be having dinner out. The phone call lasts all of nine seconds, so her mother doesn't have time to ask questions. She doesn't want to get dressed, so she doesn't. For years she has hidden herself, all but erased herself in her uniform. There's something revolutionary about being naked. As for him, he must be used to it. It doesn't even cross his mind to cover up. He's comfortable in his skin, he's not ashamed of others' eyes on him, he likes himself, or he's at least reconciled to himself. Maybe it's his age. Maybe at forty people stop expecting to be better, stop suffering because they don't look the way they'd like to, and simply accept themselves as they are. She may never know. She never thought she'd live to be forty. They wrap themselves up in the comforter and move the plates to the bed. While they pick at the clams, slurp down the spaghetti, and slowly empty the bottle of wine, Mattia tells her that he has never been to Afghanistan, and at this point he never will. But it's a place that has always drawn him like a magnet.

His father was strict and conservative. He was a surgeon, the head physician in the hospital in his hometown. Entirely devoted to his work, always absent, uninvolved in his children's lives. He never could have imagined that his father, so committed to making money and toeing the line, had once been a nut who hitchhiked all over the world. After he got married, did his residency, had kids, and made a name for himself, all that remained of his travels were a few exotic words, a few incongruous objects in the bourgeois living room of their apartment (a Kurdish amulet, a sitar, a narghile) and an encyclopedia from 1974, even though by then all he cared about was his career as a surgeon at the public hospital. He never read; he wasn't interested in books. All he talked about were medical conferences and golf. But every once in a while, on those rare evenings he spent at home, his son would catch him flipping through that encyclopedia. It made Mattia curious, too. He picked up the first volume and couldn't put it down. He read the whole thing, from A to Z.

The encyclopedia was called *Peoples of the Earth*. Twenty or so hard-cover volumes bound in white cloth. All about the habits and customs of the most bizarre peoples on earth. The Padaung in Burma, whose women elongate their necks with gold rings, the Bushmen, the Fulan, the Nuba, the Indios tribes in the Amazon, the Maori. Complete with color photographs of women whose bottom lips are deformed by disks as big as plates, of Siberians in the taiga, of Eskimos on the polar ice cap, of pygmies in the forest, of bare-breasted Polynesian women in the lagoon. But the photographs that intrigued him the most were of Afghanistan. A country closed for centuries to foreigners, who were allowed to venture there only during brief windows of time in the 1920s and 1930s and again in the 1960s and 1970s. Photographs of mountains as sharp as knives, the crests adorned with snow; thirsty hills; prehistoric-looking villages clinging to the edge of a cliff; caravans of nomads and camels crossing the desert; proud, wild warriors in boundless landscapes. But the most surprising photograph of all was of a dead goat. Its carcass, rather: decapitated, gutted, stuffed, and blown up like a balloon. Men on horseback were using it like a ball. The caption explained that this was the ancient national sport of Afghanistan, played only by noblemen. It was a violent game without rules, in which the goal was to gain possession of the carcass—or what remained of it—by the end of the game. A sport, but also a metaphor for the war that simmered constantly between rebel tribes in the highlands, among people who—finding themselves first at the crossroads of important caravan routes and then of powerful empires— were constantly invaded and conquered, trampled and beaten like that goat; yet they never let themselves be defeated. The principal characteristics of the Afghani people were a disregard for danger and a love of liberty. Mattia was young then, intolerant of everything, authority above all, and he sided with the rebels, whether they were Sandinistas or African activists like Biko. And so Afghanistan was at the top of his list of countries to visit when he had the money to travel. Those impassable, uncharted mountains would have given him the chance to forge new mountain trails, to become famous even. But then there was the war, the mujahedin against the Soviets, and he had to wait until it ended. But it never did. It was followed by the civil war among the mujahedin, then by the Taliban, then the Americans against the Taliban, then ISAF, or whatever the "coalition of the willing" was called. So he could never go. Now Afghanistan was as hard to get to as Mars. "You've been there. You've lived there, spilled your blood there, left behind a part of yourself. It's like you've come from outer space. A messenger. Tell me about it. Take me to Afghanistan."

"You wouldn't be interested in the things I can tell you," Manuela says. "I never went to see a game of buzkashi. I don't even know if they play it anymore. Now they pack dead goats with TNT, and if you see a carcass on the side of the road you just hope there's no one hiding behind the hill with a cell phone to set it off as you go by. And the virgin peaks you would have liked to climb might not even exist anymore, because the Americans bombed them to smithereens when they were looking for Bin Laden. And anyway, the mountains are all filled with caves stuffed with PETN and plastic explosives: it wouldn't take much to blow them sky high. I went there like you'd go on a business trip. For me, Afghanistan was just like any other place. Like Kosovo, Lebanon, Macedonia, one of those countries you only know by name, or because our soldiers are there. But when I signed the rules of engagement, Afghanistan became my reward. It was a promotion, which I didn't expect to receive so soon, but which I wanted to honor. I knew I was good, but I hadn't had the opportunity to prove it yet. Not everyone—in fact, almost no one—gets the chance to have the job they want. You can't imagine how hard I had to work, how much I had to prepare, for my deployment. Being a soldier doesn't really make sense these days, unless you're deployed. We don't have borders to defend anymore, in fact, we live on a continent that has abolished them. What was I going to do in Italy? Stamp leave requests? Train pimple-faced recruits? Collect trash? Guard an embassy, or a monument? A soldier isn't a garbage collector or a policeman. I wanted to test myself, to grow, as a person and as a soldier. Afghanistan isn't Kosovo or Albania, it's high risk. For us, it's the highest goal we can aspire to. Afghanistan was my opportunity. But it was more than that. I don't know if you can understand. In the barracks, during training, they explained the purpose of our mission: we were going there for peace-building, to help the weakest, poorest, and most unfortunate people on earth, so they could rediscover their right to live and work. To improve security and guarantee the development of a young nation, a young people; forty-five percent of the population there is under eighteen. In short, we were going to help build the future of the world. I know you don't believe in these things, you think they're all fancy words invented by politicians in order to sell a war to a distracted public that doesn't ever want to get involved in anything.

"But they weren't just words. There were lots of projects to manage, joint efforts to supervise, schools, hospitals, bridges, and roads to build, soldiers to train, things to teach—justice, the meaning of the word *democracy*. For me, this is what it means to be Italian, and to be proud. But words, even these words, wear out if you use them too much or too sloppily. After I'd been there awhile, even I realized that; when some staff general on an official visit to the FOB for a day would dish up those words in a little speech, they annoyed, basically offended me, offended us, because inside that base, under that bitter sun, in that burning sand they sounded hollow, like empty rhetoric. No one—not even me—had the right to speak them without violating the memory of those who had died, for or because of those words. So I forgot about them, and if I hear them now, I'm ashamed. And yet it was precisely because of those words that I went to Afghanistan. I had convictions, ideals. I believed in them."

Manuela stays in room 302 until midnight. She had written something similar in her diary, but she'd never spoken this way to anyone before—and now she feels relieved that she finally has, at the Bellavista, that she's told these things to Mattia. And she still believes in them. Mattia held her close in his arms, and at a certain point she felt a drop, like burning wax, on her shoulder, and she realized it was a tear. She didn't ask him why he was crying—if it was out of tenderness or joy, regret about the past or the future, for her words, for her, or for himself. Or for all those things put together. She gets dressed and goes to sleep in her house across the way. "To save your reputation," Mattia jokes. "Because I've only ever slept with my comrades," Manuela insists. "In an armored vehicle. In the barracks. In the trenches. Out in the open, in the woods or sand. But you're not one of my comrades. You're different, and I like that."

She takes her fifteen drops of BZD, lights one last cigarette in the dark, and watches Mattia smoking on his balcony across the way; they blow kisses on their fingertips, like teenagers. Then she slides under the covers and barely has time to think with amazement that today has been the strangest day of her life, that she has behaved in a way she could never have imagined herself capable of since becoming a sergeant. Frivolous, immoral, deplorable behavior—censure and official reprimand on her record. She's not unhappy about it, though, her superiors and her men don't know about it, it's her secret, not shameful in the least, in fact, it's joyful, she wouldn't take any of it back, and she falls asleep, flattened by the soporific. And she doesn't wake with a start, sweating with the sensation of having had a dream too horrible to be remembered.

11

HOMEWORK

peration Goat 4's target—I learned during the morning briefing—was an insurgent responsible for several attacks. The last—a truck bomb driven into a barracks—had resulted in the death of twelve ANA soldiers. His name was Mullah Wallid. The previous regiment had already made three attempts to capture him before winter set in, in analogous operations: Goat 1, Goat 2, and Goat 3. But some infiltrator had always warned him in time, and he always managed to vanish. Like a ghost. Many years earlier, when the Russians fought against the mujahedin, they called them "ghosts" because they never saw them. Like shadows, they would appear suddenly, strike, and vanish. It's difficult to fight a war against ghosts. But Mullah Wallid wasn't a ghost. Intelligence had located him, he was hiding in a village in the Gulistan Mountains, about forty kilometers from Bala Bayak. And now the Panthers had to help Afghani security forces flush him out. *Shona da shona*, shoulder to shoulder.

We assembled in the square of the base, in total darkness. We were given the radio frequency, the abbreviated code for confidential information, and the village code name. We used Italian wines for places. Ninth Company had already done cordon and search at Refosco, Amarone, and Nebbiolo. This time our destination was Negroamaro. Some units were to be transported by helicopter, and would spend the night out in the open, in the mountains. Others would go by land. When

Captain Paggiarin read out the assignments, I could barely contain my joy when I realized that Pegasus wasn't going to be left behind. It meant more to me than praise, than a eulogy, than a medal: the only true prize after weeks of humble and unrewarding work, in which everyone—like assassins lurking in the shadows—was waiting for me to make the slightest error, to give in. My platoon was waiting for my first real test on the ground, too, and I knew it. As we headed for the armored vehicles, Jodice noted sarcastically that he was surprised to see me. He thought I'd be asking for a doctor's note. Don't women have a right to three days' rest when they get their periods? How odd that I hadn't managed to get my period right before our mission. "I swear I'll reprimand you this time, Spaniard," I answered. "You can forget about your leave."

We proceeded without headlights on a moonless night. As he drove, Zandonà peered through the night scope at the ghostly green outlines of the vehicles in front of us. Jodice was being jerked around in the turret, and was having trouble keeping his balance. Despite the tangle of tightly fastened seat belts strapping me in, I had to hang on to my seat, and with every jolt it felt like they were cutting into my uniform. Puddu was huddled over the radio, murmuring under his breath. He was giving our coordinates, but to me it sounded like a litany. The fifth member of our team was Venier. I chose him because he was the worst gunner in the platoon, and I was hoping my presence would inspire him. Everybody deserves a chance. Assailed by nervous hunger, he nibbled fitfully on an energy bar. His fear had an acrid, sour smell that permeated the tank cabin. We advanced along a rough road that turned into a track, then a path, until eventually even that disappeared into a dry riverbed of white pebbles. The crackle of the radio was the only proof that all of this was really happening. I could feel my heart pounding against my ribs, and I was afraid the others could hear it, too. I'm ready, I kept repeating to myself, I know what I have to do. I've trained five years for a night like this. It's a great privilege to be here. Try to be worthy, Manuela.

Time became an illusion. My bones hurt from being slammed around, my neck muscles burned from being tensed for so long, and my head ached from peering into the dark with my night vision goggles. The valley finally opened up. For the first time in months I caught sight of rows of trees. Zandonà slowed, braked, then wedged the Lince alongside the others in a defensive semicircle. "Remember, no going rogue," I said, "just follow orders. Everything will be fine." When we opened the doors, the smell of grass and humidity assailed us. "Good luck, brothers, an eye on your feather," Zandonà said. "You, too," I whispered as I jumped down. Jodice kissed his Padre Pio medallion. "Let's go," I said, making my way into the night.

The column of soldiers clambered up the riverbed, the only access to the village, which, in the pitch black, stood out from the rocks only because its shadow was more intense, the houses thicker and darker. The escarpment was steep and my loaded automatic rifle and bulletproof vest weighed me down. The altitude caught at my breath, but I climbed through it. I would have scaled a mountain with my bare hands. Pumped with adrenaline, I gave and received orders with my heart aflutter, as if I were finally on my way to some long-awaited appointment. We ascended in brief spurts, quick and disciplined, a technique inculcated in us since our first days of training. I was supposed to keep the platoon together, but Venier fell behind; he was leaning against the low terracing wall, panting. I went back to get him. "What's that smell, Sergeant, is it opium?" he whispered, pointing to some plants in the shadows. "Move it, Fox," I murmured, "don't get us into any shit. I know you won't." Silently, orderly, we fanned out to encircle the village whose code name was Negroamaro and whose real name I've now forgotten. A handful of mud houses in a valley in the middle of the mountains on the border of Helmand, which was also the border of the area under Italian control. On the other side of the Khash River were the U.S. Marines.

Helmand rhymes with Hell-land, and it was as feared as Hell itself. Starting with our initial prep training in Italy, it was always described to us as one of the most problematic regions in the entire country because it has the biggest poppy plantations; all Afghan opium has to pass through here on its way to the Pakistani border. A symbolic border really, because the Taliban already controlled the area below Lashkar Gah. When, in 2007, our paratroopers installed themselves in Delaram, aiming to regain control of the valleys leading north, the drug traffickers felt threatened and reacted by attacking. There were some fierce clashes, even a siege. Their COP, or combat outpost, was renamed Fort Apache. Headquarters explained that the rebels were linked to the drug traffickers. In fact, the peasants who cultivated opium were the rebels. During the harvest they'd all be in the countryside with their poppies, but as soon as the work was done they'd pocket the money from the sale of their crop, unearth their AK-47s, and go back to making IEDs and planting them along the roads. The harvest began in mid-April. Which is why Mullah Wallid had to be captured first.

We spread out around the crumbling, cube-shaped houses, which jutted up precariously from the undulating earth like rotten teeth, separated one from the next only by the narrowest of alleyways. They seemed more like heaps of ruins than houses, and the few still standing were deserted. The inhabitants must have fled years ago, and clearly not even the coalition forces' promise of financial compensation had convinced them to return. In my night vision goggles the landscape looked mysterious, a ghostly twilight: the walls and burned-out cars were black, the soldiers green, like creatures from outer space. The night belongs to us, I kept telling myself, our technological superiority makes us practically invulnerable, darkness is our Achilles' shield. The hoarfrost crust crumbled beneath my boots. The stench of shit and sheep came from the houses. So they weren't deserted. It was up to the ANA soldiers to make sure. To open doors, rend the night, violate its secrets. To search every house, one by one, leaving none unchecked. They disappeared down the alleyways, shadows among shadows.

In the silence, the only sounds were the snow creaking under our boots, our labored breath, doors slamming in the distance. Not a single voice. House by house. From the radio came the order to tighten the cordon and take up position one hundred meters farther in, beyond a group of innocuous-looking buildings where ANA hadn't found any suspicious elements. We advanced silently, like spirits. The doors were all wide open, the wooden frames like white flags in mud walls. I couldn't help looking. Bare rooms, walls riddled with bullet holes, the smell of feet and sheep fat. A freshly trampled carpet over which a cloud of dust still hung. A pair of shoes on the threshold, but no one inside, as if the owner of house and shoes had fled barefoot through the window. Teenage shepherds gathered around an old man with a white beard, bodies lost in sleep on the bare ground, a curtain drawn, like on a stage, behind which women were probably hiding. We advanced farther. An emaciated invalid stretched out under a prickly blanket, his head on a high pillow, bent to one side, his neck like a thin stalk. Three bearded men drinking tea, barefoot on a dusty carpet, indifferent. Images stolen from the night, from the naked intimacy of poverty-stricken lives. They blur together in my mind—threadbare carpets; small glasses for tea, chipped and opaque; worn-out shoes; slippers; an oil lamp; a Koran.

We halt again and wait, making eye contact with each other while the ANA soldiers continue their search. House by house. We're looking for a killer. But we can't arrest him. The rules of engagement forbid it. We're merely cutting off his escape route, flushing him out so that others can take him. We're like the dogs in a fox hunt. American helicopters hum behind the mountains, making the ground shake. The radio calls me, it's Spina. The Afghani commander asked Spina to surround the corner building: there's something inside, but ANA can't stop to check it out because they've identified the suspects. But Spina can't move, he's in position on the other side of the alley. So it's up to me. I send Puddu ahead, to reassure the Afghani soldier who has stayed to guard the building. He shows him the mud on the threshold: freshly made footsteps I can tell right away weren't made by army boots. The rickety door is ajar. Cold seeps through the cracks in the walls. Dirt floor, the roof partly caved in. There's no one there. But the unmistakable odor of agricultural fertilizer stings my nostrils. Fertilizer is what they use to make the explosives with which they blow us up. I'm supposed to radio in my suspicion, request authorization to enter. But what if they don't give it to me? What if Vinci steals my find and claims it for himself? He hates me and lets it show, even in public. I'm the one here, and I want the credit for me and my men. Four of us enter: the Afghani soldier, Owl, Fox, and Mulan. Crates and sacks, dusty but neatly stacked, as if ready to be loaded and taken away. Transceivers. Detonating fuses. Five petrol drums. Ammunition belts. This hovel is really an arsenal. They left it all behind, they're still here.

I radioed the captain. His operation code name was Libra. Mine was Ripley. My very hairy deputy's was King Kong, the bomb disposal unit's was Hare. Beaming, I informed Libra that there were at least three hundred kilos of ammonium nitrate in there. He told me to wait for Hare.

ANA had reached the far spur of the village. We were behind them, beyond them was only the precipice. There was no way out: our man was trapped. When the ANA soldiers passed us, I heard them praying under their breath. Men and boys, I couldn't say how old, with baggy uniforms and thin, ancient bulletproof vests. Born to fight and accustomed to war, even though their OMLT trainers said they had trouble understanding that they were supposed to follow orders, trouble believing that discipline was not servility but rather the first duty of free men. Their courage was enviable: they despised death, and we all respected them. If I were fighting to defend my family and my country, I wouldn't be afraid to die. And tonight I'm not afraid. Pegasus is my family. Silence covered the village like a lid. There was enough fertilizer piled in that dump to make bombs to kill us all. But now it had been neutralized. I was the smallest cog in the machine, but even I was good for something. I'd made my minuscule contribution to the cause. As the proverb says, if you never stand up, you'll never know how tall you are. Now I knew.

All of a sudden a rifle shot, followed by a machine gun. Mullah Wallid had been spotted in a cave used as a sheep pen, under the rock face. The gunfire lasted only a few minutes, then the shouting started, a sort of chant. The radio informed me that he'd been taken alive. ANP handcuffed him and took him away. There were five other men with him, cut, bruised, and bleeding. Six insurgents arrested in a single operation: that exceeded all our expectations. Paggiarin would get a medal. The Panthers had reason to celebrate. "I can smell leave time, Owl," Venier whispered. I only caught a glimpse of our target as he stumbled amid the houses, pushed by some ANP officers: a gnome in a turban and filthy white rags. Mullah Wallid looked straight ahead as he walked, his expression proud and fearless.

"Congratulations, guys," Zandonà said when we climbed back into the Lince. We earned it. Not a single mistake. A textbook operation, fast, clean, no accidents or losses—apart from a goat, hit head-on by a machine gun. And an old geezer from Cerberus, who dislocated his ankle on the rocks. But he came back with both his legs.

I suggested he concentrate, because it wasn't over yet. In fact, the return was the most dangerous phase of Goat 4. It's like when you're in the mountains; the tension drops when you reach the summit, and you tend to get distracted, but the descent is more treacherous. We were at least four hours from the base, and night was beginning to fade. We were going to have to cross hostile terrain—a long, narrow valley—at first light. A few miles from the clearing, after crossing the dry riverbed, the track dropped into a sort of canyon, a narrow gorge between sheer cliffs that the Linces would have to traverse single-file. Impenetrable barriers of all-but-vertical rock faces that reminded me vaguely of the Dolomites, torn by deep crevices and ravines. There was no way out. I didn't like it at all.

We entered the gorge at 0447. According to my calculations, we should exit it by 0507 at the latest. Before sunrise, in other words. We drove as fast as possible, though given the rough terrain, we couldn't go more than ten kilometers an hour. Jodice kept his Browning aimed at the crest of the mountains, at least four hundred meters above us. He kept seeing dark shadows, but they might have only been pyramids of stones. The mountains rumbled, the rocks amplifying the echo, and then silence fell over the valley again. It was 0459, and we were in the exact middle of the gorge.

The vehicle in front of ours braked suddenly, and Zandonà slammed on his brakes as well. "King Kong, what's happening, King Kong?" The radio worked only intermittently, the looming rock faces blocking the signal. All I could pick up was that 06, the sixth Lince in the convoy, had hit an IED. In the gloom of the vehicle's interior I could just make out Zandonà's drawn face, he was biting his lip nervously. Puddu was exhaling forcefully, as if in a trance. All I could see of Jodice in the turret were his legs. All the vehicles were stopped in a line, single-file. Stone chips rained down from the sheer cliffs, landing like confetti on the windshield. Greenish spots, filaments of bodies in the dark. "The gunner went flying, like a scrap of paper," Lance Sergeant Spina said over the 07 radio. "I saw him with my own eyes. Who is it?"

Info was racing from unit to unit. Names of Cerberus platoon guys. But no, I realized with a shock, if it was 06, he was one of mine. Iota Squad. It was Michelin! Pieri, the rubber man. "Medevac, medevac right away." I can't lose one of my men. Why did fate choose Michelin of all people?

The radio reports that medics have already reached the wounded. But he doesn't seemed injured, he bounced on the snow, he really is the rubber man. He's moving, moving his legs, no broken bones, not even a scratch, Saint Lince has granted him a miracle. "The other four in his squad are unharmed as well, only a few abrasions," I radioed. No response. "Can you hear me? King Kong, Skorpio, it's Ripley. The Lince held, but the hull has been gutted, it won't start, there's no room to go around it, we're stuck." I looked up at the imposing mountains, the sheer cliffs, the setting stars, the lifting darkness. If someone was spying on us from above, they could see us clearly now.

The wreck was wedged among the rocks. The heat of the explosion had welded metal to stone. Three hundred kilos of deformed door now looked like part of the landscape. I kneeled over Pieri. They had laid him out between the wheels of Spina's vehicle. He seemed dazed, but kept trying to get up, repeating, "I'm fine, I'm fine," over and over. Zanchi and Montano had to hold him down. "The chopper's on its way, Michelin, you'll be evacuated, you'll be in Sollum in half an hour," I told him. He gave me a dull look. "The Browning's done for, I think" he said. He didn't seem to realize what had happened to him; he looked surprised by the fear he read in our eyes.

A Lince costs two hundred and fifty thousand euros—three hundred and forty-five thousand dollars—but all it takes to destroy one is a hundred and fifty kilos of TNT, which they sell here for a few dollars. Numbers always prove you wrong in this country. I knew that Paggiarin would be upset at losing a Lince, he would have preferred a clean run. This was the first IED to hit Ninth Company. The captain was almost as attached to his vehicles as he was to his men. But 06 was totaled. I thanked it silently, as if it were a dear friend. I was sorry to condemn it to death, but not even a scrap of metal can be left for the enemy. I radioed in its coordinates so our planes could destroy it as soon as the field was clear. I tried contacting my superiors, to ask for orders. Were we supposed to wait until the area was cleared? The sun would rise at 0524, the sky was already growing light.

But all I got in response was an electric short, like fingernails on a blackboard. I'd lost contact with headquarters. The only person I could talk to was Skorpio—Vinci, that is—the Cerberus commander, who was in 01 behind the ANA vehicles. "I'm already past it, I'm going to keep going," Vinci said, "we'll position ourselves at the mouth of the canyon. It's too risky and pointless for all of us to stay trapped in the gorge." "Roger, over," I confirmed. But I had my doubts. "Should we divide up the column?" I wanted to ask him. It had been beaten into my head: never divide up the column. But it wasn't just numbers that didn't add up here in the Stan. The rules didn't either. I told myself that you have to decide for yourself sometimes. You have to assume responsibility. There's no such thing as an absolute right and wrong. It all depends on the circumstances. In the wrong circumstances, nothing is right. It wasn't right to divide up the column, and it wasn't right to keep it together. Only a few seconds to evaluate the pros and cons. If this was an ambush, then maybe he was right, it was better for one group to make it to safety. And if it wasn't, even better. All in all, there were seven vehicles trapped in the gorge. Two of my squads and one Afghan squad. Thirty-five men. I looked at my watch. We still had twelve minutes of night. I gave the order to turn back: we had to get ourselves out of there as quickly as we could.

"What the fuck," Zandonà protested, as he shifted into reverse. It was a tricky maneuver, the gorge was as narrow as a birth canal. The Lince veered, its sides scraping against the rocks. "When I was in Bosnia," Jodice was saying, "a Serb shot out one of the tires on my Jeep. I swerved off the road. So I climb out the broken window and go looking for the bastard. That asshole could have killed me. He was the size of a bear, sure, but to shoot at a headquarters jeep! So I jot down his house, his street, everything, but there's nothing I can do, I'm unarmed. Two days later, I'm on leave and I run into him in the bazaar. Turns out he's the butcher. He's slicing up a bull's balls. I jam the punctured tire around his neck, like a life preserver, and throw him in the river. The tire's popped, the asshole starts to sink, nearly drowns." I didn't find Jodice's acts of bravado very amusing, but at that moment I was grateful he'd come up with another story, because it diffused the tension, put some distance between us and the shadow of death which had passed over us all; we could still feel it. And as the seven vehicles slithered slowly back up the canyon, I could clearly see the white trail of a rocket-propelled grenade above us. An antitank rocket whizzed by and exploded against a nearby boulder before I had time to yell "RPG left." Rocks as big as plates crashed against the windshield. So it wasn't just an isolated IED: this was an ambush.

Flashes of light on the rock face to our left. The last vehicle in the column was hit. It came to a stop, blocking our escape. We were trapped in the middle. "Killing zone!" I yelled into the radio. "Killing zone!" What is it they taught me? What did I do during training? Get into position? Stay in the vehicle? Take shelter? But reality doesn't look like the simulations. Decide in a split second what can save your life, and the lives of others, or lose it. "Everyone out!" I shouted. We threw ourselves on the ground, dragging grenade launchers and assault packs full of ammunition, sliding between the wheels. Another RPG hissed past us and crashed into the motor of the Lince that had already been hit, sowing metal shards that bounced off the rocks and rained down on the whole column. Bazookas fired ruthlessly on the vehicles at the head of the column, but there wasn't anyone there. Spina didn't think my order was stupid, he had followed it.

I slid behind a rock and retrieved my SC 70/90. My face was covered in dirt. The heat burned my throat. But the water and provisions were back in the Lince. "It's an ambush, they're firing on us from seven and five o'clock," I reported over the radio, forcing myself to remain calm. Dozens of rockets had hit the FOB. But it wasn't the same thing. In that gorge we were exposed, beyond the protective barriers. And I didn't know any better way to indicate our coordinates, or what the enemy position could be, because we were surrounded by rubble and ruin, a warren of ravines and caverns. The insurgents could be anywhere. They were firing from the left ridge, but also from higher up, as well as from the rocky terrain behind us, and we couldn't tell how many of them there were. We couldn't see them either; they really did seem like ghosts.

"Where are they? Where are they?" Jodice shouted as he brandished his Browning, aiming a volley at the crest of the rock face, where—three hundred meters above him—tentacles of smoke were twisting upward. I recognized the brief, disciplined volleys of a well-trained gunner, who knew not to overheat the barrel. "Get down, Spaniard," I yelled. Bullets whizzed past my ears, but our attackers' aim wasn't perfect. They were probably still at least four hundred meters away. The radio squawked, too many people trying to talk at once, a muddle of voices, all on top of one another. I had lost contact with Spina's squad, which had sought refuge in a deep cleft between two rock faces. I tried to use the infrared strobe to indicate our position. Cramps low in my belly. While Venier babbled on about a bloody nose, shrapnel maybe, and I was trying to figure out where Zandonà had gone—I'd lost sight of him—I realized that in those months of solitude, everything had changed. I was scared for that twenty-year-old kid. I finally found him, curled up behind a low rock that only covered him up to his shoulders. "Get out of there," I said, and he rolled next to me, shaking like a leaf, terrified, rifle between his knees. He was just a driver. He'd been trained to step into any role, just in case, but he'd never fired a shot in action, and hoped he'd never have to. Me neither, for that matter. They didn't let me participate in what were considered high-risk operations. I was scared for Owl, who never slept, for Lance Sergeant Spina, who treated me like a schoolgirl, for Venier, who went around smelling poppies, even for the Spaniard. Not for myself, though, because I didn't consider myself important to anyone except my mother. Each of us individually was nothing, but together we were everything. If something happened to my deputy, my gunner, or my driver, it happened to me, too.

Libra's calm voice came over the radio to inform Pegasus that the QRF had already been activated, we'd be exfiltrated as soon as possible. "They won't be able to rescue us," Zandonà said coldly, "it'll take too long, they're getting closer. I saw two coming down, they're hiding back there." We were being hit with hand grenades now, which struck the wheels of our Linces and bounced against the windshields, while bursts from AK-47s swept the snow.

The familiar noise of the Browning fell silent. Jodice was trying to get the ammunition belt unstuck. The overheated metal burned. I heard him swear as he fidgeted with the mechanism. The gun was jammed. We had no more cover. Jodice climbed out of the turret and ran on all fours, zigzagging through the slush. "Jesus Christ, I'm not even twenty-one," Zandonà whispered, "I don't want to get myself killed like this. There's a lot I want to do with my life, why can't you just take them out? What the fuck does it take?" We aimed in the direction of the flashes. We all fired, even me. I couldn't say how long it lasted. An eternity or an instant. Amid the racket of our rifles I distinctly heard the thud of something falling. So they weren't ghosts. "King Kong," I said to the radio, even though I didn't know if he could hear me, "there's one at four o'clock, I'll send up a tracer bullet to show you his position, our Browning is down." Jodice holed up behind the rock at my back and pulled out his pistol. "I'm sorry, Sarge," he said, "that's never happened to me before, I was careful not to overheat it, I respected its rhythms, it must have been defective." He was afraid I didn't believe him. The smell of cordite and smoke. The sun cast a splash of yellow on the highest jag of the mountain. The light glided quickly across the rocks, the shadows retreated. "I got him," Venier babbled incredulously. "I lifted my head, aimed where I saw the flash, and I got him." But the others didn't stop. Shots were coming closer. "I saw his head explode, Sarge," Owl whispered, "a red cloud, then there was nothing left." My watch said 0531. They'd been firing on us for almost half an hour.

I was sure we would end up like the French in the Uzbeen Valley two years earlier—attacked, surrounded, besieged until all their ammunition ran out, and then tortured, throats cut, butchered, their mutilated bodies taken around from village to village so that people would know what happens to foreign soldiers. In Italy no one ever heard about it, the story didn't even make the papers, but for us it was a nightmare, and even though we never talked about it, we thought about it all the time. The Uzbeen Valley was too deep and narrow for the helicopters to intervene, to fire missiles and save the French soldiers. And now we, too, were in a deep and narrow valley, and maybe we wouldn't be saved either.

That was the moment I understood what war is. To be a puppet in the hands of a puppeteer who doesn't know you, doesn't care about you, doesn't even know you exist. My destiny didn't depend on me anymore, on my ability or my courage. The name of my platoon, the position of my Lince, the effectiveness of our Browning, even the weather—these were the things that could make a difference. It was just like the stories my grandfather told me about the battles between the Greeks and the Trojans under the walls of Troy. The warriors fight and kill, but above them are the gods, and it's the gods who decide who shall live and who must fall. In the end, all their courage and heroism doesn't matter. The mysterious gods who worked the strings of my destiny while I was under fire in a gorge seven kilometers from a village whose name I didn't even know were in the TFC in Shindand, in a room lined with computer monitors, an NCO who takes the call at the FOB at Bala Bayak, an officer who requests authorization for American helicopters to intervene. Either the helicopters come roaring from behind the mountains, kicking up flashes of smoke, white plumes dancing on the mountain crests and in the crevices, or our request gets bogged down, authorization is delayed, help doesn't arrive in time, and the insurgents climb down the rock face undisturbed and slit our throats one by one.

But none of this happens. While the helicopters circle too high above the gorge, we realize we're shooting at the wind. It was the wind that was blowing against the snow. Whoever it was that attacked us, whoever it was who laid the ambush, has vanished, has been repelled. A dreadful silence settles over the valley. All you can hear is the wind whipping against the rocks, and stones falling on stone.

That evening, back at the base, while the men were washing away the sweat and mud, the adrenaline and regret, the fear and dust that were plastered to our skin like paint, I slipped into the Lambda tent, figured

out which cot was Jodice's, and left a blood-soaked tampon in his sleeping bag, in plain sight, right on his pillow. Because I really did have my
period at Negroamaro. And cramps. But I went anyway. Because Manuela Paris was not a dead dog or someone's sweetheart, or some little college grad protected by headquarters. She wasn't a woman either. Manuela
Paris was an Alpino.

When the Spaniard found that bloody bullet in his sleeping bag, he
simply picked it up and threw it in the trash; he didn't grumble that it
had stained his pillowcase, the only one he had, or that he had to sleep
with his mouth on my blood for three months. We never talked about it.
But from then on, he respected me not merely because of my rank, but
as a person—and he became my friend.

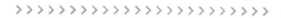

12

LIVE

attia leaves the Bellavista at nine in the morning. A coal-colored wool suit and tie; maybe he really does have a work meeting. He doesn't take the Audi from the garage. Instead he gets in the dark car with tinted windows that's waiting for him, motor running, by the glass doors of the lobby. Manuela, who has just gotten up, is still dazed from the benzodiazepine, and can't see who is behind the wheel. Mattia sits in the backseat. Like an important passenger, someone worthy of a driver.

Vanessa, who is spying down to the street from the living room window, notes that it looks like one of those politicians' cars. "No," Manuela assures her, "Mattia's not into politics, I'm sure of that, one hundred percent. He's an anarchist, a libertarian, he minds his own business, he wouldn't be the least bit interested." "If you ask me, he's some kind of secret agent," Vanessa pronounces. "He's in hiding here, waiting for orders to kill some terrorist in a sleeper cell, an Iranian nuclear engineer, or a member of some clandestine organization. I don't like this at all, honey," she says. "Apart from the fact that secret agents aren't assassins," Manuela protests, "he's not an agent, one hundred percent. I know what they're like, those secret agents, there were two of them at the FOB, and I can promise you he's nothing like them." "Don't get involved with a secret agent, Manuela," Vanessa urges her. "It'll complicate your life."

They rush to get dressed because Vanessa is late, her class at the gym starts at ten, and Manuela wants to go with her, to exercise on the treadmill. The doctor had told her not to interrupt her rehab regimen for any reason, but yesterday she didn't take a single step. In fact, she twisted her ankle rolling around in bed with Mattia, and now the pain is worse. "I have to ask you to go to that party in Rome tonight, at the Gas Works," Manuela says as Vanessa's car, a banged-up Yaris that's missing a headlight and smells of vanilla, pulls onto the Aurelia. "Why?" Vanessa asks, surprised. She looks at Manuela and almost hits a truck. "Because I want to go to Passo Oscuro with him. I'm sorry."

Manuela walks on the treadmill for almost an hour, her eyes fixed on the mirror in front of her. It occurs to her that she talked to Mattia a lot about her ideas, but not about her friends; she didn't even mention them. And yet in the end, that's all she has left from Afghanistan. Everything else has scattered, like dust in the wind. She didn't dare mention them to Mattia, afraid of saying their names out loud, there in room 302 of the Bellavista Hotel. Afraid for them, and for herself. Is this what cowardice is? She has never been a coward. Is it possible to lose yourself so completely that you can no longer recognize yourself?

While she marches on the treadmill—as if she needs to get somewhere, though in reality she's only trying to put some distance between herself and her friends, to leave them behind, to forget about them—on the other side of the glass wall Vanessa is teaching salsa and bachata to her troops. Her students' outlines skip along in the mirror. Eighteen women, all rather pudgy, and three men who aren't so young anymore move gracelessly across the polished parquet floor. Vanessa watches them, keeps them in check, corrects them, a smile on her lips but unsparing in her words: in her own way, her sister is a platoon leader, too. She makes herself respected. Or rather, she expects her students to respect her work, and the art of dance. She doesn't presume to transform them into an actual dance troupe, but she would be disrespecting herself if she let their mistakes slide. They understand, and take it seriously. Those awkward, clumsy recruits, eager to make a good impression, remind Manuela of Pegasus during their final days of joint training, their final exercises before deployment. Thirty-six soldiers, they, too, eager to make a good impression, yet strangely awkward, wearing their desert camo in the green fields of the Dolomites. She's in the lead, climbing tortuous paths, her rifle strap cutting into her neck, and she's thinking, not yet, I'm still not worthy of the brown feather in my cap, as the old-timers would say, but I will be soon. She's incredibly nostalgic for the enthusiasm of those final days in Italy—and for the Manuela Paris who was preparing to deploy, unaware of all that would come. But she wouldn't want to turn back. She looks at the numbers on the treadmill display and forces herself to evaluate them objectively. Unfortunately, they're discouraging. She has walked two point three kilometers. She has to stop. The pain in her leg is unbearable.

The Parco Leonardo shopping center is nothing like how Teodora Gogean described it. To Manuela it just seems like a giant brick-and-glass box. The Paris sisters wander past shop windows. To make up for taking over her grandfather's cottage, Manuela plans on buying Vanessa a spectacular outfit for New Year's Eve. They haven't gone shopping together in ages. And there are more stores here than in all of Ladispoli. In the end they enter the funkiest one: the window features mannequins in black leather bustiers, latex boots, and red garters. They make their way to the dressing room with a slew of outfits under their arms. Manuela assumed she would only have to help her sister choose, but as Vanessa gets undressed she begs Manuela to give her the satisfaction just once, just for tonight, of dressing like a woman.

Manuela notices the difference only when Vanessa takes off her T-shirt. They both used to be the same size, 34 AA. It didn't matter to her in the least—in fact, as far as sports and her future military career were concerned, a big chest would only have been a nuisance, a handicap, a source of problems. But those adolescent buds, which always seemed on the point of blossoming and yet never did, were a trial for Vanessa. Hereditary bad luck, she complained, Paris women have bogus genes: they have anemia, microcytosis, are likely to pass on cystic fibrosis, and, worst of all, are as flat as the seabed at Ladispoli. But now Vanessa shows off perfectly sculpted, magnificent breasts.

"I got them redone," she says gleefully. "My thirtieth birthday present to myself. Do you like them?" "They must have cost you a fortune," Manuela says, sizing them up. "You're always complaining you don't have any money." "You can't put a price on feeling good," Vanessa laughs. "And they'll last forever. Just think, I'll be a toothless old bag and I'll still have tits that turn heads. Why don't you get yours done, too? You know you can choose the size, even the shape? Champagne flute, pear, torpedo, you can even have an F cup if you want, and you can make your nipples bigger or smaller, too. I opted for something modest, 36C." Manuela observes that for something modest, they're pretty attention-grabbing.

Manuela takes off her jeans, bumping into her sister in the too-narrow cubicle. She has always hated dressing rooms, the stagnant smell of other people's underarms, the suffocating heat, cloudy mirrors, and cruel overhead lighting that accentuates your blemishes. She has never liked going shopping. Naked, Vanessa is a dancer, lean with sculpted muscles, while Manuela is a pasty anchovy, with those horrendous bloodred scars that disfigure her leg. "They'll be gone in a few years," Vanessa says, seeing how discouraged she is. She shows Manuela her cesarean scar, a line like on a musical stave that runs above her pubic hair, where her tan line is. "In the hospital, the first time I saw it, while they were changing my dressing, it was so gross, I nearly had a heart attack. I swore I'd never wear a bikini again. But it faded. And I didn't even have plastic surgery. But maybe you can get it for free in the military, so you could make yours go away even sooner." "He wants to do it with the lights on," Manuela murmurs, "but he'll faint if he sees my scars." If I understand anything about men, Vanessa thinks, as soon as Mattia sees them, he'll want to protect her, save her, and will fall madly in love with her. But she doesn't say anything. She's not sure she approves of their affair. She wiggles into a little black sheath cut high on her thigh and contorts herself to see the price tag. She doesn't want Manuela to spend a fortune on a stupid dress, who gives a shit about New Year's anyway.

But her sister rips off the price tag and hides it. "It's a gift, Vanè," she says, "I've got some money set aside, I got paid well in Afghanistan. And now I'll get disability, too." "You try this one on," Vanessa says, handing her a red evening gown, satin, strapless, narrow at the waist, 1950s style. To wear with elbow-length gloves, like Rita Hayworth. Manuela hesitates, protests, but in the end, laughing like it's a game, she puts on the gloves and even the dress. "I look ridiculous," she observes cruelly, "I look like an artichoke all dressed up for carnival."

She peers at the girl in the red dress in the mirror without recognizing herself. I'd never have the balls to wear it, she thinks, it's not me. But she doesn't say anything, because a faraway voice suddenly echoes in her head. "I fantasize at night, Sergeant." The first thing you forget about a person is his voice. It's impossible to remember. It simply fades away, evaporates, like all things without form or consistency, like water, like music. But now the voice is here, in the dressing room of a clothing store at the Parco Leonardo shopping center. It's the voice of Lorenzo Zandonà, that gentle singsong voice, a melody of sweet s's and c's and z's that soften his words. There are dialects and cadences that sting, exasperate, or snarl, and others that soothe and subdue. The Venetian accent caresses. "The most hellish thing about Afghanistan isn't the insurgents or even the IEDs," Lorenzo was saying, "it's being without a woman for six months. I'm twenty-one, I'm used to doing it every day, you know. I'm going crazy, I've worn my hand out. I can't show you the pictures I brought with me because you'd have to reprimand me. But I've rubbed myself on top of them so often, they don't do anything for me anymore, they might as well be pictures of a priest's ass. I'm not a pig, Sergeant, I'm a romantic, I need poetry. Do you know what my Afghani poem is?" "Don't tell me, Nail, or I'll have to reprimand you for real." "I'm going to tell you anyway, I want to tell you, because you're like a sister to me, or a brother really, I have a brother so I know what that means. If you're truly my brother you can't get offended. So this is my poem. There's this Manuela Paris who's the singer in a smoky bar—I'm the piano player and I give her the rhythm—she moves onstage with these gloves up to her elbows, she's wearing red lipstick and a bright red dress, her shoulders are bare. Manuela Paris's collarbones stick out like violin strings, she's so hot she makes my blood boil." "You're out of line, Zandonà!" she interrupted, slapping him on the face. "You disappoint me. You sound like a typical misogynist: I'm a woman, so for you I'm just a sex object. But I'm not a stereotype, and I won't let you offend me." "But I'm not trying to be offensive, this is something pure," Lorenzo protested as he massaged his jaw—she'd hit him hard. "You're my commanding officer, I'd obey you even if you ordered me to drive the Lince over water. We're friends, brothers, epigones, and always will be. I have a girlfriend back in Mel, I love her even though she's probably already cheating on me; my heart belongs to her. But during these miserable Afghani nights, you take away my fear of dying, you make me happy, Sergeant, and I'll be grateful to you forever for that."

Corporal Zandonà, not even twenty-one years old. For a second, like a hallucinatory flash, the red dress in the mirror becomes Lorenzo's blood, which oozes onto her face. He's on top of her—and inside her. The violence of the explosion hurled him on top of her. Flesh in flesh.

His blood is hot, viscous, it gushes, spurts, trickles. His voice comes from somewhere impossibly far away, and follows her down into the void where she is vanishing. "Manuela," he babbles, terrified, "Manuela, am I hurt?" She faints, falling to her knees, sliding into Vanessa's lap as if she were an inanimate object.

They lay her out on the floor of the shop and hover over her. "Is anyone a doctor here?" the manager asks hastily, annoyed that this unfortunate incident had to happen in her shop right when it's most crowded. No, there's no doctor, no one steps forward. Manuela isn't coming to. Her face is the color of death. Vanessa tries to shoo the customers away: "Get back, she can't breathe," she protests. She calls her name, shakes her by the shoulder, "Manuela, Manuela, honey." Manuela doesn't respond. The shop girls press her, should they call an ambulance? The customers stare wide-eyed at the lifeless girl in the evening gown. So young. One of them notices Manuela's crutches leaning against the dressing room wall. What a relief, a sign that she's sick. These things don't happen to healthy people. Vanessa lifts Manuela's head and brings a cup of sugar water to her lips. The liquid wets her clenched mouth and drips down her chin and throat. Vanessa dries Manuela's face with her fingers. Manuela opens her eyes. She's not in Qal'a-i-Shakhrak. She's in a dress shop, under a strip of neon, surrounded by female faces and perfume.

"Everything's okay, I had a flashback," she tries to explain to Vanessa. "When a memory suddenly seizes me, I see the whole scene again and it's too much, my brain disconnects. Fainting is my defense mechanism, I'm fine." Vanessa is kneeling over her, caressing her forehead, it's hard to say if her expression is one of fear or pity. "Please, don't tell anyone it happened again," Manuela whispers.

She gets dressed quickly, climbing into her jeans and lacing up her boot by herself. She leans on her crutches and makes her way to the counter with dignity, the salesgirls stepping aside as if she has some contagious disease that might ruin their New Year's Eve. She buys the black dress and a clutch for Vanessa, the elbow-length gloves, and even the red satin dress. She spends three hundred and eighty-one euros without batting an eye. And tonight she's going to wear that red dress. For Mattia. But also for herself, and for Lorenzo. As if he could see her, wherever he is. Brother. Epigone. My boy.

Vittorio Paris built the house himself, on Sundays, brick by brick. He had bought a hectare of land, a small plot wedged between the railway and the beach at Passo Oscuro. At the time the coast consisted of wild dunes, rows of eucalyptus trees planted to combat malaria, and only a few inhabitants, who lived in reed and wood huts, fishing and poaching, as if in a bygone era. It was an uncultivated plot, buried in briars, with nothing but a chicken coop and a boat shed. He pulled down the chicken coop and moved it to the far end of the field; the boat shed he enlarged and transformed bit by bit into an actual house: a wall, a window, a bathroom, a guest room. He planted two tamarisks in front of the veranda and hung a swing on the umbrella pine, in case his granddaughters wanted to come keep him company. He never would have asked them, though. He didn't expect affection or respect: if someone wanted to bestow some on him, he accepted, but without feeling any obligation to return it. For forty years he lived alone, separate from everything, in that little beach cottage, which, as Passo Oscuro grew into a modest beach town and then a Roman suburb, became quite valuable.

With time he became more cantankerous, or maybe his character was distilled. Vittorio considered everyone but himself an enemy. He hid his pension under his mattress, near a WWII rifle, which he'd never registered or returned, and kept in perfect working order. He did his exercises on the veranda every morning, and walked regularly on the beach for hours, to keep his body working perfectly, too. He washed his hair with olive oil, because, he said, shampoos contain carcinogens. He didn't use soap. He lived on the meager vegetables from his small, sandy garden, a few fish, *telline*, the birds that he caught with a line, net, or gun, and the eggs his two hens laid like clockwork. He didn't buy anything and didn't ask for anything. He was divorced from his age and from Italy. He'd never wanted a television, but he kept up with what was happening in the world by listening to the radio news religiously. He lived alone, with his hens, Pina and Nina, his memories of the war, his friends who had fallen in the Libyan desert or the Apennine forests, and his wife, who died when she was thirty. He cursed everyone who came near him, and trusted no one, not even his only son.

Yet Manuela was always glad to go see him. She wasn't afraid of him, and was happy when her mother would drop her in the garden in front of his little house—which to her was as welcoming as a palace—on a Saturday afternoon. She had fun with that strange and intractable old man.

She liked hoeing the soil, fertilizing the plants, picking tomatoes, feeding the hens, watering the garden, exercising on the veranda, inhaling the scent of sage and rosemary, listening to his horrifying stories of war and resistance. Manuela had only happy memories of those tiny rooms with low ceilings, linoleum floors, and paper-thin walls that trembled in the wind. Which is why she spends New Year's Eve there with Mattia. She hungers nostalgically for new happy memories.

They get takeout at Ladispoli's finest gourmet market. All ready to eat, because the Paris family stopped paying the utility bill, so the gas had been cut off. Vanessa told her there's no electricity anymore either, but that she'll find a cardboard box with a good supply of candles. There's also a gas heater, which Vanessa brought there to warm the place up when she started going there with Youssef, though they've left no trace of their trysts. Apart from the sand and dust, which makes its way through the cracks around the windows, which don't close properly, the house is clean. But empty. Even the furniture is gone. Vittorio's rickety furniture, remnants from every house he'd ever lived in—the master bed, the sideboard, the couch—is no longer there. Teodora Gogean got rid of it without asking his granddaughters if they wanted to keep anything. She didn't want to store it in her house, so she sold it to a used-furniture dealer. A gesture that Cinzia and Vanessa considered an affront to the family's memory of the deceased, and which earned the family less than a hundred euros. The illegal sale of that furniture, which they considered pretty much theft, was the pretext for the lawsuit Cinzia and Vanessa brought against that woman. Manuela notes that the furniture has left a lighter mark on the walls, almost like the negative of what once was. But she's not sorry or regretful. Like Teodora, she's not sentimental. She doesn't believe that the creaking bed or the couch coated in chicken shit held the memory of their owner. She is the final keeper of Vittorio Paris's life and legacy. And as long as she remembers him, her grandfather is still alive.

"I should have carried you over the threshold," Mattia says. "People used to do that, I think. A man wasn't supposed to let his bride step on the floor on their wedding night. Superstition, I guess. To bring prosperity and good luck to the house and the couple." "But we've already slept together," Manuela laughs, "and besides, I don't believe in those things."

They spread a red synthetic tablecloth on the floor and set it with paper plates and plastic cups and forks—but with attentiveness and care, as if they were made of porcelain, silver, and crystal. What's more, they're both dressed as if they were going to dinner at the Posta Vecchia restaurant, the five-star *relais* near Palo Castle, where Manuela has never set foot. She's wearing the red dress. But she's ditched Vanessa's shoes, with their six-inch heels: too risky for her knee—so under her evening gown she has on her orthopedic shoe and the same old army boot. The movie-star dress made quite an impression, though, if not quite the way she had imagined. Mattia liked it, but he also revealed that the erotic fantasy she aroused in him was quite another. Completely the opposite. He wants to make love to her when she's wearing her Alpino uniform. "That's such pornographic trash!" Manuela says with surprise. He's like one of those pigs who gets turned on dressing like a Nazi or watching women in French maid's outfits . . . Mattia blushes, protesting weakly. "Never," she tells him. "A uniform isn't a disguise or a costume: it's a way of being. It's my life."

They load little dishes with baby artichokes, *burrata*, and goose salami. They set out the soup tureen filled with lentils and homemade *cotechino* that Cinzia cooked two hours earlier, turn on the portable stereo Vanessa lent them, tune in to a local radio station playing trance music, light the gas heater and candles, and huddle on the tablecloth. "To us, and to you, Mattia, whoever you are," Manuela says pointedly, hoping he'll finally tell her something about himself. But he doesn't take the bait. "To you, Manuela, whoever you are," he echoes, raising his glass. Outside, the wind whistles and bends the tamerisks, working its way through the windows. The sea laps against the beach. Every now and then a passing train makes the panes tremble and the fragile walls shake. They eat slowly, silently, savoring the food and each other's company.

At ten o'clock they go out onto the beach. With their coats, scarves, and hats, they're transformed into woolen ghosts. Manuela says that in Italy the sky isn't real, light pollution has suffocated the stars. Mattia says the stars are still there, even if they can't see them. "Things don't need us in order to exist." As their eyes adjust to the darkness, constellations start to emerge. But looking south, toward Rome, the city lights project a whitish reflection onto the sky, a glimmer that fringes and dispels the night. They walk in the opposite direction, following the darkness, until Manuela's knee starts to protest. At eleven they're stretched out on the mattress—that, too, on loan from Vanessa and Youssef—he in his socks and she in his coat, because the heater has a limited range, beyond which you freeze. They're so intertwined, so intent on penetrating each other's body, on exchanging fluids and moods, on breathing and drinking each other in, on touching each other and whispering words, if not exactly of love then of something pretty close, that they don't even notice when the overexcited DJ starts counting down to the stroke of midnight—ten, nine, eight, seven, six, five, four, three, two, one, Happy New Year!

Manuela's cell phone finally rouses them. It's Vanessa, calling to wish them a happy new year. The former Gas Works is pumping out techno music at a hellish volume, Vanessa is totally wasted and spits out incoherent phrases, Manuela can't understand a word. "Who are you with?" Manuela asks, alarmed. "Who's there with you?" "A shitload of people," Vanessa shouts, "I met some real nice people, honey." A man's voice butts in, annoyed. "Vanessa's giving me a blow job, I'm sandpapering her tonsils . . ." "Fuck you," Vanessa laughs, "Happy New Year, hon, Happy New Year to your friend, too, the KGB spy, I love you, honey, have fun!" "Vanessa? Who are you with, Vanessa?" but her sister has already hung up.

A second later, Giovanni calls, she hears music in the background again, but more suffused this time—George Michael, Boy George: 1980s throwbacks, like at a house party. They exchange perfunctory greetings. Her mother calls, Traian and Teodora Gogean, Puddu from Barbagia, Pieri from Como, Giani from Ortona, Vito from Siracusa, her cousin Claudio. Lots of Pegasus and Ninth Company guys send text messages, Sergeant Piscopo from Logistics and Serra from EOD, Lance Sergeant Spina, the Alpini on duty at the Salsa barracks in Belluno, the nurses from the Celio, and Scilito from the hospital in Turin. Even an "unidentified caller." "Manuela?" says a musical feminine voice, "I love you, *amore mio*, Happy New Year." "Who is this?" Manuela asks, the voice is hard to make out, as if it were coming from very far away. "It's Angelica, Angelica Scianna." "Oh God, Angelica!" she exclaims, because she really wasn't expecting to hear from her, "I love you, too, Happy New Year, but where are you?" The voice is gone, though, the call dropped. The texts keep coming, at least forty of them.

"You have a lot of friends," Mattia says. "Some are numbers I don't recognize, I don't even know who they are," Manuela says, making light of it. "They probably sent a group text to everyone on their contact list." She doesn't want to depress or hurt him, because she realizes that while she was answering calls and fiddling with her phone and wishing parents, friends, Alpini, sappers, cousins, and strangers a happy new year, Mattia's cell was silent. Not a single call from his mother, father, relatives, or friends. As if he were all alone in the world. Well, he does receive one phone call, which he answers. "Thank you so much for thinking of me," he says formally, as if speaking to his boss. "Happy New Year to you, too." A pause, the other person says something, but he turns away, to keep her from hearing, and she can only make out one word: *soon.* "Thank you, I know, I understand. Happy New Year." Manuela would like to ask him who is the lone interlocutor who has modestly inserted himself in their celebration. But Mattia didn't interfere with her calls, so she can't.

They pop the champagne—kept cold on the veranda—at 12:46. They wish each other a happy new year, link arms, and empty their glasses. She's not used to drinking, and the alcohol goes straight to her head. They go out to the beach and watch the glow of fireworks erupting above Palo Castle. There's a huge party going on there. In town, someone is still shooting off rockets, firecrackers, and cherry bombs, too, but fortunately they're far away, so the noise is muffled, innocuous. "We should have bought some fireworks, too, Catherine wheels and fountains," Mattia says. "I bought some from a Chinese guy last year. They shot out green, red, and white, like the flag, you would have liked them." "I don't like fireworks anymore," Manuela says. "They remind me of tracer bullets, smoke bombs, things I saw over there. You know what I'd like?" she adds nostalgically. "I'd like to have my Excalibur here. That's what I called my rifle, a Beretta SC 70/90. I was used to having it with me all the time. It became a part of my body. I miss it, I don't know where to put my hands anymore—don't laugh, you can't understand. Excalibur has a cadence of six hundred and seventy rounds a minute, and an effective firing range of four hundred meters. I'd put a bottle on the shoreline and fire at it from here. My aim wasn't very good—to tell you the truth, I was hopeless. When I was a private, my instructor told me it was because I'm left-handed. That I'd never become a good shot, never get my dream job. I dreamed of becoming a mountain explorer, or a gunner even, imagine. Not even if I tied my left arm behind my back and learned to use my right, he said. There would always be someone better than me. But I tried, and I improved. My hands stopped shaking, and they still don't. I wouldn't miss the bottle at this distance. It would shatter into a million pieces, and bring us good luck. You have to break things on New Year's Eve."

"Shoot it without bullets, without hurting it," Mattia says. He places the champagne bottle at the far end of the yard, near the fence, on a wooden crate. Manuela positions herself to take aim, rests her elbow on her knee, closes one eye and pretends to place the other on the scope, to grasp the barrel, to chamber a round. She's about to pull the trigger but instead she gets up, biting her lip in pain. "I can't hold that position anymore," she says. "I guess I should give up. But I never give up. I don't surrender."

Mattia puts his arm around her shoulders. "You're young, Manuela, you see everything in black and white. For you, things are either right or wrong, good or bad. But that's not how things really are. Nothing is white forever. Everything changes color. A piece of fruit, a baby's hair, voices, even shadows. Sometimes white becomes black, bad becomes good, and vice versa. Refraction, that's the secret. When light rays enter a medium with a different density—and this is true for sound and thermal waves, too—they bend. Things act on each other, they don't exist in a vacuum, one without the other. They influence and change each other over time. They change color, understand? One day, what now seems to you a punishment and an unjust penalty may turn out to be an opportunity."

"I don't believe it," Manuela says, "and besides, I don't have time to wait, I want things now, now is what matters to me." She hurls a stone at the bottle and knocks it off the crate. Palo Castle has quieted down and they can hear the sound of the sea again. The temperature is near freezing. They go back inside. But she says he has to take her home now. "Why?" he asks, surprised. "Because I don't want you to see me sleeping," Manuela says. "I take sleeping drops, but I still scream, and I wake up every night and throw up. I don't want to ruin everything." "I snore, I broke my nose playing rugby," Mattia says, "and in the morning my beard's already a quarter of an inch long, it grows on its own, like on dead people. But I won't scare you and you won't scare me. I can't even imagine not sleeping next to you tonight, Manuela. You're the person I want to see first thing tomorrow morning, as soon as I open my eyes." "Are you superstitious?" she teases him. "Do you really believe you'll have good luck if the first person you meet on the first day of the new year is a woman?" "I'm not superstitious," he says, blowing out the candles. "I'm happy."

13

> >

HOMEWORK

Pegasus had accrued ninety-six hours of leave. Since there was nowhere in Afghanistan to spend it, the only possible destination
was Dubai. But there wasn't enough room on the C-130 for everyone, and just getting to Herat was already complicated enough. The
helicopters that delivered supplies and spare parts were overloaded,
and besides, there were too few of us, the commander couldn't leave
the base undefended at such a critical juncture. The soldiers realized
that only those who were wounded or had suffered a serious family
tragedy would be granted leave. It didn't exactly help morale but no
one complained, at least not to me. They found out that Colonel Minotto's sister had died the month before, and he wasn't even allowed to
go to the funeral. But after the firefight in the gorge, the captain authorized the four guys from 06, the Lince that got blown up, to take some
time in Dubai—even though they only had mild abrasions—and maybe
one other who was showing signs of psychophysical breakdown. Better
one less stressed-out soldier than one more ineffective one. The difficult season had begun. As for Andrea Pieri, the doctors insisted he be
shipped back to Italy. He was still shaken from being thrown from his
Lince, his tour of duty was done. Michelin was desperate to stay,
though, and he begged me on his knees not to dishonor him like this,
he wanted to remain at his post, with his comrades. He had a right to.

He'd recover, so we decided instead to send him to Dubai with Zanchi, Curcio, Montano, and Mason. But who else?

Lance Sergeant Spina and I held long and painful secret meetings. The soldiers spied on us, anxious. We agreed on some right away: no leave for Martelli, Schirru, Lando, Rizzo, Venier. Spina suggested Giovinazzo, Good Egg: he was married and his wife was prepared to pay her way to meet him. Or else Puddu: his mother was dead and his father had had heart surgery the year before. I should have remembered Zandonà. Our guitar player performed more than honorably during the attack, but the experience had shaken him badly. He was drained; he needed to recharge his batteries or he wouldn't make it through his whole tour of duty. But I made a different choice, and I paid for it. "Jodice," I said. "His girlfriend's pregnant, when he left he didn't know, and when he gets back she'll practically be due, he has a right to get used to feeling like a father."

Corporal Giani wanted to go to the TFS base at Farah. She'd been begging me every other day for a month to put in a good word for her with First Lieutenant Russo. "He listens to you," she would say, when I explained to her that I didn't have any say in the matter. "He trusts you. Please help me, I'll go crazy if I don't see him." Her boyfriend Antonello was at Farah, an EOD sapper. It was torture knowing he was less than a hundred miles away but still out of reach. She would never have believed she could be so in love. Giani was born in Cambodia, and was adopted when she was three. She told me that her almond eyes and olive skin made her feel all wrong until she joined the army and discovered that in her uniform she was the same as everyone else. Her four years of service would be up next October. But she wanted to reenlist for another four in order to stay near him somehow. Her boyfriend had already done two tours of duty in Afghanistan. When she was waiting for him in Italy, at the Belluno barracks warehouse thousands of miles away, she hadn't really realized what he did, how dangerous his job was. But now that she was here, it was a nightmare. When the platoons went out on patrol or for a cordon and search, and she stayed behind at the FOB with the cooks and clerks, she'd have crying fits. She couldn't control herself. Maybe she was having a nervous breakdown. But she didn't want to tell her boyfriend, didn't want it to weigh on him, because he loved his work. "I didn't even tell the chaplain, I haven't ever told anyone before," she confessed, turning off the shower and putting on her bathrobe. "But I trust you, Paris." It seemed that certain things could only be said in the gloomy Afghan spring, with the off-key music of war in the background. "Your boyfriend knows what he's doing, nothing's going to happen to him," I said. "And anyway, don't be ashamed that you love him. It's a beautiful thing. I've never felt that way. I'm like these Afghan rocks. Nothing grows inside of me." I trusted Quartermaster Giani, too.

"Okay," First Lieutenant Russo said, pretending not to know the reason for Giani's request. "I asked the CO to authorize her to go to the TFS warehouse with my CIMIC cell; they're getting a shipment from Herat on Tuesday, she can help sort the goods." "I'm very grateful, Nicola," I said. Russo smiled and shrugged his shoulders. "You're not leaving?" he asked. "You're tired, it would do you good to unplug for a bit." "I wouldn't know what to do in Dubai, I'd never be able to go to the beach while you're all here," I replied. "I'd rather stay, in case I'm needed." He didn't comment, but I could tell he appreciated my decision. We'd gotten to know each other by then; words weren't necessary. I would have liked to spend more time with him. The helicopter came to get them at dawn. The sand was already burning. The hot season in the Stan had begun.

I had always considered *friendship* to be a grossly overrated word. My grandfather would always say to me that a man could count on two hands the people he could truly trust in a lifetime. A woman on one. You're lying if you disagree. I had always told him I agreed. My friendships—intense, fierce, and ephemeral—lasted as long as a summer storm. They would end over one wrong word, over a heated argument filled with insults you could never take back, or simply out of indifference. I tired easily of people; my sister used to say I had a heart of steel. In elementary school I made friends with my desk mate, a boy named Khamel, who was as beautiful as an angel and as dumb as a rock, and whom I loved secretly, with no hope of reciprocation. We'd do our homework together at his house because his father was an engineer from Libya and his mother ran the pharmacy in the piazza, and he lived in a three-story house with a huge room all his own, overflowing with toys— electronic monsters from Japanese cartoons, racetracks for his cars—all of which thrilled me for years and formed a significant part of my love for their owner. I dropped him when he threw a birthday party and didn't invite me, because his father, who didn't like him playing with me, was going to be there. I never knew if his father rejected me because I was a girl or because my family was poor, but I gave Khamel up for good. My friends from the new apartment blocks lasted through middle school. Hormonal storms, Pitbull's crimes, and my own remorse separated us. I ran into Pitbull once, at the train station when I was on leave. I was in uniform; he was serving a two-year sentence for robbery. He'd be let out of Rebibbia during the day, but had to go back there every night. "You were my best friend," he said, greeting me cheerfully. "If I have to go to jail again, I hope you arrest me next time." I tried to explain the difference between a soldier and a police officer, but he just laughed. He asked for my cell number, so he could call me sometime. I made one up.

At the NCO Academy in Viterbo I developed a real sense of camaraderie with the other student sergeants in my year (the second years welcomed us with irritation and various kinds of ritual hazing, and I was never able to forgive them). We were united by the pride of rank, the dream of becoming specialists in weapons, communications, or explosives, of becoming platoon leaders or nurses, and by our common ambition to represent the future of the Armed Forces. NCOs are the ones who hold the troops and headquarters together, they're the backbone or link between the bodies and the minds, both soldiers and commanders, which made us feel doubly important. Living in the barracks and having very little free time for almost two years—until we were sent first for specialist training and then to our respective units—I was with them all day long, morning, noon, and night. We were together in class—English and IT, contemporary history and PE, lessons on driving a Puma, an Aries, and an armored Centaur, and urban warfare. We shared the gym and the mess hall, the crazy studying, the fear of failing, the highs and the lows. All of which, instead of making things easier, ended up making them more complicated. The usual group dynamics surfaced: competition, rivalries, jealousies, passions both repressed and latent, envy, gossip. The only one with whom I found I had a real elective affinity—we both loved death metal and for both of us joining the army was basically like emigrating to another country—was Vito, a Calabrese with fiery eyes. We kept each other's dreams alive: he wanted to be a dog handler, assigned to an EOD unit; I hoped to lead a platoon. Vito didn't get the job he wanted: he took an electronics course, to learn the software in a Freccia, and became a tower tech for IFV tanks, whereas I was sent to a weaponry specialization course. We lost track of each other, meeting again only on Facebook, where we exchanged encouraging messages. After the attack, Vito started a Facebook group about me, but once the first wave of sympathy passed, the number of members dropped, and after a while he closed it.

All things considered, apart from my sister, Vanessa, my only real friend in twenty-seven years was Angelica Scianna. The day she left for training at the Modena Academy, we promised each other eternal devotion. Wherever you are, I'll be there, too, we said, sobbing uncontrollably while she emptied her locker; kissing and crying all over each other, we swore we would do everything possible to be assigned to the same regiment one day, confident that nothing could keep us apart, that we were destined to be reunited, like the two halves of the gold-plated brass heart we gave each other as a pledge. I wore that pendant for years, even in Afghanistan. When I came out of the coma, in the hospital in Farah, I realized I didn't have it anymore. They didn't return it to me with the rest of my personal belongings. It must have been destroyed during the explosion; perhaps it was just as well.

Because something happened to me there at the ends of the earth, on the base and in that mountain gorge. I bonded with those Pegasus guys, some in particular, in a way I never could have imagined possible with someone who wasn't a relative or a lover, wasn't a father, a son, or a brother. There wasn't much to do during downtime at Bala Bayak. We couldn't leave the base. The soldiers loitered at the PX—a miserable little shop that sold razor blades, shaving cream, phone cards, and cigarettes—or challenged each other to pool. Venier would kick a soccer ball around, juggling it on the top of his foot three hundred times in a row. Jodice played Nintendo or chatted with his girlfriend (he was supposed to give up his post at the computer to anyone who outranked him or was older, but because of Imma's pregnancy he was often allowed the first shift). Lorenzo picked at the strings of the rubab he'd bought from an Afghani police officer, eager to learn how to play it before being shipped home, trying to compose songs on it. Angkor dried her long black hair—which she washed every evening because the dust dyed it gray—in the wind and, admiring those silky tresses, the only sign of a woman for hundreds of miles, no one dared protest the pointless waste of water. First Lieutenant Russo listened to Radiohead—"Everything in Its Right Place,"

"Exit Music," and "In Limbo"—and the other officers read or phoned home. They all had families, as did some of the older enlisted men.

The platoon sergeants played cards in the logistics shed. I never liked playing cards, and after the first few weeks, when I joined in because I didn't want to give the impression of being antisocial or arrogant or who knows what, I preferred to keep to myself. Sitting on a wooden bench in the empty mess hall, I read books about journalists, photographers, doctors, spies, and pacifists who, during or just before 1939, had traveled by car, on horseback, or even on foot across Afghanistan, the country on the other side of the barbed wire, the country from which I was barred. And every time the sun sank into the haze and the shadows slid down the mountains, slowly enveloping the tents, the Hesco bastions, and the watchtowers of the base, it seemed like nothing out there existed anymore. Only us, just as we were: imperfect, hateful, and wrong. Even though the darkness erased every shape, I was aware of the nearness of my platoon mates. And that nearness was a guarantee and a promise. I knew all their habits, and it reassured me to know they wouldn't change. When icy winds kicked up the sand and lashed the open space of the base, the guys holed up in their tents like nomads. They piled on Lorenzo's cot, which was always the messiest, even though no one pointed it out to him anymore. I could hear them laughing, strumming the guitar, and singing Vasco Rossi songs. Sometimes they squatted in the dust and smoked, holding their cigarettes in their fists to hide the incandescent red of the embers. Orders stipulated total blackout after sunset. The night was our ally, the invisible shield of Achilles that settled over us. And then I'd have to go over, identify myself, and order them to put out their cigarettes— because they're like lightbulbs in the dark, it's like hanging out a sign and saying to the mortar shooters in the hills, hey, aim right here! But I would have liked to share in that familiarity. I felt alone. Neither officer nor soldier, neither a mind nor a body, neither part of the elite nor one of the troops.

When we first deployed, they were all strangers to me. But then, day after day—at mess, in the tent, in the bunker, on the shooting range, in the Lince, on watch—invisible bonds formed among us, which grew stronger and stronger, and in the end proved unbreakable. We had a word to express all this. Fortunately it's obsolete, out of fashion. No one ever uses it. I wouldn't be able to hear it without falling apart.

Whenever he had time, squatting in the shade, undone by the heat that became more asphyxiating every day, Owl would work on the practice quizzes—multiple choice—for getting into the NCO Academy. He was hoping to apply in September. He'd ask my advice sometimes, and I'd gladly give it to him, because that dog-eared booklet reminded me of my own hopes and fears many years earlier. And I preferred responding to his questions to chatting with my peers in the sergeants' shed. After Goat 4 the divide between me and the other sergeants had become unbridgeable. The other NCOs were envious, so they said that Colonel Minotto, the regiment commander, who had written some very positive character notes on my performance in Kosovo, who gave me the "excellent" that had paved my way for Afghanistan, shamelessly favored me. They tried for a few months to find some weak spot in me, but I didn't offer them any opening. They found one anyway. My intimacy with the troops, they said, was excessive. Someone complained to the commander about my behavior—which was disrespectful of hierarchy—and Paggiarin asked the officers who knew me best if it was true. First Lieutenant Russo had warned me. Women walked a fine line, he had said. If they keep to themselves, they lack group spirit; if they're easygoing, they lack authority. If they're reserved, they're incapable of camaraderie, if they're indulgent, they're too emotional and destroy the group's cohesiveness. "I know your behavior is exemplary, Manuela, but be careful." That chat made me even more reserved around my colleagues. And made me hope that a good kid like Puddu, eager and tenacious, would take their place one day.

So the unsolved mysteries of the NCO entrance exam booklet became a torment for the whole platoon. What is the past participle of the verb "to fly"? A) flew; B) flied; C) flowed; D) flown. Who is the author of the poem *Ginestra?* A) Petrarch; B) Leopardi; C) Pirandello; D) Pascoli. Who guards the gates to hell in Dante's *Inferno?* A) Cerberus; B) Virgil; C) Hydra; D) Limbo. What is the Constitution? A) a code; B) a source of the law; C) an organization; D) a document. What does each point in the Hubble diagram represent? On a map with a scale of 1:500,000, three centimeters correspond to how many kilometers? 0.0003, 1,500,000, 15, 150 . . . What is a deciduous forest? Which of these fruits is an achene? A pear, an orange, a fig, or fennel?

"What's the synonym of *epigone*, Spaniard?" Owl asked as we were in line for the toilets. They were all occupied. We must have eaten some rotten chickpeas at mess the day before, because the next day the entire company was tormented by diarrhea. The stench of shit spread from the chemical toilets through the still, sultry air. "The choices are: polygon, polyhedron, follower, friend." "D, friend," Diego answered immediately. But Lorenzo was flabbergasted. He stopped suddenly, at the door to the john, butted into the conversation, and assured him he was wrong. "Bullshit, Spaniard, the correct answer is A, polygon. An epigone is a polygon, it even rhymes, it's the same thing, a synthesis." "You're a beast, Baby," Diego replied, "an ignoramus. It's synonym, not synthesis, and *epigone* means 'friend.' You and I are epigones," he affirmed, pushing the dubious Owl into the john, which reeked of rotten chickpeas. "Are we epigones, Manuela?" Diego asked me that evening, when he saluted me before taking his shift in the tower. "Yes," I said, before quickly drawing the mosquito net between myself and his enthusiasm.

And so that word became our secret code. I told my epigones things I hadn't even told myself. And they did the same with me. We gave ourselves over to each other completely. "Know why I'm here?" Lorenzo said one evening as we were lifting weights in the tent that had generously been rebaptized as a gym, the only recreational space on the base. "Because you're from the Tenth, and when you found out your regiment was being deployed, you didn't hesitate," I replied. "Come on," Lorenzo laughed, loading another weight on his barbell. "I'm an unwilling volunteer, a contradiction. My father mailed in my application. I didn't know anything about it, I certainly didn't want to enlist. He practically forced me to, he drove me to the barracks himself. He was afraid I'd fuck up and end up in jail sooner or later," he added with a snort. "And was he right?" I asked, stunned. "What do you think?" Lorenzo laughed. "I left high school when I was fourteen, I started a thousand jobs without learning any of them. I wanted to be an extreme ski champion, like Kammerlander, but I tore the ligaments in my knee. So my uncle got me a job in an eyeglass factory, but the work was so repetitive that I quit. I would have liked to buy a truck, but you can imagine my parents, a truck driver son seemed like a failure to them, a public humiliation—my mom's a teacher and my father manages a hotel. Meanwhile, I started an alternative rock band, we called ourselves the Puking Dogs, I played guitar and wrote lyrics. To see me now you wouldn't believe it, but we were pretty famous, they booked us for a summer tour, we played in soccer stadiums. We even opened for Pearl Jam once, at the Jammin' Festival in Venice. I was convinced I could live off my music, everything was going good. I was playing music, having fun, even making some money. But we were heading home after a concert in Pordenone one night when a patrol car pulled us over. It was a Saturday, you know those damned checkpoints, looking for drunk drivers. The singer was a real *cojòn*, he had three hundred grams of cocaine in the glove compartment. They took us to headquarters. The police chief knew my father, and he told him to make me enlist, the Alpini would straighten me out, instill some values in me. So my father sent in the application. I wasn't even eighteen. I was the best rock guitar player in eastern Italy. I curse him every time I think about it. But my father is always right."

"My father was always wrong," I surprised him by saying. "He did everything wrong, absolutely everything. At twenty he was the national racewalking champion, but his father told him he couldn't make a living off sports, and had to find himself a job. At twenty-one he started at the electric power plant in Civitavecchia and gave up racing. Then he got a worker at the local fish factory pregnant; he'd been seeing her for all of three days, and, to please his father, who told him that if he was a man he'd do his duty, he married her. Their marriage was hell. I never saw him laugh. I think he hated all three of us, my mother, my sister, and me, even though it wasn't our fault he was so unhappy. At forty he realized that sports were the only thing that made him happy, but at that point he couldn't racewalk anymore, because his tendons had gotten inflamed from working at the electric plant, so he got interested in windsurfing. He already had cancer, though, and the doctors discouraged him from taking up such a demanding sport. My mother sold his board when he was admitted to the hospital. I think it was that stupid surfboard that gave him the courage to leave her. He took up with another woman and I didn't see him for ten years. He'd still go windsurfing even when he was exhausted from the chemo and couldn't stand up anymore, because he wanted to die on the water, with the wind in his face. He died in a hospital bed instead, in a room with five other patients, all of them screaming in pain, and his new wife couldn't even open the window to let him feel the breeze because the other patients' relatives wouldn't let her. My father wasted his life. He has been a negative example for me. All I learned from him was what not to do."

I toweled off my face, which was dripping with sweat. I never talked about Tiberio Paris. He was a mistake, a dark blot on my life, and I was ashamed of him. Yet in that moment I realized that in the end, a negative example—because it would have been unfair to call him a bad example—can still be instructive. Growing up amid the noxious fumes of mediocrity and failure had helped me understand what to avoid. I was struck with the desire to hear my father's voice—sandy, coarse, scratchy, like his old car. But I had to make do with that of my brother. His voice was changing, and when I talked with Traian on the phone, I sometimes had the sensation I was talking with my father. I'm sorry, Papa, I would have liked to say to him. I'm not mad at you anymore. I'm sorry.

"I do everything wrong, too," Lorenzo said, stopping suddenly, his barbell in midair. "I'm different from you all, I don't think the same way. Do you know who the hero of my village is? A broke anarchist who emigrated, became a miner, and then came back because he dreamed of liberating Italy from tyranny. His name was Angelo Sbardellotto. He went to Rome to kill Mussolini, and had three chances, but he never went through with it because he didn't want to accidentally kill innocent people, too. He was arrested, and sentenced to death. He didn't ask for mercy, and they shot him in the back. He died for his ideals; he was only twenty-five. They dedicated a plaque to him in my village, but they didn't have the courage to put it in the piazza, only in the park, because they said he fell in a private war, not wearing an army uniform. The plaque is still there, though, and I would see it when I went to the park with my girlfriend, and I would think about that kid—he was only a little older than me—who gave his life for liberty. I wasn't born to drive a tank, I don't believe we're here to bring liberty to these people, because liberty has to be earned, not imposed, even your own liberty, especially your own, this place doesn't mean shit to me, and if it weren't for you, the Spaniard, Owl, and Angkor, for my brothers in Pegasus and Lambda, I would have already left."

"Sollum's not a hotel, Nail," I said to him, "it's not like you pay your bill and leave." "It wouldn't take much to get myself sent home," he objected ironically. "I could act crazy, fake a nervous breakdown, insult the skinny Buddha, tell the first reporter who happens to show up that this mission is a mistake. That it was a huge mistake sending soldiers to Afghanistan, that we should have withdrawn a long time ago. Sure, we're doing some good things, and I grant you that we do them with the kind of fairness that's worthy of a better cause, but in reality we're here to cover up other people's motivations, we're spending damn near five million euros a year to unfurl our flag in the desert, money we could be using to build hospitals back home. I could say these things, Manuela, and I really think them. I'd be dishonorably discharged, but I wouldn't care in the least—in fact, I'd be free. The reason I don't do it is because I took an oath. I gave my word. This time I'm going to stick it out. I've always started things and then dropped them when I got bored. The only thing I never gave up on was music. I'm a lousy soldier, but I was a really good guitar player. Maybe right now, instead of eating sand and living like a celibate Trappist monk, I could have been on tour in Holland, in Spain, who knows, with a different girl every night. Don't hate your father. If anything, you should love him more. It's awful to live your life wrong."

"But you're so young," I said to him, "you don't even need to shave yet, you have plenty of time to do something different. If you're really convinced you're a musician, when you get back to Italy, ask to join the brass band or to be discharged. Okay, so you gave your word, but it's okay to change your mind. You can't crucify yourself over an oath." Lorenzo got up, surprised that I of all people would speak to him like that. He had always considered me an unyielding champion, incapable of deviations, doubts, or compromises. "It can't just end like this," he said, "we can't lose track of each other, we're too tight now."

Sometimes after dinner we'd gorge ourselves on talk—stupid arguments—until exhaustion closed our eyes. We would talk about soccer and motorcycles (Owl would do motocross on the Gennargentu when he went back to Sardinia on leave). We would list the most beautiful places we'd ever been (I kept quiet, because I'd never been anywhere). We'd make lists of our favorite foods: for the Spaniard the number one spot went to his mother's schiaffoni with ragú sauce; for Puddu it was *bottarga*, salted mullet roe from Cabras; for Angkor, *fegatazzi*, liver sausages from Ortona; for Zandonà, *casunziei*, ravioli with pumpkin, prosciutto, and cinnamon. Other times we'd ask those big questions you have the courage to ponder only when you're young and then prefer to avoid for the rest of your life. What is evil, what's the difference between execution and assassination, is there really life after death, why does God tolerate, and sometimes even seem to approve of, injustice? Diego was very Catholic and we expected him to have an answer for everything. But other than a few recycled bits of catechism, he wasn't very up on theology; all he said was that God keeps track of the good and evil you do in life, and the wicked will be punished. He believed in Heaven, but he never thought about Hell. I once said to him that I found the idea of God as accountant ridiculous—God with a grade book in his hand. He was offended, and now I'm sorry.

We recounted childhood memories, anecdotes from when we were recruits, episodes that in that far distant place suddenly assumed an unprecedented importance. Jodice, who usually boasted to us about his tours of duty in the Balkans, once, who knows how, ended up talking about an accident he hadn't thought about in years. It was in some secluded valley in Wardak, a place of turbans and goats, filled with happy, festive people who greeted them with a smile when they went by and loved them because the war had just ended, or so they thought.

He was in a jeep with his captain, they were racing to the Kabul airport because they had to pick up some minister or undersecretary, he couldn't remember exactly who anymore, but anyway, some important politician. But there'd been some sort of hitch and they were late. So they were flying, the wind whirling through the open window. It had been a really good tour, he felt satisfied both professionally and personally. And at a certain point the lamb appeared. A tiny ball of white wool gamboling on the edge of the road. Hey, they both thought, there must be a flock beyond that hill. They were happy, because it meant that the people who lived in the valley had returned and were going back to their lives. The whole area was mined, there were still red marks on the rocks along the road and in the surrounding fields to highlight the danger.

The kid ran across the road without looking, hurling himself after the lamb. There wasn't even time to brake. They were going too fast. The impact was tremendous. The jeep came to a stop a hundred yards farther on. The kid had been flung into the minefield on the side of the road. Diego and the captain looked each other in the eye and then, without asking permission, Diego ventured into the field. Step by step, trying to weigh less than a lamb, to be all but immaterial. The kid was still breathing, but he had lost consciousness and blood trickled from his ear. He had brown hair and golden skin, his feet were bare. Diego took him in his arms.

"I didn't see him, sir," the driver babbled. The captain took the boy's pulse: it was faint, but still there. He called for medics, and for twenty interminable minutes, stopped on the side of the road, next to a minefield, they waited in a primordial silence for another vehicle to arrive. The mountains all around spread a cold shadow over them. But then they had to race to the airport, because in the meantime the minister or undersecretary or whoever it was had landed, and there was no one to welcome him, and he was furious, and headquarters was bombarding them with phone calls, threatening retaliation: the driver could forget about reenlisting, and the captain would be sent to the middle of nowhere, to some barracks in Friuli, to count stones on the Carso. Neither the driver nor the captain ever found out what happened to the boy. When, that evening, they asked for news, they were assured that he'd been taken to the American hospital, that everything was fine. Neither driver nor captain were held responsible for the unfortunate accident. But the heart doesn't let itself be fooled, and his heart said right away that the boy couldn't possibly have survived.

They waited on the edge of that road, and little by little the boy's face turned to chalk, his lips drained of blood. As he told the story, the Gladiator's eyes glistened. At the time his assignment was driver. He was the driver of that damn jeep. "It wasn't your fault, man," Lorenzo said, slapping him on the shoulder. "I know," Diego replied, "but I'll carry that boy in my heart forever. I came back to settle my debt," he whispered. And then he started to cry. He collapsed all of a sudden, sobbing. If something is too hard, in the end it will break. Lorenzo and I, sitting at the entrance to the tent, enveloped Diego in a hug that tasted of dust. "Thank you, brothers," he stammered, "thank you."

When the helicopter lifted off and took the guys destined for Dubai away, I presented myself in the captain's office and placed myself at the company's disposal for the time Pegasus was off duty. Paggiarin grumbled that he intended to assign me to CIMIC duty for those ninety-six hours. I could fill out forms for First Lieutenant Russo. Among other things, Russo was overseeing the reconstruction of the girls' school in Qal'a-i-Shakhrak. He had to check on suppliers and manpower, like a contractor. His work was nothing like mine. But I could expedite the mass of bureaucratic paper he was buried under. At that particular moment, everyone was indispensable; there was a lot to do. Patrols were going out day and night, searching one village after another. But the tumult and hostile activity were increasing: the Afghan police had suffered two attacks, and a checkpoint our combat engineers had just built had been blown up the night before. Operations were behind schedule, meetings with village chiefs turned into tea-drinking sessions, filled with smiles and enervating chats that concealed increasingly unreasonable requests and complaints that the promised electricity had not arrived, that the well water was contaminated by sewage, that the bridge had not been built, and Paggiarin, sitting cross-legged on the carpet, shuddered, trying in vain to decipher his interlocutors' actual intentions while they fingered their prayer beads, their expressions impenetrable. He would make promises. And then when PSYOPS would call from Herat, to ask what good news regarding the Italians' activities they should print on the flyers to be distributed to the local population, it was all he could do to keep from swearing.

Furthermore, an assailant dressed as a police officer had killed the police superintendent of Jawza, whom the captain trusted more than all the others put together. He was his mediator, his ear, and—in practice—his best ally. He was the one who had tipped intelligence off about Mullah Wallid; he was the one who gathered reports on IEDs that were supposed to blow us up. When I reported to Paggiarin, he had just returned from paying his last respects to his unfortunate colleague. The police station was deserted, the agents had disappeared. The commissary's body, burned and horribly lacerated, had not even been removed: it lay in a puddle of blood in front of what remained of the building. "He protected you! Shit, shit, shit!" Paggiarin started yelling in his perfect English. There weren't any Afghanis there, only the soldiers who escorted him.

Work languished. Hardly a quick win. Operation Reawakening was very far from reaching its objective, and they couldn't afford to lose a single day. Failure was unthinkable. "Ninth Company will not return to Italy without extending that damn bubble to twenty kilometers by the middle of June," Paggiarin declared. "And it will inaugurate the girls' school at Qal'a-i-Shakhrak even if I have to make the Alpini lay the bricks themselves." "They're all positive signs," I pointed out. "They attack us because they recognize our successes, because our activities have complicated things for them, because they feel defeated." Paggiarin gave me a glazed-over look. Yet all I had done was say what he'd been repeating to me every morning for almost five months. The men called Paggiarin the Skinny Buddha because he always wore an angelic smile and he never lost his cool. But he'd lost it that morning. He'd even let slip a four-letter word. The situation had to be more complicated than he was willing to admit.

I ran into Diego on my way back to my container. He was headed to the showers—bare chest, flip-flops, a towel over his shoulder. "You're still here, Spaniard!" I exclaimed with surprise. "They wouldn't let her leave," he said quickly. He didn't want to talk. "Risk of miscarriage, she's not allowed to fly, she has to stay in bed. I tried trading places with Nail, but they wouldn't let him. What was I going to do in Dubai without Imma?" "I'm sorry," I said. Then, to cheer him up, I added, "Come on, don't be depressed, a hundred and ten days down, only seventy left." "It's bad luck to count how many days till the end," Diego said.

Embarrassed, I studied the colored tattoos that studded his skin. A dragon. A cross. A rose. They were really big. Usually his T-shirt hid them, but some were still visible. Regulations prohibited tattoos. Captain Paggiarin hated them. For him, they were something convicts get. He didn't allow tattooed soldiers in Ninth Company. No exceptions. I'd had to have the sword I'd had tattooed on my neck at fifteen lasered off, or else he never would have accepted me. If he'd seen Diego like this, he would have thrown him out. Paggiarin was capable of depriving himself of an excellent soldier in order to enforce his moral code. Everyone has their prejudices. I let Diego know, and I wrapped the towel around his neck to hide his tattoos, at least until he got to the showers. Paggiarin was wandering around back there, nervous and burning with rage because they'd killed the superintendent at Jawza and because he had let the soldiers see him lose control. But nothing seemed to matter to Diego anymore. "It's clear I was supposed to stay close to you," he said suggestively as he headed to the showers. He turned around and smiled at me. "I'll never leave you again, Mulan."

14

LIVE

nce it crosses the canal, the road heading north runs parallel to the sea. The city peters out gently. Apartment buildings become elegant three-story homes, campgrounds, marinas, camper van storage lots, and finally a fragile strip of ash-colored dunes hemmed in by a wooden fence. Faded signs caution that this is a protected area, a nature preserve, the Torre Flavia wetland. A sandy path runs along the ponds and disappears among the reeds. Just a few steps inside and it already feels like you're at the end of the world, even though cars whiz by behind the marsh and Piazza della Vittoria is only a few miles away. A sign nailed to the fence informs visitors that it is prohibited to step off the walkways, trample the dunes, let dogs off their leashes, harvest sea lilies, or disturb the wild fauna. Mattia is surprised that such a place has survived the building speculation that devoured the rest of the coast, and wonders how much longer it will last. The pond is as crowded as a piazza, with hundreds, even thousands of birds: the water quivers, the reeds rustle, feathers flap, beaks emit powerful, shrill whistles, but Mattia doesn't know birds and has no idea what species they are. They all look like ducks and herons to him. He vaguely recalls that in certain seasons they abandon their nests and fly away. Not just birds, actually. Bats, caribou, lemmings, toads, eels, even herrings migrate. Driven by a mysterious yet infallible instinct, they abandon everything, cross mountains, oceans, ice floes, entire continents, merely to reach a certain destination, reproduce, and die. Their lives revolve entirely around this movement.

The migrating birds that dwell undisturbed among the reeds have stopped here on their eventful, exhausting journey in order to rest and regain their strength, protected and secure in this modest nature preserve. No one can riddle them with shot here. But wherever they've come from, and wherever they're going, they're just passing through. Mattia stops and stares at them lazing about in the brackish water. They're so close, and so indifferent to Mattia and Manuela's presence, so free of fears and suspicion, that he could almost touch them. Or throw a rock at them, or beat them with a stick. "That's a pochard," Manuela says, pointing to a small duck with red eyes intent on fishing tadpoles in the still waters. "It spends the winter here. And that's a teal. You can tell by the green mark on its eyes, it looks like it's blindfolded. That tiny one there is a sandpiper. There should be some dabchicks around, too, but they're probably hiding, they're really timid. The stilt plovers won't get here until spring." She points out the little white egret. Thin and aristocratic, it shakes its feather crest and advances on its slender black legs into the reed thicket, paying no attention to them. The birds keep preening themselves, and rooting around in the water with their beaks. Not even her voice startles them. They're so trusting, so vulnerable, and Mattia is sorry. "Manuela," he says, "I'm just passing through, too. But I don't have a destination. I don't know where I'm going." But Manuela, hypnotized by the beautiful white egret, has already made it to the end of the walkway, and his voice doesn't reach her.

The sun is at its zenith, so there are only thin, shadowless silhouettes on the beach, beaten by a western wind. A few families, a couple with a dachshund, and in the water a reckless kite surfer in a wet suit who struggles with his lines, while his sail, swelled by the wind, jerks impatiently above him. Farther down, on a tongue of sand the breakwater protects in vain, the ruins of a tower seem to rise up from the sea. "That's it," Manuela says. "This is where I wanted to bring you."

The bombarded tower, broken, rent into two stumps, reminds her of the minaret at Qal'a-i-Shakhrak. That, too, was hit by a bomb, but it refused to fall, and months later it still pointed its broken finger at the sky, another piece crumbling with every windstorm. War had touched these shores, too, this beach, these dunes, this sand. "We have a glorious history, but we're not very lucky," Manuela says, "there's almost nothing left. Think about it, Roman senators used to come here on vacation, Pompey's villa was somewhere around here—Sallust's, Murena's, and Heliogabalus's villas were here, too. Totila razed them all to the ground in 547. The barbarians didn't leave even a wall standing. Then in the Middle Ages, the nobles who owned estates here built towers, castles, and fortified farmhouses. This tower was first Roman, then it became part of the coastal defense system, there was a garrison here, and cannons, until the 1800s." "You sure know a lot," Mattia jokes. "I'm a tour guide," Manuela says flippantly.

"I thought you were a sergeant!" he exclaims. "I was a tour guide in my first life," she smiles. "After a year in the military, I was angry and disillusioned and didn't reenlist. I found a job in Civitavecchia, at a travel agency that worked with the Mediterranean cruise lines. The qualifications for being a good tour guide, the owner told me when he hired me for a trial period, are: stamina, because you have to stand on your feet for hours, sometimes in the blazing sun; a warm presence; strong vocal cords, because you have to talk loudly; familiarity with other languages, to hold people's attention, and to handle a group. Leadership skills, in other words. Basically, the same qualifications as an army officer. The only real difference is that ninety-five percent of tour guides are women, and it's considered women's work. The money's lousy, and you're paid by the hour, which means I didn't earn a thing during the off season, but in exchange, the owner helped me pass the qualifying exam and get my license so I could register as an official guide. In Italy, you have to pay for a training course and to renew your license even just to be able to tell Chinese engineers who Michelangelo was. Anyway, my family couldn't support me and I had to earn a living. Every Monday, tourists would disembark from the cruise ships at Civitavecchia and get bused to Rome. They had twelve hours to discover the capital, it was a really tight schedule: bathroom breaks, food breaks, cultural sites, one right after the other, all at a hellish, almost military pace. I had a whistle and a red umbrella to herd them along. I would escort my platoon to Saint Peter's, the Sistine Chapel, the Roman Forum. I knew how to do it. I was born to lead people."

Mattia laughs. Manuela doesn't add that she doesn't like thinking back to that time. Those years are a gray parenthesis. She started seeing the industrial technology student, the one from the coatroom, Giovanni Bocca, who in the meantime had started studying engineering at the

University of Rome. He'd go there every day, and slave over his books until late every night. On Saturdays they would go to a pub or the movies, go out dancing, or bowling, maybe; they would have sex in his parents' bed on Wednesday nights, when they went out to play buraco. The Boccas' bed smelled of stale foundation powder, and every now and then she'd find a tired white hair in the sheets. Giovanni liked oral sex; she preferred to have sex standing up. They compromised. As the months passed, she began to find her work depressing. The average age of the tourists—retirees from the Midwest, Saxony, Wales, Westphalia—was seventy-five. Many had trouble walking, some were in wheelchairs. Enthusiastic but ignorant—Barcelona the day before, Malta the day after—to them Rome was a stop like any other. The only things they really remembered were the spaghetti all'arrabbiata and the centurions with papier-mâché swords posing in front of the Coliseum. She prepared a little explanation in English for every monument, five minutes exactly—if she went on any longer their attention would wane, they'd start looking around with dead fish eyes, and besides, she couldn't make them stand for too long. She would always say the same thing.

Sometimes the ship wouldn't set sail again until Tuesday afternoon, so she would take the tourists to the necropolis at Cerveteri. They had never even heard of the Etruscans, whom they took to be the Italian aborigines. They were disappointed when she revealed that their origins had not been determined definitively and that the most reliable theories—confirmed by DNA tests—held that the Etruscans were not native to Italy, were not the Italian redskins, but were in fact immigrants from the East, from Anatolia, from what today is Turkey, which the Catholic tourists associated with Ali Agca, the man who shot the pope, so in the end the Etruscans got no sympathy after all. Eventually she realized she had to give them the satisfaction of meeting a native, so when they asked her if she was Etruscan, she would say yes, all the inhabitants of Ladispoli, northern Lazio, and the Maremma had descended from the Etruscans, those native Italians, a mysterious people, who believed in esoteric rites and worshipped death. "Wow, amazing!" the tourists would exclaim, and, enraptured, they would snap her picture, without even asking her permission. Every Tuesday, when she left them by the side of their ships and watched them disappear up the escalators, pocketing the tip that the most liberal of the group would hand her with a huge smile, she would think: I can't do this my whole life.

So, after an infinity of catacombs, Coliseums, and Sistine Chapels, after becoming an expert in gerontology, she applied to take the entrance exam for the NCO Academy in Viterbo. She was over twenty-two now, which was the cutoff for the Modena Academy. And besides, she didn't want to repeat that experience. She had developed a secret aversion for commissioned officers: their polished manners, their way of speaking, their privileges, their education, their degrees, their bourgeois backgrounds. They were too different from her, and she no longer wanted to become like them. Viterbo received thirty thousand applications for eighty-two spots. Having already volunteered for a year, she got one more point than the civilian applicants, but she didn't have much hope. There was no one to put in a good word for her. Her mother didn't know anyone, and she didn't know how to make connections. She didn't tell anyone she was applying. She got 73 points on the initial exams. They called her in for more tests.

During the psycho-behavioral test, she told some truths and some lies. But she distributed them better. The book that taught you how to pass the Armed Forces exams recommended presenting yourself as eager, tolerant, altruistic, willing to take orders and advice, and counseled against showing shyness, aggressive behavior, personality problems, or difficulty with interpersonal relationships. She wasn't afraid of failing, because she already had a job, which no one could take away from her. She replied confidently to the questions about self-esteem, and when the examiner made her draw her family, she remembered to include her mother, father, sister, brother, and herself. The first time, she'd forgotten to draw her mother, and the examiner was surprised to learn that her mother was the one who had raised her, and that she had no relations with her father. She drew herself with hair, breasts, and feet. The time before—as hesitant as a child holding a pencil for the first time—she had drawn a genderless puppet with too small a head. A small head, she later read in the book, is a symptom of obsessive self-control; feet pointing in opposite directions reveal a disconnect with reality; and a stiff, poorly proportioned figure denotes anxiety, uncertainty, and conflict about one's sexual orientation.

The results were posted on the Internet a month later. Vanessa was the first to know that Manuela had made it. She came in fortieth, and was accepted to the Army Noncommissioned Officers' Academy in Viterbo. "I'm a sergeant in training," she explained briefly to the owner of the travel agency. "I'm resigning, I have to be at the barracks next Monday." "What are you?" he said. "I'm a soldier."

"I stopped renewing my annual tour guide license," she told Mattia. "Tourists are a pain, but I was proud to show foreigners my country's monuments. It was as if they belonged to me, too. I really believe they do. We don't have oil, diamonds, uranium, or methane, but we have history, the landscape, art. In Afghanistan, it really bothered me to see how neglected their treasures were. You could make out the ruins in the mountains, in a valley several miles from our base. They looked like mud brick spires. They seemed ancient, the ruins of a fortification, or of watchtowers. But not even our interpreter could tell us what they were. Afghanis do not love the past." "Maybe because they don't have a future," Mattia remarks. "If you don't have the sense of continuity, if your history has been broken, you can't take care of anything but the present."

Manuela has the feeling he's trying to tell her something, but she can't figure out what it is. And she misses her chance to ask. "Anyway, war returned," she continues, "and hit us head-on. During World War II the Americans targeted Civitavecchia, they bombed it and destroyed everything. But it was the Germans who hit the tower in 1943. With artillery, from the hills in Cerveteri. It was too high, they said; Allied reconnaissance could use it as a reference point. It was just a monument to the past. The upper floors were destroyed. But it held. It leans toward the water now, it looks like it's about to fall. The sea has eroded its every defense, the waves lap at it all winter long, and people do nothing to protect it, they just let it die. Every year the stumps move farther apart, the cracks get bigger, the windows where cannons once stood are tilting. But it resists. It's my favorite place around here. I was supposed to come here with my friends, to celebrate the end of our tour of duty." "But you didn't?" Mattia asks, thinking it was the hospital and her surgeries that prevented her.

"My friends are dead," Manuela says. "It was the last thing we talked about. Then we left to go to that village, and a little while later, the bomb exploded." Mattia shudders. He knows he should tell her he's there for her, that he's sorry about her friends, and for her. But it wouldn't be the truth, because right now he's here with her, and if it weren't for that bomb he never would have met her, and he doesn't want to be anywhere else. The chipped bricks of the tower, corroded by the salt, have taken on a rosy color, and the travertine that reinforces their sides is as white as the foam on the waves. The tower seems made of the same inconstant material as the sea. He doesn't say anything, but he rests his chin on her shoulder, a comforting gesture. If Manuela wants solace, she can count on him. "It was silly, it started as a joke," Manuela says, her lips curled in a strange smile.

She thought she'd forgotten them, and yet here, at the foot of the tower, their words—crisp, isolated—reemerge one by one, as if from beneath an ocean of silence. "Mulan, what's the first thing you'll do when you get home?" Diego had asked her. "I'll go to the tower," she heard herself say. "I'll go to the tower and swim in the sea." "I was supposed to come here with my epigones," she explains to Mattia, doodling distractedly in the sand with her crutch. "I told them that the first thing I'd do, once I got back to Italy, was come here and swim, in a skimpy bikini, because I'd had enough of camouflage. I didn't miss anything about Italy over there, not the food or my family or the trees; but I missed the sun on my skin, the pleasure of baring my legs, of uncovering my back. I'm sure it seems strange to you, but I missed tank tops, bathing suits, feeling the wind in my hair. My company officers met often with the village chiefs in Farah, almost every day during those last weeks, the meetings were called *shure*, and the mayors, mullahs, and most important figures would go, they'd drink tea and agree on operations, take note of the people's needs. Some reciprocal trust was created. But I could never accompany them, even though I was a platoon leader and was the one who carried out the officers' requests. I had to send my deputy. Even during joint operations I couldn't talk with my Afghani equivalent, the ANA platoon leader: the lance sergeant had to do it. And if because of some unforeseen event in a village, I had to explain something to a man, he wouldn't look at me. I didn't exist, I was like a lamppost, nothing, he'd look at the interpreter, or the soldier standing next to me. I know he did it because he didn't want to offend me, it's his culture, and they taught us to respect that. I knew that all the difficulties we had encountered on the ground derived from the fact that initially there had been a serious flaw in communication, that we foreigners had behaved as if we were a superior, civilizing force, fueling the local people's resentment. If you go to someone's house and they take off their shoes at the doorstep, you take yours off, too, simple as that. So I covered my hair with a scarf, to make them understand that I respected their culture, which forced them to ignore me. But I won't hide the fact that it was really hard to show respect for an old man who confines his women to his house, who pens them in like sheep or goats, and decides whom to marry his daughters off to in exchange for a hundred sheep, or swaps them for money to end a feud, kills his wives with childbearing, and treats them like dogs. I felt humiliated, it was as if all I had earned, as a woman and a soldier, meant nothing. I'm a woman and a commander. And I represent my country. This is possible in my country. It took us two thousand years to get here, it may seem like a travesty to some, but to me it's a victory, and that's why I'm standing here telling you where to put those fucking weapons you're giving us in exchange for seeds for your fields. But naturally I kept quiet. I could never look a man in the face when I spoke; I kept my eyes on the ground, staring at my boots. It was hard. I couldn't take it anymore.

"My friends couldn't take it anymore either, but for different reasons. For them it was not having sex. It was all they talked about those last two months. They exchanged advice on contraception, positions, some things I can't even repeat, even though by that point I'd become as foul-mouthed as a trucker. Anyway, at a certain point, I don't know why, my epigones promised to come visit me in Ladispoli and to bring me a thong as thin as dental floss. We were just screwing around, but we swore we'd come here together, all three of us. And we'd go swimming at midnight, with a full moon, as naked as the day we were born, and we started shouting like idiots, hooray for Italy, hooray for Italy."

It was that last morning, as they were getting in the Lince, heading to Qal'a-i-Shakhrak—and without knowing it, heading to the instant that would separate them. They were moving toward death; she toward this lacerated and fragmented present. And yet on this first day of the year, among the fragile yet intact dunes, at the foot of the tower, with a happy, elusive, yet dear and thoughtful man at her side, this present doesn't lack something; it has almost everything.

Mattia says thank you, and Manuela, astounded, asks him why in the world he should thank her. For telling me these things, for bringing me here, he would like to say, but at the same time he realizes he needs to be quiet. She is trusting him with a secret that may be a burden or a promise or a request for a commitment, and he has already pushed himself beyond every limit and he can't and doesn't want to accept it.

"Too bad it's not August so we can't go skinny-dipping," he says lightly, "besides, it's not allowed, I think, we'd get arrested. Can you tell me why you call them epigones? What does it mean?" "No," Manuela says, "it was just between us, it doesn't make sense anymore."

They stay and watch the waves crash against the breakwater and dissolve against the foot of the tower in a gush of foam. Salt splashes and spray bead their faces and hair. The water has become a dark mirror that reflects the clouds, the ruins of the tower, and their bodies. The kite surfer has managed to untangle his lines and hook the straps to his harness, and now he bounces along on his board, dragged by the sail, racing toward open water like red tumbleweed on the barren land of the sea. Mattia envies his speed, his flight, that unbridled freedom. The whole time they've been on the water's edge, as the shadow of the tower slowly envelops them, Manuela has been moving her crutch in the sand, sketching lines, poles, circles, dots. It's only when they walk toward the reserve entrance and Mattia turns to say goodbye to the tower one last time does he realize what she has written on the shore. Three names, engraved in the black sand, already threatened by the undertow. NAIL—SPANIARD—MULAN.

The phone in room 302 rings three times before Manuela decides to answer it. Mattia is in the bathroom shaving with the radio on and doesn't hear it. "Yes," she says slowly, shamefully, as if she were violating a secret of his. But it's not for Mattia. The concierge informs her that someone is asking for her at the reception desk. "Honey," Vanessa shrieks, "I'm in a jam, you have to do me a favor, please, I'm begging you, I can't explain, just say yes." She's struggling to seem normal. But her voice comes out all strange—she's drooling, as if she had a handful of pebbles in her mouth, and she's having trouble stringing together three words. "Vanè!" Manuela exclaims. "Where the hell have you been? Mamma was in a panic, she called me five times to ask if I'd heard from you, I didn't know what to say." "I know you're with him and I'm being a pain in the ass, you don't know how sorry I am, but you have to watch Alessia till I get back. It won't be too long, I swear, besides, Grandma gets back at eight and you can bring her home."

"I can't babysit for you right now," Manuela protests. "She's right here, hon," Vanessa insists, as if, faced with such evidence, her sister would have to give in. "Mamma has to work, I left her with Grandma, but she went to the Kingdom Hall and left her alone, can you imagine, I found her whimpering in the kitchen, poor kid, seven years old, she was scared to death, what a heartless old woman." "Vanessa, how can I? What am I supposed to say to him?" Manuela whispers. She's uneasy, though, because she feels indebted to her sister. Without her stolen keys, she would never have gotten that night with Mattia at her grandfather's cottage. A night that already seems far away, but that nevertheless radiates an enchanted, almost unreal, and perhaps unrepeatable perfection.

"She'll be good, isn't that right, pumpkin, you won't make auntie angry?" "Vanessa," Manuela murmurs, "what have you done? You're being so weird!" "Who are you talking to?" Mattia asks, sticking his head through the door, his face half white with shaving cream. His eyes are filled with an exaggerated anxiety, which Manuela recognizes right away because she has learned to read the same look in her own. Fear. Total, uncontrollable fear. But what could Mattia be afraid of? That she would butt into his life? "It's my sister," she reassures him. "Something's wrong, I'm going downstairs a minute." "Okay, but come right back," Mattia urges her. Today has been too perfect to ruin it dealing with her family— the less contact with them, the better for everyone. Manuela kisses him on his wet lips, removes a drop of blood from a nick on his cheek, and puts on her jacket. It's only once she's in the elevator that she realizes she has forgotten her crutches.

Alessia is sitting on an armchair in the lobby, her little Hello Kitty suitcase in her lap. Vanessa looks as if she's been run over by a train. Her pupils are dilated, her hair's a mess, her hands are shaking. "Thank you, hon," she says, hinting at a smile, "you're an angel, tell your friend I'm sorry, he can ask whatever he wants in return. Keep the keys to Grandpa's house, you two use it, besides, I won't be going there anymore, it's all over with Youssef." "Did you take some shit, Vanè?" Manuela asks with alarm. Alessia, her eyes sealed shut from crying, dangles her feet in the air. The chair is too big for her. Manuela kisses her hair. It's sticky, and spotted with colorful blobs of Play-Doh. The girl claws her mother's wrist with both hands, as if to keep her from leaving. "I'll only be a little while, pumpkin," Vanessa promises, not very convincingly, aware she's lying—and then, turning to Manuela, she adds, as if it were nothing important, "Can you lend me some money? I need to get gas. My ATM card is blocked, but the bank will be open tomorrow and I can pay you back." "Gas?" Manuela exclaims, astonished. "Where do you have to go? You just got back!" And then, in a whisper, "Alessia expected you for lunch, Mamma says she was upset you didn't come back, she made you a cake." "Don't lecture me, fuck!" Vanessa bursts out. "Can you lend me some money or not?" "Of course I can," Manuela says, "but if you don't tell me what you need it for, I'm not giving you a cent."

"I don't think I can tell you, Manù," Vanessa mumbles, chewing on her nails. They're painted blue, with silver speckles. Manuela looks radiant, it's clear she had a nice night with her Bellavista lover, lucky her. It's only fair, the wheel turns. Manuela takes a wad of cash out of her purse, and Vanessa tries to grab it. But Manuela closes her purse. "There's no way I'm letting you drive," she says, "I don't know how you made it back here without getting into an accident." "I wasn't driving, my car's still there, in the parking lot, I have to go get it. Give me everything you have," she begs, her blue fingers reaching for her sister's purse. "It's a holiday, it'll be at least a hundred and twenty for the taxi." Manuela brightens. "Let's ask Mattia. It'll only take him a minute to come down. We can take you to get your car, that way you don't have to leave Alessia." Hearing her name, the girl suddenly lifts her head. Her eyes light up with a flash of hope. Vanessa nibbles her nails. The concierge of the Bellavista is pretending to check the reservations on the computer, but he doesn't miss a word as he sizes Vanessa up: shapely thighs, a run in her stockings, a dress that's too short, a neckline that's too low, her artificial tits irresistibly firm and round, almost shocking. Vanessa buttons her leather jacket, staring at him contemptuously. "Listen, hon," she whispers, "it's not true, my car's in the piazza, but I need the money, I need gas, seriously." "You're not making sense, Vanessa," Manuela objects, "where do you have to go?" "It's personal, please, don't ask." "I will so ask!" Manuela almost shouts. "You call me in the middle of the night, talking nonsense, then you disappear, and now you show up like this, I don't want to know what you took, but you're really pissing me off, you swore you were done with that shit, you may be reckless, but I'm not, and I'm not letting you drive." "Give me the money, hon," Vanessa whispers. "I can't find my ATM card, I lost it, my wallet, too, I mean I think it was stolen, I have to go to Rome, I'm in trouble, seriously."

"Hey, Mattia," Manuela calls from the reception desk, "there's been a change of plans, I have to ask you a favor, we have to take my sister to Rome." "I can't, Manuela, it's best if I don't go out," Mattia tries to say, but she won't take no for an answer: "There's no traffic, it's only twenty-five miles, now I can introduce you, I'm counting on you, thanks, I knew you wouldn't say no, we'll wait for you here."

"But it's personal," Vanessa protests as she struggles with the zipper of her jacket, which is obviously too light for January. "I'm embarrassed, in front of a stranger." "Mattia's not a stranger!" Manuela pounces. "I like him, you know, I really like him. We might stay together." And what will he think of me—and of you—if he comes, Vanessa wonders. But who the hell cares what the guest at the Bellavista thinks, a secret agent has to be pretty ruthless. Then again, if he's shocked, so much the better. He's too old and too weird for Manuela, and she's diving in too deep. She already has enough problems, she needs stability and security, and this guy's not going to give her either. "Let's hope your friend hurries up," she says, looking nervously at the clock above the reception desk, "it's already been fifteen hours, I don't have much time." "Fifteen hours since what?" Manuela asks, not understanding. But just then someone calls the elevator, the red arrow lights up, and the question remains unanswered.

"Hi," Mattia says, extending his hand to Vanessa. His hair is still wet. He puts on his most convincing smile. If he's angry over the unexpected change in plans, he doesn't show it. He knows how to adapt. Flexibility is a virtue of the strong. But Manuela has lost her flexibility; she hates changing plans now. "Hi," Vanessa says, shaking his hand energetically, as if she's never seen him before in her life. As if she hadn't invited him home only a few days earlier. "I'm sorry to meet you under these circumstances, I'm a little out of it, I don't know how to thank you, it won't take long, I won't ruin your night." Mattia hands his room key to the concierge and goes to get his car in the garage. "Fifteen hours since what?" Manuela asks again as they wait on the street, bathed in the lights of the Bellavista. "Since coitus," Vanessa says. She uses the medical, bureaucratic, police term, as if the neutrality of the word might attenuate the enormity of the deed. If only. Instead it adds to it. She feels something pulsing in an undefined spot on her vulva.

"From what?" Manuela is alarmed. "Didn't you tell me Lapo was busy?" "Who ever heard from him again?" Vanessa grumbles, shrugging her shoulders. "He disappeared—he doesn't answer his phone, I sent him two texts yesterday, but he hasn't texted me back; he didn't even wish me a happy new year." "So you didn't go to the party with him?" Manuela asks. She has the feeling she's missed something. "No, I went with Simone, Biagio, Melissa, you don't know them. It was a madhouse. We lost track of each other at some point." "I'm totally confused," Manuela says. "Me, too," Vanessa says. "What's the fifteen hours about?" Manuela insists. But Mattia's Audi emerges from the garage and pulls into the middle of the road, and they have to hurry to get in so he won't block traffic—Manuela in front, Vanessa and Alessia in the back, the girl clinging to her mother, not wanting to let go for even a second. "Don't be afraid, make yourself comfortable," Mattia says, looking at her in the rearview mirror. "I'm sorry there's no booster seat, but you can sit on my coat, besides, you're a big girl now." "It's okay," Vanessa says, buckling the seat belt, and thinking instantly that if a man knows child safety laws, it means he has a kid himself. And if Mattia has a child, he's not the man for Manuela. Manuela can't get herself mixed up in a situation like hers.

She'd been going out with Youssef for five months when it emerged that he had a wife and three children in Morocco. He said it was what his parents wanted, that it was a loveless marriage, he'd get a divorce if she wanted him to, but Vanessa didn't want to take on that responsibility. In the crinkled photo he'd shown her (he kept it in his wallet, behind his residence permit), his wife, a monumental woman with eyes ringed with kohl, had a kind, good-natured face. His three children—all boys, all between the ages of nine and thirteen, curly haired and relaxed—had sly smiles and looked incredibly like their father. Youssef was ready to repudiate Yasmina and move his children to Italy. But Vanessa, stunned by the disappointment and nearly prostrate with hatred for her rival, discovered she felt a certain solidarity with that fat, maternal woman who was, in a certain sense, a widow, who had raised their children by herself, albeit with the money her husband sent every month. Why should she take her husband away from her? He lived here ten months of the year already. They never spoke of it again.

Youssef had two families and divided himself between two countries, two languages, two women, two lives. He wasn't happy here or there, nor were they. Vanessa wanted to leave him, and every now and then she did, for a while. But she also wanted to have a child with him, which is why she had stopped taking the pill this summer. Youssef is a trustworthy, serious, and generous man. He loves Alessia and she's fond of him, too. He's as good as his word; when he says something, he does it. And she is sorry, really incredibly sorry, for what happened last night. Youssef didn't deserve it. Neither did she.

Manuela looks intently at the road; it's already been swallowed up by the imminent darkness, which is occasionally pierced by headlights. Every now and then she turns to Mattia and smiles, and everything—her new way of doing things, her mysterious need to touch him at every opportunity, the joy that lights up her eyes when she looks at him—makes it clear to Vanessa that her sister really is falling for the guest at the Bellavista.

At the roundabout, Mattia doesn't know which way to go, so he circles it twice. Then Vanessa shakes off her torpor and remembers to direct him toward the Aurelia, toward Rome. The night before, when she'd looked at her watch, it was three a.m. A dark place, far from the streetlights and the music, probably the parking lot because all around her all she could see were cars. Her cheek was pressed against the hood of a car, the cold metal freezing against her face, her deafened ears burning, her mind confused, a bitter taste in her mouth, her insides in turmoil. Someone was fucking her, and that realization had left her dumbfounded, because she couldn't remember leaving the Gas Works and it seemed to her that just a second before she'd been in ecstasy on the dance floor. It was like there was a black hole inside her head. "Hey!" she had yelled. "Hey, what the fuck are you doing?" But she couldn't turn around, all she could see was a hairy arm with a mermaid tattoo.

The first stop is the emergency room at a hospital on the outskirts of Rome. Vanessa gets out, saying she won't be long. Manuela, increasingly bewildered, opens the car door and runs after her—limping without her crutches. The Paris sisters disappear, both of them tottering down the ramp lined with dormant ambulances, their doors closed. There's not a soul in sight; it's like the hospital's abandoned. A stretcher, straps dangling and bars broken, stands forgotten at the entrance. "Who stole your front teeth?" Mattia asks Alessia, who sits petrified in the backseat, clasping her Hello Kitty doll. "No one, they fell out," Alessia whispers, scared. "What?" Mattia feigns surprise. "And the cat didn't come back to bring you a present?" "What cat?" Alessia asks, curious now because she had a cat for real, Aunt Manuela brought it home when she was on leave, a scabby stray she found scratching in the trash cans along the beach. A yellow tabby with round, phosphorescent eyes like golden marbles. Aunt Manuela named her Moon, like Sailor Moon's talking cat, even though she later discovered that she was a he. Manuela couldn't take him with her to the barracks up north, so she had trusted Alessia with him, much to her mother's and grandmother's dismay. But one morning not too long ago, while Alessia was at school, Moon had jumped off the balcony and disappeared.

"Do you know why he didn't come back?" Mattia explains as if revealing a secret. "Because he put on his magic boots, changed shape, and now he's on a mission for the Marquis of Carabas. I am the cat. Open your hand." Alessia perches on the edge of the seat and tentatively stretches her hand toward the big strong man who says he's a cat. Mattia gives her five crisp bills. "One for each tooth," he says. "You have to keep them, though, that way they'll grow back quicker." "Okay," Alessia promises. She always talks with her hand over her mouth to hide the gap in her teeth and her gums, red like slices of meat from the butcher, but the strange man with big blue eyes and sunglasses saw anyway. Still, she doesn't believe he is Moon, the tabby cat that jumped off the balcony, no.

"Do you know Tom Tom?" Mattia asks, turning on the GPS. "They stole ours," Alessia says. "They smashed the window with a rock." "No one ever steals anything from the Marquis of Carabas," Mattia assures her, pointing to the little gray box to the left of the steering wheel. "Just tell it where you want to go, and Tom Tom will take you there. Come sit here." Alessia, docile, climbs over the handbrake and catapults herself next to Aunt Manuela's mysterious friend. A strange man with a good smile that doesn't frighten her. "I want to go find the cat," Alessia says, "I want my teeth back right now." "Okay, let's give it a try," Mattia says, and has her enter the letters G-A-T-T-O—Italian for cat—on the display. It takes Alessia a long time, too long. When Mattia asks her what grade she's in, she murmurs that she's in second, but she's behind. Her teacher says she's slow, attention deficit disorder. It saddens Mattia how easily they can undermine a child's self-esteem. The conformist cruelty of adults. A woman's voice, metallic yet sensual, suggests they turn left. There's clearly a Via Gatto—perhaps after Alfonso Gatto, a poet in school anthologies, whom Mattia had always liked because of his feline name. "Come drive," he says, letting her sit between his knees and placing her hands on the wheel. Alessia smells of Play-Doh and Johnson's baby shampoo, a scent that stabs him in an undefined spot in his chest, near his heart.

He has to take two deep breaths to regain control of himself, emptying his lungs like a pregnant mother in Lamaze class. Then he places his hands, which are so much bigger, on top of hers, and removes the brake. The car moves through the deserted hospital parking lot, up and down the ramps, around the flower beds, while the woman's voice delivers increasingly abstruse, imperious, and pointless directions on how to arrive at the ineffable Cat. When Vanessa and Manuela reappear, they find the Audi making slow circles around the fountain, Alessia mounted between Mattia's arms and legs, both of them laughing as if they've known each other for ages and have always been great friends. The Paris sisters aren't laughing at all. "We have to go somewhere else, we couldn't find it here," Manuela says vaguely as Vanessa hides in the backseat. Mattia notes that her hands are still shaking but that her pupils are less dilated. Whatever chemical substance she took, the effect is wearing off. Manuela has Alessia punch the name of their destination into the Tom Tom, then nestles her in her mother's arms. They pull onto the highway and drive without talking, guided by the invisible woman's metallic voice. Alessia leans forward on the seat, and every now and then Mattia turns and winks at her. He's good with children, so, Vanessa deduces, he's an active and engaged father.

Manuela doesn't notice, though. She's still troubled. Vanessa asked the triage nurses for the morning-after pill. And they rudely invited her to look elsewhere, because the doctors here are all conscientious objectors and they never order it. "But weren't you on the pill, Vanessa?" Manuela asked, as she left the emergency room as red-faced and ashamed as a thief, hoping that those women, intent on watching TV in the tiny glass booth, hadn't recognized her from the evening news. "I'm trying to have a child with Youssef," Vanessa had replied, lengthening her stride. "But he's married to someone else! You're crazy, do you want to start all over again?" "What do you know about these things!" Vanessa had hissed cruelly. "You and your gun and your platoon and your gold stripes. But I'm different, I feel more feminine when I'm pregnant, breastfeeding makes me happier than anything, better than any orgasm, I want to have at least five children, I've already waited too long." "Excuse me, but why are you worried?" Manuela followed after her, hobbling on her lame leg. "You're not even ovulating, you had your period last week. You told me so yourself. In the valley of the tombs, when I left you with Lapo." "Well, I was bullshitting you." "But why?" Manuela had exclaimed. "Because you're like a cop about that kind of thing, I didn't want you to think less of me," Vanessa had said without turning around.

The GPS obediently directs them to another hospital, perched on a hill just off the highway. An ugly white barrack of a building, twelve stories tall. Hundreds of illuminated windows punctuate the night. Vanessa wants to go alone this time and Manuela doesn't insist. It's all so horrible. Mattia gets out to stretch his legs. They stroll with Alessia along the tree-lined avenue that leads to the building for the terminally ill. They take her hands, Mattia her right and Manuela her left. Mattia tells her a story that sounds like a manga version of "Puss in Boots," with an energy and conviction Manuela would never have thought him capable of. She's sorry to have involved him in this mess, and at the same time she feels that on this miserable evening, spent navigating between exit ramps and hospitals, she has discovered a different and better man. A man to whom she feels bound by something more than just sexual attraction, by something that resembles tenderness, the kind of affection that's born from familiarity. And to think that only a week ago, she didn't even know he existed.

Vanessa reappears quickly. Too quickly. "Nada," she whispers, "conscientious objectors here, too. What time is it?" "Twenty to eight," Mattia says. "Don't hate me, but they suggested I try at Terzo Miglio," Vanessa says to him. "Why should I hate you?" Mattia says with surprise as he deactivates the alarm. The headlights blink. "It's kind of a weird way to spend the first day of the year, but we're having fun, right?" Alessia nods. "Do you know he's the Cat of the Marquis of Carabas?" she confides to her mother in a whisper. "But no one knows, he travels incognito because he has to deliver a message." "What message?" Vanessa asks distractedly. She can't help but think that while they travel in comfort in Mattia's Audi, or rather Avis of Fiumicino's Audi, the sperm of the strangers she met at the old Gas Works are traveling in comfort in her vagina, from whence the lavender douche may not have evicted them. She doesn't even remember who or how many they were. Two for sure, because after the one with the mermaid there was another, in a green bomber jacket, who was practically dancing even inside of her, crooning *fuoco nel fuoco*— fire in the fire—and was so high he didn't even realize he'd come. And there could have been a third, maybe, because she remembers a different rhythm, as painful as flesh tearing, and she can hear her own voice saying ouch, go slow, you're hurting me, but her voice doesn't sound worried in the least, in fact it's cheerful, exhilarated almost. Then she danced some more, and took something—or maybe that was earlier—the fact is, she must have fainted, or fallen asleep, anyway time passed because the next thing she remembered, it was already morning. She was vomiting in a Porta-Potty, the light drilling into her brain. There was no one around now, on the floor only clumps of toilet paper, empty cans, and bottles. A strange, muffled yet deafening silence; her ears were buzzing as if a crazed bumblebee were whirling around inside. A security guard asked her if something was wrong and she said no, and he said, well, you're either peeing blood or you need a tampon, and she looked between her legs and burst out laughing because in that instant the situation seemed comical to her, and she kept on laughing hysterically as she wandered about the huge, empty parking lot searching for her car, and she laughed as she drove, unable to stop the convulsive tremors that shook her like an electric current sizzling in her veins. She nearly crashed getting onto the highway, and in fact she did manage to swipe the guardrail with the side of her Yaris, leaving a headlight on the asphalt. So then she parked in the turnout of a gas station and slept until she felt sober enough to get on the road again. She didn't want Manuela to suspect any of this. She would have hated her. And her little sister's opinion mattered to her, more than anything. I just wanted to have fun. I was too trusting. I'm not wary enough of people.

They stopped giving it out at the Terzo Miglio when the new medical director arrived. They try all the hospitals in the area, and when Vanessa gets back in the car after the sixth one, she curls up in a corner, leans her head against the window, and starts to cry—not for herself or for the pill they won't give her or for the terrifying prospect of being pregnant after such a night, but for Youssef. Because she ruined everything, and now it seems that she has lost the only certainty and the only fixed point in her life: him. She sniffles softly, but Alessia is dozing serenely and doesn't notice.

Rome is just starting to rouse itself from its holiday torpor; there are just a few cars on the street and the occasional bus, empty of passengers. On the asphalt a mire of broken glass, champagne corks, unexploded firecracker, rocket, and paper bomb cartridges. Mattia doesn't know the city well and is having trouble getting his bearings: he diligently obeys the GPS, slowing at times to look at a cupola, an obelisk, an equestrian statue. They cross the city from north to south, and then back again. They sweep past aqueducts, palaces, churches, fountains, restaurants, bars, arches, metro stations, temples, long straight streets lined with hundreds, thousands of shops, shutters lowered. He would like to live in Rome. No one notices you here. Everyone is anonymous, everyone is free.

They cross a bridge in reinforced concrete and then, in the opposite direction, a monumental Fascist-looking bridge in marble, on which a graffiti writer has sprayed a sentimental slogan in black. As he waits for the light to turn green, Mattia has time to make it out: HE WHO SOWS SEEDS IN THE WIND WILL MAKE THE SKY BLOSSOM. He reads it aloud, as if reciting it to Manuela. But she says it's not true. To make a seed bloom, you have to water it, care for it, you have to bend your back and hoe the soil, things don't take root without effort. Vanessa knows her sister is wrong. It's an idealistic vision of nature, and of human existence. A fertilized egg doesn't need anyone's effort to take root. It simply blooms. She wouldn't dream of saying so, though. She just prays it doesn't happen.

The hospital she remembered being behind Piazza del Popolo— they sewed up her knee in the ER after she fell during a school trip when she was a girl—no longer exists. It's been shut down. When she asks for the pill in the other hospital in the historic center, behind Saint Peter's, they look at her as if she were a murderer. Each time, Vanessa comes back more and more quickly; after a while it only takes a few minutes. And each time she gets back in the car, she slams the door with less force. "Don't get the wrong impression," Manuela says between hospitals, "she's not promiscuous, she's just too impulsive." "I think very highly of your sister," Mattia replies. "She's full of joy."

They even ask at the all-night pharmacy behind the train station, but the pharmacist doesn't understand what Vanessa is talking about—or he pretends not to. Mattia pulls over to the right, in front of some potbellied planters, awaiting instructions. It's nine in the evening. Dark porticoes ring the piazza. Cars circle a fountain: jets of water rise high and then fall, titillating the nipples of naked bronze nymphs. It seems to Mattia an unusually erotic monument in a Catholic city like Rome, and he would like to know the name of the artist who dared conceive of and then place it right there, in plain sight, on a hill dominating the entire historic center. His car headlights illuminate the bare, concave brick façade of a building swallowed by the gloom. Embedded between imposing ruins, it seems ancient. Roman, surely. Baths, maybe. Without saying a word, Manuela opens the car door and gets out.

"Where's she going?" Mattia asks. "How do I know," Vanessa says. "I'm sorry I dragged her into this, she's different, she'd never fuck up, she's pure, I don't know if I'm making sense. She's either in or out, she doesn't do things behind your back, she doesn't know what betrayal is." Mattia has already gone after her. The door to the church is open. Someone is playing the organ in the back. Mass is over, a small group of faithful, numb from the cold interior, emerge into the even colder January air. Mattia enters and finds himself in a circular vestibule that feels like the entrance to a museum. Dark paintings hang on the walls: Christ crucified and Christ risen, with a gardener's hat and a spade in his hand, and some tombs. Painters, the inscriptions say, but their names—Salvator Rosa, Carlo Maratta—don't mean anything to him. He walks under the big arch that leads to the nave. In a niche above him looms a giant sculpture; he wears the habit and the inconsolable sadness of a monk. To the right and left, like guardians, marble angels hold stoups for holy water. They're looking in opposite directions: one at those who enter, the other at those who exit. The welcoming angel looks in his direction, but doesn't see him. His eyes seem to open inwardly, contemplating a secret happiness. His wings are long and curved, like the volute of a harp. He is very beautiful.

Mattia is astounded by the immensity of the space. A few candle stubs still burn under the altars, but the light is on only in the presbytery, where it illuminates a keyboard. A bald priest in a white chasuble tries out the score, singing in a powerful baritone. Mattia can only make out the invocation, which is being repeated continuously: Ave Maria. He has lost sight of Manuela. But her footsteps echo in the silence, in time to the music. She drags her bad leg, and the sound of that limping wounds him.

The church is solemn, and its massive dimensions give rise to a vague anxiety. They banish warmth and erase all intimacy. Everything is theater. Minuscule human figures drift in the gloom among the colossal granite columns that support the vault, like crickets in the grass. One arm of the nave is taken up by the monument to Armando Diaz, Marshal of Italy, Duke of Victory. Mattia joins Manuela at the foot of the apse. Her hands rest on the balustrade that prevents access to the presbytery;

she is staring at the small painting on the main altar. Much older than those on the other altars, more naïve, friendlier. Mattia thinks it looks Venetian. Manuela mumbles softly. "And you, Mother of God, purer than snow," he can make out. "You who know every last breath and every sacrifice of your Alpini . . ." "Come on, we have to go," he urges, without realizing he's interrupting her, "your sister needs help, we shouldn't waste time." "This is where my funeral was supposed to be," Manuela says.

"I'm sorry," Mattia says, "I didn't know." "It was here. This basilica is called Santa Maria degli Angeli e dei Martiri, Saint Mary of the Angels and Martyrs. They always hold them here, I don't know why. Maybe because it's so big. I've seen lots of them on TV. They put the coffin on a red carpet, dress cap on top. At the end, the trumpet calls for silence, and they recite the prayer. The Alpino prayer closes with: bless and smile upon our battalions and our troops, amen. Then the priest blesses the remains with holy water and swings the incense, which means that it's all over. For us, this is the saddest place on earth. This place means death. Our Elysian Fields. I won't meet them on a journey to the other-world; I could meet them in my dreams, only I don't know how to dream. Do you remember the *Odyssey*? When Odysseus meets the shade of Achilles in the Elysian Fields and tries to console him, telling him he's a great hero, the most powerful warrior that ever lived, that he was a god in life and is now the king of the dead so there's no need to grieve over his death? And Achilles replies, I'd rather be the lowest servant of a peasant on earth than the king of this dead world."

Mattia shudders. It's freezing in the church, and their shadows are like ghosts on the dark floor. "I don't believe in another life," Manuela says. "This is the only life we have, it's this certainty that makes the time we have worthwhile. We can't waste it. We know we have to die. Giving one's death is like giving one's life. But if your death doesn't contribute to life, then your life is truly lost. I can't stand it. I wasn't here, I couldn't come, I was in the hospital. I couldn't even say goodbye to them." She breaks off suddenly and turns away. She catches a glimpse of the Virgin's red dress in the painting. That and a symphony of angels. So many angels. She dries her tears on her jacket sleeve. This is the first time she has been able to cry.

Mattia leaves her to her belated funeral. Manuela always uses the plural. We, we, we. He, on the other hand, knows only the first person singular now. They can never speak the same language. He reascends the nave, stepping on a line that cuts diagonally across the floor, inscribed with the constellations of the zodiac. It's a meridian line. It used to mark the passing of time for Rome. He wonders if it also marks the end of time, which is ritually celebrated here. Whenever he saw the ceremonies, the uniforms and flags, the false sorrow of the powerful and the infinite sorrow of the soldiers' relatives, he would change the channel. The farewell angel greets him with the same contemplative look as his companion. But this one isn't baroque, it's a modern imitation. Art pays homage to those who enter, but not to those who leave; here the dead count more than the living. This church is the cemetery of all of Italy's good intentions.

He slowly makes his way to the car. He is extraneous to Manuela's most authentic life, as she is to his. Yet he would have wept over her friends with her, and over her entire past. The lowest servant of a peasant on earth ... The surprising wisdom of Achilles. He never would have imagined that Sergeant Paris loved Homer. Prejudices.

Vanessa, looking glum, taps on the window. "Where do you want us to go?" he asks. "Home," Vanessa orders. Mattia says she shouldn't give up, they can keep looking, there are at least three hospitals they haven't tried yet. And if that doesn't work, he will take her to Campania or Tuscany, things are different there. Vanessa realizes that this stranger is worried about her, and wants to help her. Even though he's old and probably married, he is kind, and he seems to really care for Manuela. "No," Vanessa says, "enough. I don't want to be told no again, or to be asked why I'm asking. I'm a human being, I have my dignity, it's clear this was how it was supposed to go, it must be a sign, I'm converting, I don't know if I told you." She breaks off and bites her lip. Manuela wouldn't want her to tell Mattia her theories about the name of God and the Jehovah's Witnesses, it's better if she keeps quiet. "Converting to what?" Mattia asks. "I don't know, and anyway, I may have changed my mind already, I'm really fickle. And I'm about to faint with hunger," she says, changing the subject. "I haven't eaten for twenty-four hours." So when Manuela gets back in the car he resets the GPS for Ladispoli and at ten he stops the car in front of the Paris home.

"Come on up," Vanessa invites Mattia. "I'll fix something; I'm a lousy cook, but I don't want you eating crackers from the minibar all alone in your hotel room." Mattia objects; it doesn't seem right, he doesn't want to invade their home. But Vanessa insists: the restaurant at the Bellavista is already closed, it's her fault that he and Manuela couldn't go out to dinner together. Manuela expects Mattia to hesitate, or invent an excuse. He's always so elusive. Instead he smiles and accepts. He gracefully guides the car into the hotel garage, picks up Alessia, who is still sleeping, in his arms, and makes his way up the stairs after the Paris sisters.

He places Alessia on the bed and helps Manuela untie her shoes. They slip off her dress. Candy pink, with sequins, as if she were going to a party. Mattia lifts the covers and Manuela tucks her in. Alessia's so tired she doesn't even react, but lets them handle her as if she were a doll. "Where's her father?" Mattia asks. "She doesn't have one," Manuela says. "Vanessa never wanted to say who it is. And she's never wanted to live with another man because she doesn't want to impose one on her." "And how is she?" Mattia whispers. "I mean, how has it been, growing up without a father?" "Fine, she did without," Manuela replies, gently closing the door. "Maybe because she never had one," Mattia says. "She doesn't know she's missing something." Manuela doesn't want to ask herself why he wanted to know.

While Vanessa improvises in the kitchen, rustling up some spaghetti with garlic, olive oil, and pepperoncino, Manuela and Mattia go out on the balcony and look at the closed windows of the Bellavista. They seem small and insignificant from this side of the street. "Why did you tell Alessia that story about the Marquis of Carabas, that you're in disguise and have to deliver a message?" she asks him. "Because you should never lie to children," Mattia says, "it's hard for them to tell the difference between truth and lies, and we need to help them figure it out." "And what about adults?" Manuela asks. "I've never told you a lie, Manuela," Mattia says, "I just can't tell you the whole truth. It's different."

They eat in the living room, speaking softly because Alessia and Grandma are sleeping. Mattia tells them that he has invited Alessia to the Marquis of Carabas's castle—he means the Palo Castle. Obviously she accepted enthusiastically. They have to come, too. "It's private, you know," Manuela says. "The owners still live there, they only open it for receptions, weddings, fashion shows." "I guess I'll have to rent it, then," Mattia says, disappointed. "I already promised." "Why are you doing this for her?" Vanessa asks. "You don't owe us anything." "I'm doing it for myself, not for her," Mattia says. An unpleasant pulsing in the nape of her neck reminds Manuela that it's time for her drops. As soon as they're alone, Mattia asks Vanessa what day of her cycle it was last night. She doesn't remember and has to get her planner and count the days on her fingers. "The eleventh," she concludes. And her previous cycle, how many days was it? Thirty-one. And the one before? Thirty-two. "You're not pregnant," Mattia says calmly, but with conviction. "Don't worry about it anymore."

"What are you, a fortune-teller? Or a doctor?" Vanessa whispers. "The latter," he says. "Trust me." "Did you tell Manuela?" she asks. Her cat eyes scrutinize him so intently that he has to tell the truth. "No. She's had plenty of doctors, they've tormented her more than enough. And besides, I can't help her. I don't know how to heal her wounds."

"I'm almost out of my drops," Manuela interrupts them, worried. She shakes the little bottle, which is nearly empty. "I don't know how much longer they'll last. I need a prescription. Your father's a surgeon," she says to Mattia, "can't you ask him to write me one?" "No." Mattia reacts as if what she proposed were unthinkable. "Absolutely not." "Come on, would it really be such a big deal?" Manuela insists. "My father is dead," Mattia says without looking at her.

They smoke the last cigarette of the day out on the balcony, the lights of the Bellavista sign bouncing in the darkness. The B is burning out and blinks intermittently, dazzling them with blue, then enveloping them in darkness. Mattia has met nearly all the Paris women now, whereas Manuela knows nothing about his family, and she doesn't believe that his father is dead. When Mattia talked about him before, it didn't sound like he was dead. He would have been more compassionate. But not knowing where a person comes from, what he has lived through, what he has left behind, takes away substance, depth, importance. It's like being with a photograph. "Come to bed with me," Mattia says, staring at the dark square of his room across the way.

At four, Manuela flails about in her sleep, screaming. She lashes out, arches her back, protects her face with her arms. Mattia shakes her by the shoulder and gets a fist in the face. "Hey, hey, you're home, you're with me." Manuela wakes up and opens her eyes. She can't remember what she was dreaming about. She's drenched in sweat. She can't feel her leg anymore. There's a nail boring into the nape of her neck. She smells fire and blood. There's no basin under the bed at the Bellavista. She vomits everything she has inside her onto the rug, until a bitter wave of bile rises from her esophagus. It's like before, like always. She doesn't have the strength to get out of bed and clean it. She falls back on the pillow. She can't decide what's worse: the pain or the humiliation. Mattia rests his ear on her racing heart. It's like listening to a herd of bison galloping, it makes her lungs shake, her bones creak. That wild roar frightens him a little, but it also makes him sad; the pain is almost physical. "It's never going to end," Manuela murmurs. A tear of frustration and anger gathers on her eyelashes and trickles along her temples. She can't fall back to sleep.

Mattia wads up the rug and throws it in the bathtub. "I'm sorry," she says. She's ashamed. She feels naked. It's even worse than showing him her scar. He lends her a dry T-shirt and strokes her hair silently. They lie there, next to each other under the comforter, fingers interlaced, eyes wide open in the dark. He forces himself to stay awake. If he could, he'd tell her everything. It wouldn't do any good, but knowing that he understands might help. Instead, every now and then, when she moves an arm or shakes, which tells him she's still awake, he just says a word or two to let her know he's awake, too, and won't leave her. Ordinary words, but in the absolute silence of the night, broken only by the dripping of the air-conditioning pipes, they seem to glide solemnly down from above.

At dawn they go down to the beach for a walk, her horrific cries still ringing in his ears. They're sitting on the cement wall at the Tahiti when the sun appears behind the apartment buildings and projects a ray of white light on the sand. "The psychologist says I have to talk about it," she whispers, "but I don't know what I'm supposed to say. I never remember my dreams. And I can't talk about what I feel. They taught us that a soldier keeps his feelings inside, and I learned well, because I know it's important." "But we don't talk just with words," Mattia says. "We talk with our eyes, our hands, our bodies. I'm listening to you, Manuela."

15

LIVE

The first article stored on Traian's pen drive is from June 9, the day after the attack. The reconstruction of facts is perfunctory and imprecise; even the place-names are wrong. But the reporter describes the region well, he's clearly been there. Manuela may have met him, maybe even escorted him on a reconnaissance mission. But his name means nothing to her. She's sorry it's not Daria Cormon. The blond reporter was unlucky. Had it happened while she was visiting Bala Bayak, she could have sold her piece to the national papers, it could have been her big break. She deserved it, she'd been touring battlefields for years; but she really did bring the soldiers good luck: nothing ever happened when she was around, and her good fortune, which made her famous among the troops, condemned her to anonymity.

The Italian soldiers—the article states—were at Qal'a-i-Shakhrak for the opening of a school for girls. This was to be the fifth school either rebuilt or reopened during the Tenth Alpini Regiment's mission in Afghanistan. A total of fifty-five schools had been reopened since 2005, when Italy assumed command of the Provincial Reconstruction Team in Herat, but the PRT in Farah had encountered greater difficulties. The village, a cluster of dilapidated mud houses, topped by an equally dilapidated minaret, is located in western Afghanistan, on the edge of the area under Italian control: even though severe fighting continued elsewhere, a sort of truce had prevailed in Farah; unfortunately the situation deteriorated just as the Italians arrived to replace the U.S. Marines. Groups of insurgents, fleeing the fighting or flushed out over the course of the previous winter, had taken refuge in the barren hills that form the outer limit of the province, which runs parallel to the Iran border, or in the mountains and valleys that separate Farah from Helmand. With the help of U.S. aviation and intelligence, group after group had been arrested, at times one by one, in house-to-house searches. The Italians had established good relations with the village chiefs, and the district no longer seemed any more dangerous than the rest of the country. There had been no particular reports or warnings.

It was a joyous occasion, and marked an important success in the reconstruction of a province devastated by thirty years of war. The girls' school had already burned down three times. The Italian mission commanders and the highest Afghani civil authorities in Farah were expected to attend. But at the time of the explosion, only the Alpini EOD team had arrived, to search the area in front of the building for explosives and to signal any anomalies, along with a close protection team. The Alpini may have realized it was a trap and tried to intervene. The fact is that the attackers didn't await the arrival of the Afghani authorities; the explosion occurred at 8:35 local time. It was one of the bloodiest sacrifices since the start of the mission. There were three casualties, all from Ninth Company. Lieutenant Nicola Russo of Barletta, thirty-three years old, married with one daughter, and Corporal-Major Diego Jodice of Marcianise, twenty-six years old, unmarried, were within the immediate blast radius of the explosion and were killed instantly. Corporal Lorenzo Zandonà of Mel, twenty-one years old, who suffered spinal injuries and grave internal hemorrhaging, died while being airlifted to the hospital in Farah. All three were due to return to Italy within days. Sergeant Manuela Paris of Ladispoli, twenty-seven years old, who was hit by shrapnel and suffered serious head injuries, is in critical condition. Three Afghani civilians were also killed.

The June 10 article didn't add much to the initial reconstruction of facts, but it did provide further information on the victims. It noted that First Lieutenant Russo was a veteran, on his third mission in Afghanistan, and that Corporal-Major Jodice had also been previously deployed overseas. He was to be married in August. The article was accompanied by two photos: Russo, smiling affectionately at the Afghani baby girl he held in his arms, and Lorenzo and Diego in front of their Lince. Tan, relaxed, sunglasses perched on their helmets, they gaze defiantly at

Manuela from the computer monitor and seem to be saying: we've slogged through one hundred and sixty-seven days, epigone, we're at minus thirteen—then we're going home.

Only a few months have passed since Manuela took the photos that Zandonà's parents distributed to the newspapers—for she was the one who immortalized her friends in front of the Lince. They both have beards, which they didn't have when they arrived at Bala Bayak. Lorenzo's is sparse and reluctant, Diego's bushy and bristly. They'd all let them grow during their tour of duty until, little by little, they ended up looking like Afghanis—dusty, listless, slow, fatalistic. It was only at the end that their beards were so long and unkempt. And yet Lorenzo and Diego already seem infinitely younger than she is. Kids.

Manuela wants to read all the articles Traian has downloaded for her. As if the secret of the divergence that saved her might be hidden somewhere in there, along with the message that Vanessa, or the Jehovah's Witnesses' happy God, says was given to her. But at two Alessia comes knocking on the door and tells her that the man from the Bellavista rang the doorbell and is asking for her. "I was expecting you for lunch," Mattia says, "did you forget about me?" His voice is distorted, as if coming from far away. "I was in Afghanistan," she says. "Don't you want to come back to Ladispoli, to me?" His playful tone doesn't mask his worry that she has changed her mind and doesn't want to see him anymore. "To you, who?" she asks bitterly. "I don't even know who you are. You're Mr. No One. All I know is the emptiness that envelops you." "So you're not coming?" "Not now."

The articles that appeared on June 11 offer a different reconstruction of events. It was neither a radio-controlled car bomb nor an IED. The body of one of the Afghani civilians, a male, or rather the stump of his body that was left, showed trauma consistent with a SBBIED, or suicide body-borne IED, in other words, a suicide bomber with an explosive vest. The device contained no electronic components, which could be rendered ineffective by the soldiers' jammers, and was probably activated by a switch or a pressure mechanism. It contained circa ten kilos of C4 explosive. The device was rendered more lethal by six Soviet-manufactured hand grenades and up to a thousand pieces of shrapnel. The explosion was devastating. The plastic explosive aside—which, in any case, is readily available—all the materials needed to construct the vest (wires, batteries, switches) are for sale in any market.

Sergeant Paris, who underwent surgery during the night at the American military hospital in Farah, is in an induced coma. The doctors still will not release a prognosis or make predictions about what her condition will be, if she does survive; nor do they know if she has suffered permanent brain damage.

Lorenzo's father, Piero Zandonà, granted a disconsolate interview to a local paper, in which he said he was proud of his son, but didn't understand why the government wouldn't bring our boys home. The Twin Towers fell nearly ten years ago, along with the Taliban, but the terrorists are still multiplying like rats, practically every Afghani is a terrorist now, which means that maybe no one is. In fact, the word has fallen out of favor, and now even our allies refer to the enemy in a different way: insurgents, rebels. But, just like the word itself, an insurgent is someone who rises up, who protests, who rebels against his government or an invader. So what are the Italians doing? Fighting against people who, in the name of liberty, are rebelling against a corrupt and slavish government? But didn't the Italians go to Afghanistan on a peace mission in the name of liberty? And if they can't make peace there, or if that peace isn't to the liking of the people on whom they want to impose it, they can't make war either, because our constitution repudiates war. Other soldiers die with guns in their hands, but Italian soldiers are being blown up like sheep by land mines. They say it's a good sign, that attacks with IEDs or suicide bombs merely reveal the impotence of the rebels, who have lost all offensive capabilities. But he doesn't understand how it's a good sign when his son was butchered in front of a girls' school. For what? Would Afghani girls ever really have gone to that school? His son is dead, and no one can bring him back, but Piero Zandonà demands to know the truth about what happened. How is it possible that a TNT-wearing kamikaze managed to slip into a high-risk situation, a ceremony at which strict security measures were supposedly in place? Did someone betray them?

The remains of the dead have arrived in Italy. The state funeral will be held tomorrow, in the church of Santa Maria degli Angeli in Rome.

The third and final article to appear in the national press, three days after the attack, all text, no photo, just added a bit of color, riling up the readers with a few sentences stolen from the Marcianise parish priest who was supposed to marry Diego and Imma, Russo's young widow, and the mayor of Mel, who proclaimed mourning citywide in honor of Lorenzo's sacrifice. The article also stated that Sergeant Paris was still in an induced coma at the Farah hospital. The mangled body of the Qal'a-i-Shakhrak suicide bomber had not been identified. The subsequent articles, scattered in local papers or odd online publications, didn't add anything new, they simply repeated ad infinitum the little information that was already known. By July 25 the June attempt in front of the girls' school was already a statistic. The bloodiest summer since the beginning of the mission in Afghanistan.

Manuela calls Captain Paggiarin. She's never called him before, but over the past few months, he has let her know he's there for her. In the way a man who is emotionally stunted can: some awkward phone calls, three or four visits to the military hospital, one with Colonel Minotto, get-well cards, even a bouquet of roses when they transferred her from the Celio military hospital to Turin so she could begin her rehab. Even though he's only thirty-eight, just a few years older than she is, he takes pleasure in adopting a paternal attitude with his subordinates. Manuela pins her hopes on the Skinny Buddha's political farsightedness and his relations with intelligence.

The captain is on vacation with his wife in the Dolomites, but he skillfully conceals his astonishment at hearing from her. "I need to speak with you." Manuela is agitated. "May I come see you? It's important. If I take the train early tomorrow morning I can be there by three, I won't waste your time, I'll only take ten minutes. Please."

"Manuela, dear," says Paggiarin, disconcerted—it's the first time he's ever called her by her first name—"has something happened?" "I have to ask you something, but I'd like to do it in person." "I'm not sure that's a good idea," Paggiarin replies. "You need to rest instead of tiring yourself traveling the length of Italy by train, and I'm here with my family—as you probably know, I deploy in two weeks, we both have important things to do, don't you think? May I ask what it's about?"

"I didn't find anything in the newspapers," Manuela resigns herself to saying. "The story vanished right away. The attorney's office hasn't been in touch again. But the investigation must have continued, in Qal'a-i-

Shakhrak. The *shahid*—what did the Italian and Afghani military police tell you, did they find out who he was?" Paggiarin hesitates. Manuela can hear his breath quicken. Maybe he's thinking. This isn't by the book. Paggiarin is so strict, so careful to follow procedures.

"No one came forward to identify the body, or what was left of it," he finally explains. "They didn't even ask for it to be returned. He might have been a foreigner, or from another province. And as you well know, they're not in the habit of distributing pictures of martyrs there. They don't have the sophisticated investigational tools we do for identifying the subject. They did an autopsy, took photographs, and drafted a very detailed report. There wasn't much more they could do. But our analysts are still working on it." "So you don't know his name?" Manuela murmurs.

"Only that he was quite young," Paggiarin says, "thirteen at most, maybe even younger. Then again, he's not the first kid chosen to become a *shahid*. Even eleven- and twelve-year-olds have been recruited: a kid arouses less suspicion. He was probably an orphan."

"Why wasn't I told this before?" Manuela scolds him. "Why didn't you say anything when you came to see me in the hospital?" "We were all so devastated to learn how young the suicide bomber was," Paggiarin sighs. "I took it personally, it was an added burden for all of us. The Ninth Company officers who were on duty at Bala Bayak in June know, which is why I considered it appropriate to inform you now. But this news is not public. Do you understand?" "I had the right to know," Manuela protests. The Skinny Buddha does not reply. He lets her vent, and then accepts her silence. He really is a wise man. So Manuela thanks him, apologizes for having bothered him, hopes she hasn't said anything dumb, wishes him a happy new year. "I know I've been a bother."

"Take care, Paris," Paggiarin says encouragingly, forcing himself to sound warm. "Think about getting back on your feet. I hope to see you in Marcianise. Life moves on. It will be a day of resurrection for all of us."

Traian plays defense. Taller than the other kids his age, lean and lanky, he heads the ball well and anticipates passes. Manuela, clinging to the fence, encourages him, clapping every time her brother manages to stop the opposing team from scoring. And every time, Traian gives her the victory sign with his right hand, as if to say he's happy she approves, that it really matters to him. She's his secret coach, the person he really plays for: he wants to win the trophy for her. Manuela didn't ask Mattia to go with her to the JV tournament finals. She just explained that someone in the family has to watch over Traian, and she's the only one who can, obviously. Mattia didn't need to think about it even for a second. He doesn't want to waste any opportunity to be with her. They have such little time. "I don't understand a thing about soccer," he said, "but I'd even go to a curling match with you, Manuela Paris."

Mattia gazes distractedly at the kids scurrying across the dirt, dark and heavy with rain, careful merely to lean away when mud threatens to splash his clothes. After the game he intends to take Manuela to Rome, to the Hilton Pergola, the restaurant with the most stars in the entire city, so he's all dressed up for a romantic evening. He hadn't planned on going with her to a soccer field in Ladispoli's industrial park, shadowed by abandoned warehouses and a junkyard whose crushed cars are stacked behind the fence. For him there's nothing sadder than the sight of those boys, their bare legs covered with scratches, bruises, and scabs, muddy shorts and cleats, happy and absorbed under a low sky while a gloomy bank of clouds rolls in from the sea. The showy sunglasses he insists on wearing filter the light, accentuating contrasts and tinting everything an alarming lead color. Every now and then he clasps Manuela's waist and draws her toward him, as if he'd like to kiss her. She quickly brushes him away. She doesn't want Traian to suspect anything. He's only twelve, and when you're twelve, your sister is as asexual and innocent as the Virgin Mary.

The Real Ladis team, in red-and-blue striped shirts, faces Torvaianica, or TV, in green. The only spectators along the edge of the field are the players' parents and siblings, but they're all absorbed in the game as if their honor, instead of just a provincial JV tournament, were at stake. When the referee whistles for a penalty or allows a throw-in, a stream of curses and insults that could flay an ox comes from the sidelines. An African kid who plays forward for TV gets the worst of it, but the full-back for Real Ladis, with his Bolivian face and leather-colored skin, also draws elaborate insults. Monkey, bongo bongo, Congo, Zulu for the first; dried prune, cokehead, and pussy puma are among the more refined for the second. But the referee, bald, potbellied, with a vicious, sarcastic smile, won't be intimidated. At the third boo he stops the play, holds the ball, and yells to the spectators that the next time he hears an insult with racist undertones he'll call the game. An overweight mad-man near Manuela hisses "fucking faggot."

The referee whistles and hands out yellow cards; after the home team pulled ahead in the first half thanks to a goal on a questionable offside, the game got nasty. Those skinny kids hammer like blacksmiths. "There's something I don't get," Mattia says, watching as lanky Traian lets TV's number 10, an agile dwarf, dribble around him. "If he's your brother why doesn't he live with you?" "He's Teodora's son," Manuela says without turning around, "my father's wife. I was hoping he would name him Vittorio, after my grandfather. He was his only male grand-child, my grandfather waited for years for him, he'd lost hope, and so he was terribly offended, it really upset him." "But Traian's a nice name, imperial," Mattia comments. "It's a shame people are so ignorant," Ma-nuela says, "they don't know their history. To them it's a Romanian name." A car parks at the end of the street. A woman gets out, a mother, she's late, and she clatters breathlessly on her heels toward the soccer field. Manuela stretches her neck, but it's not Teodora.

Play is interrupted. A buzz rises from the field, the excited chirping of children's voices: a player is on the ground, howling in pain, the ref is surrounded by green shirts, his bald head sticking out like a melon in a field. A distinguished-looking man with plastic-frame glasses, clinging to the fence a few steps away from Mattia, curses and shouts. "Send him off, send him off!" The player on the ground is TV's number 10. "Get up," Traian says, pulling on his wrist, "he didn't blow the whistle, it's not a foul." Manuela has missed something. "He didn't even touch him," Mattia whispers to her. "He dived, he's faking it."

The TV parents call for a penalty and for Traian to be sent off. "That son of a bitch flattened him, he was going to score!" The referee tries to shake off the screaming kids and resume play. But it's too late, the field is in turmoil, a brawl has broken out, soon it's spreading from one group to the next, infecting coaches, ball boys, bench warmers, managers. Every-one's shouting, insulting each other, shoving. Manuela can pick out words like *gypsy, thief, bastard.* Number 10 writhes in the mud, whining that that son of a bitch whacked his legs. His teammates surround Traian, one of them grabs his shirt, another pulls on his shorts. "It was a foul, you fucking Romanian, and you know it," the African forward yells. Traian shakes him off, shouting "dirty nigger," and at that point the TV goalie, a small kid with blond curls and a goody-two-shoes look, spits in his face. Traian springs like a leopard, jumps on his throat, and punches him in the stomach before the others can stop him. The goalie crumbles as if he'd been gunned down.

The distinguished-looking guy with the plastic-frame glasses is the goalie's father. He darts to the gate, opens it, and hurls himself onto the field. Other parents rush in, some to break up the fight, some to defend their kids, and fists begin to fly. The goalie's father chases Traian all over the field, grabbing the coach's umbrella as he runs by the bench, and when he catches up with the boy, in an unexpected feat of athletic prowess, he jabs Traian's sternum threateningly with the tip as the referee whistles; the TV trainer tries to stop him, the Bolivian kid scuffles with the faker, and the lifeless goalie is trampled by his teammates. Traian fends off the goalie's father's umbrella as he looks around for a weapon; in a flash he grabs a bottle of Gatorade from the bench. It's still full—no one has drunk any yet—and slams it in the father's nose: he would have broken it if the guy hadn't stepped aside.

As soon as she sees the goalie's father grab the umbrella, Manuela tucks her crutches under her arms and heads through the gate. She enters the field limping, protesting, shouting, "You should be ashamed, shame on you!" But since she can't run and can't defend her brother, and the man seems ready to openly beat a boy, when she finally does reach him, she loses her head. It's like an electric shock that shoots up her spinal cord and disables her brain. She whirls her crutch and whacks the umbrella man, who falls to his knees, stunned, howling in pain, and then she hits him again and again and again.

"Stop! You're out of your mind, stop!" Mattia yells. He tries to make his way through the downed, weeping children. But a Manuela completely unknown to him, a fury of uncontrollable force, is savagely beating the kneeling man, who has dropped the umbrella and isn't even trying to defend himself: balled up like a fetus in the muck, moaning and begging her to stop, he bears her blows, the crutch and the boot that pound his head and back. Mattia tries to block that steel rod, but he misses and instead the crutch lands on his shoulder, the pain so sharp that it paralyzes him for a second. Mattia throws himself on top of her, locking his arms around her waist, and Manuela resists, lashes out, wriggles free, and it takes that vulgar, two-hundred-plus-pound madman to help Mattia free himself of the crazy woman with a crutch, as Mattia politely protests that this is all highly uncivilized and unbelievable. The crutch wheels, the boot kicks, the goalie's father moans, and Mattia tries again to stop Manuela, who now throws away her crutches, punches the madman in the face, hurls herself at Mattia, and locks him in a judo hold, which sends his sunglasses flying, clenches his neck with both hands. "Manuela," Mattia stammers, "please." She stares ferociously at him with wild eyes, not recognizing him.

Blood gushes from above the goalie's father's eye. Traian takes the umbrella from his hands, which have gone slack, and goes over to Mattia, wondering who the heck the guy in the suit is, the one kneeling in the mud and hugging Manuela's knees, and whispering in a strangled voice, "Calm down, my love." The madman spits three teeth into the palm of his hand.

Mattia gropes around with his left hand, trying to retrieve his sunglasses, but the Bolivian boy, who hasn't realized that Mattia is on the Real Ladis side and is only trying to calm everyone down and resolve the situation, crushes them with his cleats, jumping on top of them until they disintegrate. "What have you done!" Mattia shouts. He feels he has suffered a grave injustice. Without his sunglasses, he feels lost, vulnerable, naked.

The police arrive, sirens blaring. Not just one squad car, but three. Everyone settles down as soon as the boys in blue arrive, in fact, they're amazed that someone called the cops: nothing happened, just a kids' soccer game. An uncalled penalty. But parents and kids, the referee, managers, and coaches—all are in bad shape, covered in mud, rumpled, bruised. The goalie's father is hurting and touching his ribs; he has the unsettling feeling that they're out of place; he comforts his son, who is sobbing and eyeing with a look of sheer terror the crazy girl with the crutches; the madman's lips are bloody and as swollen as sausages; Traian is still clutching the umbrella like a sword, as if he might need to use it at any moment; Mattia feels an unnatural tingling at the base of his neck and a sharp pain in his trachea, and Manuela kneels to pick up her crutches, amazed they're no longer under her arms, amazed to find herself in the middle of the soccer field, amazed that she doesn't have the slightest idea what happened, as if a switch had been turned off. The game is called.

"Let's get out of here, for heaven's sake," Mattia says, taking Manuela under the arm. But the police have closed the gate to the field and an officer is guarding the exit. He wants to identify the adults involved in this disgraceful brawl. There will be consequences. And not only for the players. The managers of the two teams try to downplay things; the parents, furious, defend their own children by accusing the others; they don't want to show ID, they protest, swear. "She broke three of my teeth," the madman sputters to a police officer trying to get an explanation of how it all happened, "that tall lady with the shaved head, the one who's trying to slink off, she's a crazy woman, dangerous, you should arrest her, I'm pressing charges."

"I have to go," Mattia says, seized by an anxiety he can't control, "I have to go, I have to go." But Manuela's not listening to him because Traian, tall Traian with an adult's body and a boy's heart, is crying so hard he can barely breathe. "It wasn't a penalty," he keeps repeating, "I didn't even touch him. We were winning, only ten minutes left on the clock, the trophy was ours." It's the first major disappointment of his life.

"ID, please," a policeman orders. Mattia pretends not to have heard and tries to go around him and slip through the gate. "ID," the officer insists. Harshly, because headquarters radioed in about a brawl that involved racial insults that had broken out on the soccer field just as he was about to go off duty, and he and his wife have to go to dinner at his in-laws', out in the country, almost an hour's drive, and he has to shower first, and now he's going to be late, fucking hell. "I don't have any on me," Mattia says, forcing himself to sound convincing, "I went out without thinking, I wasn't planning on coming to the game." "I have to identify you," the policeman says, opening his notebook. "First name." "Mattia," he says quietly. "Last name." "I can explain," Mattia whispers, "it's an unusual situation."

"Last name," the policeman repeats, annoyed at having to waste time on this guy dressed in Armani, who flashes his fifteen-thousand-dollar, white gold Rolex and seems completely out of place on a JV soccer field. "Rubino," Mattia concedes. "Residence." "Bellavista Hotel on the promenade, it's named after some Savoia queen, Margherita, I think." "Don't mess with me," the policeman hisses, "I need your actual home address— street, street number, city, zip code." "I'm serious, Bellavista Hotel," Mattia repeats. "Listen," Manuela cuts in, waving her Armed Forces card under the policeman's nose, "he's with me, my brother's on the Real Ladis team, this man had nothing to do with this, he didn't hit anyone, he just tried to calm people down. I was the one who beat up that guy"— she points to the man with the plastic glasses—"but he wanted to beat up my brother, a twelve-year-old boy, and I couldn't let that happen."

"She broke three of my teeth," the madman blabbers as he comes over, "there are witnesses, she's a crazy woman, she should be arrested, I'm pressing charges."

The policeman examines Sergeant Paris's ID. It's the girl from Afghanistan. He saw her on TV on Christmas Day. She's cuter in person. Eyes like a gazelle. Fresh faced, so young. "I'm sorry," he says to her, "but I have to record the particulars of everyone present, it's my duty." "Take mine," Manuela says, "I threw myself into the fight, I went a little overboard. I have trouble controlling my aggression. Mr. Rubino doesn't have anything to do with it, really. I'll vouch for him. If anyone should be reported, it's me."

Sergeant Paris who almost died at the ends of the earth. The police officer heard from a colleague's cousin that a soldier deployed overseas earns maybe a hundred and thirty euros a day, which, multiplied by six months, comes to almost twenty-five thousand. Not bad. Then again, it's only fair, otherwise, who'd even go? Why else would you agree to risk your life when you're twenty? But, money or no, Paris put her life on the line, and almost lost it. Some people deserve respect. "If the people you attacked take action," he advises her, "Mr. Rubino's favorable testimony will be useful, so it's to your advantage that he be recorded as present." "I won't need any testimony," Manuela says, "I made a mistake, I take responsibility for my actions."

On their way back to the Audi, Mattia is silent, absorbed. He doesn't know what to make of the woman who savagely beat a defenseless man with her crutch. He doesn't like a woman who acts like that, and yet he likes her even more than before, because he confusedly intuits that wielding that crutch like a club has something to do with what happened to her, with an endless rage that she masks and that she lulls to sleep, but that in reality is eating her up inside, and he wants to fish her out of the sea of that rage, even though he's the person least suited to do it.

Manuela would like to erase that whole afternoon, the game, the umbrella, the goalie's father, the madman, the crack of teeth beneath her knuckles, her all-consuming rage. She may have ended her military career right then and there in that small-town soccer field. That idiotic JV championship may have succeeded in killing Sergeant Paris, something even ten kilos of plastic explosive failed to do. She's ashamed of having lost control, and yet feels relieved, euphoric even, as if pounding her crutch into that limp flesh and slamming her fist against a stranger's teeth had freed her of a weight. She would never admit it, but she liked it.

Ignoring Traian's jealous glances, she leans her head on Mattia's shoulder and tells him sweetly that Rubino is quite a name, should she think of him as someone precious? Mattia asks if she can drive with her injured leg. "Because I really don't have my license on me," Mattia says. But Manuela can't drive: her right foot has been too badly injured. The malleolus, the astragalus, and the calcaneum have disintegrated; the hospital counted twenty-one bone fragments. The screws and titanium plates prevent her from pressing the accelerator. The whole way to Traian's house, they both scan the edges of the road apprehensively, hoping they won't run into a patrol car. He goes out without his ID, like a kid, Manuela is thinking. And he really does live at the Bellavista Hotel. He doesn't like violence, he prefers to mind his own business, but he threw himself into the fray for Traian, in other words, for me. I don't know the first thing about him.

Dinner at the pizzeria on the overpass with Traian and his mother has to substitute for the candlelight dinner on the Hilton Pergola's panoramic terrace. After all that happened, Mattia didn't feel like driving. He promises they'll go to Rome sooner or later. But it's best if he doesn't go out too much. He can't explain, but he has to stay at the Bellavista, or at least in the area. So far he's been lucky, but no need to tempt fate. Manuela warns him that Traian's mother is very lively and can seem aggressive. "Look who's talking," he says, and Manuela smiles.

Teodora Gogean sizes Mattia up right away. Fifteen years on the men's ward at the hospital have made her a kind of expert. All she has to do is feel someone's handshake. She has an aversion to sweaty palms and limp grips. Manuela's friend is a vigorous man. And an experienced lover. He knows how to act, can play the role of the attentive boyfriend, but Teodora knows instinctively what he's really like. By dint of emptying urinals, inserting catheters, removing intravenous needles, she's learned to pick up vibrations from men's bodies, intuit their desires, anticipate their whims. She's amazed that Manuela has hooked up with someone like him. But then again, she needs to forget.

She can't swallow the fact that Traian let himself be dragged into a brawl. She reminds him on a daily basis that prejudice is a wall: if you want to end up on the other side, you have to dismantle it patiently, brick by brick. It takes years to construct an image of honesty and respectability, and only an hour to destroy it. Ever since she arrived in Italy, Teodora has borne every insult in silence, and she thought she'd taught him to do the same. But Traian isn't about to take the blame. "All I did was defend myself," he objects, burying his fork in the cheese of his pizza then lifting it to contemplate the stretchy white strings. "In a fight I follow the Italian rules of engagement: I don't shoot first, but if they shoot, I defend myself, that's how it works, right, Manù?" "Not exactly," Manuela says, "first you have to judge very carefully who you have in front of you. A peacekeeping soldier can't follow the old binary logic of war and separate everyone into enemies or friends. Sometimes the person shooting at you is both, and you have to gauge your response accordingly. And regardless, your reaction force has to be minimal, and proportional to the offense." Traian shakes his head, unconvinced. Manuela lectures well, but she didn't apply minimal force with the goalie's father, and her actions weren't at all proportional to the offense. But he doesn't say anything, he would never betray his sister. And besides, he's too proud of her. She flattened them, those assholes, both of them. What a sight. Manuela is better than Lara Croft.

"If you get mixed up in something like this again, I'll pull you off the team and that will be the end of your playing soccer," Teodora concludes. "It's not his fault," Manuela tries to placate her; she feels guilty for having set such a negative example for her brother—but they did start it. "Don't defend him, Manuela, he's a savage, you have no idea how hard I try to teach him some values." Traian lets out an irritated snort. Eating dinner with adults is so boring. "Do you have children, Mattia?" Teodora asks all of a sudden. "Manuela doesn't realize they need authority figures, you spoil them if you always let them have their way." "No," Mattia says, and Manuela can't decide if that is his opinion or his answer to her question. The waiter brings them their beer and the conversation shifts. Traian asks Mattia if he's an officer in the navy. Somehow he's gotten this idea. There are a ton of naval officers in the area, because of the port at Civitavecchia.

"No, I'm not in the navy," he is quick to make clear. "Air force, then?" There are a ton of air force officers around, too, the military airport is in Vigna di Valle, behind Lake Bracciano. "Nope." "Good thing," Traian exclaims. "We have a big rivalry with the navy and air force." "Who's we?" Mattia asks, surprised. "We, the army." Traian is getting excited. "They think we're all southerners, from Sardinia or Naples, they hate us. But we're the best of the Armed Forces. I'm joining the Airborne Brigade when I'm eighteen, and putting on that deep red beret. Or I'll become a commando, or an Alpino paratrooper. I don't really care that much about soccer, I play just to beef up. You have to be a real athlete to get into special forces." "Mattia's not interested in this stuff," Manuela says, "he's not in the military." "And you're going out with him anyway?!" Traian chastizes her.

Teodora and Mattia burst out laughing, but Traian's supercilious stare silences them. "My sister helped capture Mullah Wallid, an insurgent who was hunted for months, who was responsible for acts of terrorism that caused the deaths of lots of innocent people," he explains proudly. "There aren't very many women who participate in assaults, you know, very few in fact, she's doing you a real favor going out with you if you're just a civilian." "I guess I'm the only one here who doesn't know about it!" Mattia observes, turning to Manuela. She's blushing. She doesn't feel like talking to him about her mission operations. She can guess what his opinion would be. Mattia seems to her one of those people who donate point five percent of their taxes to the most radical humanitarian organizations they can find. "I didn't do anything special," she says, playing things down. "And besides, it wasn't an assault, we're not special forces, we don't do assaults. We're just Alpini."

"Manuela's company was involved in Operation Goat Four," Traian says, as if Mattia would know the mission by name. "I realize I don't understand much about your work, I thought you went to Afghanistan to distribute medicine to children," says Mattia, who's starting to get some vague idea of what Manuela is really capable of, and isn't sure he wants to know more. "Well, sure," she comments ironically, "we distributed medicine by the truckload. But the fact is, if you want to get the medicine to the people who need it, you have to take it to them, and in order to take it to them, you need a road, and to get a truck down a road, you have to keep that road clear, and to keep it clear and safe you have to search the nearby villages, and arrest whoever is manufacturing explosive devices, and patrol the intersections, and sometimes even have a combat helicopter clear the field of hostile elements." "So you hunt insurgents?" Mattia blurts out. "It's hardly a secret," Manuela says. "The restrictions on our field of action that made us appear ridiculous to our allies were lifted. And anyway, in six months, my platoon only carried out one of these operations, fifteen weeks after our arrival in the theater of operations." "Theater?" Mattia says. "The theater of operations is where you carry out your mission," Traian explains. Mattia reflects that the military has a peculiar way of twisting language, but he doesn't say so.

"It was a routine operation, just a cordon and search," Manuela downplays, using the English phrase. "Which means?" "It means surround and capture." "Surround and capture": to Mattia, it's a sinister phrase, one that ought to be avoided. Maybe headquarters thinks the same thing, which is why they prefer to use the English. In an attempt to encrypt the code and make it incomprehensible to outsiders, the army—every army—uses a private language, a monosyllabic slang stuffed with acronyms and technical terms, euphemisms, and foreign words. "Basically," Manuela explains, "you encircle a village, search the houses, or have the Afghani soldiers search them rather, because at this point they're capable of doing it on their own, and whoever flees is blocked by the cordon of troops. That's what we did, and we flushed out an insurgent." She stops. So much time has passed. She's not even sure she's the same person who advanced in total darkness among the partially destroyed houses of Negroamaro. "It was a bloodless operation, we didn't fire a shot, and I was hoping we wouldn't have to." But as she speaks she realizes that this is how she feels now, a thought of this moment, born in the overpass pizzeria, while looking into Traian's excited face and Mattia's myopic eyes, wide with astonishment, because he can't seem to reconcile his Manuela, the girl who moans in his bed at the Bellavista, with the sergeant armed with night vision goggles and an automatic rifle who searched a remote Afghani village in the dead of night. In that moment she was ready; her hands didn't shake. "They ambushed us on the way back, and we had to defend ourselves. That was my big action in Afghanistan. There's nothing heroic about it. I didn't kill anyone. I never killed anyone, Traian."

"Whatever happened to Mullah Wallid?" Teodora joins in. "I don't know," Manuela responds, "it wasn't our duty to try him, we're guests there, our job was to offer ANA support in the capture of the wanted individual." "If he was an insurgent he was probably tortured until he revealed who subsidized him and then shot," Mattia theorizes. "Not necessarily," Manuela says. "A leader is worth more alive than he is dead. He might side with the government one day, you never know. Alliances are unstable, nothing lasts. And everything has a price. I learned not to ask myself what will happen when we pull out. To live day by day, and to do the right thing at the right time. I wouldn't have been able to survive there otherwise."

That night at the Bellavista, when he turns back the comforter and slides in bed, Mattia sees her scar. Manuela's leg, slender and white, is visible between the rumpled sheets. She was too tired to wait up for him and has already fallen asleep. Instinctively he runs his fingertips along the wound. The hard, compact flesh is the color of blood. The edges are uneven, the line wavy and wandering. Her flesh, ripped apart by the shrapnel, has been stitched back together, but along the edges the skin is rippled, and little knots have formed, rough to the touch, like rope. A transparent membrane has formed where the epidermis was destroyed, as smooth as a baby's skin, forever fragile. A hieroglyph of pain.

He doesn't want to wake her, and yet he can't keep from bringing his lips to the scar and kissing it, from her knee to her ankle, following the painful hem of flesh. He shivers at the touch of her skin, as if it held the memory of the metal that had pierced her so deeply. "What are you doing?" she murmurs, feeling around for the sheets. The room is dim, and lines of light cut across the bed. "I'm listening to you," he says.

16

HOMEWORK

We have a problem, Sergeant Paris," Colonel Minotto said, as soon as I—sighing with relief—crossed the threshold of the command hut. June was suffocating. It was already 86°F at seven in the morning, and might reach 122°F by noon. The sun was an incandescent brass disk that burned in a cloudless sky for weeks, the heat turned our rifles red-hot, singed our hands, and cooked the soles of our boots. The glare seared our eyes, the dry air flayed our lips. It was hard to breathe, and agony to go outside in the daytime. Inside the sealed Lince we roasted like meat on the grill. During downtime I would gasp for air on my cot, or drag myself to the shower, where the refreshing water would make me shriek with delight, but it lasted only a second; after only a few steps toward my bunk I'd be drenched in sweat again. The tents and containers were cremation ovens, so hot that the day before, my thermometer exploded. The wind had kicked up—an obsessive, furious wind that the Afghanis call the *sad-u-bist ruz*, the 120-days wind. It had raged for five days and the weather report warned us that this was only a brief reprieve. It was sandstorm season in the Persian Gulf. The *sad-u-bist ruz* would calm down at night, but then it would pick up again, worse than before. It was like a tornado, but instead of forming a spiral turbine, it moved at ground level, like the hellish breath of a dragon. The earth had turned to dust; the sand inflamed our eyelids and scorched our lungs.

At that moment it was 115°F in the shade outside the command hut, and my fatigues were tattooed to my skin. I was swimming in sweat, I felt I was melting like ice cream. My skin, my hair, and my underwear were all boiling wet. None of my physical training had prepared me to handle this climate. I was afraid I would faint. And I worried about the kids on guard duty at the entrance to the base, in their helmets and bulletproof vests under that murderous sun. It must have been like wearing an iron breastplate in a furnace. The command hut had air-conditioning, but it couldn't be turned on because it used too much electricity and shorted out the system. Three fingers of sand had collected beneath the rusty window. The colonel was suffering from the heat, too, and trickles of sweat ran down his cheeks. I remained at attention, wary. Minotto was forty-six, with a basketball player's build, a pelican's nose, and beady eyes that sank into his cheeks, as if they'd been chiseled absentmindedly in his face. From his grim expression, I expected to be bawled out.

The rapport among officers, NCOs, and troops had broken down. Once we'd passed D+120, in other words two thirds of our tour of duty, the platoon leaders limited sorties from the FOB as much as possible. Even though it brought bad luck, the soldiers were counting the days till they could go home. The officers were tired, and the slowness, the bureaucracy, the lack of coordination, the delays, and the unexpected difficulties, which they had faced boldly in the beginning, now discouraged them. Captain Paggiarin nearly wept with rage over the cancellation of a cooperative project—the construction of a bridge on the Farah River—that had cost the regiment a great deal of effort and the Italian government a great deal of money. It was whispered that Carlo Paggiarin of Feltre, the imperturbable Skinny Buddha whom no one, in his thirty-eight years of life, had ever seen get angry or lose his cool—until he came to Afghanistan—had broken his hand punching a wall. And sure enough, his right hand was bandaged. The soldiers' discontent was even more physical. Fights broke out over nothing—for refusing to lend a cigarette, or cutting in line, or over a box of cookies that went missing. Some people's nerves gave out. Others sought doctors' excuses, the infirmary was always crowded. Complaints of crippling stomach pains and headaches that the doctors were convinced were made up. Nevertheless, orders came from headquarters to eliminate all dead weight, so as to avoid slander spreading about the competence of the health care. Private Rizzo—who faked an asthma attack every time he was supposed to leave the base—was sent home. A soldier from Cerberus platoon was repatriated for insubordination. But I didn't want to go home. I felt I was just beginning to understand Afghanistan.

Still, I was scared of what the colonel wanted to tell me. One of the NCOs from the Ninth—I could never figure out who—had complained to the captain, accusing me of causing hierarchical confusion among the troops and their superiors. He insinuated that I was having a relationship with Corporal-Major Diego Jodice, which was—in addition to being regrettable—also prohibited. He therefore requested that Sergeant Paris be sanctioned with repatriation.

"What do you know about Karim Ghaznavi?" Minotto asked without any sort of preamble. "The interpreter?" I replied, relieved. No, it wasn't about me. The captain hadn't given any weight to the complaint. He had plenty of other things to think about besides gossip. The colonel nodded. Ghaznavi was a bright little man, with amber skin, refined manners, and sad eyes behind his round glasses; he wore tired leather moccasins, and too-short, Western-style pants that revealed a pair of droopy, coffee-colored socks. He was always sweaty, dusty, breathless. He slept in a hut at the entrance to the base with the other two interpreters, younger than him by at least thirty years, and much more resourceful. His every gesture displayed the exhausted, impoverished dignity of a man who has seen better days. When I was introduced to him, I instinctively called him Professor, and I could tell that he appreciated the nickname. I didn't trust the Afghani officers, whose pasts, I imagined, included stoning women and cutting off the hands of thieves; I was suspicious of the Afghani police who collaborated with our regiment; at times I was afraid of the impetuous, arrogant, and careless ANA soldiers who roamed the base with guns loaded even though it was forbidden; I found the other interpreters greedy for money or gifts and superficial in their imitation of Western ways with their slicked-back hair and stylish sunglasses—or else unscrupulous and ready to betray us. I was always apprehensive when I went on patrol with them, afraid they'd sell us out to the insurgents by communicating our movements, our coordinates, or our itinerary, which I would choose with my squad leaders right before leaving the base. Whoever was planting IEDs always knew when and where the Alpini were going: my platoon alone had identified and defused five of them. Someone had to be informing them. But the sad Professor seemed trustworthy to me.

"For what it's worth, sir, in my experience Ghaznavi is reliable," I said warily. I didn't want to go too far out on a limb because I gathered from the colonel's grim expression that he, on the other hand, had a low opinion of the interpreter. I thought I knew Ghaznavi well. Ever since I arrived, I'd had the impression that he wanted to strike up a conversation with me, but wouldn't let himself because I'm a woman. The pleasure of discovering that we shared a passion convinced him to overcome his reluctance. He'd surprised me one evening holding a book and said, rather ceremoniously, that Sergeant Paris must be a special person: soldiers and NCOs never read. "Maybe in Italy one has to be at least a lieutenant or a captain to love books. But that's strange, because poetry is for everyone, and anyone can appreciate it. Poetry is like a flower growing in a field. It doesn't ask permission to be there, it takes root wherever it pleases." I've always loved reading to learn or to escape from the world, but I'd never read a book of verse: my indifference to poetry seemed shameful, so— to keep Ghazvani from realizing the misunderstanding—I slipped my volume on strategic analysis into my jacket pocket. "If I had met someone when I was young who knew how to talk to me about poetry with so much conviction, perhaps I wouldn't be here," I responded. Then I started to cough, because it was the time of the 120-days wind, and the blowing sand burned my throat. "Poets say that the wind is the voice of God," Ghaznavi had commented. "He prefers to speak to mortals in a language that only sensitive people can understand." "And do you believe them?" "Poets always speak the truth," Ghaznavi assured me, "but my grandfather used to say that the summer wind is the army of angels that travels the country in order to inspect the battlefield before the Apocalypse, and my grandfather always spoke the truth, too."

The Professor was from Herat. As an archaeology student he had worked with Italians on the restoration of Qal'a-i-Ikhtyaruddin, or the Citadel—sometime around 1976. It was a magnificent site, a fortress with eighteen towers over a hundred feet tall, covered in Kufic inscriptions, majolica, and frescoes. Almost totally destroyed. According to Ghaznavi, most of Afghanistan's archaeological treasures had been lost, and the rest were at risk. No one understood art here. But Italians, then and now, always ask a lot of questions. And every time I saw a mound of stones I would ask him, "Are they ancient?" Ghaznavi had learned Italian from the archaeologists. He'd never been to Italy, though.

I sensed that the colonel wasn't interested in the Professor's archaeological experience, however, and I didn't allow myself to express too forceful an opinion. I was only a sergeant, after all. "We've received a report from the Afghani police," Minotto said, scribbling in a notebook. "It seems that Ghaznavi is selling drugs to someone on the base." "Drugs!" I exclaimed. "Impossible." "That's what I said, too." The colonel sighed. "It has to be a lie, someone who wants revenge, or his job, you know he earns in a month what an Afghani working at a ministry earns in a year," I added, and then repented immediately because a subordinate answers only what is asked, and doesn't make inferences. "It's a very detailed report," Captain Paggiarin cut in. "It seems it's been going on for a while. It mentions two female soldiers. Now, Paris, other than Lieutenant Ghigo, the only women at Sollum are you and Giani. The military police have already questioned Giani, discreetly because it's a serious case, and the corporal swears she knows nothing about it. Besides, she handles supplies, she's only been off the base once, it does not appear she has had any contact with Ghaznavi—whereas you, Sergeant, have often been seen conversing with him."

It was true. But they were innocent chats. We either talked about books or theology. Ghaznavi told me he would have liked to be able to give me a volume by Rumi, the greatest classical poet of Persian literature. He wrote the *Mathnawi*, a fifty-thousand-verse poem in rhymed couplets, the *Diwan*, and a collection of maxims. Ghaznavi used to have an English version of Rumi's *Selected Poems*, from the end of the nineteenth century, it had belonged to his grandfather. Jalāl ad-Dīn Muhammad Rūmī was a poet but also a Sufi mystic, an enlightened man, it's said he was crazy for God. "Do you believe in God, Sergeant Paris?" "Yes, yes," I was quick to say, because during mission prep our instructors had coached us not to offend the Afghanis with our lack of faith. And to say that we were Christians, regardless of what we really believed. For them a life without God was inconceivable, and they wouldn't trust anyone who did not fear him. The Koran teaches that God is closer to us than our own blood. "You really should read him," Ghaznavi said. He believed that Sergeant Paris appreciated the beauty of light. Every thought that is not a memory of God is merely a whisper. And no one knew how to speak of God like Rumi, he had even written him a love song.

But Ghaznavi no longer had the book, unfortunately. During Afghanistan's darkest years, he had burned all the books in his library, one by one. Out of fear. He wept as he poked the fire. All that beauty, flying away in the smoke and turning into a pile of cold ashes. He had learned a few bits of the *Mathnawi* by heart, and he would read it in his mind, eyes closed. As he told me these things, I wondered if I could accept a gift from him, and I told myself no. So it was just as well that he didn't have that book anymore, or else I would have had to insult him by refusing. "Books are our truest friends," Ghaznavi said. "They are your companions through good times and bad, they never desert you. You may abandon them, but they know how to forgive you." And he was in need of companions because he had no one left. His brothers and nephews had emigrated to Canada. His wife and children were refugees in Iran, and he rarely saw them; it pained him. "Why don't you have them come back?" I had asked naïvely. Ghaznavi looked at me with a sorrowful smile. And it took me weeks to understand what he couldn't say: it was too dangerous, he'd been working for the foreigners for too long, by now a lot of people knew he was an interpreter, they would be hung.

"But even now," Ghaznavi continued, ignoring my question, "it's difficult to buy a book." If any Alpini, when their tour of duty was over, wanted to leave him theirs, he would be grateful. "I'll spread the word," I had promised him, "I'll collect everything I find." And I had. Ghaznavi's future library included Russo's *The Road to Oxiana*, my history and travel books about Afghanistan, two novels from Barry Sadler's series about the immortal soldier Casca Rufio Longinus that belonged to Spina, Lorenzo's *Jonathan Livingston Seagull*, Giani's *Twilight* books; other Panthers contributed *The Lord of the Rings*, three mysteries, and a book by Mauro Corona. Ghaznavi recited some verses of Rumi:

> A narrow passageway runs between your heart and mine, my love.
> I have found the door, and now I know what spring is.
> My heart is a pool of clear water that reflects the moon.

Ghaznavi was quick to explain that the erotic language is a metaphor: the poet sings his love for God. I reflected that love, be it for a man, a woman, or God, called for the same words. I would have liked to have someone to say them to.

I tried to remember what else I talked to him about. Oh yes, I had asked him about the customs of the nomads, whose black goat-hair tents had appeared along the banks of the Farah River in the spring. Were they Taymanis? Or Kuchi? And about the local men's gestures, which I couldn't work out, and why they held hands, like lovers. About the *kareze*, the traditional canal irrigation system, which a cooperation project was supposed to restore. Operation Reawakening had already cleared two square kilometers for use. About the danger of the brown-and-white striped viper I'd spotted near the latrines. (Ghaznavi's answer was comforting: hemotoxins, as deadly as a cobra, watch where you step, especially if you get up in the night, because it is an irritable nocturnal predator.) I'd asked him all sorts of things, and I'd also asked his forgiveness. "The wise man knows and asks," he had replied with a smile, "the ignorant man doesn't know and doesn't ask." But Ghaznavi never asked questions. He knew he couldn't, and he didn't want to step out of line, so he was saving them for a day when he might be able to get some answers. The accusation was insulting. But a river doesn't become dirty just because a dog puts his paws in it. They could say what they wanted; the sad Professor was not a spy or an opium dealer, I refused to believe it.

"It's ridiculous," I protested stubbornly. "Just yesterday when we were searching the village of Tamyrabad, we confiscated six drums of gas from a truck driver suspected of supplying drug dealers." "Paris, can you repeat the argument you made to me a month ago, in the mess tent?" Paggiarin interjected. "No, I don't remember," I said hastily. But I remembered all too well, unfortunately. I wanted to swallow my tongue. Fiery rivulets of sweat streamed down my spine.

"Sergeant Paris was struck by the quantity of poppies surrounding us," Paggiarin reported, looking Minotto in the eye. "She asked me why the ISAF countries couldn't legally purchase opium, to use in hospitals in the West. That way, the Afghani peasants would have an income and the Taliban would lose their principal source of revenue. That's what she said. I didn't report it because I hadn't grasped its potential danger."

"I know it may seem like a risky idea," I said, trying to endure the radioactive gaze of Colonel Minotto. "But it's not, actually. My father died of cancer, he suffered like a dog because the hospital wouldn't give him any morphine. Not everyone understands the importance of pain relief therapy, and morphine is expensive, too expensive for many. It seems a tremendous waste to let all this opium enrich the drug dealers and the Mafia, to let it ruin the young, Italians included, when it could be doing good, helping Afghanis to live—and Europeans to die—with dignity."

"It is not your job to come up with strategies to fight drug trafficking,

Sergeant," the colonel cut me off. "The best think tanks in the world are working to find a solution to this plague. Which, however, cannot be dealt with until the safety of this country is assured and its development set in motion. I am sure you will never propound such an argument again." "Yes, sir," I said.

"Have you ever noted any strange behavior in your men?" Minotto insisted, scrutinizing me. I knew what he was thinking. That he had discovered me when I was just a student at the NCO Academy, that he had believed in me. And had challenged me. The first time I met him, during training, he told me I should think of myself as a mosquito larva. If I settled in the first comfortable pond I found, I'd certainly be able to grow and to fly eventually, but I wouldn't go far. If, on the other hand, I humbled myself and hid in the tire of a plane, if I survived the difficulties of the journey, I would travel the world. I accepted the challenge, and he taught me everything I knew; he had encouraged, supported, rewarded me. And I had disappointed him. I was sorry he suspected me. His esteem meant more to me than anything. At least up until that moment. "Nothing unusual," I assured him. "It would be a matter of unprecedented and intolerable seriousness, and it would be my duty to advise my superiors immediately." "Keep an eye on Ghaznavi. And report to the captain if there is any suspicious talk among your men," Minotto concluded wearily. "Yes, sir," I said. The next time I saw him was at the Celio military hospital. We never spoke about that conversation in the command hut at Bala Bayak again. But the fact that it occurred can never be erased.

As I walked in the sun toward my tent I was aware that I hadn't been honest. I had not told the colonel that my men said suspicious things all the time. But what could Minotto have done to us? Set the military police loose on us? Asked the dog unit to intervene with their drug-sniffing canines? And what would TFS have said? He would have disgraced Ninth Company and the Alpini—for nothing. Besides, what else were the men supposed to talk about? We were literally living in the middle of a poppy field. In April their purple, white, pink, red, and yellow petals inflamed with color the valleys we crossed to get to the villages to be searched, cleared, and assisted. There the desert retreated. It was like a carpet of colored silk. We were surrounded by opium, growing out in the open. Something had to be done. The Americans had initially tried to use force. They wanted at first to bomb the poppies with napalm, though later they decided to simply uproot them. But good intentions do not always bring about good results—almost never, in fact. In reality, they condemned entire peasant families to abject poverty; the poppy harvest was their only means of subsistence, and when that was taken away, the Americans lost the peasants' initial sympathy and ended up pushing them to the rebels' side. So they changed their strategy completely: the allies promised incentives to peasants willing to grow saffron instead. They distributed bulbs and fertilizer; in fact, most of the convoys we escorted that winter carried tons of bulbs and fertilizer. The first harvest, the previous year, had been encouraging: a hectare of saffron crocuses yielded four times what a hectare of poppies did. But some of the peasants had their throats cut and their fields burned, and the changeover proceeded slowly—and in the meantime, the ISAF commanders, who were eager to conquer the hearts and minds of the Afghani people, preferred to resign themselves to tolerating the poppy fields to ensure if not benevolence, then at least neutrality. Whenever we left the FOB, we made our way through fields of flowering poppies.

If you cut the seed ball open with a knife, a milky white juice oozes out, which turns brown with contact with the air. It's sticky, as thick as cream, and the smell goes to your head. The soldiers would talk about it when they thought the officers and NCOs couldn't hear them. The peasants began the harvest in mid-April. Men, old people, and children moved through the fields, each with a knife in hand and a container hung around his neck. The soldiers could see, and they wondered how it worked. How that dark paste was transformed into opium and heroin. And where they refined the drug. But that one of them could think of buying it, or taking it, or smuggling it into Italy seemed impossible to me. We'd been living side by side for months, in such close quarters that we even knew how many times someone went to the shitter. Curcio had a brother who smoked heroin and had ended up in rehab, but you can't suspect someone because of a relative. Nevertheless, I promised myself I would send him on patrol as soon as possible so I could inspect his kit.

Then I remembered that one torrid night in May, Lorenzo told me about the time he'd overdosed on opium oil. It was so hot I couldn't fall asleep. Neither could he. We were sitting in the sand. I could see the whites of his eyes gleaming in the dark. We'd never been this close before. We were playing a sort of game of truth or dare, telling each other the very worst things we'd ever done. The moments we were most ashamed about, and which all the same we couldn't truly regret. I had told him about Mrs. Ferraris. I was still in middle school and was hanging out with the gang from the new apartment buildings. When spring came, it was as if the cage I'd felt trapped in all year opened. Instead of going to school, I'd pedal my bike along the shore, my textbooks in the basket and the wind in my hair, go for swims at the Torre Flavia beach. I'd been bragging to my friends about how I'd been going swimming since the end of March, and the colder the water, the more the others respected me. I had chronic bronchitis, I could spit mucus ten feet, blowing it out my lips. I was so good at forging my mother's signature on my excuses—Cinzia Colella, with little circles over the i's—that not even she would have noticed the difference. On the days I skipped school, I'd wander around Ladispoli with a short, stocky kid with curly hair, whose nickname was Pitbull. He would tease the boys and make the girls fall in love with him. He made fun of the weak and timid kids in our group, calling them lice and making a show of humiliating them. Whoever caved became his groupie and slave, scorned by everyone else. I was the kind who never held back. To show I wasn't afraid of anything, I'd cross the highway on foot, from one lane to the next, climbing over cement guardrails, indifferent to the tractor trailers that blinded me by flashing their high beams. I drank an entire liter of wine (I vomited so much afterward, it might be the reason I later stopped drinking). I stole T-shirts from a clothing store and bottles of whiskey from a roadside diner, in plain view of the security cameras and the watchmen. One morning in April, Pitbull asked me to get Vanessa's motor scooter because he wanted to buy a cell phone. I like to think now that I didn't realize the connection between those two things, but the fact is I did and I didn't say anything.

I'd already been driving my sister's scooter for a while, on the sly. Pitbull told me to circle around the market piazza, to maintain a good speed and not to brake. We went by the post office twice. "Keep going," Pitbull said. I saw her first. She was crossing the street right on the white stripes, her blue leather purse dangling from her shoulder. She was slowed by age and the shopping bags she carried in both hands. As we pulled up alongside her, Pitbull shouted, "Gun it!" and so I did. I didn't even turn around, I just kept my eyes on the road in front of me. But evidently he didn't pull hard enough—lack of experience—or the leather strap was too resistant. The fact is, the old lady clung to her purse for a few feet and then took a disastrous fall, face-first, tomatoes, zucchini, and peppers rolling across the asphalt. I slalomed among the cars and fled along the promenade while passersby shouted and rushed to help the unfortunate woman. In the rearview mirror I could see a spot of red blood on the white crossing stripes.

After we rounded a turn, Pitbull tossed the purse and had me drop him at his brother's garage. He said he was sorry; the old lady was dressed well and seemed rich, but she had only fifty thousand lire in her wallet. He handed me two ten-thousand-lira bills. I told him I didn't want them. I hadn't done it for the money. He kissed me on the mouth and I bit his lip. I didn't do it for him, either. I revved the engine and took off. The beach clubs were closed, so I hid between the beach huts. I was afraid these were my last hours of freedom. I was afraid of going to jail. Of all the buildings rising up in the distance, the jail was the one that always terrified me. I'd look the other way when we drove by. A strange thought came to me as I sat there, teeth chattering from cold and shock. That the incident wasn't really what it seemed. I hadn't dragged to the ground, injured, and maybe even killed an old lady: it had been me—the other Manuela, the real Manuela, the one still waiting to be born. I'd killed her. They'd come for me now, I'd be tried and locked up in that frightening building, and the warrior Manuela would never exist. I wept, huddled in a damp changing room that smelled of mold and salt. But time passed and no one came. So I calmed down. Maybe they wouldn't find me. They hadn't recognized me. Maybe I could still salvage my dream. I abandoned the motor scooter at the dump and set it on fire.

When the police came looking for the owner of the blue Free motor scooter, my sister was shocked. She hadn't ridden her scooter that day, she'd gone to school with her boyfriend, and he picked her up at eight. But the passersby had gotten the license plate, and it was hers. The police wanted to see it. Vanessa went down to the street with them, not worried in the least. It was a misunderstanding, it would all be cleared up. But her Free wasn't parked downstairs. They searched for it all along the promenade, in case she'd forgotten exactly where she'd parked it. But they couldn't find it. It had been stolen. "What happened?" Vanessa inquired, suspicious now. "Mrs. Ferraris got her purse snatched, she fell and hit her head. It was your motor scooter, and now it's a real mess, because you didn't report it as stolen," the officer explained. "But what does it have to do with me?" Vanessa protested. "I was at school, ask my prof, she even quizzed me in class."

"Is she dead?" my mother got right to the point. Knowing how insurance companies work, she was afraid she'd have to pay damages. And she didn't have any money, her account was always in the red. She avoided looking at me, perched on the edge of the couch pretending to watch the soap opera *The Bold and the Beautiful.* At the time I was wild about Stephanie Forrester. My mother had guessed what had happened, she had a sixth sense about the trouble I got into. But she also had a powerful sense of clan, and she never would have turned her daughter in. My mother's concept of justice was very malleable. Mrs. Ferraris. The name sizzled in my head. I knew her; she was the principal of my elementary school. A kind old lady, always smiling. I adored her as a child. She'd give you candy if you behaved. I would have liked her to be my grandmother. My real grandmother—Leda Colella, my mother's mother—would smack me on the head so hard I was always afraid she'd knocked the sense out of me. "She broke her nose," the officer said. My mother gave a sigh of relief and practically kicked them out of the house, accusing them of wasting her time. "It was you," Vanessa hissed when we were alone. "You're a devil, Manuela, you're out of your mind. I'm not going to start spying on you, but you have to buy me a new motor scooter." I denied it. I swore falsely on my mother's life, my sister's, even my own.

"I couldn't admit I helped Pitbull steal Mrs. Ferraris's purse. It was too stupid a thing to do for the person I thought I was. I never fessed up. You're the first person I'm telling this to. I ran into Mrs. Ferraris at the market in July. She had a sort of rubber mask on her nose. I was still afraid she would recognize me, so I stopped saying hello to her.

"When exams were over, I enrolled in tourism school and stopped hanging out with my friends from the new apartment buildings. I would read war comics, watch soap operas on TV, listen to my sister's romantic confessions while I helped henna her hair, but I was never able to right myself and turn my mistake into an opportunity, like my grandfather recommended. I lost track of Pitbull, but I acted just like him. I enjoyed tormenting the new girls at school, whom I considered weak and timid. I would worm money out of them; I'd force them to pay me to leave them alone, to write my papers for me, do my homework. The superintendent called me into her office and informed me that my bullying would no longer be tolerated. I didn't deny it that time, in fact I behaved as if I didn't care at all. The superintendent felt threatened. She was afraid I would slit her tires with a box cutter, and from then on she would park two blocks away from school. I was solitary, arrogant. I was about to lose myself, Lorenzo. But I didn't. If I hadn't broken Mrs. Ferraris's nose when I was thirteen, I might not be who I am today."

"I was fifteen," Lorenzo whispered, "I'll never forget. We smoked this enormous pipe for half an hour—opium oil, a clear, harmless-looking liquid, it didn't seem to do anything. Then all of a sudden I was flat on the floor. It was the most awful and most beautiful thing that had ever happened to me. I was dead for half an hour. Cold, frozen, completely numb. My friends wanted to dump me at the emergency room and disappear. I could hear them talking, I was totally conscious, in fact, my mind was a thousand times more expansive than before. I could hear and see everything. I could make out ants' footsteps, hear the electric current crackling in the wires, and see what my friends were doing behind my back. But I couldn't move. It was like I was suspended over my body, hovering a few feet above it, weightless. I moved through the air, drifting; I climbed the walls like a shadow, floated beneath the lamp like a cloud of smoke. Every barrier between my body, my mind, and the world had crumbled. I was both myself and everything. It was a beautiful feeling, Manuela, one of complete freedom. I would do anything to get it back, but I've never been able to. That's when I understood what death is. Maybe that's how it'll be when we're dead."

But so what, what did it mean? He smoked opium when he was fifteen. Adolescence is a time of experimentation, challenges, mistakes. I'd changed, maybe he had, too. I didn't report him. I couldn't and didn't want to believe that Nail was involved in something like that. In spite of everything, he was a good soldier. And when he had to, he, too, picked up his rifle and fired.

It could have been Schirru, though, an amiable slacker who had been counting the days till his departure ever since he arrived, and once I heard him theorize about the supremacy of black Afghan. Hashish, in other words. I could inspect his gear, maybe announce a bug extermination or a hygiene check as an excuse. But then I'd have to get the clinic involved. And explain everything to the military police, and that didn't seem right. The other Alpini considered him a dead dog, and hoped they wouldn't end up in the same squad as him. Even Venier shunned him. They had ostracized him, which already said it all.

The next day when Ghaznavi hurried to the meeting with the Ghor province chief of police, who had come to Sollum for a briefing at headquarters, I didn't let him out of my sight for an instant. Ghaznavi didn't even deign to look at the soldiers. He passed them, walking beside Captain Paggiarin, translating in a low voice for the police chief. But the soldiers—all of them—kept their eyes glued on him. I had the feeling they shared some secret, and I shuddered. My eyes sought out Lorenzo. My little brother, my epigone. He was in the piazza, tinkering with a flooded Lince motor. Sand had corroded the gears. I read no malice in those clear eyes of his. Just curiosity. As if he merely wanted to understand what that bright, agitated little man was mumbling, his eyes fixed on his dusty shoes.

Forgive me if I doubted you, Nail. If you are right, if death is like ODing on opium, you're floating outside your body somewhere right now, maybe you're close by, drifting like smoke, weightless, painless—free.

A few days after my conversation with Colonel Minotto, Ghaznavi, on his way from the infirmary, surprised me as I sat at the door to the hut, staring intently at the stars. Millions of them, emerging from the immenseness, nameless constellations in a darkness so complete, so pure, it was like a swath of velvet studded with incandescent embers. The Milky Way looked like the frothy wake of a ship. I'd always thought that only the sun and the moon lit up the sky. But that's not true. In Afghanistan even the stars give off light, they can cast shadows. There were times, when all was quiet, not even a motor mumbling along the distant road, that the silence was so thick I could hear the sand rustle and the dunes crumble. Ghaznavi hesitated a second, then asked me if I knew what the Milky Way was. "It's our galaxy, it's where we are," I answered coldly. "To us," Ghaznavi smiled, "it's the stardust that Mohammed's horse Buraq kicked up when he crossed the sky on his way to Paradise." I was afraid of being spied on, of someone noticing that we were talking, so I ignored him. Ghaznavi moved on, disappointed. His worn-out moccasins sank silently into the sand.

At dawn I was in the watchtower, binoculars aimed at the mountain that overlooked the base. An intelligence report had indicated suspicious movement up there. Nearby, Ghaznavi was on his knees praying, his forehead pressed to his dusty rug. From a distance came the call of the muezzin, carried on the wind. The first light of day sketched the empty contours of the hills, and I had the feeling that this was the instant of creation, that the world was yet to be born. Sand and sky, peaks and valleys all seemed to be awaiting something. An unspoken, infinite potential. As if all was yet to begin. That was freedom.

When I came down from the tower, I ran into Ghaznavi putting on his shoes and rolling up his rug. I couldn't avoid him. "Perhaps you will be able to achieve what it is you desire," he said with a smile. "This is what I wish for you. Sergeant Paris appreciates the voice of beauty, even though she doesn't want anyone to know. But it is nothing to be ashamed of, it is a gift to be able to comprehend the poetry of the world. And Sergeant Paris has received that gift, even though she hasn't realized it yet. But it is due neither to her merit nor to her fault. Unless something has been decided since the beginning of time, it cannot occur. The essential things are determined by destiny. To deny this is to limit the universe. Destiny can turn stones into water, and stars into dust."

I waved my hand in greeting and quickened my step. I didn't tell him that the beauty of his country had swallowed me up, or that I thought I now knew how to listen to the voice of the sand, the sky, and the wind, nor did I ask him what he meant. I never spoke to him again. It grieves me now, but there's nothing I can do about it.

Karim Ghaznavi—I learned in an article that Stefano sent me—was the last to be identified, because no relative had come forward to claim his remains. Which is why he was originally counted among the anonymous civilian victims. Besides, Ghaznavi probably wasn't even his real name. To protect themselves and their families, the interpreters chose new names, known only to us inside the base. Not even their relatives always knew what they did. Only one extreme left-wing newspaper spoke of Ghaznavi. The other papers dedicated not a single line to him. Their accounts of Afghanistan were abstract narratives, situated in a country without people; a tragedy performed only by stock characters: savage

Taliban fighters, oppressed and abused women, *shahid*—incorrectly called kamikaze—devoted to martyrdom, and nameless victims of bombings and other attacks. They were the incarnation of principles attributed to them by those who wrote about them, or who watched the tragedy from the audience—not actual individuals. They were a mass, they were numbers—and no one feels sorry for numbers. If anything, those numbers, which were constantly increasing—the count of civilian victims had tripled in recent years—were a source of embarrassment and horror.

The person who wrote the article that mentioned Ghaznavi expressed a harsh, critical judgment of the mission and reflected bitterly on the fate of the interpreter and—more generally—the Afghani people. These reflections hurt and offended me, even though I shared them to a certain extent. But the author transformed Ghaznavi into an anonymous symbol of the massacre: he'd never seen him. Only I could have written about that man, who was an individual with a past and a life story, with good qualities and bad, memories and dreams, like Lorenzo, like Diego, like Nicola Russo. But no one asked me, and after that meeting with Colonel Minotto, I ripped the pages where I'd written about him out of my diary and burned them, fearing that someone might read them and blame me for being kind to a man accused of a crime. I'm sure Ghaznavi would have forgiven me, because he, too, had known the bitterness of reducing to ashes words that were essential to him.

Now the Professor exists only in a few scattered images in my head. The last one catches him a few seconds before the end. On June 8, Ghaznavi was working for Ninth Company headquarters, as always. Impeccable, sweaty, tired, with his dusty yellow moccasins and sad eyes. At the moment of the explosion he was standing next to First Lieutenant Russo, translating for him words that could have been essential or inconsequential, which now no one will ever know.

17

>>>>>>>>>>>>>>>>>>>>>>>>

LIVE

Transcendental meditation is the confluence of an individual intelligence and the cosmic conscience, it allows us to discover ourselves and the divine within ourselves, and permits the body to enter into a state of deep relaxation. It's easy and natural, at once universal and personal. For normal people it can improve their health, help them reconnect with the primordial energy source, and develop individual potential, but for those who suffer from nervous disorders, it can also serve as therapy. Vanessa knows a Vedic master in Cerveteri who practices transcendental meditation, and she takes Manuela and Mattia to see him. It seemed like a good idea to Mattia, and he insisted he needed it as much as Manuela did. So all three of them enter a bare room—the only thing on the wall is a photograph of Maharishi Mahesh Yogi—take off their shoes, and sit on the carpet, imagining they will close their eyes, breathe deeply, enter a state of well-being, and be cured instantly, during the first session, as if by magic.

But the Vedic master, whose disappointingly normal name is Mario, as thin as a rail and of an indeterminate age, disabuses them of this notion. He congratulates Manuela for choosing to embark on the path of transcendental meditation, which is well suited to her symptoms, so much so that even some traditional doctors recommend it, though military doctors often categorically deny the existence of PTSD. But the road to enlightenment is long and complicated. There are seven steps, and only at the end will she and her friend be able to taste the first fruits of their journey. First of all, they have to join the association. Then they have to attend a group presentation in which he will elucidate the benefits of transcendental meditation and offer some initial instructions on how to actually practice it. Next they will have an individual encounter, because meditation is an experience and a wisdom that is transmitted directly, and never through a third party. At that point they can begin their sessions, which last about an hour and a half, and which must take place on four consecutive days. Only after having completed all seven steps will they be able to practice transcendental meditation.

"But I'm already convinced of the benefits, can't we skip the first two steps and start right in with the individual encounter?" Manuela asks. To her it seems like her last chance. The drugs she was prescribed—tranquilizers and antidepressants—didn't resolve anything. The cognitive behavior exercises, which she has begun since coming home, don't seem to be delivering concrete results either. She started showing symptoms only two months after the attack. If they last more than three months, they're considered chronic. Her three months are already up. She can't let herself become chronic. She attacked two people for no real reason, sent them to the hospital. She is waiting to be called to police headquarters at any moment, where she'll be told she's being charged with assault. She immediately informed her superiors of the deplorable incident with which she had sullied her record, and was greeted with an embarrassed silence. Paggiarin reminded her of the Afghan proverb that says "Don't take off your shoes before you cross the river." He noted that those unlucky individuals had ninety days in which to take action, and it was completely pointless to worry about it in advance. "Try and keep calm, Paris, you'll tough this one out, too, one way or another." She stood there, phone in hand, pensive. She wanted to try and convince them not to press charges—even though she couldn't imagine how to go about it. If someone had broken three of her teeth, she would have filed charges, and no prayers or pleas or offers of money would have made her change her mind.

The Vedic master explains with an ineffable smile that the seven steps are required, and in any case he could only teach Mattia, not her, because women must have a female teacher. "What difference does it make?" Manuela asks. "I'm used to working with men, and they're used to working with me, it's always been fine." "My sister has a very manly profession, she's a rather unusual woman," Vanessa ventures, "so maybe it could work out." "I'm sorry," the master says, "for us there are no unusual women, there are only men and women, it's a principle of nature, you are one or the other, and one of the aims of meditation—which is a science of being and an art of living—is, in fact, to reunite our masculine and feminine halves in order to rediscover our primordial energy."

"Okay, we'll join the association," Mattia says, tactlessly pulling out his wallet, "but we'd like to start right away. We don't have a lot of time." "Unfortunately everyone's away over the Christmas holidays," the master explains, "we don't have enough people to organize a session. You'll have to come back on January fifteenth." "Please," Manuela says, "I really need your help." She would do anything to be able to sleep again, to rid herself of the nightmares, of the headaches, and of the rage that is devouring her, to restore her body's natural energy.

Mattia tries to insist, even to bribe him, but despite his association's humble aspect and evident poverty, the master is a serious individual and refuses, scandalized. Manuela glances sadly at the yogi on the poster. His black eyes are bursting with such otherworldly bliss that it's almost offensive. He is visibly serene. And that serenity has been denied her.

When they get back in the car, Vanessa says that she had read up on the topic, too. She read on the Internet that ecstasy has been proven to help with PTSD. Manuela could give it a try. She knows quite a few people who sell it. And it's a fact that it improves one's mood and suppresses self-destructive tendencies. "You're out of your mind, Vanessa," Manuela says. "You're not on duty," Vanessa protests. "And it's not like Mattia's going to go around telling people, you're not a police officer, are you?"

"No, I'm not a police officer," Mattia confirms. "Try it," Vanessa insists, "one tab's not the end of the world, it'll make you feel better, really." "You don't have the slightest idea about military ethics, Vanessa," Manuela sighs. "I wouldn't do it even if it were my only hope, why can't you see that? I can't take shortcuts. I just can't, end of story."

"Manuela and I aren't cut out for chemical substances," Mattia comes to her rescue. "We'll keep trying our own transcendental meditation at the Bellavista." After all, the Vedic master said that meditation is a science of the consciousness, an expansion of the mind. That it's mechanical rather than intellectual. All of this sounds to him quite a bit like sex.

In room 302, they sit on the bed in the dark, legs crossed and eyes closed, and try an autonomous version of transcendence. They concentrate on freeing themselves of negative thoughts, on contemplating nothing, on breathing in such a way as to oxygenate the brain. "Do you feel your mind expanding?" Manuela whispers after what seems like an eternity. She's bored. She has never been able to sit still. Or to think, really. Loftiness of the spirit is foreign to her. Hers is a practical, connective intelligence, as her aptitude tests have shown. Mattia feels something else expanding.

"How many women have you slept with?" she asks him afterward, nibbling greedily on his ear. "I don't know, the only one that matters is the last one." "More than thirty? More than fifty?" Manuela inquires, not angry, not even jealous. She doesn't regret Mattia's past and has no intention of going back to look for it. And she doesn't want to think about the future—his or theirs. "I liked them all," Mattia explains. "I've always had my own idea of beauty. The body is everything, but it's also a boundary you have to get beyond in order to arrive at the source. I'm interested in the origin of things rather than in the consequences. I prefer clouds to rain, flames to ashes, beer to foam. I prefer the way a woman moves, the light in her eyes, the shadow of hair at the nape of her neck, the boldness of a jutting chin to the regularity of forms, a pretty nose, or a nice ass. I've found a reflection of something in every woman."

"Maybe because you're really full of yourself, or a really deep thinker, I don't know, I haven't figured it out yet. I'm not so transcendent, though," Manuela reflects. "The body already says everything, and often it says very little. We're a mass of cells that join together and reproduce without knowing why. For me, they're not two separate things, the mind's nothing more than the brain, the mind's what regulates the body. The body falls ill when the mind falls ill. And vice versa. If my leg doesn't heal, I'll go crazy and they'll institutionalize me. If my mind heals, maybe I'll be able to walk normally again, run even."

Mattia raises the shutters just enough to see that it's getting dark. From the street comes the distant sound of screeching tires, the echo of a horn, music from a radio speeding by. He searches for her mouth. For a second he tells himself he's taking refuge in her because only she can make him happy, even though it might not be right or loyal or fair. But then Manuela opens her lips and the thought disappears.

Closed up night and day in room 302 without even raising the shutters, eating in the room, thinking about nothing, in other words about everything, until they're completely drained. January 3 passes in this way, then January 4. Time has stopped, only the variations in the light filtering through the slats tell them if the sun has risen or set, if the moon has finished its journey across the sky. The bed is big, Mattia's body firm, his breath regular in the darkness. Something opens up inside her as she looks at him, lying on his side, cheek on the pillow, arm over his eyes, forehead bare. *A narrow passageway runs between your heart and mine, my love. / I have found the door, and now I know what spring is.* The verses come to her suddenly. Who was it who taught them to her? When? *My heart is a pool of clear water that reflects the moon.* It's easy and natural, universal and personal. Their bodies finally enter into a state of deep relaxation.

Vanessa had taken her Yaris to the car wash, so when they pull onto the Aurelia early in the afternoon on January 5, the sun glints on the shiny hood. "Three people and only one license, a world record," she says, winking to her sister in the rearview mirror. But she doesn't mind this detour to Torvaianica. Her dance class won't start up again until after Epiphany, and she doesn't want to spend too much time alone because otherwise her mind spins back to the parking lot at the old Gas Works, and the mermaid tattooed on the arm of some man she can't remember. And she doesn't know what hurts more, the metal of the car hood against her cheek or the vision of her empty purse, the physical violence or the idea that someone she trusted and was happy to meet had betrayed her. Mattia clings to the handle above the window. He's not used to such spirited driving, or maybe just a woman's spirited driving. Every now and then he courteously suggests: "You might want to put it in fifth." "You might want to downshift to third." "The speed limit might be ninety here." It's clear that he's the driver back home, he's the one who decides the speed, the gear, the trajectory on the curves. But where is his home?

"You talk like this friend I met in Ibiza," she says, looking at him askance. She can't really check his facial reaction because she's attempting a daring pass, a white van is right on her tail, flashing its lights threateningly, and she has to get back in her lane somehow without running the car next to her, which is going faster than she is, off the road. "He was from Brescia, no, Mantua, maybe you know him, his name was Faustino Silvestri. You can't not know him, he was really something, he used eyeliner, always wore black, a rose behind his ear, he taught tango in a club, I can't remember what it was called." "I'm not from Mantua," Mattia says. He grips the handle with alarming force. I nearly got him, she thinks.

Manuela is sitting in the back, not listening to them. She stares at the scrubby oleander hedges quivering in the cold wind between the guard-rails, the cars racing in the opposite direction, the numbered overpass signs, the ads for restaurants and shops selling garden supplies, furniture, lamps, and bathroom fixtures, one after another for miles and miles along the Aurelia. Six miles to go till the turnoff. Italy is one big, endless store stocked with useless things. If your desires are completely satisfied, you have nothing more to search for. She has to close her eyes. Watching the line in the middle of the road makes her nauseated.

The Torvaianica goalie's father lives in a three-family house sur-rounded by a high wall gleaming with glass shards. The black eye of a security camera blinks above the doorbells. No names, only numbers on the gold-plated brass plate. Manuela presses the first button. A foreign voice answers. Manuela says she would like to speak with Mr. Rota. "Who is this?" the voice grows alarmed. Manuela moves so that the cam-era can see her better. "I'm Sergeant Paris, the woman who attacked him on the soccer field in Ladispoli." The voice, whoever it belongs to, hangs up. Manuela turns toward Vanessa and Mattia, sitting on the hood of the Yaris. They smile encouragingly at her. Neither of them was especially sold on this visit. But Manuela had been adamant. Who knows what she was expecting. "He's home, at least, not in the hospital," Vanessa notes. "That's already something."

After five minutes, the voice comes back over the intercom: "Mr. Rota does not wish to see you." "Please," Manuela insists, "tell him I would like to apologize and to ask how he is." The edge of a curtain in a third-floor window is raised. Someone is looking out at the street. "I don't think he'll file," Mattia says. "He was the one who attacked Traian with the umbrella. A girl was killed with an umbrella, they can say it's a deadly weapon. And he's better off not going to trial against a wounded soldier." "Manuela will never forgive herself for this screwup," Vanessa says. "I know her. She wants to be perfect, she doesn't let herself make even the slightest mistake. She thinks she's somehow to blame for those three guys' deaths, I don't know if she told you. The support-group psy-chologist told me. He says that Manuela was obsessed with the idea when she was in the hospital. That when they had to tell her that those three actually weren't in the hospital as they'd led her to believe at first, but had been dead and buried almost a month, she had a breakdown, they had to sedate her because she wanted to throw herself out the window, she even broke the glass, she tried to cut her throat, but her hands weren't strong enough, she barely scratched herself, if you look you can still see the scar. She can't forgive herself for not having saved them, for being alive instead of them. But it's crazy, I read all the articles, I even talked to her commander, Captain What's-his-name, really stiff, like he had a stick up his ass, he met with the victims' families, you could see he was really broken up about losing his best men because of some stupid ceremony that shouldn't even have taken place, because that school wasn't even ready, I don't know if Manuela told you, but they wanted to inaugurate it anyway, even though the roof was still missing, no desks, just an empty shell—it was a chain of unfortunate events, the people who were supposed to be there weren't, and the people who were there shouldn't have been. You know, one of the soldiers who was killed, the youngest one, the driver—my sister had left him at the base so he wouldn't have to take this last risk, his father told me, he just can't wrap his head around it; Manuela had chosen someone else from her team, someone who'd volunteered, but for some reason the guys who were supposed to film the ceremony were stuck at another base, I don't remember why, and at the last minute the commander asked that kid to go with Manuela to film it, and so he went. In six months he'd never even gotten out of the Lince, can you imagine? All the other guys who are still alive have to deal with the fact that they're here instead of someone else. A guy with a vest full of TNT blew himself up, or someone blew him up as soon as the Italians got close. Such unbelievable atrocities. What could Manuela do? How could she have kept him from doing it? She's good at her job, really, she's the best. You know what my mother says? That she has an economy car and a luxury sedan. I'm the economy car. She thinks of me as a nonentity." "A mother would never think such a thing," Mattia comforts her. "You don't know my mother," Vanessa says. "Why don't you introduce us," Mattia retorts. He smiles happily, as if he really wanted to meet Cinzia Colella. What a weird guy.

The Torvaianica goalie's father doesn't come out. His wife stands on the doorstep and gestures for Manuela to leave, then closes the door. When she realizes that Manuela is still there, in the camera's eye, she opens the door again. She's a tall woman, hair pulled back in a chignon, nice clothes and jewelry, as if she were going out, but slippers on her feet. "You cracked his rib and broke a bone in his hand," she shouts, "he can't work for thirty days, isn't that enough for you?" Manuela approaches the gate, and a dog growls. "I would like to apologize," Manuela says, "if I could crack my own rib and break a bone in my own hand to make it up to Mr. Rota, I would; tell me what I can do." "We're not in the Middle Ages," the woman says, "it's not a question of retaliation, an eye for an eye; there's the law, the judge will decide how much it should cost you." "I know, but I'd still like to speak to him," Manuela says. The dog growls. "You did what you did, you set a fine example for those kids. I know who you are, they told us. I'm sorry. But it doesn't give you the right to beat someone up. You could have really hurt him."

On the third floor, the person behind the curtain stays and watches until she gets back in the car. Manuela is pale, serious, expressionless. Mattia keeps quiet, doesn't comment on her defeat. He understood almost nothing of what Vanessa said. Manuela never talks to him about what happened. What words could she use? Only the flesh speaks the truth. "Where is it the other guy lives?" Vanessa asks, because she doesn't feel like sitting there stewing in front of this rich, merciless man's home and have him see that an Italian army sergeant lets herself be driven around in a banged-up car. Manuela had written the madman's address on a piece of paper torn from a notebook. She wads it up in her hands, and as Vanessa grinds the gears and heads back toward the intersection, she drops it out the window.

LIVE

P alo Castle juts out into the sea. Compact, graceful, with round towers, orderly crenellations, windows neatly spaced along the façade, and a grand marble doorway: it looks like a child's happy dream. The freshly cut grass at the entrance is still damp with frost. Manuela doesn't ask Mattia what he did to get them to open the gate or what story he'd told the custodian. They're here, on a clear January morning, and in the end, that's all that matters. She's never been here before, she never even thought about being able to come, except on her wedding day. Yet now she's walking on the gravel drive, one step behind Mattia, who is telling Alessia a story—clearly a funny story, because Alessia is laughing. Manuela feels vaguely guilty that Alessia is here today, on Epiphany, and not in Piazza Navona, choosing a figurine for the nativity scene and awaiting the arrival of the Befana, as Manuela had promised. But Alessia has forgotten about that. Manuela is surprised to find herself thinking that this could become the new family tradition someday, Epiphany at Palo Castle. She regrets it immediately. The future does not exist.

The door is wide open, and movers are unloading crates from a white truck parked along the drive. The company name is stamped on all the crates. The castle has been rented. "They're holding a convention here after the holiday, but I don't know what it's about," Mattia says.

Manuela follows him through a series of rooms furnished with immense stone fireplaces topped with deer heads. Their footsteps are silent, muffled by the carpets. It's odd to be strolling through Palo Castle with Mattia. She'd come here only in her dreams. In her wedding dress, carrying a bouquet of roses, wearing white shoes, and a veil. A traditional, conventional wedding, because at the time she believed that, in spite of everything, she wanted to be a traditional, conventional girl. She and Giovanni had sent an e-mail to the owners, requesting information. It seemed phenomenally expensive. But after studying the estimate line by line and doing the math, Giovanni decided they could swing it after all: when she got back from Afghanistan they wouldn't have to scrimp and save, she'd be making a heck of a lot of money. She'd gotten insulted. They'd argued.

"You don't deploy in country for the money, only an idiot could think that a person would risk her life for a few thousand dollars, life isn't bought and sold," she had said bitterly. "Are you calling me an idiot?" Giovanni objected, incredulous. "Yes." "That's it. You can't talk to me like that, take it back." "Take it back? You're the one who should apologize," she shouted. "I don't even know what I'm supposed to apologize for, but okay, I apologize," Giovanni tried meekly to calm her down. But his servile submissiveness irritated her even more. "Let's have the reception at the Miraggio in Fregene," Giovanni suggested, "it's really fancy, there's even a pool." But it was too late. Something had broken between them. Manuela suddenly felt she was seeing her boyfriend for the first time. A weak, indecisive creature, a spineless slug who made a show of giving in so he could fling her choices and mistakes back in her face, that way he could feel sorry for himself and be absolved. Sharing her life with someone like him would be a kind of suicide. Giovanni had never understood her, and with time he'd understand her less and less. But it's not like she could blame him. Everyone has their strengths. You can't make a car out of paper, a pot out of wood, or a parachute out of lead. She left him two days later, without even bothering to tell him. She simply changed her Facebook profile. She wrote "Single," and he knew it was over.

Alessia admires the glass lanterns hung from slanted poles on either side of the door, but she likes the wooden model of a sailing ship on top of a cabinet best. Manuela steps aside to let a couch pass. "Are you the owner?" a man of about thirty addresses Mattia. "We're having a problem with the electrical system, could you please tell us where the meters are?" "I'm sorry," Mattia smiles, "but none of this belongs to me. I'm only here on behalf of the owner, the Marquis." The electrician looks at him doubtfully. "The Marquis of Carabas?" Alessia whispers excitedly. "Of course," Mattia replies with a wink. Manuela is astonished that he takes that stupid game so seriously. He never takes anything seriously; it always seems like he's passing lightly over things, not wanting to leave a trace.

They head outside. Away from the castle, the vegetation becomes thicker, the tangle of shrubbery denser. This whole area must have been covered with woods like this once. Marshes, impenetrable branches, solitude. Fragments of ancient walls emerge from the grass. Manuela remembers confusedly that the ruins of a Roman villa are around here somewhere, but she wouldn't know how to find them. When she was in her second year of tourism school, she had been tested on the castle's history. The twenty-eight girls, ignorant about everything else, were well prepared when it came to local attractions: they assumed these were the only things they would need to know. Manuela wanted to write an essay on the castle's owners, whom she found immensely fascinating: Felice Della Rovere Orsini and Leo X, the Medici pope. The noblewoman had purchased it at the beginning of the sixteenth century for nine thousand ducati, and the young pope would lodge here, along with his entourage, while hunting in the woods of Palo. He was a pope, but also a keen hunter, and his unusual, almost transgressive skills with a lance and musket had sparked her admiration for that man of the cloth, who was not supposed to hunt or kill. At fifteen, Manuela imagined that she, too, was skilled in a field theoretically prohibited to her—she already saw herself as a soldier—and the self-assurance with which the pope gratified his passions for hunting and fighting encouraged her to cultivate her own. But her professor had pointed out that both were too eccentric to be the subject of a thesis for a professional school aimed at producing tour guides and secretaries for travel agencies. The first was the daughter of a pope, and the second a homosexual who, with his scandalous behavior, had helped undermine the Church's authority and contributed to the success of the Lutheran Reformation. Manuela was disappointed, offended almost, by the revelation. She promptly forgot about them, cobbling together a scant two pages on the garrison installed in the castle to protect the borders of the Papal States in the eighteenth century. Zouaves. Mercenaries. Warriors without a history. She got a lousy grade. Warriors without a history. Like her.

"No, no, no," Mattia is saying, "you can't take a picture of the Cat, absolutely not, he's on a secret mission, you don't want to betray him, do you? Nobody can know he's here." He tries to grab Alessia, but she wriggles free and runs and hides behind a scaly oak tree. She's having fun pointing her cell at him and snaps another photo. But by now he's crouched down, so all she gets is bark and bushes. "Be a good girl and erase it," Mattia says, dropping his playful tone. Alessia laughs, waving the hand that holds the cell phone, but keeps her distance. She pulls up the image on the display. Mattia came out good, she thinks he's handsome, with his rock star hair and blue eyes, she doesn't want to erase it. She sticks out her tongue at him. She doesn't buy his cat story. Who does he think she is? She's a big girl, she'll be eight in October. There's no one else amid the ancient trees. The silence is broken only by the screech of seagulls, the obstinate call of a blackbird, and Alessia's wicked laughter. Mattia's anxiety does not escape Manuela. Why doesn't he want his picture taken? She would like to have a photo of them together. Photographs preserve memories when nothing else is left.

"This forest is just like the one in Limbo," Alessia says. "Let's play?" "I don't know what that game is," Mattia responds, "I'm old, I'm still stuck on hide-and-seek. And besides, I'm not going to play with you anymore if you don't give me that phone." Alessia explains that it's a new video game, her friend Ginevra's brother has it: there's a boy looking for his little sister, she disappeared in the woods, got lost. The player who controls the console is the boy. He meets men and monsters in the forest, and they all try to kill him. "I don't understand what the point of the game is," Manuela says. "To find the little girl," Alessia explains, "but I've never gotten to the end, they always kill me first, but it's still fun. It's better with PlayStation, but it works with real players, too, too bad there's only three of us. I'll be the boy, Manuela, you're the men, and Mattia, you're the monsters. You have to knock me down so I'm flat on the grass." "It sounds pretty violent, I don't like it," Manuela objects. "But I don't really die," Alessia says. "In this game, you don't die just once, you die all the time. You go to Limbo and then you come back to life. So you get back up and start over again, right from where you left off."

"Interesting," Mattia says, forcing himself to cover up his bad mood. "I'm in. What monster am I?" "First you're a spider, then you're a worm." Alessia is getting more and more excited. "When you're the worm you have to slither on the ground. Manuela throws pinecones at me. If you hit me I die. But let's say I escape and you chase me, you have to kill me before I make it to that tree over there, you have to trick me, jump on me from behind, lay traps, if you catch me you win and I'll let you erase the photo." Mattia pleads silently with Manuela, begs her collaboration. Alessia laughs. The man from the Bellavista is in her power. Now he'll do whatever she tells him to. He'll play the monster, get dirty crawling on the ground. "I'll count to ten," she says, "and then I'll start to run."

When Alessia gets to seven, Manuela drags Mattia behind a hedge and kisses him. "Come on, don't be mad at her, it's just a photo." Alessia's footsteps fade in the opposite direction. They chase her, showering her with pinecones, which they deliberately aim at a bush. "You go after her," Manuela says, "I can't run, but I don't feel like telling her that." For a few seconds, all she can hear is the rustle of the wind in the trees. A spider arpeggios on the silk threads of his web: perfect and empty, it sparkles in the light. Everything is suspended, simple, neat. Every religion represents Paradise as a garden. "Do you realize you've brought me to Paradise on Earth?" she whispers with a laugh. Mattia says he'd gladly bring her there again right now, but they have to wait till they get back to the hotel. Even though it would be wonderful to make love here, among the spiders and pine needles. But he wants to erase that photograph. It's really important. He straightens his hair and runs after the little girl, grumbling. Manuela hears Alessia's little scream that confirms she's been killed, she's in Limbo now. Mattia returns to the hedge. They hear Alessia get up and start running again. Mattia assumed she was just joking about the Earthly Paradise. But it's true. Her grandfather once told her that in the 1960s some American movie people came to Palo Castle. Hundreds of them, it was like an encampment. At the time, Vittorio's moving company had put him on disability because the war was still raging in his head and every once in a while his brain went all topsy-turvy. So when he heard that the producers were looking for manual laborers, he showed up, and they took him. He worked as a chauffeur for about ten days. But he wasn't driving around American actors or the director or the fabulous diva whose sexual exploits he fantasized about, just some dreadful Roman from Cinecittà. He'd drive him there every morning and then he'd roam about on set, poking around among the props and cameras, while no one paid him any mind. The guy was a snake trainer. Which meant that every morning Vittorio had a green, ten-foot-long snake as thick as a ship's cable in his van. In the floodlit park, an actor and an actress would move about half-naked. Chilled, they would put on overcoats whenever they could and drink hard liquor. The actor was always drunk. The director—a bearded American who looked a little like Noah—wasn't afraid of the snake. He claimed to secrete an odor that charmed the animals. The snake, however, was not of the same opinion; once, it wrapped its coils around him, and the snake trainer had to step in to save the director's skin. After the Americans left, Vittorio found out that the film was *The Bible*, the actors Adam and Eve, and the Palo Castle grounds the Garden of Eden. Manuela had never seen that old film, not even on TV, but people from Ladispoli still talk about it.

"Worm, you have to hit me," Alessia yells, and Mattia crawls out of his hiding place, firing a handful of pinecones at her. Alessia zigzags across the grass, rejoicing at having escaped. She's laughing, shouting, having fun. But her cell phone has fallen out of her pocket. Mattia prudently sheds his worm identity, snatches it, and then lies down on the grass again. He shows Manuela the photo. Alessia caught him smiling, looking good-natured, disheveled, and alert. But also evasive, catlike. "Erase it for me," he says. "Why?" "Let's keep the memory of today just for us, as if we were alone here, just you and me." Manuela erases the photo. "Now it's the men in the caves' turn," Alessia shouts. "Manu, come get me!!! If you don't send me to Limbo, I win." "I'm coming," Manuela yells. "I'm coming."

But she goes on hiding behind the hedge, holding her breath. Immobile, patient, the spider is still lying in wait. She hears Alessia running, panting, climbing over trunks, charging through bushes. When Alessia runs past without seeing her, Manuela gets up, and in so doing, destroys the spiderweb. The spider sinks into the leaves. "Don't catch me, Aunt Manu! Don't catch me! I win, I win!" She spots him there on the grass. Mattia doesn't move. His big body supine, his eyes to the sky, his arms crossed, hair rumpled, smiling, undoubtedly more serene than she has ever seen him. They don't make the most convincing Adam and Eve. She does feel she has been expelled from the Garden of Eden, but this park isn't it. It's the uniform, the company, the fraternity. And she doesn't know how to reconcile Mattia with all that. She drops to the grass next to him. The tall trees sway in the wind, dark green against a lapis lazuli sky. At times winter on the Tyrrhenian can be limpid and crystalline, supernatural almost. "I made it to the end and I found the little girl," Alessia's voice startles them. "I won. But you two are stuck in Limbo."

Mattia takes her hand, he doesn't want to get up, neither does she. "I think something's happened to me," Mattia says. "Did you get bit by a spider?" Manuela misunderstands. "I've found myself in you," he says, his fingers wrapping around her wrist. He can't explain it. But it's as if Manuela were his reflection in a pool of water.

Vanessa and Cinzia join them at the Posta Vecchia restaurant. Mattia has reserved a table. They're seated in front of the large window, framed by flowing red drapes. The sea in the window looks like a painting. There are only American and Japanese tourists, and the five of them, dressed as they are, seem like intruders. But the waiters pretend not to notice and treat them, like all the others, with professional kindness. "I don't want to steal Manuela away from you," Mattia says to her mother, extending his hand, "but I thought you might feel better if you met me." "You're too kind, you shouldn't have gone to all this trouble," Cinzia says, intimidated by the sumptuous dining room and the insistent presence of waiters in white livery. "What are you doing? This will ruin you," Vanessa whispers in his ear, "it's not worth it, we don't know the difference between a trattoria and a Michelin two-star." "Neither do I," Mattia replies, "but I've been eating at the Bellavista for almost three weeks, and I felt like something different."

It's not true, of course. You can see that from how he decodes the menu, which is incomprehensible, might as well be written in a foreign language as far as the Paris family is concerned (what are Jerusalem artichokes, sea truffles?), from how he chooses the bottle of wine from hundreds of labels in a leather-bound book that looks like a reliquary, from how he smells and tastes it, clicking his tongue, and by the tone he uses when he speaks to the waiter. He orders for everyone: fried zucchini flowers with caviar, raw weever with annurca apple purée, cannoli stuffed with lobster and artichoke tartare, roasted shellfish on a bed of toasted fennel, licorice, and ginger. Self-assured, easy, he shows that he doesn't take the place or the occasion too seriously. Cinzia doesn't know what to say, so she doesn't say anything, to avoid making a bad impression. Even though he's a tad too old, Mr. Rubino is distinguished, polite, and clearly rich: in short, he has class. She can't understand what he could possibly have in common with a soldier like Manuela, but she begins to hope that this unlikely relationship of theirs is the prelude to Manuela's farewell to arms—for which she is ready to forgive his difference in age and bless him forever.

The Parises are not very talkative, so Mattia ventures an odd soliloquy on city street names. He says he liked Ladispoli instantly. Oh, not for its monuments or even for the sea. But for the names. He's had to pass through Rome pretty often lately, for work. And he's struck every time by the harshness of the place-names. Il Muro Torto—the Twisted Wall; Via dei Due Macelli—the Street of Two Slaughterhouses; Via delle Fratte—the Street of Thickets; Via dei Cessati Spiriti—the Street of Dead Spirits; Via della Femmina Morta—the Street of the Dead Woman; Via del Fosso di Tor Pagnotta—the Street of the Pagnotta Tower Ditch; Tor Sanguigna—Bloody Tower; Borgata Finocchio—the Fag Neighborhood . . . In the city where he was born, the streets are named after, for example, Italy's founding fathers, Cavour, Garibaldi, Mazzini, or scientists, philosophers, battles. Then he realized that the secret of Rome is disenchantment. The lack of rhetoric. Romans, oppressed by the nearness of power, have a crude fondness for truth. They don't embellish reality, the flaws of which they know well; instead they serve it up and take it as it comes. Apparently the people of Lazio are the same. A city where the streets are called Via dell'Infernaccio—Real Hell Street; Via dell'Anatra—Duck Street; Via delle Folaghe—Coot Street; Via della Caduta delle Cavalle—the Street Where Mares Fall; has a simple, straightforward soul, and he feels at home in Ladispoli.

"Are you thinking of moving here?" Vanessa tosses out as she empties her wineglass with a studied indifference. Manuela's eyes sink into her lobster cannoli, she'd like to bury herself in them. Yet that question—which she never would have dared to pose—makes her heart race. She begins to fear she has forgotten every safeguard, every strategy, that she's gone too far with him. So far that she wouldn't know how to turn back. "I could live here," Mattia replies. "I'm sure I could live here happily."

An hour and a half later, when even the peach soufflé with star anise and violets is nothing more than a pink shadow on their plates, Alessia starts getting restless and Cinzia, relieved, takes her to see the swimming pool. "I made a terrible impression on her," Mattia observes. "Mamma really doted on Giovanni," Vanessa says. "Manuela was supposed to marry him, I don't know if she told you, Mamma wanted to see her married off, my mother and I don't have any luck with men, we fall for the ones who can't be trusted, but Manuela had this good kid, studious, serious, Mamma hoped she'd have a solid marriage, it's better for soldiers not to divorce, they're traditionalists, they still worry about those things, Mamma was really counting on it, and she still hasn't accepted the fact that they broke up." Manuela blushes with embarrassment, but Mattia doesn't ask her about Giovanni. He's very sure of himself. Or maybe he just doesn't care. He smiles at her, relaxed, satisfied, calm, and all of a sudden Manuela suspects that he's playing a part. That his excessive intimacy with Alessia, the idyll in the Garden of Eden, the official lunch with the family, that nonsense about street names, the conversation, the declaration of love for Ladispoli—that it's all an act. Theater. Once the show is over and the curtain drops, the stage will be empty. Mattia has no intention of living in Ladispoli. He took the risk of meeting her mother because he knows he won't have to see her again. She had offered him her confused heart and he accepted it, but he could just as easily throw it away tomorrow without even realizing it. A rage that she can neither repress nor control rises up inside her.

Mattia is telling Vanessa, in his usual smug, slightly forced voice, that mothers usually like him. They find him reassuring, think he's the ideal boyfriend. He's sorry he's disappointed so many of them. Evidently their mother is more shrewd. She's right to suspect him, he can't be trusted, just like the men Vanessa and Cinzia like. As he speaks, he gazes too attentively at Vanessa, and his blue eyes, the pupils encircled by contact lenses, gleam maliciously. For a second, Manuela has the impression she has unmasked him, and she hates him for it. She clenches her fists and crumbles her *grissini* onto the tablecloth. She needs air. She stands up so suddenly that the diligent waiter doesn't have time to move her chair aside. It falls over loudly. "I'm going out to the terrace to smoke," she informs him curtly. She intentionally bangs her crutches on the marble.

Vanessa watches her leave, and when the glass door closes again, she bends over him, so close that her hair tickles his nose. She tells him that when Manuela went off to war—because that's what it was—it became her job to defend her. "How?" Mattia asks. He tries to catch the waiter's attention by raising his arm, because he's afraid of Vanessa's confidences. He doesn't want to talk about Manuela with her. He doesn't want to talk about Manuela with anyone. It's all too new and fragile to sustain other people's opinions. "I thought about my sister at least five times a day," Vanessa explains, "I'd mentally review her gestures, her smile, the memories we share, the things she had said to me, her gait, her reserve, her determination, her idealism, her innocence. It was my way of enveloping her with my aura, because at the time I was convinced I had developed significant spiritual powers. Positive powers, I mean, like I could emanate goodness. In short, I watched over her in order to save and protect whatever of Manuela needed to be saved and protected. I kept her alive and true to herself. I knew that terrible things could happen over there, things that could change her, but I was trying to hold on to her real personality so I could give it back to her whole when she came home. But Manuela, the Manuela I tried to protect, still hasn't come back."

Mattia doesn't know what to say. He's not sure he has quite understood what Vanessa means, but he doesn't believe in these things anyway. No one can protect someone else, you can't even protect yourself. No one preserved the best things in him. When the waiter comes to ask if they would like bitters, limoncello, grappa, herbal tea, Mattia tells him just to bring the check. Vanessa presses her hand in his. "Manuela still isn't well," she says, "I don't know if you really understand how sick she is." "Yes, I do," Mattia says. "Listen to me," Vanessa says, almost threateningly. "If you hurt her, I swear I'll come find you, wherever you are, and I'll make you regret it."

Mattia looks distractedly at the bill, without even checking the math. Vanessa is surprised when, despite the not insignificant sum, he pays in cash instead of with a credit card. The bills are new, smooth, intact. Mattia slips the money into the leather folder. "The last thing in the world I want," he says almost sadly, "is to hurt Manuela."

The Posta Vecchia restrooms smell of lavender. Enormous mirrors over the sinks. Stacks of pure white towels, the size of handkerchiefs. The four white doors are all ajar. No one's there. Manuela fights the annoying but irresistible urge to cry. She doesn't know what exactly she blames Mattia for. For having deceived her, or for simply having involved her. Because it's as if she's been under anesthesia all these months. Her indifference was her protection. And now it's like she's walking through hostile terrain without a bulletproof vest, exposed to every shot. It's too much. She locks herself in the last stall, out of old habit, looking for a little privacy. In the barracks she learned how to control her bladder and pee without making a sound. You have to aim the jet at the porcelain, avoiding the pool of water. Years ago, she had been proud of her ability.

It made her invisible, and therefore invulnerable. The liquid slides silently into the toilet. She can still do it. It seems she has forgotten everything about military life. All that's left is this pathetic habit.

She reaches for the toilet paper, but there's none left. She swears, angry at not having noticed earlier. She hops toward her purse dangling on a hook, opens it, rummages around, but doesn't have any tissues. She's about to open the door and grab a strip from the next stall, when she senses a presence. A woman approaches in high heels, closes the door, the rustle of a skirt. Ever since Manuela came home, she'd been washing herself constantly. Hands, face, body. She feels dirty all the time. She can't imagine simply pulling up her jeans and leaving, as if it were nothing. The immodest dripping in the next toilet. "Fuck it," she whispers and cleans herself Afghani style, with her left hand, the impure hand. She stares blankly at her fingers.

The woman flushes, the water gurgles down the drain, and it takes a second before she hears the strange sound coming from the next stall. A lament, a moan almost. She hesitates, then hurriedly washes her hands, dries them on a cloth towel, throws it in the wicker basket, and, her heels ticking, goes out into the atrium. Behind the closed door, someone is crying.

Manuela has fallen between the toilet and the plywood wall, her good knee against her chest, the other leg stretched out on the floor, her hand pressed against the door. Her heart is racing. Her fingers leave bloody prints on the white wall. She keeps her eyes stubbornly closed. She can no longer stand the sight of blood. At the hospital she would faint whenever she had to have her blood drawn. And she threw up when the nurse passed her pushing a trolley of samples to be analyzed. She almost threw up at the discount butcher counter, distraught by all those plastic-wrapped cuts of meat and the acrid smell rising from the packets. She even worried she'd get sick when Alessia scratched herself in the woods. But now it's even worse. It's her own blood dripping from her fingers. She hasn't gotten her period since that night in the Gulistan gorge, more than eight months ago.

When she consulted with Lieutenant Ghigo, she told her it was normal. It happens to a lot of women during a tour of duty, their bodies are transformed. It's as if the brain sends the body a message. There's no need to inhibit menstruation with some hormonal bomb. It simply disappears: the women become soldiers, nothing more. The doctor at the military hospital told her not to worry as well. It's a result of trauma, he explained. When you're feeling better, your period will start up again on its own. But she's not feeling better at all. On the contrary, she's having a meltdown, she can't control anything anymore, she's a heap of broken shards. Dumbfounded, she waits for who knows what, balled up in the bathroom of the Posta Vecchia, her heart pounding, her body bleeding, and her mouth tasting of rust.

She wants to go home with Vanessa in the Yaris. She says goodbye to him in the restaurant parking lot, kissing him coldly on the cheek. Mattia, surprised, just stands there next to his rental car, turning the key over in his fingers. Alessia presses her nose against the back window and waves goodbye. He hesitates, as big as a bear, stunned and shaken among the cars, the sun already setting. He seems lost. When he buzzes her apartment at six to ask if she wants to go for a walk on the beach, Vanessa tells him Manuela's not home. She went to the doctor. She wasn't feeling well and wanted to get a prescription for those stupid drops of hers. "Did I do something wrong?" he asks her hesitantly. "How should I know?" Vanessa replies. "Please tell her to call me when she gets back."

She doesn't call. She locks herself in her room, turns on the stereo, and after a long time, puts on a CD: *This Is Resurrection*, by Krysantemia, an Italian death metal group she discovered before deployment, which she took to Bala Bayak. The doleful voice of the singer and the obsessive torment of the drums helped her ease the tension. Serene Nicola Russo, who loved the rarefied melodies of Radiohead, had never been able to fathom how she could love that brutal, oppressive music, those strangled, cavernous voices that sounded like a pig being slaughtered, those lyrics that spoke of death, autopsies, insanity, cannibalism, and blood. The malicious names of her favorite groups were scary enough on their own: Amputation, Vader, Hades, Sadist, Deicide, Cryptopsy, Necrodeath. But that corrosive, blatant violence was useful. It was like it absorbed the no less brutal violence of the world and made it bearable.

As the notes of "Hope in Torment" hammer her ears, she surfs the Internet—the Ministry of Defense website, for news from the theater of operations: a hospital was inaugurated in Shindand yesterday, the other day an attack on the Eighth Alpini Regiment was thwarted; an English-language Afghani newspaper site: a teacher in the province of Uruzgan was killed, the brother of a police officer hung, a checkpoint on the road to Gereshk destroyed. A Belgian filmmaker who shot a documentary on kites declared he didn't have any problems at all in Kabul, except from the Americans when he picked up his equipment at the airport. Then she goes on Facebook, to Angelica Scianna's page. Her profile still says "Single." Angelica had posted a photo of herself in officer's uniform standing next to a Mangusta helicopter. In some ways they look alike, both slender, as if they want the smallest surface areas possible exposed to the enemy. Angelica is pretty, strong, and free. Her twin sister. Manuela wanted to be like her, but Angelica had left her behind. She has two gold stars on her epaulet. She's in Afghanistan. Lieutenant Scianna's last post is about a return flight through the mountains during a snowstorm. White above, white below, white everywhere, snow on her windshield, almost out of fuel, emergency landing impossible, hostile region, fear of an ambush, low flying, adverse weather conditions, I did it, I'm still here! Enthusiastic comments, a shower of smiley-face emoticons. She would like to write something, but you can't revive nostalgia. She's lost her. As she hesitates, fingers hovering on the keyboard, it occurs to her that no, she wouldn't want to be in her place. She wouldn't want to fly a combat helicopter. She wouldn't want to see Afghanistan from the sky, to consider the hills and streets and villages below her as threats and targets. But she's disappointed in herself for thinking such a thing, a thought that does not belong to Manuela Paris. She hates herself for having conceived it.

She rummages in her duffel and dumps the contents out on the floor. Her bags were sent to her from Afghanistan when her regiment rotated out. They followed her to the hospital and then home, but this is the first time she's opened them. The mere sight of her duffel nauseates her. Things tumble out higgledy-piggledy, giving off the stale smell of dust. There's the white-and-black kaffiyeh and the scarves she covered her hair with when she met with the village elders. Her prepaid Banana phone cards for calling Italy. The postcards she'd received from her cousin Claudio on vacation in Sharm, and the black-and-white ones of the Herat Citadel and the Jam minaret she'd bought from the son of the beggar woman who looked like her mother and who came to Sollum one cold day in January. The beggar woman's name resurfaces intact from the past: Fatimeh. Her tattered diary. T-shirts, socks, a wad of dirty laundry. Fine pinkish yellow sand from the Farah desert falls from the pages of her diary, her clothes, and postcards, and filters onto the tile floor. A little bag of glass beads. She bought them for Vanessa, but forgot to give them to her. A pile of blue shards, once an elegant blown glass bottle that didn't survive the turbulence of the C-130. And a blue-green rug, rolled up and wrapped in a dirty rag. All that remains of six months of her life. A few smelly objects ruined by the journey. Nothing came back whole. Nothing survived. Neither things nor ideas—no hopes or dreams or memories. Not even herself.

> >

19

HOMEWORK

can't find anything to blame myself for. I respected military ethics, or maybe just ethics in general. So did Diego. Still, I felt uncomfortable eating dinner with him in the mess tent. The thought of his son haunted him. Lots of thoughts haunted him. I couldn't understand him. He was my friend, but I couldn't understand him. Once when we were digging into a breakfast covered in stubborn desert flies, he asked me if I wanted to have children. I told him no. He didn't believe me. "Don't you wonder what your child would look like? When you hold him in your arms and you ask yourself, will I be able to raise him? How can I teach him things I don't know?" I was quick to explain that I didn't think about it at all, I didn't feel cut out to be a mother.

"What sort of logic is that?" Diego interrupted me. "You're not born feeling cut out to be a mother or a father, you just do it. It happens. Imma and I, before I deployed, during those last three months of training, we never saw each other, and we only made love once. By the laws of probability it should have been fine. But it happened anyway. Now, when I think about it, I wish I'd never left the barracks. I wish I'd been more careful. I'm only twenty-six and I have a family to support." I tried to convince him that he'd be a terrific father. "I know," he answered, "I love my son already, more than anything. But I could have had a career. I'm the best, and you know it, and instead I took myself out of the running all by myself. I'll never have the heart to leave them for another tour of duty." "You've done plenty of them already," I said, trying to downplay things. "You should be happy about that. Bosnia, Lebanon, Kosovo, you've been all over the place. They've gone to your head, all those tours of yours." He told me I couldn't understand. "You only really grow up when you have a child. You realize you're mortal."

Time started moving more quickly. Paggiarin informed me that we had twelve hours to get ready: Lambda squad would leave on Saturday for the COP in Khurd, on the edge of the security bubble. It was the last week of May, twenty-five days till we went home, and Reawakening's objective still hadn't been reached. And I knew it.

Just like its name said—*khurd* means "little"—the outpost was a hole, a stone pit protected by sandbags, not much more than a trench, dug during the night with a pick and shovel, carved into the top of a barren hill on the edge of the desert. When I saw it, it seemed anachronistic; it reminded me of the trenches on the Carso. I had studied WWI defensive fortifications at Viterbo, never imagining I'd have to man one. But the Ninth had built several outposts like this one, laid out in a star shape around Sollum. Every time a section of land was cleared and secured, they'd build another one, farther out. The COPs were five kilometers from the base the first month, nine the second month, then thirteen. Khurd was at eighteen. The whole company was supposed to take turns, either in platoons or in teams of twenty or so, spending nine consecutive days at the COP, keeping watch on the mountains and the road below. There were Afghani soldiers there, too, separated from the Alpini by a wall. They communicated by shouting, in terrible English.

Sometimes nothing happened there, and the only event worthy of note was the arrival of provisions, tossed from an airplane, so the team's shift seemed like a survival course or a meditative retreat. The men came back sunburned, or battered by boredom, cold, or heat, and whether they'd seen God or minded their own business, they were happy to return to the Spartan civilization of the FOB. Other times they shot at you, from a hole just like ours, dug with a pickaxe on the opposite hill, a heap of white rocks gleaming in the sun. Light weapons, machine-gun fire, antitank rockets, even mortar fire. My Gamma team was lucky. Only flies bothered it.

When I got there, all was calm. Once I'd coordinated the rotations, Spina asked me if I wanted to go back to Sollum with Gamma. He could stay with Lambda. Khurd hadn't been designed for a woman.

There wasn't enough space to carve out separate quarters. He also told me that time never seemed to pass there. Keeping watch for an hour frayed your nerves more than a whole day driving around in a Lince because—for the first time in all those months—you knew those weren't just ghosts in front of you. The rebels' position was less than a kilometer away; the only thing that separated us was a gravel riverbed, which ran dry in the hot season. We could almost see them with the naked eye. The soldiers, on their cots, waited their turn to keep watch, and then time became an endless circle again. "I'll stay," I said. A commander who does not share the cold, the heat, the lousy food, the boredom, and the danger with her men isn't a good leader. Spina laughed and said he knew it, he'd already had them put up a dividing curtain for me.

Our shift proved to be more eventful. Our hearing had grown exceptionally acute over the months, and we were able to analyze the slightest sound for clues as to a projectile's trajectory. The interval between the thud of the shot and the roar of the explosion told us the distance from which it had been fired. A rustle in the air alarmed us, but not enough to make us move; the projectile would land far away, at most sending up some sand spurts. A whistle similar to a birdcall, on the other hand, indicated a serious threat. Which is why Jodice recognized it right away. When it was launched, at 1708 hours on our one hundred and sixty-second day, it made a sinister hiss. "Mortar, Sarge!" he shouted, pulling me to the ground. The first round hit very close by with a terrifying crash, shattering the roof that covered the trench. The second ripped the door off the storehouse; the third landed in the sandbags.

We radioed FOB immediately that we'd been attacked by Russian-manufactured mortar bombs, 122 mm, judging by the dimensions and explosive power. I asked our bombers to intervene, and was told that first they had to verify there were no civilians in the area. "Can't you divert some Black Cats?" "Negative, the AMX are engaged to the north, assisting a Spanish patrol in difficulty." A drone had taken off from Herat, they said. A drone flies at one hundred and fifty kilometers an hour, I was thinking, it will already be dark when it starts surveying the mountain, and the sniper, or whoever it is, will already have taken cover; it will be impossible to locate him. And that's exactly what happened. I ate disgusting combat rations with the Lambda guys, prosciutto cubes and vinegary peaches in syrup. I settled down on a cot. There were no more privileges at COP Khurd. We really were all equal there.

At dawn the mortar rounds started falling again, with the same monotonous and implacable regularity. But more precise this time. One gutted the chemical toilet, forcing us—until the ingenious Giovinazzo managed to get it working again somehow—to crouch in the sand and scatter our excrement in an already restricted space, shedding any remaining modesty. Taking a shit became a test of one's courage. The explosions shook the ground and rumbled in our heads. I was tormented by migraines. The ability to react to exhaustion and stress is what distinguishes a good soldier from a mediocre one. I knew it, and so did my men. I felt trapped. I didn't want to die in a trench like a rat. Of all possible combat deaths, that seemed the most inglorious. Hunched over, I crept from one hole to the next in a tunnel that smelled of smoke and stank like an animal den. I didn't dare raise my head. Now, when I collapsed on my cot, exhausted, I had to really make sure that whoever was on guard duty didn't fall asleep, didn't get distracted even for a second. And when it was my turn, on duty with another soldier, squeezed so tightly into the hole we could barely move, the heat suffocating us, the other guy's sweat soaking my uniform, plastered so tightly together that I couldn't have said where my body ended and his began, I had to make sure that he saw what I didn't, noticed whatever escaped me. That sleepy, stinking, sweat- and dust-encrusted comrade held my life in his hands. In a certain sense, I was him and he was me. I put my life in Diego Jodice's hands. And I held his in mine. When you have shared that waiting, there's no going back. You can no longer be just yourself. His life will belong to you forever. And yours to him.

"If it weren't for the baby," he said to me the second day, without taking his eye off his sight, "I would have left Imma. I thought about it every night, all the time. She's not the one for me. The woman for me would like what I do, really be able to appreciate it, she'd accept that she came second to or alongside this, she wouldn't try to take it from me because without it, I wouldn't be me. Do you understand what I'm saying?" "No, Diego," I said. We waited in the surreal silence for the hiss. Buzzing flies tormented us. I was crouched in the hole, behind the sandbags, shoulder to shoulder with Diego, hands numb, nostrils profaned by the humiliating odor of human feces. "Nothing's going to happen to us, Mulan," Diego said. We had given them the correct coordinates this time, we had the technology and the capacity, we could blow those fucking mortars to smithereens in three seconds. But even if something went wrong, and we weren't able to take them out, the risk wasn't very high. It was a question of math. An elementary calculation.

"You have to consider the caliber—let's say it's a 122 millimeter—the explosive charge, the weight of the projectile—at least fifteen kilos—the number of rounds a minute—five, I think, even though he hasn't fired more than three so far, maybe because he doesn't want to overheat the tube. We're not exactly in ideal target range, because the angle's not so good; what's more, he can't see us, and there's enough space around us for chance and destiny to work in our favor. And besides, mortars explode upward and outward, and we're holed up in here. Let's say the mortar is about ten klicks away, and the firing area is the outpost surface, six hundred square meters more or less. Each one of us occupies less than a square meter. So now calculate the radius of action of every hit. Let's say twenty square meters. Divide the space—six hundred—by the radius of action—twenty—and you get the rate of probability that we'll be hit before that fucking mortar is eliminated. Thirty. So there's a twenty-nine-to-one chance we'll survive. That means that in one minute we have sixty out of one thousand, seven hundred and forty chances of being hit. The situation's not as bad as it seems."

"I don't understand the first thing about math, and I don't think you do either, Spaniard," I said, trying to wedge myself deeper into the hole. "If your probability calculations work as well as the one you made with Imma, we'll all go on ahead, we'll all meet our death, and they'll take us back to Italy wrapped in flags." A mortar explosion, which hit just beyond the edge of the trench, deafened us. We had to keep cotton in our ears for a whole day. "If you really look at life up close, it's just a shitload of things that happen to you by chance," Diego observed. "Irrational, improbable things. No rhyme or reason. But from far away you can make out the pattern. You know those Nazca drawings in Peru? I saw a documentary on TV. You can only see the designs from the sky, from the ground they're just furrows in a field. But from above you can make out birds, animals; none of those lines are by chance. Well, it's the same thing with life. Seen from afar, there is a rhyme and a reason." "And what might that be?" I asked skeptically. "I'm still trying to figure it out, Mulan," Diego said, scratching his helmet. But his bizarre probability calculations worked. No one was hit at the outpost. We sang on our way back to the FOB.

By now it was over. I could consider my tour of duty a success. I had resisted—physically and psychologically—for one hundred and sixty-seven days. I had shown character and I hadn't let anyone trample me. I had kept my emotional nature in check, but without suppressing it, because it turned out to be a gift instead of a limitation. I had united my men. We had become a very stable unit. We had cordoned villages, located explosives, and helped capture insurgents. I had designed itineraries that might be used in the future. I had been prudent but not devoid of initiative. I had lost only one Lince, in a textbook ambush that we still managed to thwart in a real armed conflict and without any helicopter backup. The Ninth's mission could be considered a success as well. A moderate success, yes, but a success nevertheless. We had completed numerous projects, and were leaving others at a good point for the brigade that would replace us. We had respected Operation Reawakening's calendar and achieved our objective. Or almost. The security bubble around the FOB had been extended to eighteen kilometers, not the twenty requested. But the two thousand missing meters disappeared from the report. I don't think anyone can blame us for having erased from the map three villages lying in ruins and already buried by sand. The school for girls at Qal'a-i-Shakhrak wasn't ready either. After it was destroyed by fire in March, there had been some problems with the local laborers. Three weeks before it was finished, the construction workers disappeared. But Tenth Alpini Regiment headquarters wanted to inaugurate it anyway. It would have been unfair, after all the work we did and all the sand we ate, to deny the Alpini this satisfaction. It was a question of prestige, of image, and also of money. The schools in the small towns in the Dolomites where the regiment was stationed had gotten involved, participating enthusiastically in the project. They'd raised money and bought teaching supplies. Blackboards, felt-tip pens, notebooks. Italian children had drawn pictures and written notes to Afghani children their age. You couldn't disappoint all those good people.

Colonel Minotto finally informed Paggiarin that there would be a purely symbolic ceremony, a simple ribbon cutting in front of the unfinished building. The Tenth would send only a small CIMIC delegation to represent headquarters, along with the Media Combat Team cameras to immortalize it all on film. Paggiarin informed me that, other than for the school ceremony, Pegasus would not be leaving the FOB again. We had not been designated as one of the platoons to initiate reconnaissance and flank the first parachutists, who had already arrived at the base.

Outreach missions were over, too. The Ninth had done nine of them, which, given the unstable situation, was respectable. When I informed my men that there would be no more activity for them beyond the base, just guard duty inside the FOB, they applauded. Now we could start looking back; the mission was already beginning to seem like a memory.

During our last weeks there, some enterprising Afghanis began entering the protective barrier at the base. The merchants, who arrived on motorcycles or in ramshackle Toyotas, were eyed with suspicion by the sentries in the towers, who kept them in the crosshairs of their machine guns; the Afghanis stopped at the proper distance from the entrance, subjected themselves to the bomb-sniffing dog's nose, and hauled their wares in on their shoulders, like traveling salesmen. They sold homemade knickknacks at prices that were exorbitant for the locals but affordable for the Alpini. Metalwork, embroidery, glassware, kilims, carpets, embroidered tablecloths, ceramics, even lapis lazuli. The Afghanis knew that when a company nears the end of its mission and prepares to go home, military spirit fades inexorably: once they get through two thirds of their tour, the countdown starts, and at minus thirty, everything begins to slide. An apathy that no order managed to remedy, a sense of departure, of conclusion that broke down discipline, efficiency, everything. In the end the only thing the soldiers wanted, what they longed for, practically demanded, were souvenirs.

Ghaznavi had told me that after almost ten years of forced cohabitation, the Afghanis had learned to distinguish the various contingents—and their characteristics. They had drawn up a list. The British were the best in terms of military capabilities. In terms of resources, equipment, and arms, the Americans. For the combination of the two—the French, with the Polish and Canadians right behind them. For logistics and organization, the Germans. The Italians prevailed in human potential and adaptability. But when it came to spending, well, then the classification was reversed. The Italians took first place, hands down. The Germans were good, the Americans, Spanish, and Canadians fair, the Danish and Czechs poor, and the French and Brits dead last. The Italians bought everything, though most preferred carpets and jewels, presents for their wives or girlfriends. (We were also number one in this: there wasn't anyone who didn't have a wife or girlfriend, and so the Afghanis, who by twenty were all married and had fathered families, related better to us.) Some even bought burqas for their wives or girlfriends. They bargained energetically, showing off the Dari and Pashto words they'd learned in the past months, not so much to save money but because it was fun.

The second to last Sunday, D+165, or −15, Russo and Jodice were inspecting a burgundy red carpet. I was curious and went over to take a look. The vendor swore that it came from Herat, handmade, an authentic antique. "Don't get shafted!" I warned them, convinced as I was by then that the Afghanis were the best liars in the world. "It'll turn out to be made in Pakistan, woven by tiny fingers. Children go blind weaving carpets." "Come on, Paris," Russo laughed, "do you always have to be so politically correct? Whoever made it made it, it's beautiful, we like it, we want it. How much do you want for it?" he asked the vendor in Dari, who replied by flashing him a price with his fingers. It was too much. Seventeen thousand AFN, about three hundred dollars, two hundred euros. The lieutenant and the Spaniard burst out laughing. "Here carpets are a part of the bride's dowry," Nicola explained to Diego, "you absolutely have to buy it for your girlfriend." "But you saw it first," Diego objected, flattered. "I bought one the last time," Russo sighed, "my wife says all it's good for is collecting dust. My daughter is allergic to mites. Her skin turns pink, like a pig, she scratches herself until she bleeds, poor angel." "Okay, I'll get it, then," Diego says. "But you have to swear you'll come to my wedding. Imma and I are getting married on August ninth, in the Marcianise cathedral. You must have plenty of vacation days, you didn't use a single one here."

"Inshallah," Russo said, making a vague gesture. He was reserved, he guarded his private life, and did not speak willingly about his family. He showed me a photo of his little girl only once, on his cell. Brown curls and sparkling eyes. She turned two that day and they had thrown a party for her, with a cake and pink candles. He was distraught at the thought of not being there, but before I could say anything he slipped his phone into his pocket. The Afghani pushed the carpet toward the lieutenant because he knew how to decipher the ranks on their epaulets and was hoping an officer would spend more than an enlisted man. In fact, Diego offered him a tenth of his asking price. "It is not good done," Diego said in his southern Italian English. "Look, mistake, defect, not good." The Afghani protested energetically in Dari. "He says the irregularity is intended," Russo translated, "it keeps away the evil eye, perfection attracts the envy of wicked elves." "Son of a bitch!" Diego laughed and repeated his offer. The Afghani repeated his request. "Keep at it, Diego," Russo said good-naturedly, "if you can get it for less than ten thousand, it's a good price." Diego was stunned; it was the first time the lieutenant used his first name. "Aren't you going to invite me to your wedding, Spaniard?" I teased as soon as the lieutenant moved on. "Or aren't I important enough?" "You're too important," Diego said with a sigh. He got the carpet for a third of the original price, and both of them—vendor and soldier—were convinced it was a good deal.

The carpet I brought home is not the burgundy one that Diego had bargained over that day. It's blue, with a tangle of green leaves. Maybe it wasn't made in some factory in Pakistan. Maybe some widow in Herat really did weave it on a loom, in some rural workshop, financed by the military co-op that supported women's work. I found it on my cot Sunday evening, unrolled like a blanket. "It's from Baluchistan, at least that's what Russo told me," Diego said, coming up behind me. "He knows these things, he's already done two tours here." "But didn't you buy the red one?" I asked with surprise. "It's yours," Diego said. "Consider it a wedding gift from the Spaniard. A bride can't not have a carpet."

"But I'm not getting married," I objected with a smile, "not when I get back or ever. I'm a free spirit. I'm not made to be somebody's wife. I prefer to be wholly myself than half of something." "Maybe you'll change your mind one day and you won't be able to come back and get one," Diego said. "And besides, I already bought it, keep it, that way you'll remember me." "Thank you," I said, "it's really elegant. What's the design?" "It's the most beautiful thing in the world," Diego said, enthralled. "The tree of life."

The next day, at 0700 hours, I learned I had to choose a team to escort the lieutenant to the inauguration of the girls' school in Qal'a-i-Shakhrak.

20

LIVE

iego Jodice's son is baptized at noon in the Marcianise cathedral. Diego Lorenzo Nicola Jodice. Godfather: General Astorre, commander of the brigade in which the deceased young father served. Godmother: Sergeant Paris, picked up at her house by Lieutenant Gautieri and taken to the ceremony in an army car. Some Panthers are there, Ninth Company comrades-in-arms, and a sizable contingent from Pegasus platoon, twenty or so emotional men in uniform, their black feathers flying. Almost all of Lambda team is there. In Lorenzo Zandonà's place is his older brother Fabio. It's a moving ceremony, but not as sad as Manuela had feared. The Jodice family turns out to be a tribe of about a hundred people, including at least two dozen wild children, excited by the unusual presence of so many men in uniform. When they exit the church and stretch their legs in the churchyard, the bells are pealing, like on Easter.

Manuela is amazed to see that Imma, Diego's brown-haired and buxom girlfriend, is only twenty or so. During mass, and even at the baptismal font, she avoided meeting Manuela's gaze. Outside the church, Manuela makes her way among the soldiers to greet her. She doesn't really know how to act. She feels tender toward her, because Diego spoke about her every day, tormenting them all by singing her praises. Manuela is meeting her for the first time, but in truth she already knows her well. Knows what she likes to eat, what her favorite beer is, what outlet she buys her clothes at, where she goes on vacation, what her sign is, even what she says when she makes love. Manuela goes to hug her, but Imma turns her head and presents her cheek for a formal kiss. Manuela is about to say something appropriate to the occasion, but Imma is swept away by a whole host of festive girlfriends who compete for the newborn, squealing in admiration, and Manuela is pushed to the end of the line. General Astorre has to leave, an unavoidable commitment. He asks her hurriedly how she is, promises that the army will not forget about her, we're all family. Paggiarin has to leave right away, too. Unfortunately he can't come to the reception. He's rounder than before, and there are some gray hairs in his beard. Manuela recognizes the merit cross for Afghanistan on his chest and the tower of new ranks on his epaulets. He has been promoted to major. "I appreciate that you found the strength to come, Paris," he tells her. "This child is the son of the entire regiment. We can't forget about him. We're taking up a collection, so the family knows we're here. They're good people, and they need it."

Fabio Zandonà looks like his brother. He has the same freckles and the same copper-colored hair. Uncomfortable in his double-breasted blue suit, strangled by his tie, which he clearly never wears, disoriented because he doesn't know anyone, timid like Lorenzo and with the same meek smile on his lips. She gins up some courage and introduces herself. "I'm Manuela," she says, extending her hand. "I know," Fabio replies, embracing her warmly, "Lorenzo would send me photos, you were always in them." "He was like a brother to me," Manuela says. "Lorenzo would be glad to know you made it," Fabio says with embarrassment. "He really loved you. He would always write and say that Afghanistan was terrible, if the cold doesn't kill you, the heat will, the people smile at us and thank us and meanwhile they're making explosives to kill us, you can't trust anyone, I feel more like a civilian volunteer after an earthquake than a soldier, but then there's Sergeant Paris." Manuela smiles. "You must come visit us in Mel," Fabio adds, "my mother would like to meet you." "I will," Manuela promises, "as soon as I recover and am back at the barracks."

Fabio wants to settle on a date because his mother really did insist he bring Sergeant Paris to Mel, but he can't detain her any longer because the Pegasus soldiers have all crowded around her, showering her with questions. They haven't seen her since the day they visited her in the military hospital, right after they got back. But she was still immobilized in bed then, foggy from the painkillers, dazed from the drugs, she could barely speak, couldn't even see straight. On the young faces bending over her she saw solidarity, grief, gratitude, even friendship. But also relief, and embarrassment at their own overflowing good health. It had happened to her. She was on the other side of a divide, in a world of sickness and disability, and no one could or would want to accompany her into that kind of afterlife. After they left, she had the doctor ask Captain Paggiarin to spare her any further visits, she just didn't feel up to it. And now they all want to know how she is, what she's doing, when she's coming back.

But Manuela wants to know all about them. Some have served their time and left the military: Giuseppe Lando is a policeman, Dennis Venier works for the Veneto region, Ettore Zanchi found out in October that he was accepted for permanent service; Francesco Montano was promoted to lance corporal, he received his stripes in Bala Bayak, before leaving; Andrea Pieri received a commendation. Not a medal, they only give out those to the gravely wounded or the dead. Lance Sergeant Spina is about to deploy again: he'll be attached to Twenty-Third Company. He gave Diego's son a magnificent gift, an antique dagger with a curved blade and lapis lazuli on the handle, you should see it. And Angkor, why isn't she here? She'd like to see Sokha Giani again, with her silky hair, almond eyes, and fear of scorpions. "Don't you know?" Good Egg is surprised. "I haven't heard from her in quite a while," Manuela says in way of apology. "Giani married that bomb disposal expert of hers, a really sweet wedding, in Belluno, she invited us all, we drained every wine cellar in the province, she's on her honeymoon now, that's why she couldn't come, too bad, she really wanted to."

The guys are warm, friendly, like at the FOB, like at the COP. Manuela spent nearly six months with them. She was responsible for them, encouraged and reprimanded them, at times even punished them, but for the most part she defended them. They trusted one another. They called each other brothers. But now it's like she doesn't know them. The explosion shattered the group, broke their ties, scattered them, just as it did Diego's body. They share the memory of the past, the cult of the dead, the mourning—but nothing more.

At the restaurant, even though Puddu claims her, she sits next to Fabio Zandonà. She feels calm next to him, whereas seeing Owl's face only causes her pain. Puddu had always been the radio operator in her Lince. But on the morning of June 8 he had a fever, 100.4°F, devoured by a cough from the dust that tarred his lungs, he was spitting bloody red mucus, and didn't feel like sacrificing himself yet again, his tour of duty was almost over and he didn't have anything left to prove: he was granted a medical excuse. Lieutenant Ghigo gave him two days of rest. So Russo, who was supposed to go with another team, had taken his place, and had taken Ghaznavi along. Puddu is one of the walking dead, just like her, and she doesn't want to see him again. *Avoidance.*

Fabio talks about Lorenzo's funeral, but not the state one in Rome, at Santa Maria degli Angeli. The private one in Mel. "Private so to speak—the entire town came, six thousand people, they're going to name an elementary school after him. They buried him in the part of the cemetery reserved for WWI soldiers, Alpini who died on the Piave or the Grappa, a great honor. Lorenzo didn't really think of himself as a soldier, but as someone who was just passing through. In his letters home he would write that he was not worthy of licking the others' boots. But that's how he was, generous with everyone else and critical with himself." Anyhow, being buried alongside the Alpini of WWI is an important recognition, and he deserved it.

Manuela doesn't want to talk about Lorenzo dead, though. She wants to talk about Lorenzo alive. And besides, she doesn't want to hear those things about him. Nail wasn't a dead dog. He never held back. He'd driven his tank over dunes, through mud, and under fire. And he always did his duty, even if he didn't believe it was his duty, even though he'd never believed it.

She tells Fabio Zandonà how Lorenzo would offer his music to the wind in Bala Bayak. "He wrote songs in Afghanistan, and he'd play them in the mess hall after dinner. He was learning to play the rubab, but he was better on guitar. Everybody stayed to listen, even the commander. Lorenzo asked us to write the lyrics. He knew how to choose the notes, he said, but his uniform had taken away his inspiration. None of us managed to come up with anything decent, though, only clichés, and so the interpreter recited some verses by a mystic poet. Lorenzo was thunderstruck. One song went: *one day the flowering branch will bear fruit, one day the falcon will long to hunt, but we have appeared like the clouds and disappeared like the wind.* You have to try and imagine these words sung in his young voice, and the sound of an acoustic guitar in the desert at dusk. I wish I'd recorded it, so I could listen to it again. But you probably found his songs. You must have, in his duffel . . . He can't have improvised them on the spot, he must have written down something." "My mother wants to

ask you about the last moments of Lorenzo's life," Fabio suddenly interrupts her. "She wants to know if he told you anything."

The roar. The roar that rips open the earth. The flash of light. The
nail in her neck, her heart beating wildly and her leg gone numb. And
Lorenzo's blood pouring onto her face, her lips, down her throat, hot,
dense, viscous. And the fear, the boundless fear in his distant voice that
follows her into the void into which she is vanishing. Those desperate
syllables—Manuela, Ma-nue-la am I hurt?—that spurt out of his mouth
along with his blood, torn out with his last breath, as if she really could
help him, save him, instead of lying under him, immobile, on the verge
of crashing into unconsciousness. Intrusion. Pain. The sickly sweet smell
of blood and burnt flesh. The resurrection of the memory. To go back
there, to live that scene again and again and again. It's too vivid. She can't
bear to think about it. Not even for his mother. *Avoidance.* "I'm sorry," she
whispers, "but I don't remember anything."

Manuela manages to talk with Diego's girlfriend only at the end of an
interminable lunch, when Lieutenant Gautieri informs her that they
have to leave soon, it's a long way and the driver has to return the car to
the ministry garage in Rome. Imma thanks her for coming. "You don't
have to thank me," Manuela says with difficulty, "it's I who must thank
you for choosing me to be the godmother of your child. It's a great honor,
I'll try to be worthy." "Ah!" Imma exclaims. "It wasn't me who chose you,
it was Diego. We had agreed that my sister would be the godmother.
Then in June he changed his mind. He called me two days before he
died, a strange phone call. He was so agitated, you know how he could
get, maybe he had some kind of premonition. 'Listen, Imma,' he said, 'if
something terrible happens to me and I can't be there when our son is
baptized, I want Manuela Paris to be the godmother.' Who's Manuela
Paris? I jumped on him, furious. 'My platoon leader,' Diego said, 'she's
real tough, but she doesn't pull rank, she's my best friend in Lambda.' A
woman! I said. 'What's wrong with that,' he said. He'd never even mentioned you before. His best friend is a woman and he never bothered to
tell me. I got angry, I knew something was going on. I'm real hot-blooded,
I got all riled up right away. I'm crazy jealous. I asked him if he was in
love with this Manuela Paris. He denied it, but I didn't believe him. The
godmother of your child's a big deal, you don't just ask the first person

who comes along, not even if you were in the war together. A godmother is forever. We believe in this stuff, it's not just for show. Diego was an altar boy, he carried Baby Jesus on his shoulder in the procession, he still went to mass, and so do I. Baptism is a sacrament, you are presenting your child to God, welcoming him into the Christian community, and it's not like you ask just anybody to present your child to God. It's sacred. We fought. You know, the next day we didn't talk because I couldn't get through, so the last thing I told him was fuck you. I really loved him, he was the love of my life, we were going to get married, I already had the ring, we were supposed to grow old together, and because of you, we told each other to fuck off. Can you imagine?"

"I'm sorry," Manuela mumbles, blushing. "But this is ridiculous, you shouldn't have accused him, Diego talked about you all the time, you and the baby. He was going nuts being so far away from you. He didn't know you were pregnant when he signed on for Afghanistan, and I remember when you told him—because you didn't tell him right away, you didn't want him to worry, that was really good of you, you were really brave—it was April, I remember because we were at mess, eating some disgusting tomato-and-meat soup. He showed us the DVD of your ultrasound. He was practically in tears. Someone suggested he get himself sent home. Captain Paggiarin would have understood. But you know how he was. He liked being there."

The baby chirps feebly and Imma gently rocks his carriage, to soothe him. Diego junior is a little bundle in a blue blanket. "He's pooped all over, can't you smell how stinky he is?" Imma's sister says leaning over him. "I'll go change him." "No, let him be," Imma stops her. Manuela doesn't know what to do with babies. Her colleagues don't have children, and when Alessia was born she was far away. By the time she got her first leave, Alessia was already sitting up on her own.

"I have a sixth sense," Imma says. She speaks without resentment, leveling Manuela with her black eyes. She keeps her eyes fixed on her as she takes the sleepy, rosy bundle out of the carriage and presses her son against her abundant chest. She's still breast-feeding him. "I could tell by the way he denied it. In fact, the more he denied it, the more I knew I was right. I figured it out, and he was sorry to ruin everything. I had told him not to go. I didn't want him going over there, I told him he had to settle down if he wanted to be with me, I didn't want to move up north and be a soldier's wife, I'd already seen it with my cousin, alone for months, glued to the computer—but you can't make love to a computer—constantly terrified she'd lose him; it wrecked her health. We would have found the money somehow. But he wanted to get married. He was fixated. I didn't want him to go for permanent service, he'd already reenlisted twice, he'd served for eight years, that's a lot, too many, find another job, something safer. My uncle has a pizzeria, he would have taken him on. I'm not made to be a waiter, Diego would say, I want to bust up the world. That's how he was, a born gladiator. I'll do six months in Bala Bayak, he'd tell me, I'll take the money, and we'll get married. And then I'll go back, I'll do two or three more tours and then my soul will be at peace, we'll settle down in Belluno, there are mountains there, it's as clean as Switzerland, no dioxins like here, we'll buy a house with a yard, our kids will grow up healthy. I knew something would happen if he went. He was crazy about you, Manuela. Which is why I respected his wish and made you the godmother of my child. Just go fuck yourself, Diego, I told him, and then I slammed down the phone. Understand? Thirty-six hours later he was dead, and I slammed the phone in his face. Do you want to hold him?" she asks all of a sudden, holding out the baby to her. "He's so good, he doesn't cry, he's an angel, this little one."

Manuela holds Diego junior awkwardly in her arms. He's so light! He weighs less than a bulletproof vest. She's afraid he'll start screaming in a stranger's arms. Six months old, black down on his head, tiny hands with transparent fingernails, puzzled, half-closed eyes of an indefinable color. But he doesn't cry. I am your godmother, Diego junior. But what does that mean? I'll never see you again. And the other Diego Jodice will never see this sweet, minuscule creature. He waited for him every damned day, and he would never see him. Diego junior's skin smells of lotion, but his little blue onesie gives off the unmistakable stench of shit. He really did need his diaper changed. Manuela doesn't know what to do with the little bundle in her arms. Imma stares at her, sad but not resentful. It happened. And there's nothing she can do about it. Or Manuela either. Manuela brings her lips to the baby's warm head. She kisses him. Diego junior opens his eyes and looks at her in surprise. Oh, what the eyes of a child can see.

Sunk into the backseat of the army car, Manuela doesn't say a word the whole way home. She stares at the driver's shaved neck and sees Fatimeh.

She stares at the bare banks of the Volturno, the splashes of snow, and sees Fatimeh. The three lanes of the Rome–Naples highway and sees Fatimeh. The tractor trailers and Fatimeh. The white headlights of the cars on the other side of the median strip, and Fatimeh. She closes her eyes and she sees Fatimeh. It is neither a hallucination nor a memory. It is a presence. She can even smell her—goat, sweat, hair, and something unidentifiable, maybe the soot of the fire, a pleasant mixture of ashes and wood. A silent ghost who insinuates herself between the barriers of the base and slides along the protective wall without making a sound, her dirty feet in rubber flip-flops. A bundle pressed to her chest, her eyes glued to the ground. An emaciated boy precedes her, dragging a cart piled with rosaries and postcards, Chinese sunglasses, and phone cards. Bright green eyes and thick, jet-black hair, the body of a malnourished child and the hard gaze of an adult. Manuela could not have said how old he was. Because she was a woman, Manuela had been assigned the task of asking Fatimeh what she wanted: she had refused to say a word to the soldiers on guard duty who had interrogated her.

Fatimeh didn't understand English, and Manuela knew only thirty words in Dari. Water, capture, arrest, cold, weapons, desert, village, well, dust, canal, old man, mountain, pass, mosque, street, river, prison, friend, words like that, useful for orienting yourself, for imposing order, describing a place, or expressing a need. Besides, maybe Fatimeh didn't even speak Dari. The linguistic and ethnic tangle of the province exceeded her expertise. And Ghaznavi, Shamshuddin, and the other interpreter had left Sollum on a village medical outreach mission. Manuela and Fatimeh were a few inches apart. Fatimeh stared attentively at her uniform, her helmet, the black-bordered gold bars on her shoulder. In Fatimeh's bright green eyes, lively and intelligent, Manuela read neither curiosity nor admiration nor desire to be like her, nor the vaguest aspiration for the authority and liberty she enjoyed. But no hatred or rancor or scorn either. Merely a cosmic distance. And an absolute desperation. The last thing that woman wanted to do was to ask for help, but that's what she did.

Without ever looking Manuela in the eyes, Fatimeh held out her bundle and practically forced her to take it in her arms. Manuela moved aside the filthy blanket and glimpsed the gray face of a baby girl, just a few months old, racked by fever. The woman had come in search of the doctor. But Lieutenant Ghigo was out on the medical outreach mission with her assistants. The only one in the clinic was a nurse Manuela called the Skinner—she wouldn't have let him treat a cat. She had to detain Fatimeh until Ghigo came back. She gave her back her bundle and gestured for her to follow her to the clinic. Fatimeh looked at her son, as if asking his permission. The boy merely moved his head slightly.

Fatimeh laid the baby girl on an infirmary cot and opened the blanket so that Manuela could see her belly, which was monstrously bloated. Then she collapsed into a folding chair. She looked like a heap of dirty rags. Mother and child were exhausted and starving, and Manuela sent a soldier to the kitchen to get something for them to eat. The cook—happy to have an excuse to get away from the hot stove—came carrying two plates, still hot. "Korean frozen fish," Manuela said, stupidly, because the woman didn't understand English, "it's like chicken, some say like tuna, anyway it's tasty." But neither the boy nor his mother touched the food, and the cook withdrew, mortified. He really did try his best, and he did a good job. He would gladly have bought goats from the shepherds to make a tomato meat stew, but after the company was decimated by dysentery, Captain Paggiarin started worrying about food poisoning and preferred to order cases of frozen and prepared foods from the TFC warehouses in Shindand.

The whole time mother and son waited in the infirmary, they didn't utter a single word; didn't answer even one of Manuela's questions. As if they wanted to keep their contact to a minimum. Maybe they just didn't understand her. Every now and then the woman coughed, hiding her mouth with a rust-colored rag. Manuela noted with disgust that she was spitting up blood.

When Lieutenant Ghigo finally returned, Manuela left. As she was heading out of the infirmary, she felt a hard slap on her arm, and—surprised—she turned. The woman was whispering something to her. She pronounced the word two or three times, but Manuela didn't understand, because she'd only been there a few weeks, she'd only left the FOB once, and that word wasn't part of her meager vocabulary. The village patrols and the children's insistent requests would teach her that the word meant "pen." She must have asked for her son, because she, like ninety percent of Afghani women, was illiterate. When she opened her mouth, Manuela saw that she was missing three teeth. Her gums were inflamed, like those of an eighty-year-old. But she knew now that that worn-out old woman, devastated by tuberculosis, was her age. The boy said something to her in a reproachful tone, and Fatimeh lowered her head, bit her lip, and fell silent.

Lieutenant Ghigo told her that the baby girl was very ill: she had a temperature of 102°F and had lost almost half her body weight. Visceral leishmaniasis. An infectious disease transmitted by sand flies that swarm on excrement. It destroys the internal organs, attacks the spleen, liver, and bone marrow, causes anemia and terrible hemorrhaging. It's the disease of the world's poor. She saved her just in time, one more day and there would have been nothing she could do. Ghigo said bitterly that Fatimeh never would have brought her to the FOB if she weren't at death's door. A child's life is worth less than a dog's. The hardness of these people is inconceivable. "But she brought her," Manuela said. "Between the life of her child and the contempt of the community, she chose the life of her child, and that's what matters. Fatimeh is a brave woman."

Fatimeh came back three more times to get the antimonials for her daughter's treatment—but she refused to let herself be seen by the doctor. Manuela would see her walking in the dust, her head lowered. She avoided looking up. But twice Manuela intercepted her lively, intelligent eyes. Twice she smiled at her and twice Fatimeh gave her a half nod before quickly lowering her head again. Then she disappeared. Her relatives had not appreciated the fact that she had turned to the kafiri. Manuela would never have known any more of the baby girl's fate had not the youngest of the interpreters, Shamshuddin, told Ghigo that the little one had made it. She was already feeling better seven days later, even her belly was returning to its normal size. He had seen her in a basket, watched over by her brothers in front of their house. If it could be called a house. Fatimeh had nine children. She was a widow, her husband was killed in an air raid last year, in May, her brothers were refugees in Pakistan, and she earned her bread by begging, but she couldn't survive without her son's cart of tchotchkes. A twelve-year-old boy, already the head of the family. Fatimeh's son—Amir, Ahmad, or whatever his name was—stayed at his mother's side while they waited for the doctor, while the doctor examined his sister, and then while the medicine was being administered. Protecting her, but also keeping an eye on her. When Manuela invited him to eat the good Korean fish that tasted like chicken, he proudly refused, lifting his chin. And he looked at her as he did so. And, looking her in the face, he blew himself up.

Because he was looking at her. His eyes, bright green like his mother's, his thick hair, his gaunt face and his adult expression. She recognized him. She was so surprised by the fact that that boy happened to be in a village miles from his own, that she stopped. "Nicola!" she had exclaimed merrily. "It's Fatimeh's son." And at the same time her blood ran cold, because how had Amir or Ahmad or whatever his name was gotten to Qal'a-i-Shakhrak, who had brought him, and most of all, why? "Nicola!" Amir had recognized her, too, he quickened his pace and stepped in among the soldiers. "Nicola!" she cried. Amir kept turning around to look at her, and he was looking at her right in that instant. The instant in which the roar erased him. The roar. The flash of light. And then the buzzing. The helicopter blades whirling, whirling, whirling.

She calls Mattia on his cell, but it's off and a recording repeats that the person you have called is not available at the moment. She calls the Bellavista and asks to be connected to room 302. The concierge knows her by now, he has been spying on them, he has seen her come out of his room at seven in the morning, and spend three days in there, he knows that Manuela Paris is having an affair with his guest. But after letting it ring for a minute, the concierge comes back on the line and reports that room 302 is not answering. Manuela goes out onto the balcony. She sees the dirty yellow shadow of the hotel atrium, but she can't see the concierge, or even the reception desk, hidden by the overhanging roof. She is dizzy. Nauseated. The light of a television filters through Mattia's shutters. The roar. The flash of light. The helicopter blades. Amir's green eyes. Inexpressive, cold, without a flicker of gratitude—not even when, during that interminable wait at the FOB, she had offered to buy all his faded postcards. Postcards that showed a green and orderly Afghanistan that no longer existed and that in any case that boy had never known. He had tucked the money under the gray rags that covered him and that had once been a man's overcoat. The same overcoat he had on that day in June, to hide his explosive vest. A boy who had never been a boy, and who instead had proven to be worth more than a man because—unlike many others who for fear or inexperience didn't manage to activate the device and got themselves arrested, in a market, in front of a barracks, or at a police block—he hadn't made a single mistake; he had accomplished his mission. Caused as much damage as possible. A good suicide bomb kills on average six people, and Amir had taken out six and a half, even though only three were kafiri. Two were Afghani, so they don't count, and the sixth was himself. But his gesture had enormous resonance, it created a sense of vulnerability and made the Italians tremble with fear. Amir, raised in hatred, already killed by poverty, humiliation, and frustration, was not afraid to die, and in fact, in dying had killed the foreign occupants and their lackeys, had assured respectability and assistance and a future for his marginalized, despised family. But Manuela is alive. Alive in every fiber of her body.

She needs to hear Mattia's easygoing voice, he who knows nothing of the roar, the flash, the sickly sweet smell of blood. She needs his rough tongue. The hairs above his lips. His back. The raised little circle from the smallpox vaccine on his shoulder. His faded, rumpled hair, his myopic eyes. His cold feet and light hands. The transparent drip of semen on the slot of his foreskin. Near him, in bed with him, she is the same Manuela as always, but also different, new. She has to see him, now, right away.

She throws a clothespin at his shutters. The dull thud sounds like a shot and makes her jump. The light goes out in Mattia's room. Mattia, Mattia, it's me, Manuela, what are you doing? I know you're there, turn on the light. Nothing happens. She stands there for an hour staring at the dark window, distraught. The hotel is a skeleton, white as snow, the façade illuminated by the blue neon sign. She's going to need twenty drops in order to fall asleep. So that had been the act of divergence: that encounter with the son of the woman who had the same exhausted, proud expression as her own mother. Or more precisely, that thought. Because—for a fraction of a second—before asking herself what Amir was doing there and why, before realizing that he shouldn't be there and shouting "Nicola!" she had been happy to see him again. That woman who had reminded her of her own mother had disappeared, and as weeks, then months, passed, she worried about her, wondered if she was gravely ill, perhaps already dead. But she was wrong. She had thought that Fatimeh's son's presence at Qal'a-i-Shakhrak was a message, that Fatimeh was still alive, and hadn't forgotten, because it was a day of festivity and reconciliation. She felt infinite compassion for Fatimeh and her son, a pity born not from distance or condescending compassion, but from solidarity, from a kind of recognition. Manuela had stopped, and rummaged in her pockets; she had to give that boy something. Not alms, even if masked by the purchase of a pile of faded postcards. She had something for Fatimeh's son. She'd been carrying it around for months.

A pen. But she was holding her automatic rifle, and was hindered by her bulletproof vest, and she couldn't find it in the too many pockets of her jacket. And when she finally extracted it, she realized that Amir had moved past her, had insinuated himself among her friends, while continuing to turn and look back, keeping an eye on her, and only then did she call out to the lieutenant.

To search your pockets for a lowly pen that would cost fifty cents in an Italian supermarket. An instant stolen from the bare economy of duty. That negligible gesture had been enough to alter the chain of connected events—get out of the Lince, accompany the lieutenant to the front of the school where they were supposed to wait for the local authorities—to deviate them from their trajectory and thus dislodge the logic of the intersection. She owed her life to that infinitesimal delay, imperceptible on any watch, to an impulse, the recognition of a common humanity. Diego had kept walking, flanking First Lieutenant Russo and Ghaznavi, protecting them, and Lorenzo had followed, his video camera in his hand, but she had remained behind. One step, two, four, five—not more than ten. Enough to project her into a different, unpredictable reality where she fulfilled something that could be called her destiny.

That night she cries—for all the dead, and for herself, too, for her guilt over still being here, which nothing and no one can ever remedy, and for the shameful joy of being alive. She soaks her pillow, so much that she hurls the cold, wet blob onto the floor. She cries without stopping, till her eyelids are too swollen to open. Sealed shut, as if she were never going to see anything other than the soft, dense darkness pierced by a flash of light. Then she tumbles into the cold shadows, and awakens at eleven, befuddled.

Only her grandmother is home, curled up in her chair, with a woolen cap on her head, wearing three sweaters, and a blanket over her knees, because by now neither wool nor the radiator nor the space heater she sits in front of can warm her. "Don't listen to people who complain about being ill or blind," she had said to Manuela back when she still deigned to speak with the impure. "The worst thing about growing old is the cold. You can't get warm, you're like a rotten log that won't burn." But now Grandma Leda doesn't even talk about the cold, and she doesn't have regrets about the past. The VCR plays her prophet's sermons about

Jehovah's Judgment Day, when he will sweep the evil from the earth. Her world has been reduced to a voice. But it's clearly enough for her, because she sits there without moving, a faraway smile on her lips.

Mattia has gone out. She waits anxiously for him, but also happily, because she absolutely has to explain to him her selfish behavior the other day. Everyone makes mistakes sometimes. There are misunderstandings. But she can't allow doubts and fears to ruin their lives. It's such a miracle that they have found each other. You have something I have been searching for. I don't know what, but I don't want to lose it. She calls him three times, but his cell is always off. She goes over to the Bellavista, leaves a note for him. Direct, unequivocal, because that's the way she is, and he has accepted her. Don't make a sergeant wait. Soldiers have no patience. And besides, it's not possible to be patient and in love at the same time.

She takes up guard duty on the balcony, so she can intercept the Audi as soon as it appears on the promenade. She stands for hours in the cold, without ever letting her mind wander, but then again, she's used to it. The Audi does not return. At two she eats a salad with no dressing with her grandmother, who only drinks a cup of milky coffee. "Assembly is today. Can you take me to the Kingdom Hall?" she asks her, unusually sweet since she needs a favor. "I can't, Grandma, I'm waiting for someone," she replies, "I'm sorry, forgive me." "Are you engaged?" she asks, curious now, turning off the TV. She doesn't hear well, and after a while the racket confuses her. "No," Manuela replies, "but I'm going out with someone." "What does that mean, going out? I go out, too, but I'm as lonely as a dog, and if Jehovah weren't here I would be the loneliest person on earth. But I'm old, I'm like the moon at dawn, I only have a little while longer to live." "Going out means I see him, spend time with him," Manuela explains, embarrassed. "Do you sleep with him?" Grandma wants to know.

"Yes," Manuela admits, surprised by her grandmother's frankness. She has never talked to her about these kinds of things; it never would have occurred to her. But perhaps old age is also—or above all—freedom. Freedom from habits, from shame, from taboos, from everything. If she could only accept it. "Sex is the most important thing," Grandma declares. "If you're not happy with a man even in bed, it's not worth it. Believe me, it's not worth it."

"Thanks, Grandma, I'll keep that in mind." She feels the same way. The loneliness of the heart is something even friends can satisfy. But the loneliness of a body that no one knows how to touch, listen to, understand, is absolute, and of all the bodies that there are in this world—all made in the same way, in the end, all furnished with the same organs, identically arranged—there might be only one that completes us, without which life loses its taste. She missed Mattia's breath last night. Missed the sag of the mattress, the obstacle of limbs between the sheets, the pressure of her shoulder against his. When she had opened her eyes on January 6, the first thing she had seen was his hair on the pillow, an ashen smudge falling across his forehead, a tuft holding on in a spot where the rest had already fallen out. Then and there she had been struck by the proof that Mattia was too old—and that he would only get older, and if they stayed together, with time, the difference in age, which seemed insignificant now, would only grow more pronounced, and would push them apart. Yet now the memory of that thinning, faded hair torments her, because it seems she missed an opportunity; they can't waste time blaming each other for misunderstandings and throwing their respective shortcomings in each other's face. His thinning hair and her scar only testify to the fact that they met each other late, late for both of them, they both lived for too long not knowing about each other, and so now they have to make up for all that lost time. And she longs to tell him so.

"You've gotten prettier," Grandma observes, scrutinizing her through her thick lenses. Her eyes look huge, two grayish globes in which a malicious light flickers. "You almost look like a woman." "I'm still the same, I think you need new glasses." Manuela laughs. But it makes her happy that Mattia has changed her.

At four she sends him a text, telling him that she'll wait for him at her grandfather's cottage. Then she takes a shower, washes her hair, applies clear nail polish, uses Vanessa's cosmetics to make herself up, puts on a pair of her sister's jeans—covered in sparkles and artfully ripped at the knees like a contemporary painting—calls a cab, and goes to Passo Oscuro. She waits for him on Vanessa and Youssef's mattress, reading the book on veteran rehabilitation that Colonel Minotto gave her. It's interesting, all things considered. The smell of smoke from their New Year's Eve candles still lingers in the air. The smell of their bodies, too. She sinks her mouth into the pillow. It smells of Mattia. When it grows dark, she goes out to the veranda to wait for him. It's cold, but she doesn't flinch. At eight Mattia's cell is still off. At eleven she calls a taxi and goes home.

The concierge at the Bellavista doesn't know what to say. Mr. Rubino has not checked out of his room. The chambermaid who made his bed didn't notice anything unusual this morning, his things were still in their usual place. Her message is still there, folded in quarters, in pigeonhole 302. "Would you like it back?" the concierge asks her. Manuela rips it up and throws it in the trash.

At three the vibration of her cell phone, which she had left on under her pillow, yanks her out of a deep yet calm sleep in which shards of everyday life float. Maybe she was dreaming. A message. I'm at the cottage, came in through the window. You left. Your imprint on the bed, your perfume on the sheets. I will come to you in your dreams.

She calls him. He answers on the first ring. They talk until dawn, whispering, pausing whenever a train goes by because the rumble is so close it overpowers their voices. They talk about everything and nothing, about important things and foolish ones. About trips they've taken— she a commuter on the Belluno–Rome train, he once went all the way to the Caucasus to climb Mount Elbrus. About Sailor Moon, the warrior of love and justice. About Vittorio Paris's chickens, Diego Jodice junior's baptism, John Huston's *Bible* at Palo Castle. Mattia tells her how much he likes the knots of her spinal column, the relief of her shoulder blades, her protruding bones, the brown fuzz against her white skin, the red scar that he will never tire of running his fingers along, like an open vein, a path of blood that leads him to the very center of her. They talk about her titanium plate, about Amir's pen. Mattia says that she is in every part of him. They utter words both indecent and tender. Then Manuela tells him not to worry if they don't get to see each other tomorrow. She has to catch an early plane, she's going to Turin. She has to get some tests done for her doctor's visit. She'll be away one day, two at the most. She'll be home by Thursday evening at the latest.

"Come back soon," Mattia says, only then realizing to his horror that his battery symbol is flashing. LOW BATTERY appears on his screen. "Without you I can't—" But his battery dies and Manuela doesn't hear the rest of the sentence.

21

> >

LIVE

t's snowing in Turin. When the Alitalia ATR lands at Turin-Caselle Airport, the windows are streaked with ice. Manuela deftly maneuvers her crutches down the aisle and the sloping exit ramp, carrying her bag herself and refusing the help of the steward assigned to the disabled. She's wearing her uniform for the first time in several days, and her Norwegian cap with the eagle in the center. People turn to look at her as she crosses the arrivals hall. Tall, thin, a perfectly pressed uniform, polished boots, gold epaulets—and crutches. But no one recognizes her. When people see an injured soldier, they think: athlete with a torn meniscus. The four thousand soldiers eating dust and TNT in central Asia exist only for their families.

For forty-five minutes, as the taxi fords the traffic, dodging trucks stuck in the snow on the bypass, she chats with Mattia on her cell, giving him an up-to-the-minute report of her journey. It's always a treat to take a comfortable civilian airplane after those C-130s and Chinook helicopters. She spent nearly three months in the Turin hospital, but it seems as if she's seeing the city for the first time. The river is wide, the trams deafening and cumbersome, the avenues sketched with snow, the balconyless buildings sealed up like battlements. "Why didn't you come with me?" she asks all of a sudden. "You didn't ask me." Turin is white, geometric, cold. The symmetry of the streets and the repetitiveness of the intersections suggest an immutable order and make her feel safe. "Would you have come?" Manuela asks in astonishment as she rummages in her pocket for her wallet. "Even if you had to sit and wait for me in the lobby all day?" "Listen, Manuela," Mattia starts to say, "there are a lot of things I should have told you. But it was all so new, you can't start something on the end of something else, it wasn't because I lacked courage, but because I trusted you so much." "Forty euros, do you need a receipt?" the taxi driver says, pulling up in front of the military hospital gate. "Yes, please," Manuela says, even though she doubts they will reimburse travel expenses, and then to Mattia, "What are you trying to tell me? I don't understand." "Good luck," he says. "Just relax, it will all be fine."

The hospital again. The ticking of her crutches on the opaque marble floor again. The high windows. The perpetual glare of the livid neon lights. The dark uniforms against the white walls. The guard's glass booth at the entranceway. The Dardo and Mangusta helicopter posters. The Armed Forces calendar on the glass door of the ward. The smell of disinfectant. The sadness of injured bodies moving up and down hallways. Legs, clavicles, vertebrae imprisoned in plaster casts, braces, collars. Bones compromised by accident or disease. Disharmony, imperfection, pain. It feels like months have gone by, but it's only been twenty days. "Welcome back, Sergeant," Nurse Scilito greets her merrily. "What did Santa Claus bring you?" "Love, I think," she says laughingly.

"Lucky you," Scilito sighs, gesturing to the door. They've gotten her old room ready for her, but she hopes she won't need it. The last flight for Rome isn't until after nine. The medical evaluation board is waiting for her. She wants to get it over with as soon as possible. She goes in.

They test her knee and ankle function, then send her underground to the radiology department. She hangs her uniform on a hook and stiffens in front of the X-ray machine in just her underwear. She holds her breath. She's had so many X-rays! And every time the doctor holds those black sheets up against the light, revealing the crumbled imprint of her bones. The white part—which should show her kneecap, fibula, tibia, malleolus—breaks off, as if whoever drew it had lifted his pencil from the page, and fades to black: a sign that her fractures had not healed. But a myriad of dark stars dot the X-ray. Metal fragments, the shrapnel still inside her. "You can get dressed now, thank you," says the voice of the radiologist, barricaded behind a protective wall. "Can't you tell me anything?" she asks without much hope. The radiologist has already seen. He already knows.

She goes from one building to the next, from one wing to the next. She subjects herself patiently, as docile as a lamb, to every kind of test, including an encephalon-rachis-cervical-lumbosacral MRI. She emerges from the radioactive shadows of the basement into the brightness of the surgical orthopedics ward. She goes from one specialist to another, finally ends up in the secluded neurologist's room. When she enters, he's talking on the phone with his daughter, he's in no hurry to deal with her and lets her wait, on the edge of her seat, nervous, angry with that girl, or woman, who demands her father's attention and delays the truth. They stick probes in her knee, apply electrodes to her skull and clamps to her heart. She explains to the physical therapist that she has been scrupulous about doing her rehab, and it's worked: her crutches are a habit now more than anything else, they reassure her, but she doesn't really need them, in fact she's thinking of buying herself a cane. Her foot is responding well, she can walk, though still only for short distances. Her knee is stiff, that's true. But the movement is fluid and harmonious. Her back isn't bothering her, neither are her vertebrae. She's about to tell him she made love curled up on her epistropheus, contorting herself like a snake, without breaking in two, but refrains: military ethics.

She answers the same questions over and over. She tells the truth, but not all of it. She downplays the pain—which, every time she walks on the beach, stabs at her heels so sharply it paralyzes her, forcing her to rest. She mitigates but doesn't hide certain unpleasant symptoms: muscular tone weakness, dizziness, loss of balance. Lying on the table inside the MRI capsule, she tells herself that science is a utopia and machines are of no use. They're X-raying her brain, and will be able to see the tiniest abnormalities. But they can't see the only thing that's really in there, a strange man who says his name is Mattia Rubino.

At two, Colonel Rocca, the president of the medical evaluation board, invites her to the officers' mess. A withered man with huge ears and curly lobes, piggy eyes. He has a reputation as an old-school officer who's still not used to the idea of women in the armed forces, so the invitation surprises her. There's no one in the mess because the hospital is still practically empty after the holidays. She eats a bland risotto and some overly salted braised beef that makes her thirsty all afternoon. The colonel informs her that General Ercoli will be coming up from Rome tomorrow. He's expecting her at the Pinerolo barracks at eleven. "Tomorrow?" she asks, disappointed. The last plane for Fiumicino will take off without her. And she won't sleep with Mattia tonight. "Perhaps there's been some mistake," she tells him, "I don't think I know General Ercoli, and I'm not in the Taurinense Alpini Brigade. I'm in Julia, Tenth Regiment, from Belluno, I'm being treated here instead of Belluno on Colonel Minotto's advice." "General Astorre assured me that you have a very high IQ," Rocca says bitterly. "He's clearly mistaken." Manuela nervously jabs her braised beef with her knife. Who is this Ercoli? She's never heard of him before. And what does he want from her?

At four she meets with the psychologist. She's nervous and her heart is beating too quickly—she fears this exam even more than the X-rays, the MRI, or CAT scan. She wants and needs to seem cured, capable, of sound mind. If the psychologist decides she's still suffering from PTSD, that it has become chronic, she can forget going back to active duty. No more in-country tours. Offices, orderly rooms, dying of boredom in some provincial barracks. A desk jockey, more or less. And not even twenty-eight years old. The best, the perfect age for a soldier. Not too young and not too old. The summer of one's life. She forces a smile. She looks for affirmation in the gray eyes of the mustached man sitting behind the desk, but finds only an inexpressive, impenetrable wall. The psychologist asks her how her insomnia is, if there have been any incidents of vomiting during the night. "I'm sleeping better," she replies, "and the vomiting has decreased, only three or four times in twenty days." (Honesty, she thinks, you're not being honest, Sergeant Paris. Nine times, you have vomited nine times.) "Medication?" "I'm taking the drops," she explains, "but really more out of habit, out of fear, than necessity." "Flashbacks? Numbing? Nightmares? Hyperarousal? Emotional anesthesia?"

"Pretty good," she says, "numbing only once." Some intrusive flashbacks, but she considers their effect positive because they have helped her overcome her amnesia and restored her memory. Stress is more or less under control, and she is no longer emotionally detached. She can't tell him about Mattia, or that perhaps—probably—she has fallen in love. In a certain sense for the first time. She has never experienced such powerful emotions. She feels an irresistible urge to say his name. To touch him. She blushes when Mattia looks at her. And she feels herself blossom like a rose when she looks at him. But a soldier keeps her emotions to herself, so she simply assures him that the resumption of old habits, going home, being in a familiar place, but one that is extraneous to her professional life, has been very good for her, just as he had predicted.

"And your aggression?" the psychologist asks without looking at her. "Colonel Minotto informed us about the unfortunate incident you were involved in." "I'm pretty good at keeping it under control; unfortunately, that day I lost it. I made a mistake. I don't know why it happened. But I didn't try to hide it, I notified my superiors immediately, I called Captain Paggiarin that same evening. The captain, I mean the major, tried to reassure me. He helped a lot." The psychologist jots down something on the piece of paper in front of him. The Torvaianica goalie's father appears before her eyes, cowering in the mud, all curled up in an attempt to escape the pain. She would curl up like that, too, in her hospital bed, when the painkillers wore off and her shattered bones seemed to want to pierce her skin and climb outside of her. "Nurse!" she would cry. "Nurse!" The nurse explained that she was trying to get into what is called an analgesic position, but that it was bad for her. She had to remain in traction. Finally they hung her leg from the ceiling with a pulley, and anchored her neck to the bed. They crucified her. "The victims still haven't filed against me," she notes. "So it seems less serious to you if the people you attacked don't turn you in?" the psychologist insinuates. "No, it's very serious," she whispers. "But it won't ever happen again, I know it, I'm absolutely certain, you have to allow me one mistake, just one."

"And have you done your homework?" he interrupts her. "Did you bring me your self-monitoring diary?" "I haven't had much time to write," she confesses. "But I've thought a lot about the things you told me, I've done the cognitive reconstruction exercises in my head. I've recognized my automatic thoughts, have focused on goals, I've practiced what you called exposure. You remember how I really didn't want to go to the baptism of Diego Jodice's baby? You told me I had to address my avoidant behavior and take advantage of an event like that to relive the trauma, that it could help me. Well, I went to the baptism, I saw the guys from my platoon, and it happened. I relived everything. It was incredibly painful, but it did me a lot of good. I'm definitely better now." She repeats it several times, and it's true. He has to believe her.

The psychologist takes notes. Manuela cranes her neck but can't decipher the words he covers the paper with. His handwriting is tiny, cryptographic practically. "I feel freer now," she explains, "it's been a while since I've had a crisis." "How long is a while?" the psychologist asks. "Well, since I've been home," she says with conviction, because the fainting spell in the Parco Leonardo dressing room seems so remote to her now. "I can talk about what happened to me. I've remembered a lot of things, even the sequence of the attack, I can handle the memory, I can live with it, accept it. It's a part of me now. I realize that I'll never be able to erase it, I'll carry it inside of me my whole life, but that doesn't scare me. I feel I'm a stronger person now."

The psychologist asks her if she considers herself capable of handling a new situation. "New in what sense?" she asks suspiciously. "A radical change," the psychologist explains. Manuela thinks about Mattia. But the psychologist probably means something completely different. "Yes," she says, "I think so."

"When are you coming back?" Mattia asks her when she's finally able to call him. It's 8:53 p.m. Her meeting with the psychologist lasted nearly five hours. "Tomorrow afternoon, I hope," she says to him, "I still have one more appointment, and then I have to get my leave stamped. It expires tomorrow, you know, but they'll give me an extension. I still can't return to active duty." Her voice echoes too loudly in the silence of the hospital. Darkness sticks to the buildings. In the pavilion across the street only one light is on, and the solitary window looks like a lantern in the night. "I'll pick you up at the airport," Mattia says. "Let me know which plane you're on." "So you found your driver's license?" she asks. Jokingly, because it seemed funny to her that a forty-year-old man would go out without any form of ID. "I don't have a license," Mattia says. "I mean, I have one, but they have to issue me a new one, it's a bit complicated to explain, but what's the worst that could happen? At most they'll give me a ticket, and I'd have to be really unlucky to run into the cops, it's only a few miles to Fiumicino from here. I want to come get you, it means a lot to me."

"Who is Marco?" she asks, gesturing to Nurse Scilito to leave her dinner tray on the table. "Why?" he asks after a second's pause. "The other night while you were sleeping, you called out to him." "I don't remember," he glosses over her question. "I've told you everything and you haven't told me anything about yourself," Manuela says. "Sometimes I feel like I'm with no one and it scares me."

No reaction. Silence. For a few seconds all she hears are the nurses laughing in the hallway, and Thom Yorke's voice in the distance, singing I'm lost at sea, don't bother me, I've lost my way, I've lost my way. She really hit home. "Who are you?" she asks. "You know how to transform fear into energy, Manuela," Mattia tells her. "So you're also capable of facing a man without a shadow. Because that's what happened to me, more or less. I don't cast a shadow, I lack substance, I'm empty, there's nothing inside me."

"So you've been bit by the camel spider," Manuela says. "Did I tell you I killed dozens of them in Bala Bayak? They would hide in our helmets and shower shoes. They're real scary-looking, a cross between a spider and a scorpion. They're afraid of the light and are always looking for dark spots. They follow you, to hide in your shadow. An Afghani I knew—the only Afghani I knew, the interpreter, his name was Ghaznavi—said that according to legend, if a camel spider bites you, it steals your shadow, in other words your soul." "That must be what happened," Mattia allows. "We'll talk about it tomorrow," Manuela says, changing her tone, "it's too important to talk about over the phone, when we're three hundred miles apart." Mattia says that in truth there's really not much else to talk about. When she hangs up, she's sorry she didn't say something a little more intimate. I miss you, too, I think about you all the time, I think I love you, something along those lines. But she has never been able to talk like that.

General Ercoli doesn't waste any time on formalities. Sitting in a swivel chair, stiff in his ribbon-covered uniform, he tells her that someone spoke to him about her—but he's careful not to say who. Manuela Paris's human qualities and professional competence have not passed unobserved. In the highly likely event that she is declared permanently unfit for military service and discharged, she will still have an opportunity to serve her country. "But I don't want to be in the reserves!" she says impulsively, then immediately falls silent, turning red in the face at the incredible lack of discipline she has just shown in interrupting a general. It's just that she is shocked. Is this mellifluous dinosaur telling her they've already thrown her out? Without even awaiting her test results and the board's recommendation? Or does he already know what they are thinking? Have they already made up their minds? "In the highly likely event that you are discharged," General Ercoli continues, pretending not to have noticed her outburst, "you still have the opportunity to serve your country. Might you be interested?"

"I'm not sure I understand," Manuela says, making an effort to stay calm. To control herself. She used to be able to do it. Interested in joining national intelligence? A position of great responsibility and much sought after. "We receive hundreds of letters every day, from aspiring volunteers. But you have to be recruited. Naturally the job demands total commitment. But you've always said you feel you were born for operational life and want to dedicate yourself to serving your country." "Wow, I really haven't thought about this," Manuela says. She doesn't know how to react. She certainly can't blow him off right away, on the spot, without knowing who sent him and why. Without knowing if they have already thrown her out of her life, without any hope, or if she's still a sergeant. She would like to explain that a soldier is the opposite of a spy. There was an intelligence guy in Sollum, the same rank as her, who for six months did nothing but spy on the officers and enlisted men, meet with shady characters, and act as if he owned the place. He didn't deign to speak to us and no one ever found out his name.

"You don't have to decide right away," the general says. "Think it over. Sleep on it. We'll be in touch." Manuela gets up. She wants to run away, but she forces herself to express her gratitude for the opportunity she has been offered. She handles it well, the general will never know what is going through her head. This is the way a soldier behaves. "Yes, sir," she finally says, clicking her heels and bringing her hand to her hat in salute. I don't need to sleep on it, she should have said. I've already decided. The answer is never. I'm an Alpino, and always will be, even if I never go out on patrol with my men again, even if I never end up in some distant outpost that looks out over nothing. Alpini are in trenches and under fire. Alpini build roads and dig through rubble and even pick up trash. We don't serve politicians, we serve Italy. We don't have secrets and we do our duty in the light of day. We wear our past on our uniforms, and not merely in our ribbons and badges: and anyone can read it. Our names are sewn onto our uniforms, right over our hearts.

When she tries calling Mattia, a little after eight, there's no answer. She lets it ring for almost two minutes. Maybe he's still running on the beach, and he can't hear it over the sound of the waves. Or maybe he's in the shower. She tries again at nine, but at that point the voice mail picks up. "Hi, it's me," she says, a bit uncertain, "where did you go?

Good thing you were going to sit by your phone waiting to hear how things are going here . . . When the cat's away the mice will play, right? And to think that I'm all alone here, in a hospital room . . . It's freezing cold, dead silent, I'm the only one on the whole floor. Anyway, I wanted to say that we've spent so much time together that it feels strange not having you here. Okay, call me if you get this message, I'll leave my phone on, have a good night." When she turns out the light two hours later, the display on her cell still emits an azure glow, like a little altar. But no calls.

That night, in her room on the second floor of the military hospital in Turin, she dreams of Mattia for the first time. He's sitting on her bed, naked, in a completely empty space. It's not room 302 of the Bellavista, or the mattress at Passo Oscuro, or any other place they've been together. The walls are gray and there's only one window, high up, a dull light coming through it. Mattia is looking in her direction, but he doesn't seem to be expecting her. "Mattia?" she calls. "Sorry I'm late, I got held up." He stares without seeing her, as if she were talking to someone else. She calls him again but he doesn't answer. She starts to run, but the room seems to expand, it becomes a hallway with no way out, and the bed on which Mattia is sitting retreats into the distance, so that no matter how far she runs—light-footed, pushing with both legs, like before June 8, a feeling that fills her with an irrepressible joy—she can't seem to reach him. And then the gray walls disappear, she's on the beach in Ladispoli, the raging sea is pounding the shore, the tower is crumbling and she tries to hold it up with her shoulder. She hears a roar, and bricks and bones come crashing down all together.

At ten the doctor summons her. She's eager to know her test results and at the same time she never wants to know. There are moments that break a life in two, and this could be one of them. Her file is on his desk. The medical evaluation board has expressed a provisory opinion. Three noes, two maybes, and one yes. "No what?" Manuela asks. "Three of the specialists think there is no possibility that you will fully recover, either at the physical or psychological level. They've suggested another year of leave—the maximum allowable by law—after which you'll be declared permanently unfit for service. Two of them, thanks to your youth and force of character, think you have recovered surprisingly well, and they have suggested you be discharged, placed in the reserves, that is, as provided for by law, and assigned to office duties in the barracks of a nonoperational regiment." "Is this a joke?" she asks. The blood drains from her face. In the reserves at twenty-eight? It's worse than death. "One thinks you need to continue your rehab and psychotherapy, because you might be able to recover, medicine's not an exact science, and you're very young, so, if no complications arise, he thinks you could be reassigned to your regiment, on regular duty, maintaining your rank and duties."

One. One in six thinks she can still be Sergeant Paris. God bless him! Who is it? The orthopedist? The neurologist? The colonel? "In short," the doctor concludes, "they didn't reach a consensus and are taking more time. They have judged you temporarily unfit for military service, and granted you leave for another six months."

"But I can't stay in limbo for another six months!" she blurts out. Lost time. Wasted time. So much can be done in six months. Six months is a tour of duty. An eternity. "Hey, Paris, calm down," the lieutenant says. "Look, it turned out pretty well. Six months ago you were in pieces. A wreck. Your head was a mess. No one would have bet a cent on you. They've given you another chance. Take it easy. Look after your leg, look after your mind. Take a vacation. Go to the beach, enjoy life. Do whatever you want. You're scheduled to meet with the medical evaluation board again on July 12, here. If you're really better, you'll be reassigned to your regiment. Rest assured, they won't let you go so easily."

"So I can go home?" she asks. The lieutenant hands her her stamped leave. Home, she'd said. Home is the Belluno barracks. But for the first time in years, she meant Ladispoli when she said home. The waterfront, the black sand, the tower, Mattia. She stuffs her toothbrush and pajamas into her bag. At the elevator she runs into Nurse Scilito. "Farewell, Sergeant Stan," he says. "Why farewell?" she laughs. "Because you won't be back," he says. "They always do this. They extend your convalescence hoping that you'll be the one to ask to be discharged. You're a woman, you're young. They're counting on the fact that you will decide to focus on your family, that you'll get pregnant, that you'll make yourself unfit on your own." "What a strange way to see things, a conspiracy theory," Manuela says, unperturbed by the nurse's insinuations. She feels optimistic. Positive. "I accept their verdict. I'm taking six months' vacation. I'll be back in July. You can count on it. See you."

She turns on her cell in the taxi. Three messages. At 12:45 a call from an unknown number. At 1:00 and 1:05 Vanessa called. It must not have been urgent, because then she gave up. Mattia's cell is off. She sends him a text to let him know she's on her way to the airport, she'll catch the first flight home. The snow is melting. There are dirty piles along the street and on the roofs of the industrial warehouses. Why not? she says to herself as Turin slips past the window, already swallowed up by a gray fog—neighborhoods with signs in Arabic, halal butchers, kebabs rotating on spits, twelve-story buildings, straight streets, crowded tram stops, and bearded men and veiled women, whose presence alienates her. A six-month vacation. She's never taken a real vacation in her life. Never gone on a trip. Never been to Paris. Or London or Berlin or anywhere else. Just one town in Kosovo. And Afghanistan. The most inconvenient and dangerous country in the world. Six months all to myself. To get to know Mattia, the man with no shadow. To live, finally. There's a line at the ticket counter. Unhappy passengers eager to file who knows what kind of complaint make her lose time. The first seat she can get is on the 6:45 p.m. flight. When she places her cell in the tray at security, she sees that she still hasn't gotten any messages. Mattia's phone is still off.

The red light goes on, a beeper sounds, something's not right. A policewoman comes up to her and rudely orders her to raise her hands. She obeys. The policewoman pats her down with professional immodesty, her gloves going from her armpits to her ankles and buttocks, but doesn't find anything unusual. She orders Manuela to turn around and go through the metal detector again. But the red light goes on again, again the alarm sounds. Manuela turns out her pockets—empty—and she's not wearing a watch or earrings or a pendant. Then she gets it. "I have four titanium plates in my leg and I don't know how many screws," she says. "Maybe that's what's setting off the alarm." The policewoman can't take her word for it, she has to see her medical records, her X-rays. "They're at the military hospital," Manuela says, "I can't take them with me." The policewoman doesn't know what to do. The people in line behind her are growing impatient. Some are in danger of missing their flights. So—even though she's standing under neon lights with hundreds of annoyed, intolerant eyes glaring at her—Manuela pulls up her pant leg, rolls down her sock, and shows the policewoman her scar. The woman looks away and gestures for her to go through.

Manuela whiles away the hours watching the departures board. Compared with the one in Dubai, the Turin airport, recently renovated for the Olympics, is small, provincial, modest. But reading the list of flight destinations makes her happy. Istanbul. Katowice. Barcelona. Casablanca. The world is at once big and close at hand. She daydreams about going somewhere with Mattia. About traveling for two or three months, getting to know Europe. She'd like to go to Spain, to Vilnius, to the Baltic Sea. The Spanish and Lithuanians were under the Italians at Regional Command West, they'd come through Sollum on the way to their bases, they all got along well. She'd talked about Beethoven in English with a female sergeant who had the strange and beautiful name of Fuensanta. She was Catalan and played the violin. What is Mattia really like? Does he know how to adapt, can he handle the unexpected, the inconveniences, the differences? A trip is like a particle accelerator. A chemical detector. There's nothing like travel for getting to know someone. But they understand each other, it will work out. They've hardly said anything to each other, but life is stronger than words and it bursts forth everywhere. They've said even more than they needed to. In some way they've chosen each other. She feels oddly free.

She gets to the arrivals terminal at Fiumicino at 8:12 p.m. A bunch of guys are crowded near the sliding doors, leaning against the barriers, waving signs for passengers on her flight. A pharmaceutical company is waiting for Mr. Takeshita. A travel agency for Mr. and Mrs. Robertson. A Rome hotel shuttle for Mr. Di Donato. Then there's a father waiting for his son, and a kid with a ponytail waiting for his girlfriend, who, as soon as she sees him, all but flies to meet him, leaping into his arms. Young love is a feast for the eyes. But she doesn't see Mattia anywhere. Maybe he's late. Now that the holidays are over, there's traffic in Fiumicino at this hour, with all the commuters heading out of Rome. But he still hasn't sent her a message and his cell is still off.

She waits patiently, trustingly, without letting herself be assailed by anxiety. She sits on a stool at the bar near the bookstore, orders an orange juice, then a sandwich, then a coffee. She doesn't take her eyes off the glass doors that lead to the street for even a second, as if Mattia's massive frame might appear out of the darkness at any moment. Disheveled, smiling, maybe with a new pair of glasses. He was really upset about losing those glasses at the Real Ladis soccer field. When she asked him why he wore sunglasses even on a rainy day and in the evening, he said that he suffered from photophobia, that light really bothered him. She hadn't believed him. But she didn't press the issue, because she didn't want to force him to lie. She thinks again, this time with a chill, about the camel spider. Can you really lose your shadow? And if you do, how can you find it again, your shadow—or your soul? There's nothing in the legend about that, it's gone for good.

The glass doors open constantly. Gypsy cabdrivers, chauffeurs, passengers with suitcases who have taken the wrong exit or are desperately looking for the escalators to the train tunnel, friends, relatives, suspicious characters, maybe even thieves: the whole world seems to be at the Fiumicino arrivals terminal. Everyone but Mattia. She tries calling him at the hotel. And she chastizes herself for not having thought of it earlier. No one answers. The phone at the Bellavista just rings and rings. At 9:50 Manuela pays for her orange juice and coffee, gets in a cab, and has the driver take her home. The signs at the Bellavista are dark, the door locked. The hotel is closed.

Her mother is working the night shift at the roadside diner and Vanessa is spending the night somewhere. Alessia is at Uncle Vincenzo's. Grandma Leda can't tell her what happened, she didn't notice anything. Manuela stays out on the balcony until midnight, anxious, staring stubbornly at the lowered shutters of the room across the way. In the end, she puts out her cigarette in the potting soil, dilutes her sleeping drops in water, and resigns herself to going to bed. Mattia isn't there.

Vanessa wakes her up at noon, shaking her by the shoulder. She slept for twelve hours. A deep sleep, without nightmares but also without dreams. "I made you some coffee, honey," she says and—without giving her time to ask any questions—disappears into the kitchen. Manuela takes her time. She has the feeling she needs to delay her encounter with her sister. Something bad has happened. And she's afraid she doesn't have the strength to face it. She wallows under the shower, puts on her sweats, and when she finally sits down at the kitchen table, her coffee is like cold dishwater. "They took him away, hon," Vanessa says. "I don't know exactly when it happened, I wasn't here. Yesterday I realized that the Bellavista was closed." "Why didn't you tell me?" Manuela asks. All of her serenity of these past days has disappeared. She snaps a cracker in two. She has to keep herself from screaming. "Listen, I don't know what happened," Vanessa says as she loads the cups and glasses from her mother's and grandmother's breakfast into the dishwasher. "The police were here, they asked me questions, they wanted to know who he spent time with, where he went. I told the truth, that I know him, that we even went out with Mamma and Alessia, that he spent time with our family, that you had been seeing a lot of him these past few weeks, I didn't say that you two were an item, but I think they already knew."

"But who? Why?" Manuela blurts out. "I don't know, they were really rude, they probably want to question you, too." "Where is he, Vanè? Where is he?" Manuela practically shouts. Vanessa collapses into her chair. "I don't know where he is. Yesterday, it must have been around one o'clock, because Alessia was on her way home from school and I was here making her lunch, he called. He said your cell was off so he was calling me." "I was talking to the doctor, fuck!" Manuela exclaims. "He had to tell me what the medical evaluation board decided. I never turn off my phone, but I had to then, out of respect, it was important. . . . So that call from an unknown number at 12:45 was him."

"He was calling from a phone booth," Vanessa said. "He was really nervous. He was in a rush, super-abrupt. He said he couldn't tell me where he was and that I had to say two things to you. The first is that you have to talk to Gianni, the waiter at the Bellavista. He has something for you."

"And the second?" Manuela asks. Vanessa bites her nails. The blue speckled nail polish from New Year's is chipping off. She avoids Manuela's gaze. "I don't know how to say this, honey, it's really hard." Hard? thinks Manuela. "It can't be harder than what I've been through." "But it is. He said not to look for him."

Gianni Tribolato lives in the middle of the artichoke fields, on an out-of-the way farm on reclaimed land, patrolled by a dozen snarling dogs that surround Vanessa's Yaris, pissing on the tires and rubbing their teeth on the body. Without his white uniform and bow tie, in gardener's gloves and rubber boots, the Bellavista waiter looks like what he probably would have been had he not attended hotel school: a hearty farmworker. With a surprisingly small voice unsuited for his rough, stocky frame, he silences the dogs and guides Vanessa and Manuela to the house, apologizing for the mess. He's a good waiter, but a lousy housekeeper. Then again, no one ever comes here.

Empty bottles everywhere, flasks of wine, and ashtrays full of cigarette butts, bags of fertilizer, spades, rakes, pruning shears, and two fat cats splayed on the only couch in the living room. There's also an old man in a wheelchair, apparently not devoid of his senses, who wags his head and opens his mouth when he sees the Paris sisters come in. "My father," Gianni says. "He had a stroke, unfortunately, and lost the ability to speak." So this is why Gianni was so chatty at the hotel; at home he went for hours without hearing a human voice. He doesn't have a wife, his animals are his family. So this is why he bonded right away with Mr. Rubino. Loners understand each other.

He doesn't really know how to explain what happened. The hotel usually closes in the winter, because in January, once the holidays are over, it's really dead. But this year the company informed them that they would stay open. The owner was pretty pleased with the arrangement because high season had been abysmal—the recession meant a sixty percent drop in reservations this year—and with this unexpected change at least operational costs would be covered. But then on Thursday evening, it must have been around eight, the police showed up. He saw them arrive because he was in the kitchen, whiling away the time till dinner with Adel, the Egyptian cook. Not that they had "police" written on their foreheads. Plainclothes policemen, completely normal-looking, no uniforms or squad car. But they flashed their cards at the concierge. Two of them stayed in the lobby while one went up to room 302. Ten minutes later Mr. Rubino came down with his suitcase and computer bag. He said he wanted to talk with Gianni, but they said there was no time. Mr. Rubino started shouting, he was completely beside himself. This surprised Gianni because Mattia was always so polite, a real gentleman. He'd been working at the restaurant for thirty years, he had a lot of experience, and Mr. Rubino was a rare sort of guest. It was clear that he was upper class, but he knew how to act with everyone, and he even enjoyed talking with Gianni, a simple soul, a waiter. Gianni knew his conversational skills were limited, so he told him anecdotes about Ladispoli and his cats. Mr. Rubino really loved cats. The concierge called him and Gianni came out of the kitchen and Mr. Rubino said he wanted to have a word with him alone so they stepped into the restaurant. It was closed—there weren't any customers—they talked in there, among the tables in the gloom.

Mr. Rubino said he had to go away. He thanked him for having taken such good care of him and then he gave him a big tip. Unfortunately he didn't have time to say goodbye to his friends who lived across the way, Miss Vanessa Paris and her daughter, Alessia, and he was very sorry. He begged him to say goodbye to the little girl and to tell her that the Cat had to go on one of his voyages for the Marquis of Carabas, but that he would help her find her teeth soon. She had to touch her gums with her finger every evening, and every time she felt the bump grow a bit, she should think of the Cat, because the Cat was thinking of her. "That's exactly what he said," Gianni swears on his father's head. It was an odd conversation, but Mr. Rubino was really shaken up. Then he begged Gianni to keep something that belonged to Sergeant Paris. And not to tell anyone—not a soul—that he had given it to him. And to give it to her as soon as he saw her. He had to give it directly to her, not to anyone else, ever. The "something" is an iPhone box. Manuela shakes it, but there's no phone inside.

"He didn't tell you anything else, for me?" Manuela asks. Her mouth is dry, her heart topsy-turvy. She feels she's in a bizarre, evil dream. The cats brush against her legs, their yellow eyes glisten in the dark living room. "No, I'm sorry," Gianni says. "Mr. Rubino was really upset. That's for sure. I think he didn't want to go, but that it wasn't up to him. Then he got in a dark car, and the two who had stayed in the lobby showed us their cards and questioned us, first the concierge, then me, then Adel. They asked us all the same questions, we talked about it afterward. They wanted to know who Mr. Rubino had seen in Ladispoli, who knew he was at the Bellavista, who had called him. Oh, and if we had noticed anything unusual. Suspicious characters, people not from around here. I'm just a waiter, I explained, other than our regular clients, everyone is from somewhere else, this is a beach town. They wanted to see the reservations, and wrote down the names. They criticized us because we don't ask for a phone number when someone reserves a table, but I explained that this is a simple place, and besides, we're never full in the off season, if someone who reserved doesn't show up, no harm done. The concierge recalled that last Monday two men came asking if we had a room. He couldn't take reservations—the company had informed him that the hotel was reserved—and so he told them no. The men took a good look around. According to the concierge, they weren't tourists and they weren't interested in a room, but there are lots of strange people around, and he assumed they were our competition, come to spy on the new décor."

Vanessa and Manuela decline his offer of coffee or an aperitif. Unfortunately they're in a hurry to get back, they say. Gianni apologizes if he chattered on too long, he's a gossip, everybody always tells him, even Mr. Rubino. The Paris sisters thank him and wish him a pleasant vacation. "This is my vacation," he sighs, gesturing to his father, the dogs, and the cats. He is a sad, kind man, and it occurs to Manuela that he was Mattia's only interlocutor for all those days, and then they stole Mattia away from him. Mattia talked with Gianni Tribolato every morning and every evening—about inconsequential yet necessary things. About spaghetti, clams, mascarpone cake, cats, nothing at all. Mattia said something to the Bellavista waiter, something just for him, but for her not a word.

As soon as Vanessa starts up the car and pulls into the bumpy track that cuts through the artichoke fields and connects with the main road, Manuela opens the box. Inside is a packet of letters, all in envelopes from the Bellavista Hotel. And on each one is written—by hand—MANUELA PARIS, nothing more. No stamp, no address.

22

REWIND

BELLAVISTA HOTEL, JANUARY 6

I died on March 16, three years ago, in the parking lot of a restaurant overlooking the sea. The strangest thing is that I didn't realize it. It was midnight, give or take a minute. I'd had a few glasses of wine, but I was completely sober. I was sleepy, really tired, in a bad mood because the evening had gone all wrong. I don't know if you've ever gone to a conference: I go to at least two a year—one in Italy and one abroad. The organizers usually choose a pleasant spot—a city with plenty of cultural attractions, an island, or a castle—to tempt people to attend. Everyone prepares a paper to read, and they listen distractedly to those of their colleagues—it's really about networking. You're there to be seen, catch up, make connections. You meet people, go out to dinner, sometimes you end up in bed together. The whole thing lasts three days, then everyone says goodbye, maybe you see them again at the airport, and then you forget about everyone for a year.

I can't tell you the name of the city, I'm determined never to mention it. My silence is my insurance. I ask that you burn this letter when you get to the end, if you even get there. I am violating an agreement, I know you didn't ask me to, but I owe it to you. You left almost without saying goodbye, went away without warning me, you're angry with me and I think I understand why. You talk a lot about honesty. I'm not—and couldn't be—required to be honest with you, but I will be. It was a beautiful city, windy, on the sea, in southern Italy. I'd never been there before, and I'll never go back there again. All things considered, I even have some happy memories of the place. The sun was shining, and you could see the cliffs of the port from the conference hall.

I was scheduled to speak on the last day. My paper was on experimental cataract microsurgery. I showed a film clip of an operation where I used a new method, made possible by the invention of an intraocular acrylic lens. Then I highlighted the advantages of making a micro-incision—just 2.2 millimeters—in the crystalline lens, which could drastically reduce the duration of the operation as well as the risk of endophthalmitis and post-op complications. The whole thing lasted twenty minutes: that's how much time each participant was given, and I never run overtime; I respect the other speakers because I expect them to respect me.

During the coffee break the members of the American delegation complimented me; they thought my working hypothesis was very intriguing, we exchanged e-mail addresses and planned on sharing the results of our latest experiments. They asked me if I might be interested in working at their institute for a while. I indicated that I was open to the idea. Three years ago cataract microsurgery occupied more or less sixty percent of my day. The rest I dedicated to my family, sex, and mountaineering. A pretty simple life, all in all.

At the end of the afternoon session I met a colleague I'll call Livia—in any case, her name doesn't matter. She's two or three years younger than me, she lives near Turin and is a good, ambitious ophthalmologist. I won't hide from you that we had a casual relationship. We'd see each other almost every year, at the ophthalmology convention, and more than once I ended up in her room. I should tell you right up front that I have always liked having sex in hotel rooms. I hope you're not offended. Maybe I'm an exhibitionist, but the idea that someone might hear me turns me on instead of making me anxious. I love leaving my own viscous fluids behind on the sheets, towels, the carpet. Maybe it's the animal in me, marking my territory. The fact is that fucking in an anonymous place where you have no memories is relaxing; it helps empty the mind of all of life's junk. Sex with my colleague was pretty detached, devoid of any sentimental implications. I didn't even have her phone number, nor she mine. When I said goodbye to her, I never knew whether I'd see her again, and it didn't much matter. Over the course of a dozen or so years, we spent a few happy hours together, and that was really it. I respected her, but I can't say I particularly liked her. She was a fun distraction for me. And I for her. We were equals. I wish I had never met her, but I know it's not her fault, and I can't blame her.

Livia wasn't alone, though. She was talking with two colleagues I didn't know in the lobby of the conference hall. From her deferential behavior I gathered that they were important. I distrust powerful people. The Greeks say that it's risky to be friends with them, it's like riding a donkey. She introduced me. We shook hands, with that courteous indifference of strangers. The older one, tall, elegant, with a white mustache, was the director of a private clinic in the city; the other, a plump, sweaty doctor with a crackling voice and a red, veiny nose, was probably about my age. Unlike us, they weren't wearing plasticized name tags on their lapels. Livia and I locked eyes, silently questioning each other; we were both thinking the same thing. She whispered that she had to have dinner with them, but she'd really like it if I went with her. It was clear that she really wanted to get to know the older one, but was counting on being able to get away early, and wanted to spend the night with me.

I had a seat on the 8:00 plane the next morning. I was complicating my life, because we'd get back to the hotel around eleven at the earliest, and if I spent the night with her I wouldn't get much sleep. I was thirty-eight, not twenty, alas, and certain activities were starting to take their toll. But Livia insisted, and I was happy to end my trip in her bed—she hadn't come to the conference the previous two years because she had a small child and had stayed home to care for him. So I told our two colleagues—whose names I had already forgotten but could no longer ask—that I was grateful for the invitation, and that I'd be happy to join them. We agreed to meet at the waterfront restaurant a few miles out of town. Livia and I caught a cab, and held hands when it entered the underpass. "You look great," she told me. "But you should cut your hair, it's too long, it's messy, it makes you look less authoritative, more like a student." Her comment annoyed me. And if I had told her I preferred not to go, if I had eaten at the hotel buffet with the other conferencegoers and gone to bed early, I would still be alive now.

The restaurant was very fancy, the fish very fresh. But I was in a hurry to leave with Livia, so I didn't eat much. Experience had taught me that there is nothing worse for sex than a heavy meal. Every once in a while, to encourage me to sit through the boredom, Livia would rub the toe of her shoe along my calf, and that contact held me in a state of permanent excitement. I wasn't very talkative because all my energy was concentrated there. I know you won't understand, it's different for women, I guess. But at ten o'clock—they still hadn't brought us our main course—Livia got a phone call. "Oh my God, no," she exclaimed, getting up. Confused, upset, she said she had to go back to the hotel right away to get her bag, she was going to try and catch the last flight to Turin, her husband had been in an accident, he had been rushed to the hospital, it was an emergency. I offered to go with her, but she didn't want me to. She felt guilty, which I can understand. She barely even said goodbye. I never saw her again, and I'm not sorry. But she should have sought me out, she owed it to me. Of all human weaknesses, cowardice is the most repugnant, and I can't forgive her.

So I found myself having dinner with two strangers. They were understanding about the emergency and very pleasant, but the mood was far from relaxed. I sensed a powerful tension between the two of them, which my presence served in some way to soothe: I was involved in a game whose rules I did not know. I wanted to get up and leave, but didn't know how. Unfortunately my parents were old-fashioned, bourgeois, and I was raised with impeccable manners. We talked about medicine, so as not to sit there in silence. But they weren't oculists or microsurgery experts and at that time I was very specialized. The younger one was a gynecologist—I instinctively think less of men who stick gloves, mirrors, and that phallus-shaped ultrasound machine in women's vaginas. I didn't understand what they had to do with the conference. The gynecologist was passionate about sailing, he had a boat in the marina, too bad I was leaving tomorrow, or we could have sailed out to the islands, the weather was supposed to be perfect. The older one boasted about his clinic, an oasis of excellence in a region with poor health care; he told me he had offered Livia a job in the ophthalmology department, he knew she wanted to move back home. "Oh, I always thought she was from Turin," I said. They seemed like two completely normal guys, a bit arrogant, but people in my profession often are. The older one got up from the table first, without waiting for coffee, and I stayed with the younger one.

He was really anxious, but in no hurry to go. I don't know how, but I ended up having to sit through a depressing harangue about the statistically proven increase in tumors in the area, potentially due to the radio-active waste dumped into the sea, just a few miles off the coast. He wanted to know what effect radioactivity could have on the visual system. I explained that the retina is not particularly radiosensitive, but the crystalline lens, if exposed to radiation, can lose its transparency and develop a cataract. I know I didn't seem terribly eager to express my opinion on radioactive waste. I never tell my colleagues what I'm thinking, it's not worth it, even hospitals have become political minefields, you have to know how to navigate them. When I was young, I was quite an environmentalist and took part in antinuclear demonstrations, but frankly I'd only be interested in the problem now if criminals were dumping radioactive waste in my sea. But I vacationed in Greece, I'd remodeled a house on the island of Santorini, in Imerovigli, a village as white as snow on the edge of the caldera—for me it was the closest thing to an earthly Paradise. When I looked at my watch, it was 11:50. It was late, I really had to go. I wanted to pay for dinner, but the gynecologist explained that we were the older man's guests. We couldn't be rude. I asked the waiter to call me a taxi, and again the gynecologist said it was out of the question. I was a guest, he would drive me back to the hotel in his car.

It was drizzling. The parking lot was dark except for two streetlights that cast a yellow glow on the gravel. When we'd arrived, there was a kid showing people where to park, but he wasn't there when we left, and the chair next to the gate was empty. The restaurant was still crowded, and the guests milling around the parking lot cast dark shadows. Their voices blended with the murmur of the sea. I remember one couple with a BMW because of the woman: she'd had a terrible nose job but was still very beautiful. We didn't have an umbrella so we jogged to his car, a Porsche Cayenne Turbo, which costs a hundred and twenty thousand euros. I noted the make because I would have liked to buy one myself, but I'd hesitated—in part because of the cost and in part because it polluted a lot. My last thought—I am ashamed to say—was that if a hick gynecologist from the provinces can afford one, then so can I. Not to brag, but I was an established professional. In my private practice alone—not counting my hospital salary—I made ten thousand euros a month. There were times when I would go home with pockets full of money. I'd pull bills out of my jacket and pants pockets, sometimes I'd forget them in my clothes and the dry cleaners would give them back to me perfectly washed and pressed, as if they'd just been minted. At that moment I decided that as soon as I got home I would buy myself a Porsche Cayenne, to hell with environmental scruples and particulate emission impact; it was a terrific car. I gazed at it admiringly, grateful for my good fortune, my talents, my life. I had it all.

And there it was. A motorcycle appeared from the farthest corner of the parking lot. The front headlight, a white glow through a veil of rain, lit up the hood of the SUV. There were two people on the bike, and the passenger wasn't wearing a helmet. "Calogero," he said. "Christ," the gynecologist said. Then I heard two bangs. Not particularly loud. Like a thud. But I knew right away that they were shots. I didn't think anything; I wasn't even scared. It seemed like a bad movie I'd ended up in by pure chance. But I instinctively crouched down behind the car door, which was still open. Stupidly because, if they wanted to do me in, all they had to do was go around the car: I was exposed, no cover, like a sitting duck. But the motorcycle accelerated and took off. I stayed crouched on the gravel, petrified. I don't know how much time passed. A few minutes, I think. The rain dripped from my hair onto my neck, an icy rivulet creeping down my back. I was cold. There was an eerie silence. The voices had disappeared, now the only sound was the waves on the rocks. I kneeled down: a puddle was spreading out from under the SUV, and since the ground was slightly uneven, it flowed toward me. And then I saw a hand, still clutching a set of keys.

I didn't even know the guy. I'd seen him for the first time in my life just three hours earlier. Now that name, Calogero, was lodged in my brain. If they hadn't called out to him, he would have remained a stranger. I stood up. There was no one in the parking lot. The shadows that had been milling about a minute earlier had disappeared. I didn't know what to do. But I'm a doctor first and foremost. I went around to the other side of the SUV, kneeled over him, and checked his pulse. As I held his wrist in my fingers, I noticed that he had two bullet holes in him, one in his forehead, the other in his chest, right at heart level.

I thought about my flight at eight the next morning. I just wanted to go home. There was nothing more I could do for that Calogero, whoever he was. But I couldn't leave him there, lying in a parking lot in the rain like a dog. You don't know how many times I told myself that I should have just started walking toward the city, which was only a few miles away. A lot of people had seen me with the dead man—in fact, I was the last person to see him alive, and that's never a good start. But Livia and the older man had dined with him, too, and they could have explained everything. I was just a speaker at an ophthalmology conference. I lived six hundred miles away, in a quiet place where things like this didn't happen, I didn't know the first thing about him. I could have said I was scared, and no one would have blamed me. I should have vanished, like that couple in the BMW. Like everyone else in the parking lot and inside the restaurant. But I didn't. I can't explain why. I couldn't imagine. But in a certain sense I could. I was a stranger there, but I'm not an idiot. And I'm a doctor first and foremost. That man wasn't dead yet. He had no chance of surviving, and I knew it. But my fingers had felt the echo of a pulse. I think that's why.

I went inside the restaurant and told the waiter to call an ambulance because someone had shot Dr. Calogero. The waiter pierced me with a cold stare, as if I were a nuisance. But he picked up the phone. I sat on a chair and waited. The gynecologist was no longer breathing when the ambulance arrived. I died at midnight, in the parking lot of a restaurant overlooking the sea. My name is not Mattia.

I didn't take the 8:00 a.m. flight. At that hour I was asleep. I had spent the night at the police station. All things considered, the police were very understanding. Keep in mind that I have always had a complicated relationship to authority. Perhaps as a reaction to my father's being so overbearing, I don't know, I'm not very interested in psychology. The fact is that until that night I'd only had three run-ins with the police in my life, and it was my fault each time: I'd broken the law, or helped someone else break it. At sixteen, on my way home from a party, I was stopped for drunk driving and driving without a license. At nineteen I was involved in a brawl at a stadium after a game. Soccer didn't interest me in the least, you must have realized I don't get it the other day, but I'd gone with a friend who was crazy about our city's team. She had a knife with an eight-inch blade in her backpack and they loaded us both in the police van. At twenty-two my girlfriend got herself arrested for insulting a public official: she spat at a riot cop during the evacuation of a community center where she taught illegal immigrants Italian. She was really committed, a radical who wanted to make the world a better place— that's why I fell in love with her, even though I didn't do anything to help her, all I did was waste my father's money: to keep my motorcycle running, to pay for cigarettes and plane tickets to climb pristine mountains in Nepal, Alaska, and Chile. I was an okay mountaineer and a pretty good rock climber. As you can see, behind all my troubles you'll find a woman. But anyway, now I was thirty-eight and I hadn't set foot in a police station since I'd had to renew my passport. I don't like uniforms, as I think I already told you.

And now I was surrounded by uniforms, I was in their hands. They brought me coffee, asked me if I wanted to see a psychologist in case I was in shock. I didn't feel like I was in a state of shock, though. I had seen a man killed. But I'm a doctor, after all: I'd seen people die as far back as med school; when I was interning at the hospital, a little girl with heart complications expired in my arms. They questioned me a little disrespectfully at first, then—once they had verified that I really was a speaker at the ophthalmology conference—more courteously. When they finally let me go, it was five in the morning. I had told them what I knew, in other words nothing, and I felt relieved; I went back to the hotel, climbed in bed, and crashed. I was exhausted. I woke up at noon, feeling fresh and rested, I checked out and took a taxi to the airport. I got a seat on the first plane. I was home by three.

I had a nice house. I'd lived there for five years. First I'd lived in the historic center, in an old building, a labyrinth of stairs and courtyards. You could see the cathedral's bell tower from my windows, a slice of the façade with its rose window, and a swath of red tiles. I liked it and would have stayed. But Denise kept saying that there was too much pollution, that the smog was dangerous, and that our son needed to grow up in nature. The sight of trees teaches respect for life. Denise—not her real name, but you have to forgive me for concealing it—worked for the Green Party; she handled public relations for the regional headquarters, and had strong convictions about the fate of the planet. So we went to a real estate agency and they found us a house on the outskirts, in the foothills. Close enough to the center so you could bike there, but far enough away that we could see the mountains from our porch, and I think I chose it mostly for that. Three stories, a recent construction by a trendy architect. It had a rec room, a yard with tall trees and a swing, and a whole slew of bedrooms. I would have liked a big family, and was counting on convincing Denise over time. It took us a year to decorate it. She did it all, because I've never cared in the least about furniture. A bed is a bed, a table a table. Over time, Denise began to regret moving to the countryside. She quit her job when Marco was born, and the bucolic solitude of that enormous house—shared only with a newborn and a Moldavian babysitter whose vocabulary was limited to about a hundred words—turned out to be really hard for her, almost unbearable. I was never home before nine. But by that point I liked our house, I'd fallen in love with the trees, the birds, the mountains, I wasn't up for moving again. And we'd also gotten a cat—a Persian, Soraya, who quickly became the queen of the yard, and I never would have confined her to a city apartment. It may sound strange to you, but as the years passed, Soraya's happiness became more important to me than Denise's.

I didn't tell Denise anything about Calogero's murder. It was something that happened hundreds of miles away. There was only a brief article in the newspapers, and she never read the news unless something happened in our city—and nothing ever happened in our city. When Marco ran to greet me and I held him in my arms, it was like the whole thing had never happened, at least not to me. Like a hallucination, a nightmare, but one from which I had awoken into my previous existence.

I have experienced just about all the sensations a man can experience in life. I never denied myself anything. But nothing feels more amazing than the gentle weight of your son's head on your shoulder as he wraps his arms around your neck and slobbers your cheek with kisses, quivering with joy because you've finally come home. It's hard for me to write about him, but if I didn't, I would be hiding from you the only good thing I've been able to do in my life. Marco is his real name. I know I shouldn't write it, but I can't help myself. It's a way of having him here with me, even if only for an instant.

He has blue eyes and blond hair and everyone says he looks exactly like me. But the most recent photograph I have of him is from last Christmas, and maybe he looks different now. I haven't seen him in a year. I'm sorry I haven't told you about him. It wasn't because I wanted to hide his existence from you, but because I can't talk about him without doubling over in pain. It's a physical pain, as if someone were twisting a knife in my guts. I know you can understand me—in fact you may be the only person who can. Everything lessens with time. Solids sublimate and become gas. Water evaporates. Rocks crumble—even granite turns to sand in the end. Radioactive materials decay, it takes centuries, millennia, billions of years, but even uranium, cesium, and thorium become harmless. Not pain, though. Pain is indestructible, like gold, like diamonds.

My pain has withstood the passage of time, of everything; if anything, it's growing stronger.

I have to say that I can make do without everything else. My house, my work, my family, Denise. But not my child. The next day I returned to my office, my patients, my hospital rounds, my usual routine. I examined eyes affected by macular degeneration, myopia, exotropia, presbyopia. I handed out eyedrops, prescriptions, and atropine. I performed cataract surgery. Keep in mind that seventy-five percent of people over seventy have problems with cataracts, and one hundred percent of those over eighty do. Given Italy's aging population and the increase in the average life span, I'd chosen an ideal profession, and I didn't have to worry about being unemployed. Nearly eighty percent of my work was cataract related. The technical term is phacoemulsification. I would use ultrasound to emulsify the crystalline lens, aspirate it, make an incision, remove the natural lens, and implant a synthetic one. Making the incision requires real skill—we're talking about minuscule measurements, barely six millimeters in diameter, and during the extraction you have to be careful not to damage the surrounding tissue—but it had become routine to me.

Denise and I went shopping at the supermarket near our house, Marco sitting in the cart; I took the babysitter to the train in the evening; we invited friends over for dinner—I liked to cook and was pretty good in the kitchen. It seems to me now that the week after the ophthalmology conference was the best week of my life. Because somewhere inside of me I knew it couldn't last. It may sound strange, but I felt guilty. Almost as if I'd been the one to shoot Calogero. In truth, I'd shot myself, and somehow I knew it. So I tried to make peace with my life. To ignore the rough patches and celebrate the joys.

Denise and I had gone through some tough times. She was only one of my girlfriends. I'd never felt particularly bound to her. But when I was thirty-one I got it in my head that I wanted to have a child. I'd had an absent father and was a terrible son, but I was convinced I would be a good father and that my son would be happy. I know it doesn't usually happen to men, that the biological clock usually ticks only for women. But I really wanted to have a child. I was seeing three women when the idea seized me and wouldn't let go: Denise, Valeria, and Giada. Each one would have liked to be the only one, but all three knew about the others; I don't like lying to people. Giada, a third-year medical student, was too young. Valeria was a dark-haired nephrologist who laughed all the time and was an octopus in bed. She knew every trick there was to please a man. She was as promiscuous as I was; she wasn't jealous, and never would have suffocated me or gotten depressed over an affair. I was happy with her and she would have been the ideal mother. But she was already forty and I worried we would have trouble conceiving. I was very pragmatic, maybe even cynical, and I'm sorry about that—she was very hurt when Marco was born; even someone as easygoing as she was can get depressed. Anyway, I got Denise pregnant and we went off to live in the countryside with our son. But I continued to see Giada and then Giada's cousin, too, and obviously Denise found out about it, and tried in vain to make me leave them. She had put on forty pounds during her pregnancy and, diets and workouts notwithstanding, she never managed to drop the extra weight. She started feeling depressed, neglected, and ugly, even though it wasn't true; she actually looked better with a little more flesh on her. I found her new shape more reassuring. We started fighting, poisoning our relationship. I would promise her any- and everything because I didn't want her to leave and take Marco with her, but I never kept my promises. Deep down I knew she wouldn't leave: she loved me.

That week I always made it home in time for dinner. I didn't cheat on her. On Saturday we went snowshoeing in the mountains. The snow was perfect, powdery, packed—zero risk of avalanches. All alone, we walked for almost three hours, in single file in the woods. Every now and then we would come across hare or chamois tracks. The only sound was the thud of snow falling from tree branches. It was all so white and pure, and I felt good. Denise was tired so I hoisted Marco on my shoulders and carried him as far as the Alpine hut. We sunbathed on the terrace. I made Marco a snow bear. We'd been told that they cross the border from Slovenia sometimes, and make their dens in the caves below the peaks. Marco wanted to see one and was disappointed when I explained that bears sleep through the winter. On Sunday my brother and his wife came to visit and we had a barbeque. Marco didn't want to go to bed and I finally convinced him by promising him a bedtime story. He was crazy about "Puss in Boots." So I read him "Puss in Boots" until he fell asleep. The next morning I got a phone call. It was the police commissioner who had questioned me the week before. He told me there were some new developments and that they needed to talk with me. He asked me when I might have a few hours to go down and talk with them. I explained that

I was extremely busy, I didn't have any vacation time and couldn't get away. Since he couldn't convince me to go there, in the end he said that he would come to me.

I met them in my office. I've forgotten the face of his colleague, who didn't say a word; but the commissioner had bags under his eyes and was unshaven, as if he hadn't slept in days. He asked me if any other details had come to mind, anything that I might have omitted during my first deposition. But I hadn't given it any further thought, so I told him no. At that point he showed me some photographs. I had stupidly told him that the guy on the back of the motorcycle wasn't wearing a helmet, and that I'd seen his face. A kid, roughly twenty years old. I looked at the photographs, but not very carefully. It was cold but I was sweating like a pig. Because I understood perfectly well the situation I'd gotten myself into, and I wanted out, but I didn't know how to get out. And then I saw him. I would have picked him out in a crowd of a million. His face was stamped on my memory, a snapshot frozen right at the instant he said "Calogero." And now there he was on my desk, alongside my ophthalmology books and international journals, in which I managed to publish an article every once in a while, alongside the photos of Marco in the pool, Marco skiing, Marco with me in Santorini, in the dazzling white of the houses of Imerovigli. And that kid had shot a forty-year-old gynecologist in the face right in front of me.

I ask myself all the time what I would do if I could do it all over again. If I could have imagined all this. I told you, I don't believe in anything, I'm allergic to ideologies and I've never done anything for my neighbor simply because it was my duty to do so. I just tried to be happy, and I'd succeeded for thirty-eight years. I'd deceived everyone, myself most of all. I don't have a particularly elevated opinion of humanity, and I don't consider myself better than other people. When the law restricted my freedom I broke it without remorse. I'm not particularly bound to institutions; as a student and then as a doctor I knew only their most corrupt and repugnant aspects. The word *Italy* means nothing to me beyond the language I speak and the country I live in. I get annoyed when people talk to me about the homeland. For me the homeland isn't the land of our fathers but of our children. It's not an expanse of space or a history, but something alive and present, that each one of us carries inside. I know you don't agree, but for me Italy can be reduced to a passport, my son's school, and the hospital. I'm not particularly courageous—if anything

I'm reckless, I'd risk my life trying to clear a path in the Himalayas for the sheer pleasure of the challenge. But recklessness is the opposite of courage. And anyway, I wasn't thinking about any of this then. Calogero the gynecologist was not innocent, but I probably wouldn't have been either, in his place. I didn't owe him anything. I had everything to lose and nothing to gain.

And yet I believe I would do what I did again. I put my sweaty fingers on the photograph and nodded. "That's him, I recognize him beyond any reasonable doubt." The man who had traveled six hundred miles to hear those words sighed and scratched his beard. He was happy, but also sad. Sad for me, but I didn't know it then. He told me I would have to make a statement, and I had to go with him to the nearest police station. The report took about an hour. When it was over, both visitors thanked me and shook my hand. I didn't really understand what they were thanking me for.

I didn't know the kid's name, and I didn't want to know. In fact, I stated clearly that it didn't matter to me who he was. For me, he was just someone who had shot a man in the face. If they caught him, sure, I'd be willing to testify at the trial, but I didn't want to know anything more till then. The man who had traveled six hundred miles for me thought that it might not be so simple, but he didn't say anything at the time. Later, I found out that the kid was named Marco, like my son, and I still can't forgive him for that.

Some time later—I can't remember exactly when, my memory has erased the intervals, but at any rate some time later—I found out that Marco's father was one of the twenty most dangerous fugitives in Italy. With that murder, his son was proving that he was an adult and could control his father's territory even in his absence. Marco was suspected of various crimes, but they had never been able to gather enough evidence to charge him. My deposition could turn out to be decisive in upsetting the family's plans and in apprehending both the instigators and the accomplices. So I was a precious witness. To cut a long story short, the prefect's office sent a public security representative to see me. He informed me that the police had been ordered to set up appropriate protective measures to guarantee my safety. Nothing serious. Standard procedure, as provided for by the penal code. I shouldn't worry. A provisional measure, purely precautionary. Nothing bad would happen to me. I shouldn't be afraid. But I had to talk to my wife. My family had to be informed of the new protective measures, it was essential for our safety. "She's not my wife," I said. Just think: he was trying to tell me that my old life was dying, and all I could think to do was point out that Denise and I weren't married. Maybe it was a way of defending myself from reality.

"What does it mean in practical terms?" was the only thing Denise said when I informed her of the killing and my meeting with the police. "I think they'll send someone to watch the house," I told her. "Oh well, as long as they don't send a female officer," she sighed sarcastically. She was still witty despite the disappointments and bitterness she'd endured in recent years. A rather rare quality in a woman. In that moment I forgave her years of accusations and fights she'd picked, and I opened myself to her. I don't know if I loved her, but I cared a lot about her, and I was happy she was my partner.

They didn't come right away, some time passed. For a few days I even hoped they had changed their mind. But I will spare you the delays. When a dark car finally took up position in front of our gate, I picked up Marco and pointed to it. "Do you see that? It's for me. Papà's a big shot now. I have police protection, just like a politician." "Wow," Marco said. And we laughed.

On the face of it, nothing changed. I still rode my bike to work. The dark car circled our house, following me if I went out, but after a few days I managed to forget about it. And yet, almost without realizing it, my habits changed, and I started to change, too. I was being watched, after all. My personal freedom was cramped by that discreet yet nagging presence. Because I was ashamed to let the judges and police officers—who considered me a serious, honest, upright professional—know that I wasn't what I seemed, that even though I had a partner and a child, I was seeing another woman. Her name was Lara, she was a patient of mine, visually impaired. My office was like a girlfriend recruiting agency, a factory for minting admirers. Three quarters of my patients were women. In that half hour of intimacy—in which they, timid, hesitant, rested their chin on the testing instrument and looked me in the eye—something sparked. I was young. It's hard for two human beings to look each other in the eye like that and remain indifferent. They were seeking comfort, and I wanted to share a little happiness. But Lara wasn't merely a whim. She couldn't see me, so she touched me with an almost shamanic power, identifying the most sensitive parts of my body and sensitizing those that weren't, from the soles of my feet to my elbows, from my fingernails to the folds in my ass. So we made love in the dark, and she taught me to see with my hands.

Maybe I've shown you what a good student I was. Maybe not, and if so, I'm sorry. If you give me another chance, I'll try again. I haven't been able to figure out what you blame me for, and why you're avoiding me, but I'd rather not ask. If you want to tell me, you will. I'm always here, I'm writing facing the balcony, I'm looking at your windows, even though you're not home today. The car that took you away had Italian Army plates. Wherever you are, I wouldn't have been able to go with you, and this thought gives me the strength to carry on. I owed a lot to Lara, and it seemed unfair to leave her just because I had looked a killer in the face.

But in a sense my new circumstances forced me, at least for a while, to behave—that is, to behave the way society holds that one must in order to be considered respectable and therefore credible. It's hypocritical, of course. But still, I left her. I promised her the separation wasn't definitive, because I really believed I would be free again after the trial. But I would understand if she found someone else in the meantime and wished her all the best. And I would keep checking her eyes, as I had done for years. Lara responded sadly that she preferred to wait for me. I was the only sighted man who knew how to see her with his hands and not just with his dick. So, for two months, even though I didn't want to, I conformed to my new role. No women, no daring mountaineering. I lived a normal life, I came home early. Denise understood: "Thank God for Calogero," she said. "Someday I'll put flowers on his grave, he turned you into a responsible person."

One night my cell rang at midnight. I was already asleep, and I awoke with a start. My first thought was that something must have happened to Denise's mother. She'd suffered from multiple sclerosis for years, and sometimes she'd have an attack and need to be hospitalized. But it was a man's voice. He asked if he were speaking with the doctor; he said my name. I'm used to phone calls from clients at all hours of the day and night, so I said yes. The voice said something laughingly. I didn't understand. He spoke in heavy dialect. A southern dialect, which might as well be Chinese to me. "Excuse me," I said, "what is it you want?" The voice repeated it, in the same joking tone, but slower this time. Some of the words were clear. He was telling me I was already dead. At that moment

I assumed he was joking or that it didn't have anything to do with me. But his voice was so sinister that when I hung up I felt a chill in my bones, and my heart was in my throat.

I went out to the street just as I was, in my underwear and bare feet. The echo of those absurd words hounded me and their true meaning was becoming clearer inside of me. I even understood the ones I hadn't grasped earlier: there's no escaping, Doctor, we've found you, you don't go very fast on that bike of yours, something like that. The man who was supposed to be protecting us was dozing in the dark car, his head against the window. "They know who I am, they have my phone number," I told him. We drank a coffee on the porch. It was the end of June, in three days I was supposed to take Denise and Marco to Imerovigli, help them open up the house, and then come back to Italy, before joining them on August 1. The officer asked me if it was hard to become an ophthalmologist. An eye seemed to him like a difficult thing to treat, so small, so strange. "It's a muscle, just like any other," I answered. Like the heart. But with less blood. I was an impressionable med student. The smell of blood made me sick. But the eye doesn't smell even when it's diseased. Of all the branches of medicine, ophthalmology is the cleanest. If he wanted, I could show him the DVDs of my operations. I kept them, so I could show them at conferences. I would have liked to show them to you, Manuela, because you would have seen that my hands don't shake when I make an incision with a microscalpel, and that I, too, know how to hit an almost invisible target without even looking. I smiled when you told me how much you love your rifle and how much it hurts being separated from it, and you thought I was making fun of you. But I understood how you feel. My hand feels empty without a scalpel.

The next day they advised me to stay on Santorini all summer. I canceled all my appointments and left my associate in charge of the office. Sun, sea, beach, moussaka, swimming pool, motorboat—not a care in the world. Italy was very far away. I didn't let Calogero the gynecologist or Marco the murderer disembark at Santorini. We were alone— Denise, Marco, and me. I taught my Marco to swim. It was the last thing I did for him. We came home on September 15, for the start of school. On September 16 my car caught on fire right in the center of the city. It was parked outside my office. I was using high-frequency ultrasound to bombard a particularly hard, advanced-stage cataract. The girls from the hair salon across the street rang my bell to let me know. The flames reached the second floor.

Everything spun out of control pretty quickly. They informed me that they had to raise my level of protection: I was in clear and present danger, and was no longer safe in my hometown. A change of domicile was necessary. In other words, we had to leave. But everything I had was there. My whole life, within a radius of a few miles. My parents, my brother, my house, the hospital, my practice, the mountains, my clients, Marco's school, Denise's mother, my friends—everything. "We're sorry," they said. For my own good, for that of my partner and my son, we had to leave. Naturally I would receive all the assistance I required. House, work, social reintegration, I needn't worry about any of it, a situation suited to my existing way of life and my profession would be found, a job was guaranteed. We packed in silence. Denise wept, incredulous. Marco followed me around mutely, putting all his toys in bags: little cars, monster robots, soccer ball, puzzles, stuffed dogs. As we loaded the car, Soraya escaped from her basket and, even though we searched everywhere, we couldn't find her. For months I made them hang up posters with her picture on the lampposts, outside shopping centers, in the piazza, but she never turned up. Maybe she died of hunger in the woods; she was an aristocratic cat, not used to hunting for food. Or maybe she got run over by a truck on one of the narrow lanes that cut through the industrial park. She was the first victim of the earthquake that brought my whole life tumbling down.

Before closing the front door, I turned on the alarm. It was evening, the house stood out like a pink cake against the darkness of the trees. It had never looked so beautiful. I hadn't even finished paying off the mortgage. My son was in my arms. Sleepy, Marco asked me when we could come back. Soon, I told him. There was a plaque next to the gate, Marco designed it, it said MY HOME. It pierced my heart. I didn't know where we were going, or for how long. Everything was unfolding above and beyond my will. I watched the house in the rearview mirror until it disappeared in the hedges around the curve. I haven't seen it since.

I tried moving to America. I contacted the institute that had asked me to come on board with them, but they replied that it would take time. I'd have to wait until I don't know what meeting, where the budget would be approved, and only then would they know the extent of available funds, and regardless I had to present my research project, and submit my findings to a scientific commission for evaluation. If I submitted the material before the end of the year, and they decided to fund my project, they would offer me a contract: I would be able to leave the following September. But it was hard to gather all the necessary paperwork and to write my research proposal. I couldn't concentrate, and besides, September seemed so far away. By then, I thought, the protective measures will have been lifted, we will have returned home, and we wouldn't want to leave again to go to America.

We spent nine months in a northern city similar to our own, a twin city of sorts—but it wasn't the same. It, too, had a cathedral with a bell tower, a piazza with porticos and cafés, a pedestrian center, bike paths, a hospital, hills. It even had mountains—although in that part of Italy the Mediterranean breeze melted the snow early and the peaks were under ten thousand feet. Few forests, no fir trees. Olive trees climbed up the precipices. We rented a villa that was vaguely reminiscent of our old place. But the people spoke with a different accent, I had few patients, we didn't know anyone, we didn't have any friends and didn't want to make new ones, we lived suspended, uprooted, like refugees awaiting asylum. We had to believe this was provisional in order to bear having been torn away like that, in order to imagine that we would return to our lives soon. To imagine the future, in other words.

We spent a lot of time alone in that unfamiliar house, surprised by strange noises, assaulted by unknown odors. One night, it was almost spring, I suggested again to Denise that we have another child. Marco was nearly seven by then, we had to get a move on. Maybe I already sensed that only my family would be able to protect me. Denise said that she would stop taking the pill as soon as she finished that month's supply. She wasn't stingy, but she was convinced that we Westerners have forgotten the art of frugality, and was determined not to waste anything. This was her way of showing respect for those who have nothing, even if we can't do anything for them. I often laughed at her obsession, but now it strikes me as noble. I have done away with everything that is superfluous, at times even with what is necessary.

I'll only tell you the bare minimum about the trial. Recalling those moments makes me uncontrollably angry. I think you can understand that. I testified behind opaque, bulletproof glass. As I sat in that uncomfortable chair repeating what I had already said so many times that by now it was like a monotonous lullaby and—for me—devoid of nearly all reality, I realized I no longer existed. All they could see of me on the other side of the glass was my silhouette. My face was erased. My voice distorted. I had become a shadow. It was only when my mouth went dry and I had to drink a glass of water that I understood what that voice had meant on the phone that night. I really was dead. I coughed, took a deep breath, as if preparing to dive under water. I said what I had to say, and then went outside, said hello to my man, the one taking care of me, and told him that as far as I was concerned, that was it. I didn't want to know anything more about any of it. He said he understood, but nevertheless he thanked me, this country needed people like me. I told him I didn't consider myself a role model. "I'm a terrible partner, an unscrupulous doctor, a cowardly father, you really don't know me." He smiled. A few months later he called to tell me the verdict. That kid Marco had been sentenced to life in prison. I confess I didn't feel a thing, not even relief.

It was June. I remember because we were counting down the days until the end of the school year. We already had our tickets for Greece. We had decided to spend the entire summer in Imerovigli. Before, I never would have been able to stand being in one place for three whole months, no matter how beautiful. I never would have been able to stand being away from my work for so long, abandoning my patients, giving up my experiments and operations. A surgeon is like a pianist. He has to keep his hands in shape. He has to keep studying, learning, operating. But like I said, I was changing. I was no longer what I once was. I was like a snake after molting. I'd shed my old skin, but I hadn't yet grown a new one. I didn't know who I was anymore. I hadn't had an affair in months. I didn't go to the annual ophthalmology conference—neither the national one in Italy nor the international one in Paris. I hadn't even made a new video to add to my collection—no daring operations, no experimental research, no scientific publications.

I had become a provincial ophthalmologist. To build up a clientele in my new city, I worked on credit. My patients paid in installments, or not at all. Before, my patients had been city council members, notaries' wives, businessmen's daughters. My new patients were immigrants who had entered the country with veils on their heads, speaking not a word of Italian, who blushed when I told them to look me in the eyes; or they were chatty retirees with advanced-stage cataracts in both eyes; or they were gypsies I treated for free and who paid me back by playing the accordion under my window. I examined them because I didn't want to lose touch with my work, I wanted to stay in shape, even if it meant using decades-old instruments. By this point Imerovigli seemed like the only link to our previous life.

I hadn't earned much that year, and the money I'd been promised to cover my lost income never arrived. Denise never complained. We didn't have a babysitter anymore, so she would pick up Marco from school herself. On June 8, when she arrived at the gate, the porter told her that Marco had left with his uncle. Denise was very surprised, because my brother had never come to visit us; he was buried in red tape all the time, ever since he'd been given an important post at a local sanitation company, and had phoned us maybe three times since we'd moved. Maybe she didn't want to worry or maybe she was just lying to herself. The fact is that when Denise came back home, she wasn't all that upset. I was alone in the yard, raking leaves, and obviously neither my brother or Marco had come home. They had taken him away.

I barely remember a thing from those terrible twelve hours. Denise did nothing but cry, curled up next to the phone, pleading, practically begging it to ring. Every now and then she would glance at me with pure hatred, saying I had killed Marco. I understood how she felt: she blamed me and I deserved it. I was so devastated I couldn't even cry. We weren't alone, obviously the people who had been handling my case those past few months and the one I called my man arrived a few hours later. I can't tell you his name and I don't want to give him any old name. In a certain sense, he represented my fate, and fate is anonymous, impersonal, it simply unfolds. Besides, I don't know anything about him. In that moment, it was like he didn't exist. My sense of guilt tore at my soul. I couldn't think about anything other than my son's smile when we played soccer together in the yard or worked on a jigsaw puzzle together on the living room table. An extraordinary child. And they had stolen him from me. I couldn't imagine a more inhuman punishment.

I rambled. I remember saying to my man that I was recanting, to let them know immediately. I wanted to take it all back. It's too late, Denise screamed, it's too late. I couldn't bring myself even to look at her. I remember thinking that I'd kill myself if Marco were found dead in some ditch. A man who didn't know how to protect his own child doesn't deserve to live.

Marco called from the neighborhood café at about one in the morning. He's always been an intelligent, mature child, and he had memorized my and Denise's cell phone numbers. But he called me. It meant the world to me. Denise never forgave me for that. He was okay. They hadn't touched a single hair on his head. Later, he had to tell the police everything. He did so without hesitating, serious, precise, choosing the right words. A nice, fat man had picked him up from school, saying he was one of Papà's climbing buddies. Marco had believed him, even though it seemed a little strange because he didn't have the physique of a mountain climber. But since he would have gone anywhere with a friend of Papà's, and the fat man said he had to take him to his papà, he got in the car. There were two other men in the backseat, and they made him sit between them. They got on the highway and then got off, they took him to an empty house in the countryside, to wait for Papà, they said. The house was run-down and abandoned and there wasn't anything to do and he got really bored and then at a certain point he fell asleep. Finally they got back in the car, took the highway again, and then they left him at the café, with Mrs. Lucia.

When I saw him, that skinny little blond boy sitting on a stool at the counter, I melted like a popsicle. "Why are you crying, Papà," he said with surprise, "everything's okay."

But it wasn't okay at all. Our trip to Greece was canceled. We left that night. We spent two weeks in an empty extended-stay hotel in a muggy plain, a hellish, mosquito-infested landscape. All we brought with us was some underwear and a change of clothes, they'd send the rest later. We couldn't tell anyone back home, or call our families to say where we were. It was a delicate moment, or so they told us. Delicate! I made furious phone calls. I insisted I wanted to take it all back. I was tired, our life was slipping through my fingers, and I had to grab it while there was still time. And I couldn't let anything happen to Marco. No principle, no matter how noble, could compete with him. "I take it all back, I'm out," I kept saying.

My man kindly explained that it wasn't a good idea. If I pulled out, I would lose my right to get into the special witness protection program, whereas now I could submit my request, and there was a good chance it would be accepted. And even if I pulled out now I wouldn't be safe. Those people never forget, and sooner or later they would find me. "But this way we will continue to protect you. Legal witnesses have certain rights, and they must be defended. It's a pact. You do your best to obey the rules, and we'll do our best to hold up our end. All you have to do is sign the papers and behave accordingly. If, on the other hand, you choose to turn your back on all this and something happens to you, who will take care of your son?" It wasn't a threat, of course, just the truth. But in practice nothing changed. I was forced to keep running on this crazy treadmill, like a hamster.

We were on edge in that empty hotel. We argued over the smallest things. The mosquitoes, the heat, the isolation. We couldn't do anything, we couldn't even go outside. Marco and I played soccer in the half-empty rooms. I'd signed him up for soccer in our second city, he was in the youth league and really liked it. He'd even made some new friends already; it's easier for kids. And here I was, taking everything away from him again. We're like gypsies, Denise would say every now and then. There are happy gypsies, too, I would say, reminding her of an old song. After all, I told myself, I have the two of them. What else do I need, really? The rest is superfluous.

In June I got some good news. We would be moving to Abruzzo, a city by the sea, population twenty thousand or slightly more. We would be given a new house, and once the summer was over, Marco would be enrolled in a new school, a private Catholic school with a good reputation. There was only one drawback. For the time being, it would be best if I left off my work as an ophthalmologist. Too obvious. I could work in the ER. Sure, they realized that for someone at my level it was a painful step backwards. But for the moment they couldn't offer me anything better suited. There had been budget cuts, and I still hadn't gotten into the special witness protection program. Some people at the ministry thought that the protective measures for me had become excessive. Others said that in the meantime some *pentiti* had come forward, my deposition wasn't unique or essential, and therefore I didn't have a right to the program's benefits. The pettiness, the bickering, and the stinginess: it's not even worth talking about. I think you understand what it means to find yourself on the front line and know that there's no artillery to back you up, no one's covering you, your life is worthless, and they'll weep for you only when you're dead.

But my man was surprised by my reaction. "I'm really happy," I said. "It's a great opportunity for me. It'll be like being born again. I'll be twenty-four years old again, a recent graduate without a specialty, young and idealistic, with his young family. A chance to start everything all over." "Well then, I'm happy for you, Doctor," he said. "Good luck."

Denise left on January 1. I was on call at the hospital, doing a crossword puzzle to kill time. Over the past few months I'd become a master at puzzles, rebuses, sudoku. Before, I'd always thought that these kinds of games were just for old ladies. Things my grandmother, my elderly aunts, my mother did. But I discovered that filling in those little boxes helped me fill in the void I felt around and inside me. I feel at peace every time I finish a crossword puzzle: it's like putting everything back in its place. Crosswords are an oasis of order, a bulwark against chaos. It's comforting to know that a number corresponds to only one letter, that only one word fits a definition, that for every question there's only one answer. Crosswords are the antithesis of the world. I didn't see a single patient that day. The phone never rang, and the hours slowly drained away, as monotonous as the rain that fell silently from the timid, leaden sky.

We lived along the waterfront, on a street that makes me think of Ladispoli. Which is why I loved your city right away, even before meeting you. The smell is the same, even the buildings are similar. Maybe I'm condemned to live in twin cities. I'm pursued by repetition. When I parked my car not far from our building, I noticed right away that the lights were out in our third-floor apartment. Strange, because it was dinnertime, we always ate at eight thirty. We had become set in our ways.

So I knew. I didn't have the strength to climb those two flights of stairs and walk into an empty house. I collapsed onto a bench and stayed there, whipped by the frosty easterly wind, splattered by the rain, like an outcast, the last soul left on earth.

She didn't even leave a note. Then again, what more was there to say? In truth, she'd already left me that morning in November, in the gynecological ward of the local hospital. She didn't ask my opinion then, either. Those last weeks were just the death throes. She'd killed me a second time. But I don't hold it against her, I've forgiven her. In her place I would have left much sooner. I would not have been able to face or endure what she had for me. I would not have been able to devote myself to unhappiness because of something I could neither accept nor understand. What I can't forgive is the fact that she didn't kill the man I was before, the one who deserved to be punished. She killed the young, new, enthusiastic me, the better man, who deserved another chance. Denise denied me that chance. And, sitting on that park bench, I died a second time.

I'd enjoyed our Adriatic life. I'd thought it could work. We furnished the apartment together, and this time I went with Denise to buy couches and beds, because it's not true that a bed is a bed and a couch is a couch. Objects take on the identity of whoever chooses them, whoever uses and consumes them; even knickknacks have memories. In the summer we went to the beach club across the way. There were six rows of umbrellas, spaced three feet apart. And they were all occupied. Mindless music blared from loudspeakers until sunset. Denise missed the sea at Santorini, our elegant house on the crater, the solitude of the volcanic bays under the cliffs, the sea urchins and schools of fish in the clear, cool waters. But I enjoyed doing battle with the shade from our neighbor's umbrella, flip-flopping along the wooden footpath, even plunging into the shallow, hot, slimy water. I already knew I would never see Imerovigli again, and I'd managed to accept that. That house belonged to someone who no longer existed, and I didn't miss it. I sold it to an international chain that owned a five-star hotel just below us. They'll turn it into luxury suites. They paid me extremely well, and I had the money transferred to Marco's account. I can't buy him the future I would have liked to build for him, but I delude myself that at least I tried.

It was a simple life, normal even. We'd ride our bikes along the flat waterfront, shop at the supermarket, sleep a lot. I was on call four times a week. I treated lowly flus, panic attacks, and the congestion and diarrhea of German tourists. One night in September Denise and I conceived our second child. When school started, we took Marco to a crumbling old building that had probably once been a convent. The nuns were tiny and chatty. His classmates had rough, country accents that made us smile, but I liked it all because it made me feel like I was making peace with a more ancient, more humane Italy, an Italy I had never known.

In other words, I adapted. I became a pathetic country doctor, with no ambition or desire beyond raising my children to be better than myself. I worked to support my family, to treat them to pizza on Saturday night and the water park on Sunday. We'd brought the solitude of our previous life with us. But Denise and I also brought fear. We never left Marco alone, not even for a second. An irrational fear paralyzed us if he was out of our sight even for a moment. We tried not to pass our anxiety along to him, but I'm afraid we didn't succeed. Children absorb us like air, breathe in our joy but also our sadness, our melancholy and sorrow. You don't have to say anything; they understand just the same. Marco became a cautious, quiet boy. He would even ask permission to go to the bathroom. We watched our backs whenever we went out. We'd spy on the street from our windows and immediately report any suspicious car. In a restaurant we only ever sat near the emergency exit, and I always had my back to the wall and my eyes on the door. We didn't have a land-line, only cell phones, whose numbers only we and my man knew. We didn't trust anyone and made a point of rarely socializing. We were pleasant but vague with shopkeepers and neighbors. We never accepted invitations. Not that we got very many. People were suspicious of us. They thought we were criminals. One of Marco's classmates told him so, and he cried, wouldn't speak for three days, then confessed everything to me and swore that he didn't believe I was bad. So I decided to tell him the truth, even though it was too serious for a child. Every now and then Denise complained that she felt she had nothing left. But I felt like I had everything. That is, the essentials. You know what I mean.

I didn't realize that Denise was sick. She was weak, anemic, listless—I thought it was probably the pregnancy. I didn't live with her when she was pregnant with Marco, but she told me that she was sick a lot the first months. She was weak from anemia, and it was a painful struggle just to get a cracker down. Then her mother died. It was the beginning of November. It rained cats and dogs, and the humid, gloomy climate made us nervous. When my man gave us the news, Denise's mother had been dead for a week, forgotten like a dog in the clinic back home. She'd already been cremated. They couldn't tell Denise because she would have wanted to go see her, to at least be with her during those final hours, but she couldn't; the danger was still too great.

We fought. She was upset, devastated, she hated me. She told me her mother didn't deserve to die like that. That I had made her life a desert—worse, a hell. That I had turned her into a pariah, an untouchable, a damned soul. That she wanted her freedom back, wanted to leave the house without looking over her shoulder, to call a girlfriend, go on a trip, take Marco to the playground without having to worry if someone spoke with a southern accent. To find a job, do something, to stop vegetating as if she'd been condemned to death. She wasn't a criminal, she hadn't done anything wrong, she had never in her life broken the law apart from the one time she had forgotten to declare some income on her tax return, she didn't deserve this, and neither did her son. A child can't live like this, transplanted again and again from one place to the next; plants and trees have a hard time if they can't put down deep roots. And so do people. Growing up like this, he would be incapable of normal relationships, of making friends, even someday, of love. It wasn't fair. She didn't want any part in ruining her son. She loved Marco and if she had to choose between him and me, she chose him. I had to understand, I would have done the same thing.

Alarmed, I asked her if she wanted to leave me. She couldn't take Marco away from me. He was all I had left. Denise shrugged her shoulders, took a sleeping pill, and slept for sixteen hours. We never talked about it again, and I attributed those fierce words to a breakdown—understandable—over her mother's death. Denise's mother, a kind, generous, good woman, who loved us both like her own children and who had shown me more affection than my own mother had, was my second victim.

She didn't tell me anything about the hospital. She took care of it all in a day, while I was on call. She went, did it, and left a few hours later. She didn't even spend the rest of the day in bed. I didn't realize what had happened at first. Denise had been taking folic acid, she'd been told it was important for the health of the fetus. She kept a small bottle of it, with a green label, near the stove in the kitchen. One day, it must have been the end of November, I noticed it wasn't there anymore. I asked her why. Casually, as if she were relating something unimportant, she told me she didn't need it anymore, the baby was gone. It was like I'd been hit on the head. My vision went blurry, I had to sit down. I felt like strangling her. I started to cry, a sudden fit of tears, furious and uncontrollable. But by that point there was nothing I could do. It had already happened. My second child was my third victim.

Denise stayed with me for five more weeks, but in truth she was already gone. During those last few weeks, I said goodbye to Marco. An infinite sadness weighed on me, but I tried to hide it until the end. Marco pretended not to understand, and I am grateful to him for that. He was cheerful, he liked that simple city, where he had settled in right away. He was playing soccer again, another youth league, and was proud he'd been picked to play defense. Protecting the goal, preventing the other team from scoring: it suited him. I'd bought a whole arsenal of deadly Chinese fireworks, and on New Year's Eve I set them off. We played with sparklers on our little balcony, shrieking with excitement, dueling with the incandescent tips, crossing imaginary swords made of sparks, writing in the air with fire. Then, when even the last firecracker was out, Denise told me I should put him to bed myself. Marco fell asleep with his hand in mine. I don't know what he will think of me in the future, or if he will forgive me. Maybe the price he paid will seem too high and he will blame me for having let all this happen. Maybe he will think it wasn't worth it, and he will be right. But life is also—perhaps especially—about doing things that aren't worth it. I haven't seen him since.

In May I received an envelope at the hospital—with three bullets in it. The other doctor on duty gave it to me, a kid from Puglia who'd graduated three months earlier. "I think there's something metallic inside," he said, "the magnet on my badge stuck to the envelope." I opened it and held them in my hand. I don't know anything about guns. You would have recognized them immediately. They were heavy, large caliber, maybe for an automatic rifle, an AK-47, I think that's what it's called. I've always hated guns. Even hunting makes me sick. When I was young I would go into the fields or the woods with my environmentalist friends and make noise with pots and pans and drums, to chase away the deer and migratory birds. I did it with conviction, but also for fun. Now I feel tied to those migratory birds, just as if they were my family. Which is why I was bewitched by that white egret at Torre Flavia. It was the only time I tried to really talk to you about myself. But you didn't understand. And that's as it should be: you needed to find your comrades again in order to find yourself. And if you hadn't found yourself again, you wouldn't have been able to accept me.

I learned that the guilty verdict was upheld on appeal, but frankly, it doesn't really matter to me anymore. They told me I would have to leave again and that I had been accepted into the special witness protection program. This time, per article 13.5, I would receive a new identity. A new address, a new birthplace, a new tax ID, a new benefits card. A new name. I instinctively said I wanted to be named Marco. I kidded myself that I could always have my son with me that way. They told me it wasn't a good idea. Too easy. Like passwords. Everyone uses their birthdate, their nickname, their wedding date—anyone can hack them in a second. A new identity can't be tied to the past. It has to be pure, like a blank page. And anyway, I'm not the one who decides. I will be notified when the order has been approved.

So in the meantime, I am Mattia. Because of Pirandello's novel *The Late Mattia Pascal*. I don't know if you've read it—my Italian teacher in high school made me, required summer reading for juniors. I can't say if I liked it or not, but it certainly made an impression on me. I never had the urge to reread it, and maybe my memory is playing tricks on me. Anyway, it's the story of a man who dies, or rather is presumed dead, and he thinks he can make a new life for himself in another city, under another name. But it's an illusion, because his past haunts him and one day comes back to claim him. And even though he meets a girl and falls in love, he can't have a future with her or with anyone, since he is the living dead, condemned to live as dead every day, until the end. It's a sad story, but it's also the only one I knew truly suited me.

My last name I took from the phone book. I have to say it felt weird. Like baptizing a new creature: in a certain sense I was becoming the son of the man who died in that restaurant parking lot near the sea. I am my own son, I brought myself into the world. There were lots of names in the phone book I liked: Ferro, Pace, Dell'Amore—iron, peace, love. In the end I chose a precious gem. My mother had a whole box of jewelry: pendants, chokers, earrings. She knew the qualities of each gem, and decided what to wear according to her mood. Precious gems influence our feelings, she would say. She was neurotic, as testy as a wasp, but she was amazing, she really did know how to connect with minerals—better than with people, unfortunately. She still is amazing, in fact. She's fine, and I'm in contact with her occasionally, through my man. I tried to remember her sayings. Diamonds reveal the truth. But I did not consider myself a revealer of truth. Topaz facilitates spiritual growth. But I'm afraid I'm not very spiritual. Agate encourages you to be attentive to your surroundings, and it would have been a good fit for my situation, but Mattia Agata sounded like a fake name. Sapphire helps you break out of old patterns, but Mattia Zaffiro wasn't very believable either. Tourmaline helps you face new challenges without losing your sense of self, but there wasn't a single Tourmalina in the phone book. Rubies convey strength, courage, steadfastness, enthusiasm, and a joy for life. And there were Rubinos in almost every city. So that was it, my new name had to be Rubino. I baptized myself Mattia Rubino. I don't know if I can really explain its true meaning, but it wasn't merely a bureaucratic act. I really am Mattia Rubino.

I don't have much to say about the past few months. I've roamed from one place to the next, from hotels to half-empty apartments, never able to stay for long. I'm like a seed tossed about by the wind. Do you remember that saying, spray-painted black, on that marble bridge, in front of the hospital in Rome? He who sows seeds in the wind will make the sky blossom. I liked it, but you said it was stupid. You were right. He who sows seeds in the wind harvests nothing. But I can't bury myself in the ground and flower. I can't put down roots and I don't give fruit. Nothing is born of me. I'm not complaining, and I don't want to give you the wrong impression: I still know how to appreciate life, at a basic, almost primeval level. Mattia Rubino has found comfort, he has had a few casual affairs, but mostly with prostitutes. Women who ask no questions and have no expectations. For your peace of mind, let me assure you that I always used a condom. I shunned like the plague any woman who might interest me, because I can't allow myself to get attached to anyone. I agreed not to speak to anyone about what happened, not to reveal my previous identity, not to use it under any circumstances, and never to return to the places I'd left unless I was authorized to do so. In practice, I agreed to not have a past anymore. If I break even one of these rules, the legal motions to change my identity could be revoked, and then I really would be no one. Again, I ask you to burn this letter.

I swore to myself that I would be strong. I don't want to inflict my life as a captive on anyone. I cocooned myself in my solitude, and being with myself is okay. I'm resourceful and I make for interesting company. I read, write, and people-watch—I study them, empathize with them even, but always from a safe distance. I find comfort in cigarettes, in cats and birds, and in lakes and mountains. Their immobility reassures me. Lightning loves the peaks, it strikes high in the mountains rather than down in the plains. But the peaks persevere. I don't know if you know what I mean. I started exercising again. I lift weights and go running every day, as you know. I keep in shape because I've decided that as soon as I have my passport and my money back, I'm going to Greenland, to climb the virgin peaks of Gunnbjørn Fjeld. It's a serious climb, but it's under twelve thousand feet, which the old me wouldn't even have considered worthy of attention. But Mattia Rubino holds that you don't get the true measure of a mountain with cartographer's tools, just as you don't get the true measure of a person by what they do or seem, but by what they are.

I didn't even want to talk to you, Manuela. I was happy just watching you from my balcony. The soldier girl with a crew cut, a child's smile, an athlete's body, and crutches. A hard girl, but also a fragile one: enthusiastic and disappointed, scared and courageous. I never tired of watching you. But I avoided meeting you, believe me. It was you who came to me, who looked for me, who flushed me out. I tried to defend myself. I hadn't yet realized that in behaving like that, all I was doing was drawing you in, because you've been trained to attack, and the more I defended myself, the more I retreated, the more you pursued me, hunted me, cornered me; you weren't going to let me go until you'd captured me. Cordon and search . . . you're a soldier, I suppose it's your nature. You have a unique beauty that wounded me deeply. I felt your pain, in your body and in your eyes, before I even spoke to you. I realized right away that you were dangerous for me. Because you were my shadow.

My life—if you could call it a life—is strange. But I'm not dead either. Not anymore. It's as if I'm suspended, in limbo. I know that the word has become a cliché, even a child like Alessia knows it. But to me, before, it was a medical term. The corneal limbus is the border of the sclera, the white of the eye. I used it all the time. But I would like to restore the word to its former grandeur. It means "margin," "edge," "brink." One of my most vivid memories of school is of my Italian teacher trying to explain to a bunch of sixteen-year-olds who were for all intents and purposes pagan, how Dante had imagined Hell, with Limbo as the antechamber, where those who will be excluded from grace for all of eternity, even if they are without sin, end up. Words like *grace, sin,* even *Hell* meant and still mean nothing to me. Yet today the Supreme Poet's melancholy when he encounters those spirits, innocent yet deprived of happiness, touches me deeply, and the verse he devotes to them seems to me the most devastating he ever wrote: "we are lost . . . we who without hope live in desire." So, I truly am in Limbo, but I'm hoping it looks more like the forest in Alessia's game, where you don't die just once.

I have a fake ID, but it's not very convincing, it gives an invented address, and would raise suspicions if it were ever checked, which is why I didn't want to show it to the police officer at the soccer field. Forgive me for not explaining this to you, and for not helping you when you might have needed me. I'm still waiting for my new papers, along with the new identity they're going to give me, and for them to release the funds I need to embark on some activity somewhere. I want to work, I can't live like this, on a miserable assistance check, like a retiree. Before Christmas I let my man know that I wanted to live in Ladispoli. The afternoon I arrived, I took a walk on the beach. You weren't back yet. The black, volcanic sand, still warm from the sun, reminded me of the sand on Santorini. And the smell of rotting seaweed and the pitiful reddish brown shells the tide throws onto the shore reminded me of my city on the Adriatic. Mattia Rubino doesn't have a past, but he does have a memory. And it's memories of my former self that help anchor me. Necessary memories, but also useless ones—the things I've seen, the books I've read, objects, smells, words, the faces of people I've met. You can't live without memories, as you well know. Otherwise life would lose its meaning. Even freedom is worthless without limits. I don't know what to do with my liberty other than sacrifice it to you. Your city was familiar to me. You— you were familiar to me.

After our trip to Bracciano, I called my man back and asked to be transferred. Mattia Rubino is as vulnerable as a child, but he's also strong, and my selfishness died in the parking lot of that restaurant. I'm just a man, Manuela, but I am a man. I didn't want to touch you. To touch you was to carve a mark on your skin, like a curse, and you already have your scar. Precisely because you were already irrationally dear to me, I had to lose you—and right away, before I became something for you.

I got a fax, summoning me to Rome. You saw it. They told me that they were short of staff over the holidays, so they couldn't process my request, and besides, the entire third floor of the Bellavista had been reserved for me until February. The financial agreement was satisfactory to both parties, and couldn't be renegotiated now. As the days passed, I blessed the Christmas holidays. They gave me twenty days of life. They gave me you.

If I stay in Italy I won't be a doctor anymore. Maybe I'll go back to school, study to become a vet, specializing in feline care. Or maybe I'll simply become an assistant in a shelter for stray cats. I really don't know what will become of me. The protective measures expire in a few months, and I don't know if they will be renewed. I'm almost out of money. I'm not telling you this because I feel sorry for myself—like you, I hate people who feel sorry for themselves—but so that you know that soon I really will have nothing. Don't feel bad about all the money I spent over the holidays, the only riches you truly possess are the ones you spend. I don't know if I will be able to stay in Ladispoli, if this is the place I am fated for. I don't know if you are the person fated for me. I would like to think so.

Vanessa told me that you torture yourself about what it means that your life was spared. She explained to me your theory of divergence. We saw each other today; I spent the day with her, while you were in Turin.

Don't get the wrong idea, we just talked. Your sister is my sister, I'm as fond of her as you are. I only wanted to talk about you, it comforted me to hear your name spoken out loud. I like to think that the divergence, as you call it, was me. Because I was waiting for you, at the end of your dark night. That all the trivial, random acts of your life were leading you to me. I can't save you and you can't save me. All we can do is put ourselves back together again, and be something together.

The fact is that I love you. Reason tells me that, precisely because of this, I have to give you up, get myself transferred as soon as the office reopens. The only way I could condemn you to becoming no one's shadow would be if I didn't love you. A few minutes ago you accused me of lacking substance. It's true. Everything passes right through me and is lost. I'm as porous and inconsistent as a jellyfish. I've always been a reasonable person, and I will make an effort to be reasonable with you. You're a reasonable person, too. But now that you're not in the apartment across the way, now that I can't see your thin figure behind the curtains, I can't help but tell myself that Mattia Rubino is not a reasonable man. Why should he be? He was only born a few months ago, the world is new to him. He is young, innocent, unaware. He hasn't had time to be disillusioned yet. He is curious and impatient. He believes in the future. He is free.

If you returned to the barracks, I'd follow you north. And if you left for another tour of duty, I'd wait for you at home, sighing like a wife. I'd even go with you, if the army allowed a civilian doctor to accompany you. If you didn't want to hang up your uniform, I would accept that. And if you're not going to be a soldier anymore, I would follow you wherever you wanted to live—in Afghanistan even, or at the ends of the earth. I didn't do anything special, like you always say about yourself. Someone said that the very essence of virtue is ordinariness. You would say that I merely did my duty, but I don't really know what that word means. The only duty I recognize is to be human. True to my nature, in other words, to that which distinguishes me from a cat, a bird, a rifle, or a murderer. What I did restored me to myself, and made me the man I am. And Mattia Rubino is not unworthy of Manuela Paris. Your dark room troubles me. I'm like you: I don't like to wait, I'm not patient. I keep going out on the balcony and my shadow appears on the railing. The sight of it cheers me. You are my shadow. I am your reflection. Come home soon.

23

LIVE

anuela stays in Ladispoli. To avoid more family tension, she gives Alessia her room back and goes to stay with Traian and Teodora. She insists on helping with the rent. She sets two goals for herself, and is determined to accomplish them both in the shortest time possible. Quick win. To get better and to get back together with Mattia. One seems pointless without the other.

She updates her Facebook profile, changing her status from "Single" to "Engaged." She embellishes her page with the latest photos, the ones that Alessia took on the terrace of the Palo Castle, even though she's not sure Mattia knows how to use Facebook, and might be too old to even know what it is; but on the off chance that he's searching the Internet for her, he'll be able to see what she's up to and will know that she thinks of herself as tied to him. She never turns off her phone and charges it every night, convinced that sooner or later, as soon as his situation stabilizes, Mattia will call her. He said not to look for him, but he didn't say he wouldn't look for her.

She memorized Vanessa's funny little speech on the name of God, which now seems to her to hold a simple truth, elementary and therefore genuine. If you don't know someone's name, you can't call out to him, and he won't be able to hear you. And until she knows Mattia's name—his new name, his permanent name—she can't call out to him, and he can't respond.

As for the rest, she focuses on rebuilding herself, with the same determination with which she would have rebuilt a broken bridge or a demolished house. She's no longer so convinced there's no such thing as a soul. Her body, mind, energy, and will must all regain the equilibrium they lost. If any one element is broken, the others suffer as well. She also focuses on the things she'd been neglecting all along. She goes to a psychotherapist a dozen times, one who specializes in PTSD. She joins Master Mario's Vedic association, intent on completing the seven steps of transcendental meditation. Maybe she really was wrong. Maybe she is—as Ghaznavi had said—a spiritual person. She learns to contemplate the void and to expand her mind. In a specialty bookshop in Rome she buys a dozen little books by Afghanis who lived in Herat during the Timurid dynasty, in the Middle Ages, or at least before the discovery of America, all members of the Naqshbandi brotherhood. The books collect parables of Sufi wisdom and fragments of Dervish illumination. Parables and fragments that invite the reader to a greater awareness and urge him to let go, to accept suffering and love, and to seek union with the divine: at the end of his spiritual journey, the apprentice mystic discovers that God is none other than himself. Manuela is amazed to learn that the Naqshbandi practiced breath control and awareness exercises that are very similar to those of her Vedic master. The dizzying connection enthralls her.

But then she abandons her psychotherapy, meditation, and Sufi mystics, in order to start in on the homework the psychiatrist at the military hospital had assigned her in vain months before: in other words, she starts writing. For the psychiatrist initially—she plans on turning in her homework in July, at her checkup. But as the pages fill, she forgets her original intent and ends up writing for herself, and, especially, for Mattia: she believes he'll read those pages sooner or later. She would even be willing to turn them into a book, to publish them—in order to reach him.

She throws away her notebook and turns on her computer. She creates a new folder called "Homework" and tries to tell the story of Sergeant Paris in Afghanistan. One hundred and sixty-seven days. From her arrival in Sollum until her departure for the inauguration of the school in Qal'a-i-Shakhrak. It turns out to be a more labor-intensive task than she'd expected. More difficult than marching under the sun, patrolling a road, or reprimanding a soldier. It's almost like an orienteering test. She has to unlearn everything she knows, or thinks she knows. To admit disappointments she'd forgotten about, memories she embellished or selectively edited, emotions she forbade herself to feel. To tear words from the silence, and to find new ones. She rereads her diary from Bala Bayak and discovers that she and Sergeant Paris are now separated by a nearly insuperable distance. The sergeant doesn't comment on anything. She records times, dates, coordinates, temperatures, wind intensity, volume of fire, assignments, ammunition consumption, names, ranks, and facts; she obeys orders and ensures that they are obeyed by others. She is satisfied when an objective is achieved. The Manuela Paris who writes in Teodora Gogeon's ironing room, on the other hand, believes that facts and objectives mean almost nothing: behind the names and ranks are people she thought she knew but who are vanishing with each new day. And you can't say an objective has been achieved if the cost of gaining it is too high. She tries to fix on the page her epigones' words, gestures, even their secrets. At least what remains of them all these months later. Lorenzo's music. Diego's anxiety. Nicola's philosophizing about Zeno. It's too little. Almost nothing. And what remains of Manuela Paris?

She tries to see herself from a distance, to sight herself as in a rifle. As the weeks go by, she realizes that writing is like advancing in the dark with night vision or thermal imaging goggles. They reveal what's hidden in the night, in the dark of the past. Looking through her virtual goggles— writing—she can see the heat left by Lorenzo, and Diego, and Nicola, and Ghaznavi, and Fatimeh. They went on ahead, as the Alpini say, all of them, they met their deaths, and yet with her thermal goggles she senses their presence—filaments of light streaking across her black screen. Thermal goggles register the heat of a person's body even if he's no longer there. They signal a presence that is also an absence, as if they can see the past. All things considered, writing does the same thing. It doesn't console or save, it doesn't raise the dead, doesn't recover what has been lost. But it registers the past. It records absence—filaments of light in the darkness.

She goes to physical therapy behind the piazza every morning, scrupulously keeping to her rehabilitation program. Every time she comes home she asks Teodora or Traian if by any chance she's gotten any mail or if anyone has called for her. They shake their heads. They both think, though for different reasons, that she should forget about Mattia Rubino, but they never say so.

In early February she keeps her promise and goes to see Giovanni in his new house in Civitavecchia. It is, in fact, light and airy, modern and comfortable, and she likes it. Champagne recognizes her and whines with joy, licking her hands. Giovanni acts sensibly—he really is a nice guy. The ease of their former intimacy is still there. They continue to see each other, until she finds it necessary to explain that she has no intention of getting back together with him, that the most she can offer him now is friendship—that for sure. But true friendship means reciprocity: no more secrets. Giovanni says he accepts her decision. He leaves Champagne with her when he goes skiing in the Tyrol for a week at the end of March. Manuela takes the dog to the beach and lets him off the leash. She throws a tennis ball, a toy, or a rubber bone, and Champagne scampers breathlessly after them. But one bright morning when she tries to chase after him, to run in the sand, she has to stop after three steps. Only in that moment does she truly realize that she'll never be able to catch up with him. She can walk for miles now, limping, of course, but without too much pain. But she'll never be able to run again.

She keeps the discovery to herself, and doesn't alter her rehab in the slightest. But she knows. Medicine is not an exact science, the doctor had told her: it is the science of the possible. She would need a miracle. But she has never believed in miracles. Tan and happy, Giovanni comes to get his dog, calls her two or three more times, then disappears. At the end of June she receives an invitation to his wedding in Bergen to a Norwegian engineer named Niels. She sends a gift—money for their honeymoon in the Seychelles—but she doesn't see him again.

Little by little, she starts going out again on Saturday nights. Vanessa has broken up with Youssef, and is seeing Lapo now. They're not together, it's more fluid than that. Being fluid, it assumes the shape of the container, which is appropriate given how equivocal they both are. In short, it works. It turns out that the reporter appreciates contemporary dance—or at least he's able to get tickets for premieres when the most important companies come through Rome. If he's bored he bears it stoically, because he's really taken with Vanessa. He even attends the shocking performance of the Flying Ghosts, Vanessa's old dance troupe, in a theater in a former soap factory. The benches are so uncomfortable that Manuela is convinced they were intentionally designed to punish the audience. The show, which is called *Autopsy*, only lasts an hour, but despite its brevity, Manuela finds it as entertaining as a punch in the face. It's all about nudity and physical deformity, and most of the dancers, moving like wax figures, flaunt anomalous limbs, stiff or stunted or mutilated, and rigid bodies, marked with wounds, lesions, and amputations. In spite of all this, the performance, which is both ghostly and harmonious, is not at all depressing. The critics adore it. The program notes explain that Flying Ghosts is an upbeat company, and their wild, ritualistic dance is a critique of the commercialization of the body in today's world; essentially, a hymn to life.

Vanessa had left the troupe because of a fight with the choreographer after getting her breasts enlarged. The choreographer had criticized her for acting contrary to Flying Ghosts' philosophy. Vanessa had objected that what she did was instead the apotheosis of Flying Ghosts' philosophy: otherwise healthy, she, too, was now an altered body, there was silicon under her skin, she, too, had prostheses, like the African dancer who had lost his legs on a land mine. It's blasphemy to compare two tits redone for vanity's sake with a war victim's artificial limbs, the choreographer had angrily countered. Redone out of a sense of inadequacy, redone in order to become a plastic doll, evidence of our nostalgia for perfection, and thus evidence of the imperfection of human beings, Vanessa had objected. In the end, since each was convinced of being right, Vanessa quit Flying Ghosts and gave up dancing. The other dance troupes, in comparison, seemed Jurassic to her. After the performance, Vanessa, with Lapo and Manuela trailing behind, goes to the dressing rooms to congratulate her old friends, and a little while later, without ever resolving the old argument, she rejoins the troupe.

Manuela and Lapo, sitting together in the audience, anxiously watch Vanessa's debut at the Rome Festival at Villa Medici. She dances with grace and fury, as if she had never stopped. Manuela and Lapo are both moved, but they hide it out of modesty, turning their shoulders. The next day, the photo of Vanessa, magnificently naked among the other dancers—mutilated cadavers—appears in many newspapers and in all the specialized magazines. Manuela has the feeling that Mattia will see it.

She doesn't find the reporter particularly unpleasant anymore, and even Stefano, the obstetrician who is as tall as a lamppost, who hangs out with Lapo's friends when he's in Italy, turns out to be less boring than she had remembered. One night he takes her to see a heartbreaking Iranian film in a movie theater in the center of Rome. Afterward, she finds herself sitting on the edge of the Trevi Fountain, like an ordinary tourist, talking about the Ganjabad and Gerani massacre. While Stefano licks a melting ice cream cone, she tells him about the cemetery on the hill behind Bala Bayak, the mass graves, the abandoned tombs, and the uneasiness she felt thinking that there was no one to weep over those dead. The uneasiness of traveling through those villages, because yes, she did know they'd been bombed before their arrival, and she knew about the attacks and the accusations of massacre. But she never would have doubted the official version, and at any rate she couldn't find a link between her—their—presence there and that cemetery. The Italians respected the fifth commandment—"Thou shall not kill"—although certainly not for religious reasons. The fact that their allies had done it, maybe in order to save their lives, hadn't bothered her much.

When he leaves again for the Congo, Stefano, encouraged, sends her e-mails with links to subversively named sites. Manuela opens them, and finds pages that intelligence officers and insurgents probably visit, as well as curious people like herself. They introduce her to a world of outraged antagonists who talk in surprising and absurd, and not totally incorrect, ways about things she knows. She reads the articles. She endures the bloody photos of the slain children. Upending your perspective and looking at things from another point of view helps you to understand who you really are. It's like she's using binoculars. She wants to take in the full panorama of the stage. She doesn't want to sit in the end zone anymore, or be the ball boy behind the goal.

In March, the captain in charge of the public information office for her brigade contacts her to ask if she might be willing to go on TV. There's been another casualty, and Afghanistan is once again a hot topic. All she has to do is talk about her own experience, explain in simple words what our soldiers are doing in that faraway land, because it's important to sustain public consensus for the mission. He doesn't say that the military budget is up for a vote and that they need a consensus to get it approved, but he doesn't have to: Manuela already knows that.

She tries to refuse. She tells him that she's not any good at speaking in public, that regardless, she's not interested in appearing, she just wants to return to active duty and be deployed in country again. But he insists. Colonel Minotto takes the trouble to call her. He is quite commanding, and she realizes that the general staff considers the young, motivated, and attractive Sergeant Paris the ideal poster child for the Armed Forces, perfect for an afternoon talk show—that this is the future they are imagining for her. She feels angry and ashamed. But then she thinks that Mattia, alone in a hotel room, might leave the TV on so the voices onscreen can keep him company, and if he sees her, maybe he'll call. So she agrees.

She goes to the television studio and lets them put blush on her cheeks and gloss on her lips. "No eye shadow or mascara," she explains to the two beauticians who have arrayed an arsenal of nail polishes and colored tubes on the shelf under the mirror in the makeup room, "I'm a soldier." The beauticians commiserate: it's an injustice, they say, female soldiers should rebel against the limits being placed on their femininity, but she's young and doesn't need much in the way of touch-ups anyway, her eyes are very expressive and she'll doubtless look good on camera—though it's a shame about her hair. "What's wrong with my hair?" Manuela asks. "It's a bit too short," one of them observes, "it shows your skull and makes your ears stick out." Manuela feels sorry for them.

The show—which has a celebratory, hagiographic bent—drags on for nearly two hours, but she speaks only three times. The first time to try to explain the importance of the mission's humanitarian aim. She says that every war demands an ideal justification, which is necessary in order to gain consensus. In fact, when the world acknowledges the necessity of military action, no one dares dispute it. This may seem to be merely a way for those conducting the war to justify their actions, and in part of course it is; but in today's world, no one in any country—neither the government nor army nor the public—could commit to a war that it did not consider just. And today only an ethical or humanitarian motivation can be understood and accepted as "just." The host's alarmed face makes her suspect that she has ventured into terrain too difficult for a light afternoon talk show, and her suspicion is confirmed by the fact that the hostess then interrupts her in order to show the first film clip from Farah.

The second time she speaks it is to explain where the girls' school at Qal'a-i-Shakhrak is, and why it's important for the future of a country to build schools. She can't keep herself from noting that our government spends a lot of money building schools in Afghanistan, so it seems strange to her that it doesn't consider it important to support education in Italy as well. We build schools over there, but here we let them fall to pieces; there we support teachers, we protect them and consider them essential for the future of the country, but here teachers are humiliated and disrespected, and the education of the young is considered a waste of time. This hypocrisy is even more inexplicable if you think that over there we were also charged with reconstructing the judicial system. Among all the countries of the coalition, we were considered the most able, because of our own judicial tradition, to form a magistrate and establish tribunals, in short to ensure the working of the law. We export a model we are proud of, but which here is insulted and disregarded on a daily basis. Sometimes she thinks that's why we went there. In that faraway, devastated country, we project the image of what we should—of what we want—to be, but which we can no longer appreciate here. Afghanistan is like a mirror, it lets us see a better image of ourselves.

The last time is to answer the hostess's question as to whether she considers her dead comrades heroes or martyrs. She hesitates for a second and then says she is sure that they wouldn't have seen themselves as one or the other. They merely did their duty. Not that she can really explain what duty is. To her it's not so much what one is bound to by religion, ethics, or law. It's a personal debt.

The camera scans the puzzled faces of the other guests, then the film clip shot at Jodice's house in Marcianise starts rolling. Imma, together with Diego's parents, who clutch his silver-framed photo to their chests, talk about their dear one, praising his sense of justice, his time as an altar boy, his faith in God, his ideals, and his willingness to sacrifice himself for others. As Antonio Jodice speaks, his voice trembling and his eyes wet with dignified tears, the camera frames Diego Jodice, Jr., who crawls across the tile floor of their modest family home. When he charges under the table, Manuela instantly recognizes the carpet from Bala Bayak. And when the red light that indicates they're on the air comes on again, there's no time left to explain herself better. One of the other guests is the general commander of the brigade deployed there now, and she's not sure he understood what she wanted to say. Mattia will understand, though, and that's enough. Sometimes, you can only write for one person, speak for one person. No comment arrives from the public information office.

The only real result of the TV show is that, in the days that follow, 24,570 people send her Facebook friend requests. The 541 Facebook friends Manuela already has are soldiers, noncommissioned officers, or former Alpini—at most, some women from the Volunteer Training Regiment who in the years since have hidden their boots in the attic and become mothers. Her appearance on TV wins her admirers and potential new friends. Might Mattia be among them? She sets out to examine each and every profile. Mattia's not there. Not even under a pseudonym.

Most of those who want to friend her have less than pure motives. Manuela does not friend strangers, so she ignores their requests.

She never stops waiting for Mattia's call, and time, rather than shattering her hope, strengthens it. She attributes the long wait not to his decision to break up with her, but to his wanting to be sure he can settle into a new life before coming back. It seems logical to her, and right, and she doesn't blame him. She is sorry she followed orders and burned his letters. Nothing is left of him now. She can't even remember his voice. And in April she realizes that waiting is a psychological state she's just not suited for. To desire something too much is to lose it; it's precisely that desire that makes you lose it. She still prefers action. And if Mattia doesn't come back to her, then it's up to her to go find him.

On the Internet she gets information on all the ophthalmology conferences in the last ten years, picks out those that were held in seaside cities, records the names of all the participants, and starts looking up the Italians one by one. The search engines provide her with all kinds of information about the ophthalmologists—in addition to their scientific curriculum vitae, there are often photos, Facebook pages (she's amazed to discover that even the fifty-year-olds have them), sometimes even a phone number. In the end, she winnows the list of possibilities down to one name: a man who nearly five years earlier had presented a paper on advances in cataract microsurgery at an international conference. He had left quite a few traces on the Internet, which now float—crystallized in an eternal present—on the most disparate websites. Scientific articles that turn out to be illegibly abstruse. Photos of a party of climbers roped together on the Polish Glacier Traverse Route on Aconcagua. A signature on a petition to close a northern city's historic center to cars, and another to release a woman unjustly condemned to death. A photo of a marvelous Persian cat, held in his arms as he wins third prize at a cat show. The horrifying video on YouTube of a phacoemulsification: the aspiration of cataract fragments through a cannula inserted in the crystalline lens; the incision, and then the implantation of the artificial lens, rolled up like a plastic veil, with a microinjector.

At that point Manuela abandons her search. To piece together the clues to Mattia's past that he sowed in his letters, to follow his tracks and reconfigure the components of his life, will not give her back the man she loves, but rather an ophthalmologist who specialized in experimental cataract treatments he himself no longer identifies with and whom he himself considers dead. She discovers that that man means nothing to her—in fact, she hates him. It's the other man—Mattia Rubino—she's waiting for.

At Easter she goes on vacation to Santorini with Vanessa and Alessia. She reserved two rooms in a small hotel in Imerovigli, facing the crater's abyss. The sheer cliffs are so arid, not a single blade of grass grows on them. The severity and violence of that landscape, devastated by an ancient yet somehow indelible explosion, has something of Afghanistan about it. But the village has become the picture of Greekness for the world's rich, a Cycladic Capri, an Aegean Portofino. Despite the cool weather, tourists from Japan, South Africa, and New Zealand roam about in sandals and tank tops among the jewelry shops and designer boutiques that open onto the labyrinth of whitewashed streets. The houses have all been turned into luxury hotels and dream villas. She convinces herself that she has identified Mattia's house, on the highest rise in the village, in the shadow of the church. Two floors, the lower one with a panoramic terrace that gives onto the pool of the five-star hotel below. The house is being renovated. Two listless, blond workmen are whitewashing the walls and spreading a gray cement resin on the terrace floor. They speak only Albanian and can't answer her questions.

Manuela confesses to Vanessa that she's a bit disappointed. She had hoped to find him here. Hoped that he had lied to her when he said he'd sold the villa. He really loved this place, and she imagined he had been too happy here to give it up. Vanessa says she thinks it's precisely the opposite. We never go back to the places where we've been happy, it's too painful. We're more likely to go back to where we've lost everything than to where we had something. Manuela thinks her sister may be right, because she would more willingly go back to Qal'a-i-Shakhrak than to Lake Bracciano. She sits on a low wall and watches the wisp of smoke rising from the nearby islet of Thirasia. The volcano is sleeping but still alive. "You have to try and see it in a positive light," Vanessa says. "Appreciate the good you've had, and forget the rest. That's what I always do, and trust me, it works. If he didn't love you, he would already have called you, Manuela. He won't call you because he loves you." "He'll call me," Manuela says. "We have to be together, we mirror each other. I'm his shadow."

When she gets home, she uploads the photos of Imerovigli to Facebook. If Mattia visits her profile, he will know that she's gone on a pilgrimage to his past, that she has seen what he has seen and loved what he has loved. She's up to 762 friends. But Mattia Rubino is not one of them. She finds a post from Angelica Scianna, who is back from Afghanistan, an invitation to come visit her. And one Sunday in May she goes. Angelica is as blond and slim as ever. She doesn't wear the pendant with the broken heart anymore either. So much time has passed. She still has it, though, Angelica tells her, she keeps it in the breast pocket of her uniform, but only when she flies. Talismans never grow old. She gets permission from her commander to take Manuela up with her during a helicopter training exercise. She tries to scare her with tactical maneuvers and sudden nosedives, hurling them toward the earth like a bullet, brushing mountaintops, cable car wires, and power lines strung between pylons— but Manuela enjoys it, like it's a roller-coaster ride. But she no longer thinks that Angelica is living the life that should have been hers, the life that the psychiatrist at the Modena Academy stole from her so many years ago. She's not envious of Angelica's life, because she finally loves her own. She discovers that she can simply—truly—be Angelica's friend.

They walk on the deserted runway as the sun sinks into the Mediterranean and the light fades over the military airport. A fighter-bomber rolls docilely toward the hangar. Angelica's hair blows across her lips. She realizes that Manuela can't match her stride, so slows her pace. "What do you think you'll do?" she asks. "Are you going to stay in the army?" "I don't know," Manuela answers honestly. "I'm thinking it over." Angelica scrutinizes her, almost frightened by what Manuela might say. But Manuela keeps quiet and stares at the helicopter shimmering in the twilight. An object of almost artistic beauty. The light gun with rotating barrels is in place, but the rocket containers under the propellers and the props for the TOW antitank missiles are empty. "I've changed," she adds after a bit. "I'm not the same person I was before, and I'll never be the same again. But I don't feel disabled. I haven't lost a leg, I've gained one, but I don't know if they'll be able to understand that."

In June she goes back to Belluno to clear out her studio apartment. Her lease is up and she doesn't want to renew it, not knowing if she'll ever be back on active duty at the Tenth Alpini Regiment barracks. The place had been furnished by the owners, so there's almost nothing of hers other than her grandfather's military regalia, a few boxes of photographs, and her clothes. When she takes them out of the closet, they smell of mothballs.

That afternoon she goes to Mel, to see Lorenzo's mother. "I've been waiting for you, dear," Mrs. Zandonà says familiarly, as if they already knew each other. She's a delicate woman with copper-colored hair and diaphanous skin, shriveled by grief. But hers is not a life of regrets. She teaches music to children at the public elementary school, and their colorful, surreal drawings brighten the walls of her little living room. She was the one who gave Lorenzo his first guitar. Unfortunately, she hadn't understood his music, hadn't been able to encourage him or to keep him from doubting himself. Not that it would necessarily have changed anything.

Manuela tells her everything she remembers about Lorenzo's life at Bala Bayak—Ahmad Zahir, the Afghani musician he listened to, his nickname, Nail, which she had given him, the cordon and search for Mullah Wallid, his songs, even the smell of the opium poppies and the jokes about the word *epigone*: though they didn't know the word's real meaning, when they were over there they had decided that *epigone* meant "friend"—forever. She tells her she will never forgive herself for what happened, and that she has often thought about dying, because a commander who doesn't know how to protect her men doesn't deserve to live. But knowing how to bear misfortune is a sign of wisdom, and accepting it is a skill. Living means bearing responsibility. She doesn't tell her that the last word her son spoke was *mamma*, even though that's what she would like to hear, and it might even be true. Manuela was unconscious in the helicopter while Lorenzo was dying. But she doesn't feel like inventing an exemplary death for him. Mrs. Zandonà doesn't cry, the time for tears has passed.

She goes with her to the cemetery, to see Lorenzo's tombstone, there among the Alpini heroes of the Great War. His mother asks if she thinks there's any meaning in her son's death, if it did any good. Manuela says that everything has a meaning but that's not to say it did any good, individuals don't make history, certainly not an Alpino corporal, not even the brigade general, or a minister, or the president of a country. History is something beyond the intentions and aspirations of individuals; it's more like the tide. You can be part of it, but you can't stop or guide it. Lorenzo became a minuscule grain of sand in the history of that distant country, a history that for a short time was intertwined with Italy's. And maybe the meaning lies precisely in that strange tangency of parallel worlds destined to meet only in infinity—that the life of a guitar player from Mel was joined forever to those stones, sand, and mines, to the stars of that sky, because we are all one.

Lorenzo's mother invites her to visit her again, her son admired her infinitely, respected her as his commander, and considered her a friend— she will always be welcome here at Mel. Manuela promises she'll be back, and takes off on her Honda. It's been twelve months, and she feels up to riding her motorcycle again.

On July 12 she goes back to Turin for her meeting with the medical evaluation board. It's hot and the city has emptied out for school vacation. Nurse Scilito greets her warmly. He seems truly surprised to see her again. "So you're still holding on?" he asks her. "I began this journey a long time ago," Manuela says. "I'm not one to turn back. I told you I'm always moving forward."

She descends to the dismal radiology department and undergoes all the same tests again. X-rays, orthopedic and neurological controls, CAT scan, MRI. She does not give the psychiatrist her homework. Assessing these past months, she honestly reports three or four intrusion phenomena (every time she sees blood); several flashbacks in moments of weak consciousness—at the movies, for example, or right before she falls asleep, or when she is writing; nightmares almost every night; mild insomnia; and olfactory hallucinations—sometimes she can still smell blood and burnt flesh. But she has kept her anxiety and aggression under control, and the incident on the soccer field has remained an isolated event. The madman demanded money for his three teeth and for not pressing charges, quite a bit of money, which she gave him, while the other guy, the father of the Torvaianica goalie, initially filed charges, but later withdrew them. She didn't know if he'd been pressured to do so, but she hoped not. In any case, there had been no further repercussions. Her sentimental and emotional life are full and satisfying. In short, she's gotten used to living with PTSD.

The psychiatrist tells her not to kid herself: six months earlier, the only favorable opinion regarding her return to active service had been his. Manuela is surprised, and thanks him for giving her that chance. "You were the one who had to give yourself a chance, Sergeant Paris," the psychiatrist says, "you just needed time to realize it." Then he stands up, shakes her hand, and wishes her good luck.

She sits on her bed, laptop on her knees, waiting for the medical evaluation board to summon her. She's surprisingly serene. Her room is on the second floor, adjacent to the one she stayed in for so many months. She can see the same magnolia tree through the window, but from a different perspective. It seems bigger and taller, and its leaves resound with chirping. Scilito knocks to let her know that her meeting with the board has been set for ten tomorrow. Manuela goes down to the communal living room to watch TV. An army engineers officer sits in an armchair watching the news. A lieutenant, about thirty years old. His head is bandaged and his arm is in a sling. The ribbon on his uniform tells her it happened in Afghanistan. He must have been repatriated recently. "Bala Bayak?" Manuela asks. "Bala Murghab," he says.

"Did you see any action in country?" she asks. "A hundred TICs, twelve of them IDF, seven IEDs identified and neutralized, two IEDs activated, four vehicles hit, two casualties, three lightly injured, ten insurgents captured," the lieutenant says. "We had eighty TICs," Manuela says. "Not bad," he concludes. "Do you ever ask yourself if we're losing the war while telling ourselves we've already won it?" Manuela wonders. The officer switches off the TV and turns to look at her. "What are you trying to say?" he asks. "I don't think I understood, I'm deaf in my right ear. I lost my eardrum in an explosion, and I'm trying to get my hearing back in my left ear."

"It's not your ears that aren't working, Lieutenant," Manuela replies, "it's my head. I want more than anything in the world to go back there, back to that school. To see it with my own eyes. To know that it exists, that we were the ones who built it, and that girls are learning to read and write there. But at the same time I wish that Fatimeh's son had built it. I don't know if I can explain." "I'm sorry, I'm not feeling well," the officer says, mortified. "It's like liquid cement is dripping into my ears, and I have severe tinnitus. I can pick up the vibrations of your words, but they're all broken up, I can't piece them together."

She crosses the big meeting hall slowly, intimidated by the strange silence that lends an unfortunate solemnity to the moment. She's never seen so many generals up close. The lowest-ranking officer is a colonel.

Their uniforms are arrayed with ribbons and decorations. All the members of the medical evaluation board are there. That's a good sign, right? She doesn't understand. All those men, all of them old enough to be her father or grandfather, are looking at her sympathetically—tenderly, she would say if that weren't impossible. The lieutenant colonel congratulates her: serving in a theater of combat operations, she faced enormous difficulties and dangers, heightened by powerful social and political tensions, a trying social environment, and a complex and extremely risky operational situation. She carried out the mission entrusted to her with courage and utmost professionalism, offering a constant example of self-sacrifice, skill, and responsibility. The success of Operation Reawakening speaks to the courage, efficiency, and effectiveness of all the men and women of the Tenth Alpini Regiment. For these reasons, and for having contributed to augmenting the prestige of the Italian Army in an international context, he informs her that Sergeant Paris has been awarded the military cross for Afghanistan. Manuela gasps in astonishment.

But she has also been recognized as permanently unfit for military service. In acknowledgment of her merits in the field, she can remain in service on the honor roll. The amount of her indemnity for her disability and her retirement package will be communicated to her later.

Manuela manages to remain stoical while they pin the cross on her uniform. She smiles, shakes hands. She thanks them for this honor, which she does not deserve, for all the attention they have lavished on her, the care, advice, respect, everything. Then she clicks her heels, salutes, turns, and crosses the very lengthy meeting hall again. She still limps, and does nothing to hide it. She goes up to her room and slowly removes her cap, then her uniform: her jacket, her short-sleeved, summer-issue shirt, her pants and socks. Then she removes the dog tag from around her neck. Her good luck charm. She was wearing it that day at Qal'a-i-Shakhrak, and she believes it saved her life: she'd never taken it off. The Americans wear two of them, one around their neck, one on their leg, to identify the pieces in case their body is blown to bits. She'd had hers made before she deployed, in a shop in Ladispoli, and had paid for it herself. The Italian Army doesn't issue them anymore. "In Italy there's no money for things that don't bring in votes," First Lieutenant Russo had said bitterly. Even if they're necessary. Nicola. She misses his philosophizing. Then she folds her uniform and puts it in her bag. She places her cap with the feather on top, careful not to squish it when she zips the bag closed. She puts on a pair of jeans and a green T-shirt, grabs her bag, and leaves the hospital. She lets herself go only once she's in the taxi, on the way to the airport. She cries silently, her face pressed against the window. The tears roll down her cheeks and splash on her hands, hot as coals.

"It's over," she says to Vanessa when she picks her up at Fiumicino. "Which means?" her sister asks. "They declared me permanently unfit for service, basically I'm retired, I'm out." Vanessa hugs her. She cries in the arrivals hall, her army duffel weighing on her shoulder. She cries all the way home. "You did everything you could, honey," Vanessa says, "some things just don't work, you have to accept it. You have to make peace with your destiny, and it's not a defeat, there's something noble, something sweet in it." "I know," Manuela says.

Vanessa pulls up in front of Teodora's building. It's almost nine in the evening, but in the west, out at sea, phosphorescent waves of rosy light still streak across the pale blue sky. The horizon is a clear straight line. "You explain to Mamma, tell her I'll come say hi to all of you after dinner, I can't eat anything." "They'll make you a spokesperson, hon," Vanessa says, "they'll put you in communications, you'll train the girls, they'll find something you like, and if they don't, well, then they'll help you go into politics, or you'll leave the army, you'll do something else, besides, every-one's going to pull out soon, if you want to go back to Afghanistan you'll be able to go with some kind of organization, the Red Cross, what do I know, things change." Manuela forces herself to smile and gets out of the car. But as soon as Vanessa's Yaris disappears on the overpass, she turns around. She doesn't feel like talking with Teodora or Traian or anybody.

The gate to the nature preserve is closed, but she carefully reconnoiters the fence in search of an opening. She finds one and slips underneath, the barbed wire slicing her T-shirt. But it's not military concertina wire, which stabs you and rips out chunks of flesh: this barely scratches her shoulder, and only draws a drop of blood. The wooden walkway through the marsh sways beneath her feet. It's getting dark. The migratory birds have flown away, but the dunes are dotted with white spots that seem to glow in the gathering darkness. Sea daffodils, the flowers of the sand. The tower is still there, but it looks even more crooked and fragile now. The only per-son in the preserve at that hour is a fisherman, and he pretends not to see her. The Tyrrhenian is rough, turbulent, the waves crash relentlessly on the breakwater, spraying her face with a salty mist, like tears. Manuela piles her clothes on the tower's crumbling marble ledge and dives in.

Underwater, she opens her eyes. The black sand whirls around, zero visibility, and anyway this sea is dead, there's nothing to see, no fish or other living creatures—only algae, ribbons of sea grass the current pushes toward the shore, and sand. Sand, sand, sand. She swims out until the coast is just a dark line. She lets herself be tossed about by the waves, pounded, slapped, submerged. Six months ago she was convinced she would come here to drown herself if the answer was no. But she hasn't come here to die. The poet Rumi taught her that a person is like the sea, eternally in motion: he who doesn't know that sees only the waves on the surface, but their movement merely hides the sea beneath. She lets the water wash her, cradle her, renew her. She floats on her back, her eyes open to the twilight sky that slowly grows dark. Behind the dunes, shadows have swallowed up the city and its buildings: out at sea, a sliver of blue light still lingers on the horizon, and a solitary star already twinkles in the sky, sparkling like a precious gem. The beauty of it all is imprinted on her memory. She looks at it, for herself and for them. Her epigones are there with her, too, and always will be.

She gets dressed in a hurry, without waiting to dry off. Her jeans stick to her skin, her hair wets her motorcycle helmet. She takes her time in the crazy summer evening traffic, can't find a parking space in front of her building, so she parks farther on, between the yellow stripes for handicapped drivers. It's not taking advantage. Soon she'll have the right to park there. That sad thought makes her smile. The Bellavista is open. They've replaced the faulty lightbulb. Now the blue sign is visible from far away. They've even replastered the place. Now it's an intense navy blue. She walks up the stairs with the slowness of someone who has nothing left to prove. She hugs her mother and her grandmother and Alessia, and tells the little girl she brought her *gianduiotti* from Turin. Alessia, the sweet tooth, thanks her. Her front teeth have come in. Square, white, straight. Manuela stays with them in the living room until late. Her mother offers her an iced lemon vodka, something she learned to make at the roadside diner. Her family doesn't ask Manuela anything, she doesn't have to explain anything. They just sit there, all five of them, distractedly watching a variety show on TV, until Alessia falls asleep on Vanessa's knees. Music throbs from the beach clubs, along with the buzz of vacationers' voices. Summer has always been her favorite season. Ladispoli comes out of hibernation, is resuscitated, comes alive again. At midnight she goes out onto the balcony to smoke. "When are you going to quit?" her mother begs her. "It's bad for you, it'll kill you." "Tomorrow," Manuela promises. "This is my last cigarette."

The rooms at the Bellavista are lit up behind the shutters, the beach towels hung on balconies to dry flutter in the wind. It's high season, the hotel is almost full. Manuela flicks the ashes into the geranium. The plant survived winter and drought. A tuft of green leaves clings to the railing. One red blossom stretches toward the street. In the hotel across the way, only one room on the third floor is dark. Room 302, Mattia's room. The shutter is lowered almost to the floor. The iron chair is tipped up against the table. If only I knew how to find you. If only I knew where you are, and what your name is, I would call out to you. And you would come. I know it. A knot of people has formed in the street. Kids are getting drunk, laughing, making a racket. Elegant couples are coming out of the Bellavista restaurant. Gianni's corpulent profile is silhouetted in the doorway, then disappears. To the left the Tahiti is a cube of light. A procession of motor scooters heads up the promenade toward the music. There's a party on the beach, on the other side of the footbridge. She puts the cigarette out in the cracked soil, and slips it into her pocket—her old habit of hiding her weaknesses. Then she changes her mind and drops it over the balcony, down into the street. When she looks up again, she thinks she can make out a shadow in the darkness on the unlit third-floor balcony. A massive shadow. She tries to breathe, deep breaths to calm herself, but her heart is exploding. It's him. It can't be anyone else. He's come back.

She grips the railing. She walks the length of the balcony, all the way to the corner closest to the hotel. She leans out into the darkness. The shadow doesn't move. It's not Mattia, it's just some tourist, he's not there. I'm fooling myself. I don't like reality and don't want to accept it, so I invent it, change it, dream it. She's afraid it's not true. She's afraid it is true. She swallows. She pinches her arm. She closes her eyes. A faint hint of aromatic tobacco reaches her nostrils. She's so agitated she can hardly restrain herself, but she resists the temptation to open her eyes again right away. She hesitates. Waits. There's only a split second between desperation and hope. When you try to avoid something, this effort is exactly what lets you face it. Be brave, Manuela. The first thing she sees is the glow of embers and a whiff of smoke that coils and disappears into the night.

ACKNOWLEDGMENTS

Limbo is a novel. The characters and the action are the fruit of invention. The Tenth Alpini Regiment does not exist. Although Panthers, the Ninth Company name, is taken from an actual airborne company, it has never been deployed in Afghanistan. There are several Pegasus platoons, but none of them inspired this one. The Salsa barracks in Belluno are home to the Seventh Alpini Regiment. Bala Bayak and Qal'a-i-Shakhrak, like the FOB Sollum, the COP Khurd, and the Bellavista Hotel, exist only in these pages. But Ladispoli, Shindand, the province of Farah, and all the other places cited here are real. The Flavia Tower is the final sentinel of the beauty of that coastline brutalized by cement: it deserves to be saved and restored.

The tripartite classification of female soldiers—which Lapo refers to—is by Professor Fabrizio Battistelli, who pioneered the earliest research and published numerous articles on the topic.

There is a rich bibliography on this most recent war in Afghanistan. Among the works that have been most helpful to me I would like to mention: L. Kleveman, *The New Great Game: Blood and Oil in Central Asia*, 2003; R. Pape, *Dying to Win: The Strategic Logic of Suicide Terrorism*, 2005; E. Giunchi, *Afghanistan, Storia e società nel cuore dell'Asia*, 2007; AA.VV., *Suicide Attacks in Afghanistan. United Nations Assistance Mission to Afghanistan*, 2007; R. Crews and A. Tarzi, *The Taliban and the Crisis of Afghanistan*, 2008;

A. Rashid, *Descent into Chaos*, 2008; C. Bertolotti, *Shahid, Analisi del terrorismo suicida in Afghanistan*, 2010; A. Marucci, *AfghanistNAM: Analisi di un conflitto troppo in fretta dato per vinto*, 2010.

The theory of divergence was formulated by Ardengo Soffici in his book on war memories, *Errore di coincidenza*, 1920.

I am grateful to all the men and women who helped me imagine this story by sharing their memories and experiences. The soldiers of every branch and rank, from the general to the captain to the corporal—who, by so generously listening to me and donating their time and expertise, trained my language—know how much I owe them and how invaluable they have been to me. I thank them discreetly and respectfully. Further-more, I thank Lieutenant P.F., doctor and parachutist, for the stories about his tours of duty (and for our conversations); Corporal A. for allow-ing me to "drive" a Lince past the Coliseum; and R., who has no rank, but would be a veteran if he were a soldier, and knows the front better than anyone. I also thank Ahmad, a refugee awaiting asylum, who, at age thirteen, left the Farah desert and ended up in a manhole in Rome, and now sells television sets.

All opinions, errors, and inventions are mine. I summarized passages, modified procedures, altered the stage of certain rituals. A novel is a construction, an adventure, a hypothesis. I was more interested in veri-similitude than philology, in possibility than news, and so I took many liberties.

I popoli della Terra was my favorite reading in 1974. I have organized three trips to Afghanistan. The first with my friend Francesca, the second with Annemarie Schwarzenbach. Both of them went without me. The last time I made it to the border, in the desert of Baluchistan. Beyond the watchtower the road was mined. No one asked for visas or passes. Be-yond that point was war, and a regime no one knew a thing about. Only armed combatants, doctors, drug traffickers, and smugglers went ahead. I smuggle words, and I went ahead, too—without leaving any foot-prints in the sand. *Limbo* is my journey.

TRANSLATOR'S ACKNOWLEDGMENTS

Many people helped me bring Melania Mazzucco's novel to life in English; without them this project would have remained in its own form of limbo.

Giovanni Marizza, Lieutenant General, Italian Mountain Troops, and former Deputy Commander of the Multi-National Corps in Iraq, indefatigably explained Italian and coalition military hierarchies, equipment, and terminology.

George H. Calhoun, Captain, Infantry, U.S. Army, read several chapters of the manuscript, offering precisions and editorial advice that would make his mother proud.

Daniel Jewiss, former Master Sergeant in the CT Army National Guard, provided military expertise and brotherly encouragement.

Brendan Kelley, Team Leader, Third Battalion, Seventy-fifth Ranger Regiment, U.S. Army, shared precious military details and lingo from his tour of duty in Afghanistan.

Deborah Miller coached me through Traian's soccer match.

Gail Jewiss, R.N., guided me through Manuela's operations.

Dr. Giancarlo Di Maggio counseled me on psychological terms.

Patricia Caprotti, Rita Fabbrizio, and Stefano Spadoni unflaggingly explicated the intricacies of Melania's prose.

Miranda Popkey, my creative and ever-cheerful editor, refined the translation at every step.

My warmest thanks for their generosity, meticulousness, and patience.